The incomparable EJ Barnes will steal your heart. She captivates the reader with her artistic ability to paint her story and characters with imagination, vitality, and pure magic. Few writers can convey the style and bridge to cross over that EJ uses to paint a beautiful picture for young adult, children's fiction, adult fiction erotica, and riveting poetry. However, she stands out by empathizing with adults, youth, and poets internationally. EJ was born and raised in London, Ontario, Canada, where she currently resides and is making herself known across Canada, the United States, and the rest of the world.

EJ Barnes

THE ROAD TO YOU

A Story of Sexual Obsession

AUSTIN MACAULEY PUBLISHERS™
LONDON * CAMBRIDGE * NEW YORK * SHARJAH

Copyright © EJ Barnes 2024

All rights reserved. No part of this publication may be reproduced, distributed, or transmitted in any form or by any means, including photocopying, recording, or other electronic or mechanical methods, without the prior written permission of the publisher, except in the case of brief quotations embodied in critical reviews and certain other non-commercial uses permitted by copyright law. For permission requests, write to the publisher.

Any person who commits any unauthorized act in relation to this publication may be liable to criminal prosecution and civil claims for damages.

This is a work of fiction. Names, characters, businesses, places, events, locales, and incidents are either the products of the author's imagination or used in a fictitious manner. Any resemblance to actual persons, living or dead, or actual events is purely coincidental.

Ordering Information
Quantity sales: Special discounts are available on quantity purchases by corporations, associations, and others. For details, contact the publisher at the address below.

Publisher's Cataloguing-in-Publication data
Barnes, EJ
The Road to You

ISBN 9798886937213 (Paperback)
ISBN 9798886937220 (ePub e-book)

Library of Congress Control Number: 2023922835

www.austinmacauley.com/us

First Published 2024
Austin Macauley Publishers LLC
40 Wall Street, 33rd Floor, Suite 3302
New York, NY 10005
USA

mail-usa@austinmacauley.com
+1 (646) 5125767

Chapter One

It was a cold January night; outside, the wind was blowing and the snow flying. Inside, the warm fire roared and the passion was hot.

Lisa and Chad lay naked in each other's arms, as the heat from the fire beat down on their hot bodies. Chad caressed her and she quivered with his passionate touch as he slid his hand down to caress her hot moist loins.

He sucked and nibbled at her breasts, her nipples were hard with erotic pleasure, as she threw herself on top of him and rode him like a wild stallion. Feeling his massive organ deep inside of her, Lisa screamed and panted with pleasure. Her heart was pounding and her pulse racing, as she fell deep into erotic ecstasy.

Chad pulled her close and rolled her over, then getting on top, he pushed his massive organ deeper inside of her. Lisa kissed him gently and sucked his nipples. He groaned and began to shake with pleasure as he reached his peak. Lisa, so aroused and excited, felt as if she would burst with erotic pleasure. They screamed with such satisfaction, as they climaxed together, it was as though the whole room shook.

Then Chad pulled away from her and lay down beside her. Lisa was so totally satisfied, she felt like she was in heaven. Even though she knew that it would soon be time to leave, and she would have to face the real world and what was waiting for her back at home.

Lisa and Chad were lovers, two people who'd been in love for years, yet due to circumstances and their lives ending up on different paths, they were separated. It had been a long road back to each other and their love never faded. Lisa was now a married woman. Her husband David, was a very abusive man, who never truly loved her. He preferred sleeping around with hookers, strippers and any other woman who would take him. Chad on the other hand, was a very successful business man. He treated Lisa like a true princess, he loved and respected her and would move heaven and earth to keep her safe.

Chad however was also married, not to another woman but to his job, and didn't really have the time in his busy life for a serious relationship or commitment. Even though he loved Lisa with all of his heart, there was still the factor of her husband. Chad hated the way that her husband treated her, but there was nothing that he himself could do about it, without jeopardizing Lisa's safety.

David was an alcoholic and was always out at the bar, so every night while David was out, she and Chad would get together. They were very close and now that they were reunited, they enjoyed every moment they spent together. The passion between them was extreme and they got great pleasure from fulfilling each other's sexual fantasies.

Lisa got up from the floor, she kissed Chad sweetly.

"It's that time again, babe, even though I hate it. I better head home before David, gets there. I'll see you tomorrow, stallion, have the fire roaring and the wine chilled."

Chad groaned as he rubbed her shoulders.

"You know I will, baby. I'll be ready and waiting."

Then he smacked her bottom.

"See you tomorrow, love buns, and take care of yourself."

Lisa smiled and waved as she then headed back home to her violent and unsettled marriage. Rushing to get in before David, arrived home from the bar.

She knew that as always, he would be drunk and likely have been with a hooker or two. Lisa hated him for that, but no matter what, she couldn't let him find out about Chad. She quickly ran upstairs to have a shower and get ready for bed. Then she lay down on the sofa to watch television making it look as though she had been home all evening.

Shortly thereafter, David arrived home.

As always, he was in a violent mood and began throwing things around. Lisa did her best to stay out of his way, but no matter what she did, it was always wrong.

David grabbed her and began punching her and yelling.

"You bitch, what in the hell do you think you're doing lounging around like that? You should be taking care of this bloody house; doesn't our home mean anything to you?"

Lisa was terrified as she tried to calm him.

"David, it's late. Why don't we just head up to bed and I'll do the house work in the morning?"

David yelled, "No Lisa, look at this place, it's a bloody mess."

Lisa thought to herself,

Well gee, I wonder why. Stupid fool.

David then grabbed her again, punching her once more in the face.

"You'll clean up this mess now; you're not to go to bed until this place shines."

Lisa afraid to say no, as always, agreed. David then went up to bed and passed out.

Lisa did the cleaning, even though she knew the mess was caused by David's violence and then decided to call Chad. She needed to speak to somebody who cared and would listen.

"Hi Chad, its Lisa. Did I wake you? I really need to talk to you."

Chad knowing that something was wrong quickly answered,

"No Lisa, it's fine, I was still up. What's wrong? You sound upset."

The phone was silent for a second then Lisa sighed, "Only the usual, but I'm okay, I suppose." Chad became concerned as he jumped in.

"Did he hurt you? Are you sure that you're okay? What happened?"

She quietly answered, "Well he hit me several times, even in the face this time, but I think I'm okay. Really. I just needed to hear a friendly voice."

Chad was furious but not wanting to make it known, he sighed.

"Look, Lisa, I really wish that you would just leave the bum. He's no good and you don't deserve to be treated this way. What David is doing to you is wrong; nobody deserves to live this way."

Tears began to stream down her cheek and her voice become choppy as she replied.

"Chad I know, but he's my husband and it's just the way he is. Besides, eventually, I do hope to have a new life, I pray every day for things to change. It's just really hard. It really isn't easy starting over, and I guess you could say I'm scared. Anyway enough about David, I called to forget about him."

Chad was quiet as she continued.

"I'm really looking forward to tomorrow night, I can't wait to see you again you make all the problems in my life fade away. Even though it's just a few hours a night, it keeps me going."

Chad sighed, "Lisa, I'm looking forward to tomorrow too, but you really do need to talk about David. You can't keep ignoring the problem and just hoping it will go away. Anyway, I suppose we can drop it for now. We will talk about it more tomorrow though, understood?"

Lisa sighed.

"Understood. Oh Chad. I can't wait to see you, I wish I could be there right now, but I can't be." Chad understood.

"I know Lisa, I feel the same. I'm looking forward to seeing you tomorrow too. I always look forward to seeing you. Anyway, hun, I should get to bed, it's late and I've got a lot of work to get done tomorrow. I'll see you tomorrow night, love buns, make sure you're ready for an evening filled with nothing but pleasure. I know exactly what my lady likes, and you know, I love to please you."

Lisa purred like a kitten then replied.

"Oh, I'll be ready stallion; you know that I can't get enough of you. Okay I'll let you go, see you tomorrow."

"Okay bye, Hun, be careful." Chad replied.

Lisa got off the phone from Chad and headed up to bed. Then as she lay down next to her husband, all she could think about was Chad and their relationship. She knew that it was wrong for her to be having an affair while she was still married to David. Yet Chad, had been the one in her heart for years. The lost love, she could never get over and fought to find her way back too. He was her true happiness and the only excitement she had in her life for a very long time.

Deep down Lisa always hoped that someday she and Chad would have a serious relationship and be a couple again. She was a very sexual woman, yet David never saw that side of her, nor did he want to. He preferred to have sex with strangers. Lisa was no longer the light of David's life, yet in Chad's life, she was. Lisa needed and wanted both the love and sexual fulfillment that she got from Chad. He completed her, with Chad everything felt right and comfortable. Almost as if they'd never been apart and lost all of those years together.

David was constantly beating on her, and going out to get drunk trying to see who he could pick up. Even if it were just a hooker off a street corner it meant more to him than Lisa did. She told herself, that her marriage was over, in every sense of the word. All that was left was to make it legal, but David wouldn't allow it. He refused to give her back her freedom. He needed her there to do his cooking and his cleaning and to take his frustrations out on, whenever he had a bad day.

Chad on the other hand was sweet and gentle. He filled her life to the brim with caring and understanding and he fulfilled all of her needs and deepest fantasies.

The night passed quickly and once again David was gone. Off to the bar where he would drink and mess around all day and night. Lisa, was excited about seeing Chad again, so spent the entire day making sure all of her chores done and the house was in perfect order, then went and prettied herself up for Chad and headed over to meet him at his apartment, where he met her at the door.

He immediately grabbed her, pulled her close to him and began sucking on her ear lobes and kissing her neck.

"Hi baby, I've been waiting."

He then slowly slid his hand down her blouse and began fondling her breasts.

Lisa moaned,

"I've been waiting to see you too, babe."

Then as she reached down and unzipped the zipper on his jeans, she moaned.

"So, how's my wild stallion tonight?"

She then, took him into her hand and began stroking his already hard organ up and down.

Chad groaned, Lisa got down on her knees. She then slipped his jeans down to his knees and began sucking and nibbling at him hungrily.

Chad moaned and groaned with pleasure.

"Oh Lisa, yes baby, that's it, suck it baby, lick me like a lollipop That's it baby; you know how I like it."

He shook and quivered as he reached his peak.

Lisa licked him faster and faster, he could feel how badly she wanted him. Then he climaxed and his love juices began to flow.

Lisa moaned and she sucked and licked him.

"Oh yes baby, ooh you taste so good, oh Chad oh yes." She sucked him faster and faster until he couldn't take it anymore. He reached out and took her into his arms and lay her down on the floor.

"Come on baby, it's your turn. Let me taste those sweet lips of yours."

Lisa moaned as he then began licking her hot wet opening.

So aroused, she began thrashing about the floor with pleasure. Chad sucked her hard clit and pushed his tongue deep inside of her to taste the passionate love juices of his sensual lover.

Lisa shrieked with pleasure as her climax arose. She pulled Chad closer, pushing his hard organ inside of her. Then when he was deep inside, he began pushing himself in and out faster and harder each time.

Lisa raked her nails down his back as she screamed. "Harder my wild stallion, harder. Come on baby, give it to me, give it to me hard."

Chad pumped deeper and deeper. With each thrust of his hardness, Lisa shrieked with excitement and sexual satisfaction. She was soon so overcome by erotic waves, she grabbed him and rolled him over. Then getting on top of him she rode him like a wild stallion. Chad was so deep inside of her that it hurt, but the pain was surrounded by such pleasure that she didn't care. She just kept on riding him faster and faster until they both peaked and burst into massive orgasm.

Then as they sailed to the heights of sexual satisfaction, they held each other close, feeling the beating of their two hearts together.

Lisa lay down on the floor next to Chad. He pulled her closer, holding her in his arms as they panted, trying to catch their breath. The light from the fire lit a romantic scene, as Chad caressed her and rubbed her shoulders.

He bent down and gently kissed her earlobe, and then he whispered.

"You're the best, hun; I just wish that you would leave that husband of yours. He doesn't deserve you, and you don't deserve to be treated that way."

Lisa sighed, not wanting to talk about David.

"Oh Chad, please don't, please don't spoil the mood. Let's just enjoy each other."

With that, she began kissing his chest and stroking his manhood, signaling that she wanted more. Chad found the offer tempting, however knew that the matter of David needed to be discussed.

"Lisa, we really need to talk about this. You can't go on like this and you know it. David is a no-good bum, all he ever does is hurt you."

She sighed as she looked down at the floor.

"Look Chad, I know that David is a bum, but he is my husband. I don't know what to do anymore; if I leave, I would have to start my life all over again, and I'm not sure that I could."

Chad kissed her sweetly.

"Lisa I know that you could. You're a very strong woman, too strong to go on taking this abuse. You'll be fine, I promise, I will see to it."

She smiled.

"Chad you're so sweet, but really I can handle it. Like you said, I'm strong. Don't worry so much, I can handle David, or at least, I like to believe I can. Besides if I left him, what would I do? You know, I hate being alone."

Chad placed his hand on her chin and raised her head to look in to her eyes.

"Oh come on now, you know that you wouldn't be alone. You've got me and you know it, that's no excuse."

Lisa sighed.

"Yes, for now."

Chad looked confused.

"What do you mean, for now?" He quietly answered.

"Well, come on, Chad. Sure, we're together now, but what about later? You don't have the space in your life for a commitment and that is something I need, we went our separate ways before. Who's to say, that it wouldn't happen again?"

Chad hugged her.

"Oh, Lisa. Just give me some time, give me time to slow things down in my life. When I commit to you, I want to be sure that I can give you all the attention and love you deserve."

Lisa pulled him closer and kissed him.

"Chad, you truly are a gentleman. You're the best, I'm lucky to have you in my corner."

Then as she glanced down and saw her watch she jumped up from the floor and quickly began dressing.

"Look at the time! Oh no! I've got to get home before David. I'm running late tonight. Chad, I really wish that I could stay, but I've got to go, I'm sorry."

Chad sighed.

"You have nothing to be sorry about. I mean, sure, I wish that you could stay too, but I also don't want you being hurt because of me. So, go on and I'll see you tomorrow. I love you."

Lisa smiled as she kissed him sweetly on the cheek. "Thanks for understanding. Babe. I love you too. I'll see you tomorrow, got to run."

With that, she headed home.

Luckily arriving home before David. Wanting to avoid a fight, she rushed around, double checking that everything was in place, and then she headed up to bed.

But as always, it still wasn't good enough for David.

He walked in the door and few minutes later and headed straight upstairs.

"Lisa get up! Get your lazy butt out of that bed now. I'm hungry, go down and cook me something to eat. You know, like a good wife would? All you ever do is lounge around, you stupid lazy bitch."

Then he grabbed her and began punching her, closed-fisted.

"What do you think you're doing going to bed before I get home? Don't you have any respect? Get your lazy ass moving."

With that, he threw her down the stairs. Then as she lay at the bottom, he yelled.

"Now get up and cook me something to eat or else."

At this point, she had become so afraid of David, that she was terrified to say no. So, in pain, she pulled herself up and headed into the kitchen to cook something for David to eat. Which still, wasn't good enough for him.

Even after, she had done what he wanted and had taken the time to prepare him something to eat, he decided it wasn't what he wanted after all.

He got up and dumped it into the garbage and then grabbing the frying pan started beating Lisa with it.

She cried and begged for him to stop, but the harder she cried, the harder he hit. So she pulled herself together, and took the beating until he finally got bored with her and stopped.

Lisa wished that he would just die. She had thought about killing David, but she knew that doing something like that would just land her in jail.

She refused to give up her life and spend the rest of her days in prison because of a jerk like David. He wasn't worth it and death would be letting him off too easy.

Lisa vowed that one day; she would finally be free of him and hopefully once again, have a life with Chad. She knew that Chad loved her, he had for years. But if she divorced her husband, she would want a real commitment from him. Which at this point Chad wasn't ready for. He felt his life wasn't in order and things needed to be more organized, before he could fully commit to anyone.

So for now, it appeared that all he wanted was their sexual relationship and of course, his work. Nevertheless, Lisa was determined to make him completely and totally hers. She believed that she and Chad would soon be free and completely devoted to each other for life and David would no longer be a problem, nor would Chad's work.

After a very painful and restless night's sleep, Lisa decided she would go out shopping. She wanted to buy something really sexy to wear for Chad. She was sure that if she kept it interesting, eventually he would be hers, forever. She got up and started to get ready to leave, when David came in.

"Good you're up, I guess this means I don't have to drag you out of bed. Look Lisa the kitchen cupboards are really disorganized, I want them cleaned right away, and I expect you to do it, before you even think about, leaving this house."

For a brief second, she got brave and stood up to him.

"Well, sorry David, I was just heading out. The cupboards can wait until I get home, I shouldn't be gone too long." David smirked as he became furious and lunged at her, grabbing her by the throat.

"Look you stupid little whore. Did you think I was kidding? I want it done and you'll do it now."

Lisa tried to defend herself, she took her hair dryer and bashed him across the side of the head with it.

"No, you stupid jerk. I'll do it when I'm ready and not until."

That was it, Lisa had crossed the line. David grabbed her by the throat and began choking her. Then he bashed her head several times on the side of the tub, causing it to split open. As the blood began to run down the side of her face, David once again blamed her and jumped up yelling.

"You stupid foolish woman. Now look what you've made me do, why can't you just listen and do what you're told and these things wouldn't happen."

With that, he threw a wash cloth at her.

"Clean yourself up. I'm going out and I won't be home until tomorrow. I've got better things to do than sit around here watching blood gush from your head. Besides, prostitutes are more interesting then you'll ever be."

Then he laughed a fierce laugh and left slamming the door behind him.

Lisa knew that she needed help and she could only think of one person who could help her. She got up from the bathroom floor and called Chad.

"Hi, Chad Roberts, please."

Chad took the call.

"Hi, Chad. It's me, Lisa. I'm sorry to call you at work."

Chad knowing that his was unusual for Lisa, knew something was wrong.

"It's okay Lisa, what is it?"

She began to sob.

"I'm hurt really bad. David beat the hell out of me last night, and then this morning he finished the job. Listen I really need help, my head is split open, I'm not sure how bad it is, but I think that I need to go to the hospital. There's a lot of blood and it really hurts, I'm dizzy too. Oh, Chad, it was awful."

Chad was furious with David.

"Oh, Lisa when will this all end? Listen, hang on and try and relax. I'm on the way."

With that, he hung up the phone.

Lisa forced herself over to the door and unlocked it for Chad and then she lay down on the sofa with a towel under her head. She couldn't believe that David had hurt her this bad. He had never taken it this far before. She was terrified, not just of David, but of what was going to become of her, if David took his abuse any further.

Then as she lay on the sofa, she heard the sound of squealing tires as Chad pulled in the drive way.

He rushed in the door and over to the sofa. Lisa at this point was limp and motionless and just stared straight ahead afraid to move.

"Oh Lisa, oh look what he's done to you."

Lisa looked up in to Chad's worried eyes as he then scooped her up and carried her out to his car.

"Lisa, honey, you've really got to get away from him. Sooner or later, he's going to end up killing you. Now, I'm taking you to the hospital and I hope that when they asked what happened, you'll tell them the truth so that they can help you. Of course, that decision is up to you. If you don't tell them, I guess I'll have to except that, but I won't like it. Anyway, I hope that you'll think about it, you really do need help."

Lisa replied softly.

"Yes, Chad, I know. I also know that I need to get away from David. But right now there is just no way. He won't give me a divorce and if I'm not careful, he'll find out about you. If he knew that I was seeing you, he would never let me out of the house again. Please Chad, try to understand. I just can't let him find out, I couldn't handle losing you again. You're all I've got right now."

Chad shook his head with fury over David.

"Well Lisa, fine. But sooner or later all of this crap will have to end and David will have to pay for all he has done. I mean it, Lisa, David is going to be one sorry boy."

Lisa wondered what Chad had meant by that, but said nothing more. Her head hurt and she no longer wanted to discuss the matter, it was only upsetting her more. All she wanted was to see a doctor and then get back home to rest.

When they arrived at the hospital, just as Chad had suspected, the nurse asked Lisa how she had gotten hurt.

Lisa not wanting to stir anything up, explained that she had fallen down the stairs and hit her head on a table at the bottom.

The nurse wasn't falling for it, as she replied.

"Lisa, are you sure that you weren't hurt by somebody. This doesn't look like the typical accident. I've seen many people who have fallen down stairs and their injuries were nothing like this."

Lisa sighed, "Yes I'm sure, nobody hurt me. You're right though, it wasn't the stairs. I just said that because what really happened is just too embarrassing. It was just a stupid accident, that's all."

The nurse still unsure what to think then asked.

"Now Lisa, you have nothing to be embarrassed about, accidents happen. Tell me what happened. Or should I say tell me what you'd like me to believe happened."

Lisa knew that nothing she said was going to convince the nurse, but as long as she stuck to her word, they couldn't do anything.

"I was taking a shower and my shower mat came lose. I fell and hit my head on the side of the tub."

The nurse still didn't believe the story, but went along with it. There was nothing that she could do, unless Lisa spoke up and told her the truth.

Chad was displeased with Lisa for lying about what had happened, as he went to take a seat in the waiting room.

Lisa knew that Chad wasn't happy with her, but she knew if she had told the truth, the nurse would have called the police. She couldn't allow that to happen, David would freak out on her.

And probably kill her. She had no choice but to lie.

The doctor then came in to see Lisa; he examined her and found so many bruises and scrapes on her, that he wasn't falling for the shower story either.

"Lisa, why don't you tell me what really happened? We can help you, but only if you let us. Someone has beaten you, it's obvious. You don't get bruises like this from falling in the shower and you're in far too much pain. Let us help you."

Lisa jumped.

"No I told you that nothing else happened and that's the end of it. I fell in the damn shower."

The doctor shook his head as he handed her a prescription for pain medication.

"Well, all right, Lisa. But if you choose to change your story, you can call us back here any time."

Lisa nodded.

"Fine. Now, can I get home?"

The doctor nodded.

"Yes, you can go home, just take those pills as long as you need them, if you feel any other pain or anything different, give me a call."

After seeing the doctor, Lisa headed out to meet Chad.

"Hi Hun, how are you?"

She answered, "I'm okay. The cut wasn't that deep after all. The doctor cleaned it up and bandaged it. He said that I'll be just fine. Now, can you take me home?"

Chad knew that there was more to it, but answered. "Sure, but I'm not taking you home to your place, I'm taking you to mine. I'm sorry if I got upset with you, I didn't mean to. All I want is for you to get help."

Lisa sighed.

"Yeah, I know you and everybody else, too."

Chad was confused.

"What does that mean?"

Lisa was frustrated and very confused at this point.

"Oh just you, the doctor and the nurse. Everybody wants to help me, but I don't see how anyone can. Anyway, Chad, it's okay. I understand your concern and I understand why you got upset with me."

Chad shook his head.

"Oh, baby, I just hate to see you this way, that's all. Anyway we'll drop it for now. You just try and relax and let me take care of you for a while."

With that, Lisa got into the car and laid her head back on the seat to rest.

For the rest of the ride to Chad's apartment, nothing more about the incident was said.

Lisa and Chad sat on his sofa, holding each other close.

Lisa explained what she had been planning to do, when David got so angry.

"Chad, thank you for your help. I can't believe that David went this far. All I was planning to do today was go out to the mall. I wanted to buy something sexy to wear for you tonight. I wanted to surprise you and I guess instead it was me who got the surprise. I'm really sorry that things turned out like this. Will you forgive me?"

Chad sighed.

"Lisa, you have nothing to be sorry for and there's nothing to forgive. This wasn't your fault, David is a sick man. As for going out to get something sexy, baby, you don't have to wear something sexy to please me. I've always believed that if you feel sexy then you are sexy. Let me tell you, honey, you've got exactly what it takes. You don't have to hide behind some silk teddy to prove it either."

She smiled and gazed into his eyes.

"Chad, you're so sweet. I guess that's what I love about you. You're so understanding and so caring. I'm happy that you came back into my life. I needed you. I always have and I pray that this road I am on, only leads to one place. Me safe, in your loving arms for the rest of my life."

Chad kissed her as he lay her back on the sofa and began unbuttoning her blouse.

"Are you up to it, baby? Because if not, I'll stop right now. I don't want to hurt you."

Lisa smiled as she whispered.

"Yeah I'm up to it; I'm always up to it when it comes to you."

Chad moaned and growled like tiger.

"Well then just relax and let me show you just how sexy you really are and I promise to fulfill your every desire."

Lisa becoming aroused with his words moaned.

"Oh, yes, my wild stallion. Show me what you're made of."

Chad slipped off her bra and began kissing and caressing her breasts. He encircled her pebble hard nipples with the tip of his tongue, as he slowly slid his hand down her pants sliding them off. Then as she lay there in nothing but her silk panties, she felt him gently caressing her hot wet opening.

Lisa wanted him so bad, that she was sure that she would burst with erotic pleasure.

Right then, Chad put his hands on her hips sliding her down on the sofa.

"Come on baby, it's time for me to please you and make you quiver with waves of sexual satisfaction."

He then got down on his knees and began licking her hard clit, while stroking his finger in and out of her soaked opening.

Lisa shook and wriggled about the sofa. She rocked her pelvis, signaling that she wanted more, as she stroked her fingers through his hair.

Suddenly Chad got up from the side of the sofa.

"I'll be right back, baby; I've got something that will really please you."

Then he went into the bedroom, where he took a vibrator out of the drawer and returned to the sofa. He turned it on and then slowly rolled the tip over her hot yearning mound, he moved it downward and encircled her clit, causing her to shake with excitement. He continued to move the sex toy around her mound and her opening, making her want it inside of her. Her body was out of control as she began pushing her pelvis upward in a rocking motion. Then as if Chad had read her mind, he slowly slipped it deep inside of her.

Lisa shrieked with excitement, as she climaxed and burst into massive orgasm. Then as she sailed to the great heights of ecstasy, Chad continued pushing the sex toy in and out of her opening. He moved it faster and faster, deeper each time. He really seemed to be getting great pleasure out of pleasing his hot lover with his sex toy. Lisa climaxed over and over, she was soaked with sweat and her entire body quivered. Then as she lay there in complete ecstasy, Chad rubbed her shoulders.

"How was that, honey? A night just for you."

Lisa moaned.

"Oh, that was great. You're remarkable. I never imagined that playing with sex toys could be this fun."

Chad laughed.

"Oh, Lisa, you just have to know what you're doing, and what your partner likes. You, my dear made it pretty apparent, what it was you wanted."

Lisa blushed and smiled.

"Well I guess we both know what each other needs and enjoys."

With that, she got down on her knees and began sucking his rock-hard dick.

Chad moaned and twitched as he raced to the heights of sexual desire and shot his hot cum, in her mouth. She continued to suck him faster and longer, she was determined to satisfy him, the way he had her. She sucked him while stroking him up and down, as she fondled his warm balls with her other hand. Until he was once again brought to orgasm, she then moved up and gently kissed his chest.

Chad bent down and kissed her sweetly as he said.

"I guess you're right, baby. We do know exactly what the other likes and needs. That was great, but you didn't have to, you know. After all, it was supposed to be a night just for you."

Lisa smiled.

"I know and I appreciate that. I just wanted to give some of the pleasure back. You deserve it, besides I'd feel guilty if I didn't satisfy you."

Chad chuckled.

"Oh Lisa you're so great, now come here. Come and sit close to me, let me hold you."

Lisa sat on the sofa next to him and he put his arm around her. Then for the rest of the evening, they sat by the fire holding each other close.

Lisa wished that it could always be like this, she wanted to be with Chad forever and never again have to return home to David. However the way things stood, it was going to be quite a while before that happened, if ever at all.

Once again the time had come for her to return home to her loveless marriage and leave Chad there waiting for her. Her life was filled with nothing but pain and hate.

David was always hurting her, whether it was physically or mentally, there was always something he was doing to cause her pain. She wanted him out of her life for good, but without a divorce he wouldn't let her go. She and David hadn't made love in over two years and it seemed that their marriage was over.

However whenever Lisa mentioned divorce, he would become violent and beat on her. He would yell at her and tell her that she was owned by him and say that there was no way in hell he would ever give her a divorce and that he wouldn't allow her to leave him.

He told her that she married him, she was stuck with him and that trying to leave would be her biggest mistake. David truly believed that he owned her and that he controlled her every move.

Lisa had thought a lot about killing David to end her pain, she had even thought about ways to do it. However not being her nature, she couldn't bring herself to do it. She couldn't picture herself actually killing someone, no matter how terribly violent and abusive they were.

All of her life, she had dreamed about meeting a loving man, someone like Chad, who she had secretly loved for years. Someone to spend her life with and have lots of children. When she married David, she was sure that he was the man to make all of her dreams come true. She loved him and she believed that he would always love her to. Only a few years later, she discovered that she was wrong.

The man she had married and vowed to love was an abusive drunk, who turned out to hate children. Lisa wanted out and decided that she had taken enough of David's abuse. One way or the other she was going to fight for a new life and she prayed that this horrifying road she was on, would end with Chad.

Lisa sat up all night that night, trying to make sense out of the way her life had turned out, but she couldn't find the answer. A loving relationship had turned into an abusive one and she couldn't understand why. All that she could figure was that it was the alcohol and David's great love for hookers and having sex with anybody but his wife.

Then as she sat in the bedroom, thinking about all of her problems. She suddenly heard the door slam shut. David had returned home. Lisa's heart began pounding with fear, as she wondered what kind of mood he was in this time. She never knew what was coming next, David was a time bomb and the slightest thing would set him off.

There was never any warning, his mood swings were constantly changing. Lisa thought that if she just lay down and pretended that she was sleeping, he would leave her alone. But she was wrong. Right then he burst through the door and started beating her. She knew right then, that he was never going to leave her alone. He enjoyed seeing her hurting and his day just wouldn't be complete unless he was beating her.

Lisa bolted up.

"David stop, leave me alone. Please, just go and leave me the hell alone. Why can't you ever treat me with some respect? Why do you always have to hurt me?"

David laughed as he bashed her across the face several times, once again causing her head to bleed.

"You stupid foolish woman, I'll do whatever I want to you and I'll never let you go either. You're too much fun to have around. I married you and now you're my possession and my own personal maid. All you're good for is cooking and cleaning, anyway. Everything else I can get elsewhere, from real women."

David continued to hit her over and over, knocking her around like a piece of trash. Then he ordered her to go and make him breakfast.

"I'll have coffee and toast, and don't screw it up or you'll be sorry."

Lisa couldn't believe that this was happening to her, it was like a nightmare. Against David, she was powerless and felt like a little child. She was always giving in to his demands and taking his abuse. As she prepared his toast and coffee, she stood in the kitchen and cried. Her life was a total mess and more than ever, she felt trapped.

Once David's breakfast was ready, she took it into the dining room where he was waiting. As she walked into the room, she found David sitting at the table fondling himself and looking at a porn magazine. She gasped at what she saw and David turned around. He looked at the shocked expression on her face and began yelling.

"You dumb bitch, what the hell is your problem? Are you surprised to find that even my own hands are better than you are?"

Then he laughed a vicious laugh and turned away, finished what he was doing and headed in to the kitchen for breakfast. As soon as he finished, he once again, began yelling.

"Lisa, make sure that the housework is done and all of the laundry is cleaned. I have a date tonight and I need some clean clothes. Oh and Lisa I'm bringing somebody home tonight for a romantic night. So make sure that you are out and you don't return home until after three A.M."

Then he threw a hundred-dollar bill at her.

"Now get your ass moving. Get the work done and then clear out of here. I don't want to ruin my mood by staring at you for the rest of the day."

Lisa couldn't believe that David was going to bring another woman home, to sleep with her in their marital bed. But she didn't let it bother her, as this was the first time that she wasn't going to have to sneak out to see Chad. David was allowing her to go. Although she knew that if David were to find out, where she was actually going, he would keep her under lock and key.

Lisa hurried to get the house in tip top shape and finish the laundry. Then decided that she would go over to Chad's place early. She wanted to be there before he got home from work, to set things up for a real sensual evening. She planned to shock him and show him just how sexual she really was.

Once she arrived at Chad's apartment, Lisa lit the living room with candles and pulled his bear skin rug to the center of the room. Then she lit a fire in the fire place and lay down naked on the rug, to wait for him to arrive home from work.

Shortly thereafter he arrived. He walked in the door, to find Lisa spread out on the rug playing with a vibrator.

"Lisa, you're here early and boy do you look great."

Then as he watched her pushing the vibrator deep inside of herself, he became aroused.

"Oh baby, that looks fun. Oh Lisa I want you, I want you bad."

Then he got down on the floor next to her and watched as she moved the toy faster and faster, in and out of her wet opening while fondling her own breasts. She smiled at Chad.

"Don't worry baby, you'll get some too."

Chad groaned with passion as his heart raced.

"Oh I'm not worried about that. I'm just enjoying watching you please yourself this way; it's a real turn on."

Then he smiled.

"Here baby, let me join you."

With that, he began stroking his hard organ up and down with his hand.

Lisa watched him as she continued to play with her hot moist loins. She wanted him bad, as she reached out to him. "Come here baby, I want you to cum on my chest. I want to feel your hot sex juices on my body."

Chad moaned as he moved toward her allowing his sexual juices to flow freely across her chest. Feeling his excitement, she herself was brought to orgasm. Lisa groaned and thrashed about the floor, as Chad then began sucking her hard nipples and caressing her yearning mound. Then moving his hand down, he began fingering her ass.

"I want to stick it in your ass, baby."

Chad said as he then rolled her over and got up behind her. He began penetrating her ass as he fondled and caressed her breasts. Lisa had never had sex like this before, but found herself enjoying it. As Chad continued pumping at her faster and longer, she reached between her legs and began fondling her clit.

She was so erotically stimulated, she was once again brought to orgasm and at the same time so was Chad. He held on to her tight as they panted, trying to catch their breaths. Their bodies tingled with pleasure as they rolled over and kissed each other passionately burying their tongues deep in each other's mouths. As they kissed, they caressed each other.

Chad asked, "So what happened to David? You don't usually get out of the house this early."

She sighed.

"Oh it's a long story, to make it short he has some woman coming over and he didn't want me around. He actually told me to go out and not to come home until after three A.M."

Chad was stunned.

"He's having another woman over? In your bed. How can he do that? She's probably some sleazy hooker, too."

Lisa sighed.

"Yes, she probably is, but I can't argue with David. I have to just sit back and let him do whatever he sees fit, if I get in the way…Well you know what happens then. Anyway enough about him, I'm hungry, are you?"

He agreed.

"Yes I'm starved but I'd also like a shower. Why don't you join me and then afterwards we'll grab something to eat?"

She smiled a sensual smile.

"I'd love to join you; I haven't had the opportunity before." Chad smacked her ass.

"Well come on then."

As they took their shower and looked at each other's wet soapy bodies, they once again found themselves becoming aroused. They washed each other and stroked each other passionately until they soon found themselves once again making love.

Chad lifted her up against the shower wall and began entering her over and over. They kissed wildly and they groaned and shook with such sexual satisfaction, that it was as if time had stopped. They orgasmed together as they felt like one and they raced to the great heights of sexual stimulation.

Lisa pulled him close as she whispered.

"You make me feel whole, Chad. You know exactly how to please me and make me feel like a real woman."

Then she kissed him.

Chad held her close as the hot water dripped down their warm bodies.

"Well, Lisa, I believe that good sex is all in who you're with. If you're with the wrong person, you don't really care whether or not you're making them happy. You're either making love, or you're having nothing more than sex with no meaning. I guess we're just meant for each other."

Lisa was stunned as she kissed him sweetly and whispered in his ear.

"I love you, Chad."

He smiled whispered back. "I love you too, hun."

After they finished their shower, they decided to order in Chinese food. Then they sat by the fire and talked about their wildest sexual fantasies and their deepest desires.

Lisa found that Chad had a lot more to him then she had once thought when she heard about his biggest fantasy. He explained.

"Well Lisa, I've always had this really wild fantasy. It's one that I would love to fulfill, but I'm not so sure that you would go for it."

She grinned and raised her eyebrows.

"Well, what is it? You know that I'm always up for something new and exciting. Come on tell me. Maybe, I would be up for it."

Chad chuckled as he answered.

"Yes, Lisa I know, but this just may be too wild even for you. It involves another woman."

Lisa was shocked as she jumped in.

"Chad what exactly do you mean? Another woman!"

He explained, "Well I have this wild fantasy about watching two women going at each other. Watching them kiss each other and finger and lick each other. Then afterwards I have sex with them."

Lisa was astonished.

"You mean you want me to have sex with another woman and then sit by while you have sex with her to?"

Chad answered, "Well, yes, but if you would feel better about it, I'd only have sex with you. I wouldn't even touch the other woman. Come on, Lisa, you'll never know if you like it until you try it."

Lisa, still stunned, replied.

"Well, I'll need to think about it for a while, I'm really not sure that I like the idea, in fact I'm quite shocked. I never knew that you liked that sort of thing, anyway I'll think about it and possibly consider it."

Chad assured her, that nothing would change between them if she went through with it and told her that they would never have to see the woman again.

Lisa was becoming frustrated as she replied.

"Alright, Chad enough. Please just give me some time to think it over. I can't make a decision like that on the spur of a moment."

Chad leaned over and kissed her.

"Okay, baby, I'm sorry. I won't pressure you, I'll just let it go for now. Just tell me that you'll seriously think about it."

She sighed.

"Yes, Chad, like I said, I'll think it over."

The rest of the night, they sat by the fire, holding each other and talking about their dreams and their plans for the future. Lisa had no real plans, other than to be with Chad. He, on the other hand had big plans, for a big future. Lisa found herself wondering, where she would fit in to all of that and what it would mean for them. She loved Chad and he loved her, but would his plans always include her as Lisa hoped they would?

The night had now passed and Lisa was once again going to have to leave. It was already two A.M. and she was told to be home by three A.M.

"Well Chad, I'm sorry, but I've really got to get going. David wants me home by three and you know how he can be if I'm late. I've really got to hurry."

Chad passed her clothes over to her as he sighed.

"I really wish you didn't have to go home to that creep. You're too good for him, he really doesn't deserve you." Lisa smiled and kissed him passionately before heading home.

Chad once again reminded her.

"Please think about what I asked, will you?"

She sighed, not really wanting to think about it at that moment.

"Yes Chad, I said that I would and I meant it. Don't worry, I'll let you know, one way or the other. Now I've got to go, I'll see you tomorrow."

Chad kissed her at the door. "Okay, I'll see you later, be careful."

All the way home, all Lisa could think about, was what Chad wanted her to do and she wondered what it would actually be like. She couldn't imagine herself ever going through with it, but still considered giving it a try.

The whole idea made her very nervous, but she would be doing it for Chad. Pleasing Chad was her top priority, as she didn't want to lose him or destroy their relationship. Chad had done so much for her, so she decided that she would do this for him.

She thought to herself.

Well Lisa, you only live once and you're always up for new experiences. Okay, I'll do it, I'll say yes to Chad. After all, I do love him, this will make him happy and it's only a one-time thing anyway. So, why not?

She arrived at home, to find that David still had company. She walked in the door and immediately, he started yelling.

"Sleep on the sofa, you dumb bitch! I've still got company and she'll be staying the night."

Lisa was astonished as he then yelled, "Oh and Lisa I expect you, to bring us toast and coffee in the morning. You can bring it to us in bed and make sure that you don't forget."

Lisa couldn't believe what she was hearing and was furious as she yelled back.

"Yeah Sure David, I'll just wait on you and your slut like the good little waitress. Will that make you happy?"

David yelled.

"Yes, it would bitch and don't get so cocky with me. So God help me, Lisa, if you keep up your shit, you're as good as dead."

Lisa couldn't believe that David had actually said that he would kill her. He had never come right out and said it before, but tonight he did. She still couldn't believe that he was going to sleep with another woman right there in front of her. Even worse he expected her to serve them breakfast. She didn't want to do it, but knew she had to, so that she didn't get beat on again.

David was running her; he played her like a deck of cards, knowing just which card to play and when to play it.

As she lay on the sofa, she could hear David and the woman upstairs having sex in her bed. She was shocked that he would do something like that, right there in their bedroom. Especially when he knew that she was at home and could hear them. She then realized that she really didn't mean anything to him. The love was gone and their marriage was over.

Lisa knew that her sexual escapades with Chad weren't much better than David sleeping around. But at least she didn't have the gall to flaunt it and do it right there under his nose, in their home. She was furious with what was going on and the fact that she had to sleep on the sofa, only made things worse. Knowing that she couldn't interfere without being punished by David. Lisa rolled over and tried to ignore it and go to sleep.

The next morning only five hours later, Lisa was awakened by David standing over her, slapping her in the face.

"Come on, you stupid woman, get the hell up. I expect coffee for me and my date, in ten minutes."

Lisa was as angry with him as he turned around to go back upstairs, that she grabbed a ceramic vase, and threw it at him. Hitting him smack dab in the back of the head.

David laughed and turned around.

"Boy Lisa, aren't we a little testy this morning? What's the matter? Did you wake up on the wrong side of the sofa?"

Lisa yelled.

"You son of a bitch, get your own bloody coffee. I'm not serving you and that little tramp that you picked up off a street corner. Go to hell David, go straight to hell."

David was furious with her, but because there was somebody else in the house, he let it go by saying.

"Later dear, I swear you'll be sorry for speaking to me that way."

Lisa becoming brave laughed.

"Oh, will I, David? I don't think so. You won't be here later, you never are. Besides I'm going out."

David smirked.

"Oh, are you? Fine bitch, go out. Then there will be more room for me and my guest. The best part is that I won't have to look at your disgusting face. Just remember, be home before dawn, or I'll hunt you down like the dog you are and kill you."

David went back up with his date and Lisa got ready and left for Chad's. His apartment was the only place she had to go, and the only place where she knew she would be safe. There was never anybody there to hurt her or order her around.

When she arrived at Chad's apartment, he was still at work. Lisa decided that she would prepare a nice candle light dinner for the two of them, as she knew that he would most likely be tired, after a long day at the office. She prepared chicken parmesan and a Caesar salad; she chilled the wine and started a roaring fire to set the scene. Only a few hours later, Chad returned home and was surprised to see her there so soon again.

"Lisa, you're here early again. This is twice now, I'm stunned and look at this you've made me dinner. Wow, this is great; it will be nice to have a home cooked meal for once, instead of ordering out. Really, it looks delicious, it's great to be able to come home and sit down to a nice dinner. You're one terrific lady Lisa Curtis and I'm glad to have you in my life."

Lisa was pleased to see that Chad was happy with her as she replied.

"Well dear, I'd do anything for you and after dinner you're going to find out, just how far I'll go to make you happy."

Chad raised his eyebrows.

"Oh? What exactly have you got planned?" She smiled.

"Well you'll just have to wait and see, now won't you? We'll discuss the matter after dinner, don't worry, I'm sure you'll love it."

Then she leaned over and kissed him sweetly.

"Now come on, let's eat."

During dinner, Lisa told Chad about David and the other woman and she explained what they were doing, right there in front of her.

Then she went on to explain.

"I may have pushed it too far though. I told David to go to hell and I'm probably going to get it when I get home. You know that he won't stand for me telling him off, I guess I should've tried harder to control my mouth."

Chad was astonished with what David had done as he remarked.

"You know Lisa; you really do take too much crap from him. I'm amazed that you stand for it, you're tougher than this. Anyway I wish that you would just take care of that raving idiot once and for all."

Lisa was confused.

"Chad, what are you implying? What is it that you want me to do?"

Chad smirked.

"Don't worry princess, with my help you'll be free and he'll never hurt you again."

Lisa was lost, she couldn't understand what it was Chad meant.

"Chad, what exactly have you got in mind? By the look on your face, I know that it can't be good."

Chad grinned.

"Oh Lisa, don't you worry your pretty little head about it. I promise you'll find out when the time comes, now let's just enjoy this lovely dinner that you've prepared for us and have a good evening."

Chad raised his wine glass.

"Here's to the future, may it be happy and David-free."

Lisa was still wondering about what Chad had said, but she was happy to have finally heard Chad say, that he wanted a future with her. Now even more, Lisa couldn't wait to be free of the violence and enjoy a happy and loving life with Chad.

After dinner, Chad put on some slow music and led Lisa to the living room. They held each other and danced, while they kissed each other passionately, so passionately that one would believe they were committed to each. However as it stood, at this point all they were was lovers and this was all they could be until David was out of her life.

Lisa slowly unbuttoned Chad's shirt and gently and sweetly kissed his chest. Then moving downward she slid off his jeans and removed his bikini underwear with her teeth. She then continued by slowly kissing and caressing his inner thighs. Chad was becoming aroused; his manhood was erect and ready for the heat of passion to take over. Lisa got down on her knees and gently kissed and licked the head of his erection as she said.

"Do you want me, my sex machine? Do you really want me? Come on baby, tell me you do, tell me you want me."

Chad moaned.

"Yes baby, do your stuff, suck me, suck me good."

Lisa then took him into her mouth and began sucking him long and fast. She stroked him up and down as she reached in between her legs and caressed her hot moist opening. She then moved down his rock-hard shaft and began licking and sucking on his warm balls.

Chad shook with erotic excitement as she continued stroking and licking him. She moved faster and faster bringing him flying to the heights of arousal and causing a massive explosion in his loins. Lisa bent down and placed his pulsating organ between her breasts and allowed his hot sex juices to flow freely across her erect nipples.

The warm sensation of Chad's cum across her chest aroused her as she lay back. Then spreading her thighs wide, she began stroking her finger in and out of her hot yearning pussy. She moved her finger fast and encircled her clit, bringing herself skyrocketing to orgasm. Lisa writhed about the floor with sexual excitement, as Chad came to her and slapped her ass.

"Come on baby, roll over, I want a piece of the action. I want to feel the heat of your tight pussy, wrapped around my hard dick. Oh yeah baby, I want to screw your hot wet pussy."

Lisa rolled over and got on her knees; Chad came up behind her and slid his massive organ deep into her hot yearning loins. He gave it to her long and hard, she screamed and shrieked with erotic pleasure, as she rocked her body back and forth.

Chad then pulled away and rolled her over, then he began licking ferociously at her once again hard clit, longing for more. She rocked her body with the motion of his tongue, pressed hard against her love button. She felt his hot breath sweeping across her wet mound, as she then began rubbing her erect nipples. Lisa raced to the heights of sexual desire and burst into flames of orgasmic passion, as she panted and groaned with pleasure.

Chad then rolled her over and once again inserted his stiff organ, deep inside of her. He pushed it deeper and deeper, and just when she thought it was all inside of her, he pushed it even deeper. His hard, massive manhood filled her and the sensation of him stroking it fast, in and out deeper each time. Brought her such pleasure, she rolled about the floor, screaming with sensual and erotic satisfaction. Chad groaned and panted.

"Oh yeah baby, that's it, yes baby take me, take all of me." He pumped and pumped at her and wriggled with stimulation, as he pulled it almost all the way out and then rammed it back, deep inside her pulsating pussy. Lisa lay there in a complete erotic state, twisting her nipples as the waves of pleasure took over her body.

"Oh Chad, give it to me, baby, make me cum with your hard dick deep inside my pussy. Come on baby, do it to me, give it to me hard."

Chad moaned as he pumped faster, driving harder and longer as she felt the peak of her arising orgasm. Lisa knew that at any second the pleasure would dominate her every move and completely overcome her body. She screamed involuntarily as the erotic waves swept over her body. Grabbed on to Chad and pulled him deeper as she writhed about and shrieked.

"Oh yes, Chad, oh I'm going to cum. Yes, my stallion, yes, oh make me cum, make me cum good."

Right then she burst into flames of passion and orgasmed into total and complete ecstasy. She moaned and panted as she raked her nails down Chad's back and exclaimed, "Yes baby yes, that's it, baby. Oh, it feels so good, oh yes."

Chad shook as he reached his peak he groaned and convulsed uncontrollably. "Take it baby, take it, oh yeah baby take me, make me cum with you."

Chad moaned as his sexual juices began to flow freely deep inside Lisa's channel of love. He pulled her close and kissed her passionately, burying his tongue deep in her throat. They held each other tight and writhed with stimulation, feeling each other's passion.

Then as they lay there, with Chad holding her in his arms, suddenly out of the blue he said, "Darling, something has to be done about David. I want you all to myself and I don't want to see you hurting anymore."

Lisa smiled.

"I know Chad, but getting rid of David isn't easy. Now, please, let's just drop it and enjoy the moment, why ruin it by discussing David?"

Chad agreed.

"Yeah, you're right, I'm sorry honey and I understand how difficult things are for you. I guess we can just leave it alone for now, I don't want to ruin your evening, but we will talk about this."

Lisa and Chad sat by the fire in each other's arms, gazing into one another's eyes when Chad finally asked.

"So dear, have you given any thought to what I asked you yesterday? You know, about my fantasy and making it come true."

Lisa smiled.

"Well, actually, Chad, I have and I've decided that I'll do it. However I would like to wait a little while, I'm extremely nervous about the whole thing and I'd like some time to prepare myself for it."

Chad sighed.

"Well I'm glad that you're willing to do it, but are you really sure you want to wait? I was kind of hoping that if you said yes, we could do it next Saturday night."

Lisa saw the curiosity in Chad's eyes.

"Well, Chad I really did want to wait, but if it would make you happy…"

Then she paused for a moment and looked down at the floor, then looking back up she smiled.

"Okay, Chad I'll do it. Next Saturday night will be fine, I'm still really nervous though."

Chad kissed her and smiled.

"You're the best, Lisa. Really, there's nobody like you."

Lisa then decided that it was getting late and she would have to head out soon. "Listen Chad, it's getting late. Why don't I help you clean up from dinner before I go?"

She got up and headed into the kitchen to wash the dishes and Chad followed to help.

"It was really nice of you to cook me dinner tonight, Lisa." She smiled.

"Oh it wasn't a problem I loved doing it, I love doing anything for you."

Chad grinned as they finished up the dishes and Lisa got ready to head home.

"Well I guess I've got to get going, anyway. I'll see you tomorrow."

Chad smacked her ass.

"Yeah princess, I'll see you tomorrow, keep your chin up." Lisa smiled, kissed him on the cheek and headed out.

She dreaded going home to David, but knew that she had no other choice. She feared for her life and was sure that if she ever left him, he would track her down and kill both her and Chad.

Lisa prayed that someday he would just give up and let her go, but she was sure he never would. David had such a hold over her; she found it hard to even picture a life without abuse. A life of freedom with happiness instead of pain and suffering seemed like an impossible dream.

Lisa arrived home, to find a note on the table from David. The note read that he wouldn't be home until tomorrow and that he expected her to have all of the housework done. He said that he being gone all night would give her plenty of time to do her job and get the house spotless. Then he added to the bottom, P.S. you're not off the hook.

Lisa was worried about David's last remark, but didn't let it get to her. She was too happy about having a David free night. A night all to herself, without a beating or someone to order her around and make her feel small. Deep down she wished that by some freak accident, David would never return home and she would be freed from his clutches. However, Lisa knew that it was nothing more than a pipe dream and the night would soon pass by, and her abuser would return home.

Lisa lay down on the sofa and listened to some quiet music. Enjoying the peace and tranquility while it lasted, as it wouldn't be long before the yelling and the violence began again. As she lay on the sofa totally relaxed, she found herself wondering and fantasizing about sex with another woman. She wondered what it would be like and what the other woman would do. She thought about Chad watching them and wondered if she would enjoy it and she wondered how to please another woman and what she would have to do. Lisa was always up for something new and willing to try just about anything. However this was something that made her very uneasy and she was still unsure about the whole thing. Although all she wanted was to see Chad happy. He meant the world to her and she was determined to go through with it for him.

He had done so much for her and given her so much love and understanding. How could she not give him this one little thing and make his deepest fantasy come true.

Not having David at home, made Lisa happy and for the first time, she felt completely safe. It was as if she were dreaming, the house was silent and she was free from pain. Tonight would be the first night in eight years of marriage that she would get restful night's sleep.

Lisa's life was in complete limbo. She was married to one man, but in love with another and with the way her husband was, there was no possible way, for her to just walk out and go to be with Chad. For now, her life had to remain in limbo and remain a big mass of confusion.

The next morning, Lisa woke up feeling totally relaxed. She slept better than she ever had, while David was at home. She pulled herself out of bed and looked over at the clock. Then, noticing the time she suddenly panicked, she had over slept and David was due home any time. She hadn't got the housework done yet or even started his laundry. She rushed to get dressed and then quickly did the housework. She was in a complete frenzy trying to get everything done before he arrived. As she put a load of his laundry into the washer, she heard footsteps upstairs. Then as she heard the sound of keys hitting the table, she realized that David was home.

Lisa's hands began to shake as she suddenly became terrified. She hadn't gotten his laundry done and she knew that he would be furious.

Then as she turned to head upstairs, she was suddenly struck at the back of her head and knocked to the floor. David had hidden behind the door, as to catch her off guard. He was furious that the work wasn't finished and that she had deliberately disobeyed his letter.

He began yelling and screaming.

"You foolish woman, can't you do anything right? All I ever ask for is a clean house and clean clothes and you're so goddammed lazy, you can't even get that right. You knew that I would be home this morning and you never even bothered, to put on a pot of coffee. You're nothing but a selfish useless whore; you'll never learn, will you, Lisa?"

David then kicked her several times in the back and then in the face, blacking her eye and scraping and bruising her cheek.

Lisa tried to reach out for a two-by-four that was lying on the floor.

She was going to hit him back, but was caught. David stomped his foot down on her arm and he snickered.

"Don't try something that you'll regret, you stupid little bitch."

Then with one last kick to her back, David went upstairs and cracked open a bottle of scotch and began drinking.

Lisa lay on the floor and cried; she couldn't take anymore but didn't know how to stop it. There had to be some way out and she was determined to find it. David loved to see her in pain, she was nothing to him, other than someone to slap around. He was a drunk and the bottle meant more to him then their marriage. She had already suffered enough through eight years with him and she was totally worn out from fighting to survive.

She pulled herself up from the floor and went to clean herself up.

As she approached the top of the stairs, David was there.

He demanded that she clean the house, saying what she had already done wasn't good enough.

Lisa sighed and explained.

"Look David, I've already done the housework and I don't intend to do it all again, at least not right now. The house is fine; I don't know what you're complaining about."

David became furious; he picked up one of Lisa's plants and dumped the dirt all over the floor. Then he laughed and yelled.

"There, bitch. Now, you have something to do. Get a move on and get this mess cleaned up. You're such a fool, Lisa, all you had to do was listen."

Then he walked over and slapped her across the face once more.

"Get that smug look of your face, girl. I'm going out. I'm sick and tired of looking at your pitiful face, I'll be home when the bar closes and I expect dinner to be waiting for me in the fridge."

Lisa laughed.

"Yeah, fine, you stupid ass, I'll be sure and cook it before I go out."

David picked up the coffee table and threw it across the room.

"You're going out, are you? Well just make bloody sure that you're home by two A.M. If you're not, you'll be sorry. So god help me, Lisa, I'll come looking for you and if I find you, I'll kill you and anybody you're with. You remember dear, you're mine, I own you and there's no way out of this marriage. You'll just have to learn to deal with it."

Lisa shook her head as she sighed. "Yeah fine, David, just fine."

David then left slamming the door behind him. Lisa sat and cried, terrified of David and his threats.

She waited until she saw his car pull away and then she went to cook his dinner and put it in the fridge. Then she took a shower and after tried to cover up the bruises on her face. However her eye was so swollen that there was no possible way, she could hide it. She knew that when Chad saw it, he was going to be furious. He hated to see bruises on her and he wished that there was something he could do to stop it. He wanted to confront David, but Lisa stopped him. She wouldn't allow Chad to blow her cover, because she knew that David would kill her.

It was a chance that she couldn't and wouldn't take. David hated her and he believed that she wasn't deserving of anyone but him. He was convinced that he owned her and he wouldn't allow her any kind of real happiness. Finding out about Chad, would send David right over the edge and into a violent fit of rage. He would hurt her worse than ever before and she knew that she most likely wouldn't survive.

Later that evening, Lisa's bruises had become more pronounced and extremely sore.

As she got ready to go and see Chad she worried, about how he was going to react, when he saw how terrible she looked. David never usually bruised her face, because it was visible and Chad swore that if he ever did, he would kill him. Lisa knew that no matter what, she couldn't allow David and Chad to meet, because the effect would be totally devastating.

Lisa put on a pair of sunglasses to cover her eye and headed over to Chad's place. Chad opened the door and knew immediately what had happened. The sunglasses gave it away, Lisa never normally wore them, and so he knew right away that she was hiding something. Chad gently removed the glasses and looked at her face and sighed.

"Oh Lisa, look what he's done. That stupid son of a bitch deserves to die, I'll kill him for this, and I swear I will."

Chad took her by the arm and led her inside to the sofa. They sat down and he held her close, as he said in a calm and relaxing voice.

"Lisa, honey, let me help you before he kills you. You're the one who is suffering, he may have a drinking problem, but the pain is only taken by you. Suffering from alcoholism doesn't constitute doing this to somebody, you need help, Lisa."

Chad then went and got a mirror and held it up to her. "Take a look, Lisa, take a good look. Is this how you want to look for the rest of your life? That young beautiful face hidden behind a mask of bruising. Honey, this has got to stop, we've got to do something and soon."

Lisa looked in the mirror and broke down crying.

"Oh Chad, I want out so bad, but he won't let me leave. I'm so exhausted from fighting that I'm not even sure what day it is anymore. I really can't take much more, but there's no way out, at least not right now."

Chad tried to comfort her.

"Just relax, honey and let me take care of you. Just lie down here and rest, you need it."

Lisa sighed and shook her head.

"I'd love to rest but I can't. What if I fell asleep? I can't risk being late getting home."

Chad smiled.

"Don't worry; if you happen to fall asleep, I'll make sure that you're up in plenty of time to make it home."

Lisa smiled as she lay her head down on his lap. He put his arm around her and gently kissed her cheek.

"Don't worry, princess, you're safe with me."

Lisa smiled sweetly, knowing that in Chad's arms she was safe and there was nothing to hurt her. Then as she felt his loving arms around her, she drifted off into a peaceful sleep. Chad stayed with her watching her sleep; he stroked his fingers through her hair and whispered.

"Sleep, my pretty lady, Lord knows you need it."

Chad sat watching her and all he could think about, was what she was going through at home. As he stared at the bruises on her pretty face, he wondered how David could do something like this. He couldn't understand how David couldn't love her, she was beautiful and sweet and she could never harm anyone. There was nothing Lisa could do, to constitute him doing this to her. Chad hated David and more than ever, he wished him dead.

The hours quickly passed and it was nearing time for Lisa head home. Chad gently kissed her, waking her from her sound sleep.

"Lisa, princess its one A.M., you've got to be home in an hour."

Lisa jumped up.

"Oh Chad, oh. I'm so sorry. I've ruined our evening, I slept the whole time and now I've got to go. Oh darling, I'm sorry, really I didn't mean to sleep so long."

Chad smiled.

"Sweetie, relax, its fine. You needed the rest and I enjoyed just sitting here watching you sleep, there is nothing to be sorry about."

Lisa smiled and hugged him.

"Chad, you're so sweet and understanding, thank you for caring about me."

Chad held her in his arms.

"Listen, Lisa, always remember that if things get too rough or it's too much to handle, you can call me, any time, day or night. You just call and I'll be right there. I'm a man of my word, and if you need me, I'll be there, I promise."

Lisa smiled a sweet smile.

"Don't worry, Chad; I'll be fine, really. Anyway, I've got to go; I'll see you tomorrow, bye, darling."

Lisa kissed him passionately and headed to the door. Chad added.

"I mean it, Lisa, if you need me, call."

She smiled and waved.

"Good bye, Chad."

Chad put his fingers to his lips and blew her a kiss as he added.

"Okay, baby, but not goodbye. It's see you later."

With that, Lisa was gone, headed back to her life of Hell with David.

She arrived at home and ran in the door, then quickly went in to the kitchen and warmed up David's dinner, and then she sat it on the table. It wasn't a moment too soon, as he walked in the door right after. Once again David was with another woman; he left her standing at the door and came in to speak to Lisa.

"Hey bitch, how's it going? Listen you're going to have to spend the night on the sofa again, I've got company."

Then he smirked and added.

"Oh and for your sake, you had better not even try to cause a scene. I'm tired of your little tough girl attitude, so I've got a little something to help keep you in line."

Lisa was confused.

"Oh yeah, and just what might that be?" David laughed.

"What might it be? Well it's a gun, of course and it's in this house, I mean it, Lisa, if you piss me off, I'll use it and if I have to. I'll kill you."

Lisa was in shock, she had no idea that David had a gun. Now more than ever before, she feared for her life. Not only did she have to obey everything David told her to do, but she had to be extra careful not to make him angry when he was drunk. While he was drinking, David was capable of anything and she didn't want to be shot and possibly killed.

Meanwhile David had another woman in the house and his wife had to sit quiet and just try to ignore what was going on right before her eyes. David was a selfish man, he only cared about himself and Lisa's needs were of no importance to him. All that mattered was his needs and as long as they were met, then to him, life was perfect. However for Lisa, life was nothing but a shattered dream. All of her hopes and ambitions were gone and the love of her husband was a thing of the past.

Lisa settled down, for another restless night on the sofa. She turned on the radio, to drown out the sounds coming from the bedroom, where her husband

and another woman were having sex in her bed. Lisa had become a slave in her own home, while her husband partied his life away in bars and strip clubs.

She, no longer had any love or feelings for David other than hate. She couldn't stand the things he made her do and the things he got away with. She was determined that one day, David would pay for all he's done and regret his foolish actions.

The next morning, Lisa was awakened to the sound of laughter coming from the kitchen. David and the other woman were cooking breakfast together and really seemed to be having a good time.

Surprisingly, Lisa found herself becoming jealous. She and David hadn't been like that in years and although she hated to admit it, she really did miss the fun they used to have.

Lisa got up off the sofa and headed upstairs to take a shower and get dressed. David noticed her heading to the stairs as he remarked.

"Wow, the bitch has risen. It's about time. Lisa, hey, listen when we're done in here, we'll get out of your way, so that you can do the cleaning. I want to see this kitchen shine."

Then he and the woman laughed as they returned to their cooking.

Lisa was furious, she wanted to just haul off and slug him, but she didn't. She just ignored him and went to take her shower. She didn't have the strength to argue with him, all she wanted to do was avoid being hurt again, so she stayed out of his way.

Lisa took her shower, got dressed and headed back down the stairs, to do the housework as David had asked. However as she walked in to the kitchen, she was startled to find David and the woman on her kitchen floor having sex. David looked up to see her standing there; he smirked and went back to what he was doing. They were going at each other like crazy and didn't even care that she was in the room; in fact, it seemed to turn them on even more.

Lisa was disgusted as she turned and walked out of the room. However unable to contain herself, she laughed and blurted out.

"Oh, what a joke! David, you're nothing but a bloody joke."

David yelled to her.

"Oh yeah, Lisa, well at least I'm getting some."

Lisa chuckled to herself as she thought about Chad and how at least she had somebody decent, and not some slut off the street. She wanted so much to tell David about Chad, just to see the stunned expression on his face, but she couldn't. She just laughed, looking back and yelled.

"That's okay David, I wouldn't want to have sex with a drunken dog like you anyway."

For the first time, David did nothing, he just ignored her and went back to having sex with the woman and Lisa did the housework.

Lisa couldn't get over the fact that they were doing it right there in the next room, while she was cleaning. David was truly a disgusting animal and had absolutely no shame. Nothing bothered him and nothing stopped him, he was never going to change and Lisa finally realized it.

Shortly after the escapade in the kitchen, the woman left and David once again started yelling and screaming.

"You're pretty stupid, Lisa; I told you that you weren't to cause a scene."

Lisa was furious.

"Oh yeah right, David! What in the hell do you think you were doing? You're the one who caused the scene, screwing that slut right there on the kitchen floor."

David slapped her across the face and pushed her up against the wall.

"You watch the way you speak to me, woman, or I swear you'll be sorry. Now, get your lazy ass moving and get this house cleaned, I'm going for a shower and then I'm heading out. I'll see you tonight after the bar closes, you better be here and the house had better be spotless."

Lisa grinned.

"Yes master, whatever you say."

David smirked as he went to take his shower and got ready for the bar.

Then as he headed out, Lisa yelled.

"Have a good time, you drunken moron."

David turned back and pointed at her.

"Watch your step, Lisa; you're treading on thin ice."

Lisa laughed as he left slamming the door behind him.

Lisa was tired of doing everything that David wanted her to, as she decided that this time, she would just ignore his demands and leave the housework until later. She decided that she would just go out shopping and do something that she wanted to. She went to the lingerie store and anticipating a wonderful and sensual evening with Chad. She bought a sexy purple silk garter belt with black fish net stockings, black spike heels and a nice purple teddy.

Then she went to the grocery store and picked up a can of whipped cream, chocolate sauce and a jar of cherries. She had a very interesting night planned and she was positive that Chad would love it. When she arrived at Chad's, she set the room up with candles and a roaring fire. Then she moved the table into the center of the room and put on her garter belt, teddy, and stockings and heals and waited for Chad to come in from work. Shortly thereafter he arrived.

Chad walked through the door and was astonished with what he saw. Lisa was sprawled across the table in a sexual manor, waiting for him. She got up and took him by the hand; she led him to the sofa and sat him down. As she put her finger to her mouth signaling for him to be quiet, she then put on some dance music and began dancing erotically on the table, just inches away from Chad's face. She teased him, getting him hot, and as he reached out for her, she smiled and slapped his hand away.

"Later, big boy, no touching till later."

Chad sighed as he continued to watch her. She moved her body in a provocative manor, waving her pussy right in his face. Each time he reached out, she pulled away and grinned, enticing him further.

Lisa began ripping off what little she had on and tossed it at Chad.

Then she began caressing her breasts and fondling her wet opening. Chad was becoming so sexual aroused, that he wanted her right there and then. As if she knew exactly what he was thinking, she then got down on her knees and took his hard organ into her hand. She poured whipped cream and chocolate sauce on his rock-hard shaft and then placed a cherry right on the tip. Then she took him into her mouth and began sucking and licking him hungrily. She caressed his warm balls, as she sucked him long and hard, bringing him to orgasm in her mouth.

She then stood up and put whipped cream on her mound and a cherry right in the opening. Then she perched herself right above Chad's mouth as she said.

"Come on baby, eat me. Eat my pussy and make me cum."

Chad began licking her sensitive pussy. She became extremely aroused as she rocked her pussy back and forth over his mouth. His hot breath stimulated her, as his tongue slid deep inside of her. She could feel his lips pressed hard against her erect love button, as she squirmed and shook at the peak of sexual delight. Then as the sexual waves took over and she burst into orgasm, she shrieked and panted with pleasure.

Chad then lay her down on the table and drove his hard dick, deep into her yearning crevice. He was driving her so hard and so fast that it was impossible to tell when he pulled out and when he pushed back, the stroke seemed constant.

Lisa could feel his balls slapping hard against her ass, as he pushed deeper and deeper. Then as his dick was buried deep inside of her, she orgasmed once more. Then within seconds of the start of her orgasm, Chad's began. It was as if they were one together, as they held each other tight and writhed about with the erotic pleasure coursing through their bodies.

Chad moaned as he spoke.

"Oh Lisa, you really know how to plan an evening and how to satisfy a man's every desire."

Lisa smiled.

"Oh anything for you honey, I'm just glad that you enjoyed it. After all, that was my intention."

Chad smiled.

"Oh, I loved it, baby, it was fabulous."

Lisa got up and looked at her watch. "Oh damn, it's almost time for me to go again. The night really passed quickly, didn't it? I wish it never had to end, but thanks to my idiot husband, I have to go home."

Chad sighed.

"Yeah, unfortunately. You know I really hate watching you head home to him every night; I wish you didn't have to. I wish that you would just end all of this and stay here where you're safe."

She smiled.

"Oh and believe me, I wish I could. Anyway I do have to go."

Chad sighed as he kissed her.

"Well, all right then. Hey, before you go, I wanted to remind you about Saturday night."

She smiled.

"Yeah, I remember. I just hope that I can make your fantasy come true and please you. I want to make you happy; I like to see that wonderful smile on your face."

Chad smiled and kissed her.

"Baby, you already please me. Saturday will just make it better. Anyway, I'll see you Saturday and who knows you might enjoy it, just think of it as an erotic adventure."

Lisa smiled.

"Yeah maybe it won't be so bad, I guess I'll just have to wait and see. Anyway, Chad, is there anything special that you want me to wear? Or anything I should do?"

He grinned.

"No, just be your own beautiful self, relax and let the new experience take over, just enjoy yourself."

Lisa grinned.

"Yeah, okay, but I do have to admit, I'm still pretty nervous about this."

He smiled.

"Oh, Lisa, it will be great, don't worry so much, you'll do fine."

Lisa kissed him good bye.

"Well, I'll see you later then."

Chad smiled.

"Yes, darling, I'll see you on Saturday. Remember now, don't worry about it, just be you."

Lisa waved and blew him a kiss as she headed out.

Chapter Two

It was soon Saturday and the night that Lisa had planned, to fulfill Chad's fantasy. As she got ready to head over to his apartment, she worried that she wouldn't know what to do, or how to react. This was something that she had never thought of before and still couldn't even imagine. There were so many thoughts running through her head, that she thought she would go crazy. Finally she decided that she would just forget about the fact, that it was another woman and just pretend that it was her and Chad. She thought that if she imagined it was Chad, doing these things to her, then maybe she'd get through it and actually enjoy it.

As she drove over to Chad's, she wondered about the woman. She was afraid that she might be prettier and sexier than her and that Chad would want her instead. She thought about Chad watching them and wondered how he would react, when he actually saw her, with another woman. She wasn't sure, that he would actually get turned on by it. She feared that he would get disgusted and not want to see her anymore.

Lisa pulled into the parking lot, of Chad's building. Her hands started shaking and her stomach was in knots. She took a deep breath as she said to herself.

"Come on, Lisa, you can do this. You'll be fine, just stop shaking and get in there." Then as she got out of her car and headed upstairs, she prayed that the other woman hadn't arrived yet. She wanted to get there first; she thought that if she had some time with Chad, before the woman got there, then maybe she wouldn't be so nervous.

She arrived at Chad's apartment and he let her in. Luckily she was the first to arrive. Chad was surprised, to see her there so early and he could tell that she was uneasy.

He kissed her hello and then smiled.

"Lisa, honey, you look so tense. Just relax, everything will be fine. Listen if it helps at all, I asked the woman to come over a little later, I wanted to have some time alone with you first."

Lisa smiled.

"Thanks, Chad and yes, it does help. Anyway what is this girl like? You haven't told me anything about her, what is her name?"

Chad smiled and answered.

"Well I guess I should fill you in then. Her name is Candy; she's a bisexual call girl."

Lisa jumped up.

"What in the hell do you mean? She's a call girl." Chad continued.

"Lisa honey calm down, there's nothing to worry about. I had her completely checked out and I checked out the madam she works for as well. All of the girls are screened and take medical examinations once a week. There is no chance of any harm coming to either of us."

Lisa calmed down a bit, but still had her reservations about the whole situation. Then as she paced back and forth across the living room, the doorbell rang. Chad answered it and in walked Candy. She was a tall blonde, with a slim figure and large perky breasts. The first thought that ran through Lisa's head when she saw her was.

"Oh yeah, right, silicone."

She was stunned with the woman and couldn't believe that her breasts were real, they just didn't look natural.

Candy had on a long black coat and when she removed it, she was totally naked. She looked over to Lisa, whose jaw dropped and smiled.

"I'm sorry if this is a shock to you, but I thought it would help. I figured if I came naked, then you would have a chance to explore my body with your eyes before we began. Chad explained that you were nervous, so I thought it might relax you a bit and make you more comfortable with me."

Chad jumped in.

"Well, this is a new experience for Lisa, but I'm sure if we just give her a bit of time, she'll relax and enjoy."

Lisa was still stunned, as Candy then walked over to her. She took Lisa's hands and placed them on her large breasts and then began undressing her. Lisa had never felt another woman's breasts before and to her surprise, she was actually turned on by it. Then still unsure what to do, Lisa bent down and began kissing and nibbling Candy's breasts. Candy slid her hand down and began fondling Lisa's wet opening. Then she took her by the hand and led her over to the sofa, where she laid her down.

Candy fondled and caressed her, and then suddenly she climbed up and straddled Lisa's body, with her wet opening resting just above Lisa's mouth.

She then began kissing Lisa's moist loins and gently sucking her love button. Candy pressed her breasts hard against Lisa's body, and Lisa became aroused. Then before Lisa knew it, she reached up and pressed her mouth hard against Candy's opening and began licking her.

Lisa wanted to give Candy some of the pleasure she was receiving back. She pushed her tongue deep into Candy's pussy, and then began sucking her clit hungrily. Candy began moaning and rocked her body above Lisa's face.

Lisa shrieked and quivered with her crashing orgasm, sobs of erotic pleasure shot from her throat involuntarily, as the vibrations of Candy's moans, and the sensation of her warm wet tongue, sent waves of stimulation coursing through her body. Then as Candy's orgasm began, Lisa licked her faster and faster, and stroked her finger in and out of her throbbing pussy.

She pushed her finger long and hard, heightening the pleasure of her desire. Then as the two girls moved to the floor and writhed about in total and complete ecstasy, Chad came over, all ready to go.

"Oh Lisa, you were wonderful, I want you and I want you now."

Chad then mounted Lisa, and pushed his rock-hard shaft deep into her throbbing, yearning pussy. Chad drove her long and hard, as Candy fondled Lisa's breasts, and encircled her clit with her fingertips.

Lisa was so aroused she felt yet another orgasm approaching, she reached out and joined in with Candy, by fondling her body, just as she was doing to her. Then as the three of them orgasmed together, they filled the room with screams of erotic sexual delight. Chad's fantasy was fulfilled and Lisa was proud to have made it happen.

Shortly thereafter, Candy left and Chad took Lisa into his arms and kissed her.

"Baby you're amazing, you're the most sexual woman I've ever met. I swear you're truly the greatest, thank you for making my fantasy come true."

He pulled her closer and kissed her passionately, then whispered.

"I feel more close to you now, then ever before. You're the most precious thing in my life and I'm glad to have you."

Lisa began to cry.

"Oh Chad, I want you to know that you are the most important person in my life. Being with you makes me happy and it makes me feel complete."

Chad sighed.

"Well, you know what we have to do then, don't you? We have to get rid of David, so that we can always be together and have a life of our own."

Lisa sighed.

"I know, Chad, I realize that we have to get rid of David, but it's just not that easy."

Chad smiled.

"I know that it's not easy Lisa and it may take some time, but you just wait. I'm going to find a way to get rid of David and you're going to be free to be with me."

Lisa was unsure how to respond. She didn't understand exactly what it was Chad had planned. All she really knew was that she couldn't handle the abuse anymore and she wanted to be happy with Chad.

Once again, time had passed by quickly and although she didn't want to leave. Lisa had to head home to David.

She kissed Chad sweetly.

"I've got to go. I hate leaving you, but I have to, I'll see you later."

Chad smiled.

"Yeah I guess I'll see you tomorrow."

Lisa sighed.

"Yeah, I love you, Chad."

Chad smiled, "I know. Bye, sweetie."

Lisa waved and headed out.

As she drove back home to her prison of abuse, she became terrified. Her heart was pounding and her pulse racing. Going home to David night after night was truly becoming a terrifying experience. She was sick and tired of always being beat on, but because of David's threats, she returned home every night.

Lisa was determined to start fighting back against David. She thought that if she defended herself, he would give up and let her go for good. Although she still had reservations about fighting him, due to her fears. She didn't want to push him too far and end up dead. David had always threatened to kill her and at this point, she believed that he wouldn't hesitate.

As she pulled into her driveway, she noticed a light on and David's car was in the garage. He had gotten home before her. Lisa panicked, knowing that she was going to get it and she was terrified to go inside. Then she looked out the window and David was coming toward the car. He threw open the door and grabbed her arm pulling her out of the car.

"Where the hell have you been Lisa? Why weren't you here when I got home? I expected dinner on the table and the house cleaned. Now you being the bitch you are, you were out gallivanting around town."

Lisa was frantic, as she pulled away from him.

"Oh, just relax, David. I'll cook your bloody food. I was only out for a coffee, I would have been here sooner, but on the way home my car over heated. You know, David, I really wasn't gone all that long and if you had fixed my car like you said you were going to, it wouldn't have over heated."

David slapped her across the face.

"Fine, Lisa, I'll let this one slide, but don't you ever take that tone with me again. Now get your ass moving and get me something to eat."

Lisa let out a sigh of relief, as David had fallen for her bogus excuse about the car over-heating and he had calmed down somewhat. However she knew that it was only temporary so she refused to let her guard down, for even a second. She knew that as soon as she did, he would strike again.

Lisa headed into the house and began preparing something for David to eat. He remained in the living room, in a violent state of mind. He was throwing things around and ranting and raving, all because he couldn't find a cigarette. Lisa walked out into the living room; she took a cigarette out of her purse and through it at him.

"There, David. Now shut your damned mouth, before the neighbors call the police."

Then she returned to her cooking and David followed her, sneaking up behind her. He was still violent, as he hit her across the back of the head with his baseball bat and she fell forward, smashing her forehead on the cupboards.

Lisa was furious; she was tired of taking all of this crap from him. So right then without even thinking, she turned around and threw a pan of hot grease at him and it splattered across his chest burning him. David freaked out and threw the pan, smashing the kitchen window.

"You stupid whore, you'll pay for this. You've just made the biggest mistake of your life."

He then lunged at her, attempting to grab her by the throat. Lisa grabbed a piece of glass from the broken window and held it up to him.

"Back off, David, I've done nothing wrong. Just leave me the hell alone, I mean it, David, back off."

David kicked the glass out of her hand and then tripped her knocking her to the floor. Then he pushed her face into the glass, slicing open her cheek. Lisa panicked when she saw the blood, she was bleeding badly and David still didn't stop.

He just kept hitting her over and over, by the time he finally did stop; there was so much blood on the floor that Lisa was sure she was going to die. At this point, she was positive that David actually was trying to kill her. David turned to head out of the kitchen, when Lisa then took a piece of glass and threw it at him, sticking him in the back of the leg.

David screamed and fell to the floor. Lisa knew that she had hurt him bad and even though he had hurt her, she felt guilty about what she had just done. David yanked the glass out of his leg and got up from the floor. He looked over to Lisa with hate in his eyes.

"Okay bitch, you win this one, but don't you even think that you'll be so lucky the next time."

Lisa was relieved that he had given up; however a part of her, wished that she had killed him. She still felt guilty, due to the fact that she had never hurt anyone before, but she also wished that he had died and freed her for good.

Lisa went into the bathroom to clean up her face. The cut didn't seem all that deep, so she bandaged it and went to bed. All night long she tossed and turned, thinking about the incident with David. She felt terrible about stabbing him with the glass and she feared the worst possible punishment, when he got up in the morning.

The next morning, Lisa's face had already begun to heal. She was relieved because she wouldn't have to explain another freak accident to the hospital. The nurses were beginning to question; her so called accidents and she didn't want the police involved. She was tired of making excuses for David, but she knew that if the police became involved, he would kill her.

The house was quiet this morning. Actually too quiet for Lisa's liking. She knew that something was up, because when David was home, the house was never quiet and he never let her sleep in so late. It was already ten thirty and he normally dragged her out of bed by seven A.M. to make his coffee.

Lisa worried that he was going to sneak up on her again, as she crept down the stairs, trying not to be heard.

However as she walked into the kitchen, she was surprised to find a note on the table. David wasn't home, he had gone out. The note read that he had some important business to take care of, and he wouldn't be home for at least twenty-four hours. It also said, as usual, that she had better make sure that she was home and the house was cleaned.

Lisa wondered what it was he had to do and why it was so important. It was unusual for him to head out before three in the afternoon. Normally nothing could get him moving before noon. She worried, that he had found out about Chad and had gone to see him. Lisa then decided to call Chad at work and warn him.

"Hi, Chad, it's me."

Chad was concerned.

"Lisa, honey, is there something wrong? You never call me at work unless it's serious. What's happened?"

She sighed.

"Nothing, Chad, at least not yet. Anyway, David hasn't shown up there has he? He left a note on the table, saying that he wouldn't be home for twenty-four hours, because he had some things to take care of. I just wanted to call and make sure that one of those things wasn't you."

Chad chuckled.

"No, Lisa I'm fine, nothing to worry about. I haven't seen David around here and anywhere else for that matter. I'm sure he's just at the bar, you know David."

Lisa sighed.

"Yeah, I know David and he only leaves the house before three, when there is a serious problem. What if he knows? What if he keeps you away from me?"

Chad sighed.

"Lisa, first of all there's no way he could have found out about us and second of all, even if he did find out, there's no way in hell that I would let him keep you away from me, he would be one sorry man, if he even tried."

Lisa was relieved as she replied.

"Well, I'm glad to hear, that you wouldn't allow him to separate us, it really puts my mind at ease. Anyway, dear, I'll let you get back to work and I'll see you later."

Chad blew a kiss into the phone.

"See you later, my pretty lady."

Lisa was enjoying her time away from David and she was more relaxed then she'd been in a long time. She wanted to do something very special for Chad, as they had now been back together for a whole year and she wanted to celebrate the day they found each other again. So she headed to the mall to shop for the perfect gift, then she found it, a gold tennis bracelet with his name on it. She then had it inscribed, the inscription read, "You're the best stallion, love Lisa."

After finishing up at the mall, she picked up a bottle of champagne and went over to his apartment, to cook a special dinner.

She set the table with candles, then turned down the lights and put on some slow romantic music. Then she slipped into a black satin teddy and waited for her prince of passion, to return home, from a long day at the office.

Then to Lisa's surprise, Chad arrived with a gift for her. He walked in the door and expecting her to be there, he presented her with two dozen red roses and a small box. Lisa's first thought, was that Chad was going to propose, but upon opening the box, to her relief they were earrings. Beautiful one carat diamond earrings.

Lisa gasped when she saw the earrings and threw her arms around Chad.

"Oh, Chad, they're wonderful, thank you so much, I've never had anything so beautiful."

Chad kissed her sweetly.

"Dinner looks great, honey, but you…well, you look absolutely delicious."

Lisa blushed, as they sat down at the table and she handed him his gift.

"I'm sorry that it's not as extravagant as your gift to me, but I hope you like it."

Chad smiled.

"Oh, Lisa, honey, anything from you is great, you don't have to buy me anything to make me happy, you just being here is wonderful enough."

Chad then raised his glass and made a toast.

"Here's to us and many more wonderful years together."

Then he leaned forward to kiss her, as the light of the candles reflected off of her face and he noticed the cut on her cheek.

"Lisa what happened? That looks bad, are you okay?"

She sighed and answered.

"Yes, Chad, I'm fine, it's just a little cut from a broken window. Please let's just forget about it for tonight and enjoy our anniversary."

Chad raised his eyebrows.

"Okay Lisa, if that's what you would prefer."

She smiled as they enjoyed the dinner that she had prepared.

After a romantic dinner, they danced and held each other close. They kissed passionately and slowly disrobed until they were dancing there by the fire, completely naked.

Then Chad took her by the hand and led her into the bedroom, where he laid her down and began kissing her gently. Starting with her lips and then slowly moving downward, he kissed her inner thighs and then slowly moved up, toward her hot wet opening. He began licking hungrily at her yearning loins. She moaned as he pushed his tongue deep inside and then encircled her clit with the tip.

Lisa groaned and panted, she writhed about the bed, as her body tingled with erotic stimulation. Chad's tongue moved quickly in and out of her wet pussy. She pushed his head, forcing him deeper, as the pleasure dominated her body and the waves of erotic stimulation, moved from her love button and shot through the rest of her body like lightning bolts.

Suddenly she shrieked with joy, as her orgasm crept up and took over. She writhed about the bed, grabbing Chad and pulling him closer to her, she pushed his hardness deep inside of her. Lisa shrieked as he began driving her long and hard. Then in deep arousal, she latched on to the headboard, pushing her pelvis upward and forcing him deeper and deeper. The screams of pleasure that shot from her throat, aroused Chad further, as he stroked his dick faster and harder burying himself deep inside her mound.

Their bodies pressed hard together, Chad let out a groan of relief as his orgasm rapidly approached. The sounds of his pleasure, sent signals to Lisa's love button, bringing her to orgasm once more. She felt the pounding motion against her sensitive mound, as she clenched her muscles tight. So tight that Chad was immediately brought to massive orgasm.

Chad pulled out, allowing his hot sexual juices to flow freely across Lisa's belly. Then his pressed his body next to hers and kissed her slowly and passionately, as he whispered.

"I love you, Lisa, I really do."

Lisa hugged him tightly.

"I love you, too, you're the man of my dreams and I love you more than I've ever loved anyone before."

Then as the emotion took over, she held him close and cried.

"Oh, Chad, I promise you, as soon as I can get away from David and there is no longer a chance of him hurting either of us, then I'll be yours forever and I promise that I will always love you."

Chad smiled.

"Babe, you'll always be mine, anyway. David will never separate us, he's just not strong enough, our love can overcome any obstacle, and I know it can."

At that moment, Lisa felt as she were truly, a part of Chad's life. She believed that their relationship, had finally taken a turn in the right direction. Now the only thing standing in their way was the fact that she was married.

Chad loved her and she knew that with him, all of her dreams of love and family would finally come true. Chad was the most gentle and sweetest man and he always put her feelings and needs first. Unlike David who abused her and treated her like a slave.

Lisa loved Chad with all of her heart and needed to be with him. However David's constant threats were always rushing through her mind and made it very difficult for her and Chad to be together.

Lisa got up and began getting dressed, Chad grabbed her arm.

"Is it that time already?"

She sighed.

"Yeah, I've got to get going, I've got housework to get done before I go to bed. I have to make sure that it's done, in case David decides to surprise me again, by returning home early. You never know with him, he's always trying to catch me doing something wrong."

Chad sighed.

"I wish you wouldn't go. I can't protect you if you're not here. When you go home to him, there's nothing I can do to keep you safe. Lisa, honey, I'm just terrified that I'm going to lose you, because of that idiot and his violent temper."

Lisa sighed.

"Chad, really I have to go, David told me that he has a gun and ways of finding me too. You and I both know that if he finds me here with you, I'm as good as dead."

Chad jumped.

"David has a gun? Oh, Lisa now more than ever, I wish you would just stay."

Lisa sighed as she looked toward the floor. "I know you do, Chad, but I have to go."

Chad still worried agreed.

"Okay, baby, I know you're right, I just wish I could help. Anyway, if you have to leave, I guess I'll see you tomorrow, I love you."

Lisa kissed him goodbye.

"See you tomorrow, Chad, don't worry. I'll be okay, I always am. Anyway, I love you and I'll see you soon."

Chad kissed her once again she headed for home.

Lisa arrived at home, to find a woman sitting on the porch. She wondered what it was she wanted, as she walked over to ask.

"Hello, can I help you?"

The woman jumped up.

"Yeah, you can. Your husband, David, owes me three hundred dollars and I have no intention of leaving until I get it. So, where is that stupid jerk anyway?"

Lisa grinned and replied.

"Well, sorry to tell you, hun, but you've got quite the long wait. David won't be home until sometime tomorrow, you may as well just go home and come back then."

Right then the woman pulled out a gun and began yelling.

"No, I don't think so, come on, little miss perfect, shall we go inside and wait?"

Lisa was frantic.

"Look I don't know why you're doing this, it's not me who owes you, it's David and he's not here."

The woman hit Lisa with the gun and then held it to her head.

"Listen, sweetheart, if it's all the same, I think I'll just wait here with you, and then if he doesn't pay up, well, then you'll die. I'm sick and tired of being cheated by men and for once I'm putting my foot down. Anyway, lady, I guess you're going to find out, if you really mean anything to your husband. Think about it, will he pay up, or will he watch you die? I sure don't know, but I can't wait to find out."

Lisa pleaded with her.

"Please, just put the gun away and you can stay as long as you want, just put the gun back into your purse."

Lisa's pleading only agitated her further, as she then pushed her into a chair and tied her up.

Lisa was terrified, she was being held hostage in her own home, at gun point. Knowing that David probably wouldn't have the money only terrified her further. Lisa did everything she could to be nice to the woman, hoping that she would just let her go. She looked over to her.

"By the way, my name is Lisa and you are?"

She replied, "I'm Jill, now just shut the hell up, you don't need to know anything more about me."

Lisa sighed.

"Look Jill, killing me really isn't going to get you anywhere. It's only going to make things worse for you, come on, it's stupid to kill me, because of something stupid that David has done, don't you think so? Have you really thought this thing through?"

Jill laughed.

"Oh, come on, Lisa, you're his wife, I'm sure that he'll save you."

Lisa laughed.

"Yeah, right, why would he save somebody that he's always trying to kill?"

Jill hesitated for a minute and then replied.

"Look, Lisa, I want the money and if it means that I'm going to have to hold you hostage until he gets here, than that is how it's going to be."

Jill then sat the gun down on the table.

"However Lisa, if you're nice, I might just decide to let you live."

Lisa trembled with fear and for the first time, she wished that David would come home, so Jill would let her go.

Suddenly, Jill appeared to be somewhat calmer, so Lisa decided to talk to her some more.

"Jill, why don't you just come over here and untie me, then maybe we can work something out."

Jill refused.

"Forget it, you're staying right there, tied in that chair, until your bum of a husband gets here."

Lisa tried to reason with her.

"Why don't you just let me go? I could go to the money machine down the street and get you your money, I'll pay you."

Jill yelled.

"Like hell, no way, you're not leaving! Besides, I think that your husband deserves to be taught a lesson and if that means that someone has to die, then oh well."

Lisa tried to loosen the rope on her wrists, but the knots were too tight. She was terrified of possibly being killed as she exclaimed.

"Jill please, I've done nothing wrong, just let me go. I've told you that you can stay here until David gets back. I could make us some coffee and we could talk, killing me really isn't the way to solve this. I swear to you, you'll get your money, I'll make sure that you're paid in full."

Jill laughed.

"Yeah right, I'm not falling for this crap; you'll just call the cops on me."

Lisa sighed.

"No, Jill, I won't, I promise you that I won't call the police. You deserve to be paid and I want to help you, why don't you let me?"

Jill was stunned.

"Look, Lisa, I promise that I won't kill you. If anything, it will be David that I kill, but I'm still not untying you, if I did you would only try to get away and like I said, I really don't want to hurt you."

Lisa was somewhat relieved, but still worried not knowing exactly what was going to happen. She wasn't sure if she should trust Jill or not, after all she did tie her up in a chair and she was holding a gun. Lisa was positive that Jill was unstable and given the chance she probably would kill.

The hours passed slowly, as Lisa remained tied up, uncomfortable and exhausted. Jill however, was wide awake and sitting in the corner with her gun. The sun was now rising and Lisa prayed that it wouldn't be long, before David returned.

Then suddenly she heard the sound, of a car pulling into the driveway. Jill stood up.

"Okay, Lisa, this is it, the bastard's home."

Lisa began to shake and her heart was pounding a mile a minute, this had to be the most terrifying day of her life.

David walked through the door and saw Lisa tied up in the chair. He was astonished as he exclaimed.

"Lisa, are you all right? What's going on here?" Right then Jill came out from behind the door. "This is going on you, stupid jerk."

David jumped.

"Jill, what are you doing here? Have you totally lost your mind?"

She yelled.

"I want my three hundred dollars, you stupid creep. Now, hand it over, or bullets are going to start flying."

David sighed.

"Okay, Jill, just relax I've got the money, I'll pay you right now."

Then as David reached into his jacket pocket to get his wallet, Jill fired the gun, shooting a vase.

"There, David, that was just to prove to you, that I will use this thing if I have to, now fork over the dough."

David pulled out his wallet and handed her the money.

"Here you go, now please leave, before this situation gets any worse."

Jill laughed.

"Oh, not yet, I think that you should pay me another hundred for my trouble, don't you?"

David sighed.

"Well, I'm sorry Jill, but I don't have it, you just took all I had."

Jill freaked out and started firing shots, at pictures on the wall.

"Get the money, David, or it's you that I shoot next."

Suddenly there was a knock at the door and then it burst open, it was the police. One of the neighbors had reported shots being fired and then hearing more shots, the police burst right in. They grabbed Jill and placed her under arrest and then took statements, from both David and Lisa.

Lisa felt like a freak show, there was media surrounding her house. After hearing reports of a hostage situation, they had all turned out to get the story for the news. Lisa was furious, David had really screwed up this time and because of him and his foolish mistake, their dirty laundry was going to be aired on the six o'clock news. Everyone that Lisa new was going to know, what an idiot she had for a husband.

After many hours, of speaking with the police and the media, the commotion finally died down and Lisa was able to get some rest, or at least try to.

As usual David blamed her for the whole situation. He started hitting her over and over, while yelling.

"You're a stupid bitch Lisa, when you saw Jill waiting outside; you should have left and went somewhere else. How could you be so stupid? Why would you even bother to let her into our home? This is your fault, you let her take you hostage, what in the hell were you thinking?"

Lisa yelled back.

"You stupid son of a bitch, this wasn't my fault, it was yours. If you weren't sleeping around all the time, this wouldn't have happened. Don't you blame me for your stupidity, you could have gotten me killed. When will you learn David? When will you stop and take a look around you, to see exactly what you're doing. Think with your brain for a minute and not with what's in your pants."

"David you're killing yourself, don't you see that? Your drinking has gotten so bad, that you don't even know the time of day anymore. Please just listen for a minute, you have to stop, you have to stop drinking before it kills you. You're withering away to nothing; you don't even look like the man I married. Please David, if you won't do it for me, then do it for yourself. Stop this stupidity and straighten out your life."

David became furious; he hit her knocking her clear across the room.

"You stupid whore, don't you lecture me, I won't put up with that kind of talk. There's nothing wrong with my life, except for you, of course. Now I'm heading out to the bar, it's been a long day and I definitely need a drink. You get this goddammed house back into shape; this little incident has left it a total wreck. I'll be home at my usual time, make damn sure that your work is done or else."

David walked out the door and Lisa began to cry, she hated seeing the mess that David had made of his life and she wished that there was something she could do to change it. However as long as he denied the problem, there was no hope.

Lisa did the housework and then finally was able to get some sleep. She figured that she would just grab a few hours, before she headed over to Chad's.

However it didn't quite work out that way, she overslept and Chad seeing the news, became frantic and was soon knocking on her door.

Lisa opened the door and was surprised.

"Chad, what are you doing here? You should have called me; you know how risky it is for you to be here."

Chad sighed.

"I'm sorry, honey, but when I saw the news, I was worried sick. I had to come and see for myself that you were okay. I mean its seven thirty and you're normally at my place by six, I just had to be sure that everything was okay and you were safe."

Lisa was shocked at the time.

"It's already after seven? I'm sorry I didn't mean to worry you, I was just so tired. I only lay down for a few hours, but I guess I overslept. I was actually going to call you when I got up, to let you know that everything was okay and warn you about the news. Anyway, I'm sorry, now maybe we should hurry up and get out of here, we don't want to chance running into David, you never know with him, he could turn up at any second."

Chad sighed,

"Yeah, let's get going we'll take my car."

Lisa smiled and they headed out.

On the way over to Chad's, he asked what happened and she explained.

"It was just one of David's crazy hookers; I guess he cheated her out of three hundred dollars. Anyway she thought that by holding me hostage, she'd get her money quicker, which in turn she did."

Chad shook his head.

"Lisa your life is just one big dilemma after another, we've really got to do something, before you end up dead. That woman could have killed you and for what? A lousy three hundred dollars."

Lisa agreed.

"Yeah, I know. It seems that the way things are going, I'm doomed to become just another statistic. My life really is getting ridiculous."

Chad replied.

"Baby, don't worry, I'm not about to let that happen, I'll find a way to ensure your safety, I promise. I won't let David or anyone else for that matter gets the best of you."

Lisa smiled.

"You're so sweet, Chad, but I hope you're right, I hope that I survive all of this."

Chad smiled as he pulled the car into the driveway of his building.

"So Lisa, what do you say I cook you some dinner? You must be starving."

She smiled.

"Yeah I guess I am a little hungry, but you don't have to cook for me."

He smiled.

"Oh, I know I don't have to, I want to. Anyway how does a nice steak sound?"

Lisa grinned.

"Oh that sounds great, can I give you a hand?"

Chad kissed her sweetly.

"No it's fine, you just relax you've had a hard day, I think I can handle cooking a couple of steaks."

Lisa smiled.

"Well, okay then, I'll just go sit down, thanks, Chad; this is really sweet of you."

He smiled.

"Not a problem princess, now get out there and relax, let me cook our dinner."

Lisa laughed as she went and sat down in the living room to wait.

Following a wonderful steak dinner, Lisa and Chad sat on the sofa in each other's arms. Chad rubbed her shoulders and kissed her sweetly.

"Boy honey, are you ever tense, after the day you've had though, I don't doubt it."

Chad then lay her down.

"Here, honey, roll over and let me give you a nice massage."

Lisa rolled over and took off her shirt; Chad began giving her a nice hot oil massage. He massaged her from head to toe and kissed her gently, Lisa's tension was soon relieved and she was totally relaxed. She rolled over and sat up, she pulled Chad close and kissed him long and passionately. Then she began rubbing his shoulders.

"Here darling, let me massage you now."

Chad smiled as he removed his shirt and turned around; Lisa rubbed and massaged his strong muscular back, while she sweetly and gently kissed his shoulders.

Chad turned back around and smiled.

"Lisa, I love you so much, you're quickly becoming all I live for."

She felt the tears of joy pooling in her eyes, as she pulled him closer and kissed his sweet lips.

"I love you, too, Chad; you're the greatest thing that's ever happened to me."

Chad took her into his arms.

"You've had a rough day princess. Tonight, I just want to hold you close to me." Lisa leaned into the safety of Chad's arms, as she wished that the night would never end. In his arms, she was safe and secure, but once she left to go home, the security was gone and she felt like a little lost child.

Soon their time together has once again passed. This time, quicker than they had expected.

Lisa looked up at the clock and panicked.

"Oh no, Chad, it's two A.M., you've got to drive me home, oh no, what if we're late? What if David is already there? Oh no, oh maybe I should take a cab, it's too risky."

Chad sighed.

"No, I don't think so, there's no way that I'm letting you take a cab, alone, at this time of night. I'll just drop you off a few doors from your house and then I'll keep an eye on you, until I'm sure that you're safely inside."

Lisa agreed.

"Well, okay, I guess that would be all right, but I am still a little worried. What if we get caught? Then what do we do?"

Chad sighed.

"Oh, don't worry, we won't get caught, now come on, let's get you home."

All the way home, Lisa worried that David wouldn't be watching for her. She knew that if he saw her get out of Chad's car, there would be trouble.

As they turned on to Lisa's street, she looked for David's car. To her relief, he wasn't home yet, but she still made sure to have Chad drop her off down the street. Then as she walked toward the house, David pulled in the driveway. She looked back, to see if Chad had left, but noticed that he had turned his car off and was sitting there watching the house.

Lisa was extremely frightened, as she feared that Chad would be seen and David would find out about them.

Then as she walked up the driveway, David began yelling. "Where in the hell were you?"

She sighed.

"I was just out for a walk David, relax."

He continued to yell.

"No, I won't relax, you should have been home long ago, you stupid little whore."

David grabbed her by the hair and smashed her head into the bumper of his car and she fell to the ground.

Lisa then looked up to see David standing over her with a crowbar and Chad coming up behind him.

Chad yelled.

"Drop the crowbar, pal, that's no way to treat a lady." David turned around stunned.

"Who the hell are you?"

Then he turned and hit Lisa across the back with the crowbar.

Chad yelled.

"Knock it off pal!"

David asked once again. "Who are you?"

Chad answered.

"Look, I'm a neighbor, I was just walking by and I noticed you hitting this woman. Who the hell do you think you are, doing this to her?"

David laughed and went to hit Lisa again. Chad grabbed the crowbar.

"Come on pal, you want to fight somebody, fight me."

Then he threw the crowbar and punched David, right in the face. David shook it off and yelled.

"Listen pal, this is my wife, she's mine and I can do as I please with her, so why don't you take your macho attitude and get the hell out of here."

Chad hit him again and yelled.

"No, I won't, what's the matter, can't you fight a man? Come on, from what I've seen here, you're a real abusive bastard, in great need of an attitude adjustment."

David snarled. Chad grabbed him and began punching him, over and over. David was on the ground and to Lisa's surprise, he wasn't fighting back, it was as if he was afraid to fight a man. Then with one last kick to David's head, Chad winked at Lisa and left.

She was astonished with what had just happened and shocked that David hadn't fought back, he just laid there like a stupid lump. She felt honored that

Chad had fought for her, but even more she was relieved, that he hadn't let his identity be known, to David.

David pulled himself up and went inside, being so drunk and beat up, he went right upstairs and passed out. Lisa waited a few minutes, to be sure he was asleep and then she called to see if Chad was home yet.

"Hi, you're home."

Chad interrupted her.

"Oh, hi baby, I hope you're okay. I wanted to stay and help you, it was my fault you were late and I couldn't just walk away. I saw him hitting you and I lost control, I love you and I can't stand the way he treats you."

Lisa sighed.

"It's okay, Chad, and thank you, I appreciate what you did for me, but I am a little stunned though. I didn't expect anything like this to happen."

Chad sighed.

"Well, Lisa, he had it coming and let me tell you, he's lucky that I didn't kill him. He's a stupid prick; he had his nerve hitting you with that crowbar, right there in front of me. Anyway sweetie, are you okay? You're not hurt too bad, are you?"

She sighed.

"Well, my back is pretty screwed up, but I'm sure I'll be all right."

Then she gasped.

Chad jumped.

"What is it, is there something wrong?" She answered.

"I've got to get off the phone, David's coming, I thought he was asleep, I'll see you tomorrow."

Chad answered, "Damn him. Okay, honey, please be careful, I'll see you tomorrow."

Lisa quickly hung up the phone and started cleaning.

David was yelling.

"Who in the hell was that idiot and why was he so concerned with you? It's none of his bloody business; I'll do whatever I want."

With that, he grabbed Lisa and started punching her. She yelled.

"Leave me alone, you stupid son of a bitch, let me go."

Then she kicked him in the groin and when he bent over in pain, she hit him over the head with a lamp, knocking him out cold, and then she kicked him in the face and went to bed.

David remained on the floor, for the rest of the night, which only infuriated him further the next morning. He dragged Lisa out of bed by the hair and threw her down the stairs. Then he punched her over and over and gave her two black eyes. Lisa cried and begged for him to stop, but he wouldn't, he just kept right on hitting and yelling at her.

"You stupid whore, you'll learn to respect me sooner or later. Come on bitch, cry like a little baby, seeing you in pain brings me more joy then you could possibly imagine."

Then suddenly out of the blue, he stopped.

"I've got better things to do, I'm out of here. Get your housework done or else." Lisa was stunned, it was as if somebody had just flipped a switch and turned him off, he just stopped and walked away. Then he left and headed to his usual place, the bar.

Lisa was beat up pretty bad, but she had made special plans for Chad and didn't want this incident to ruin them. So she got up and fixed herself up, she felt that she owed Chad, after what he had done for her. She put makeup over her bruises and fixed her hair, and then she went to visit Chad, at his office.

He was working alone today, so knowing that, she had a little surprise in store for him. She put on a red satin teddy, high heels and a long trench coat. She walked into his office and locked the door behind her, Chad jumped up.

"Lisa, what are you doing here?"

Then he gasped when he saw her face. "Oh Lisa, I'll kill him, are you okay?" She sighed.

"Yeah, I'm all right, don't worry about David right now, I've got a little surprise for you."

Chad grinned, as Lisa walked over cleared off his desk and climbed up on it. She them slowly removed the trench coat and began dancing erotically in front of him, waving her pussy in his face.

Chad shook his head.

"Oh baby, you look fabulous, I suppose I could take a break."

With that, he began taking off his clothes. His dick was hard and yearning to get inside of her, as he grabbed her hips and guided her to the floor. Then as she lay there flat on her back, she spread her thighs and raised her pelvis, inviting him inside.

The spontaneity of their actions, sent them writhing into a frenzy of arousal. Chad's dick was pulsating and filling her mound to the brim, as she screamed with excitement. Chad pumped with the rhythm of her rolling pelvis and her pussy swallowed him deeper, as they spiraled into ecstasy. Then as they climaxed into orgasm, their sexual contractions matched each other and the satisfying feeling of their erotic release, sent them whirling into a cloud of satisfaction. They screamed and moaned, filling the room with sounds of fulfillment, as they held each other tight.

Then Lisa grinned, as she got dressed.

"Have a good day, babe. I'll be waiting for you when you get home."

Chad moaned in a pleasing manor. "Oh, do you have to go?"

She sighed.

"Yes, you have to work. I wouldn't want you to lose your job, because of me." Chad sighed.

"Yeah, I guess I do have to get back to work. Okay, I'll see you later, but it really isn't going to be easy concentrating on my work, when I know that you're at my place, dressed like that."

Lisa laughed.

"Yeah, okay dear. Anyway I'll see you tonight." Chad blew her a kiss and winked.

"Bye, sexy."

As Lisa waited for Chad to come from work, she found herself daydreaming, about another sexual escapade with Chad and becoming aroused. She began fondling her breasts and caressing her wet crotch. Then she pulled out a vibrator and began stroking it, in and out of her pussy. The sexual juices oozed from her opening, as she encircled her clit, sending herself bursting into erotic orgasm.

She writhed about, pushing it harder and deeper into her yearning crevice. She couldn't wait for Chad to come home, everything about him aroused her and the mere thought of his massive dick inside of her, made her so hot, that she had to have satisfaction.

Then once again Chad arrived home. Walking in, to find Lisa lying totally naked on the sofa, with the vibrator in her hand.

"Oh baby, starting without me, are you?"

Then he stripped off his clothes and laid on floor, alongside the sofa.

Lisa rolled off the sofa and straddled him, resting her pussy just above his face. Then she began sucking his rock-hard dick, long and fast. She lowered her pelvis and her pussy pressed hard against his face, as he began licking her hungrily, tasting the oozing juices of her desire.

Lisa sucked him long and fast, as she cried out.

"Oh, Chad, cum in my mouth, let me taste your sensual love juices. I want to feel your hot cum, shooting down my throat, come on baby, cum, cum in my mouth."

She then took him so far into her mouth that her lips pounded against his mound. Chad licked and sucked her hard clit, as he pushed his finger deep into her pussy. She pushed herself lower, as she forced his lips hard against her clit, arousing her further.

Then, as Chad came in her mouth, the vibrations of his groans sent her bursting into orgasmic ecstasy. Chad pulled away and mounted her, driving his hardness deep into her oozing crevice of passion. His thrusts were constant, it was hard to tell where his in and out thrusts began and where they ended. His hardness filled her, as she tightened her muscles causing the friction to intensify. Erotic bolts of energy sailed through their sexes, causing and irruption of orgasmic waves and filling them with pleasure and sensual relief.

Then as they lay lifeless on the floor, trying to catch their breath, Chad massaged her shoulders.

Lisa sighed and spoke softly.

"Oh, Chad, I want to be with you forever, I can't handle anymore of David and his abuse."

Chad sighed.

"I know, honey, and you shouldn't have to take it. I swear to you, someday David is going to get exactly what he has coming to him and it won't be pretty."

Lisa smiled.

"I love you, Chad."

He kissed her sweetly.

"I love you, too."

For the rest of the evening, they lay in each other's arms by the fire. They talked about the future and their dreams and they spoke of their love and their relationship. It was soon time for Lisa to head home again, even though she didn't want to leave. She wanted now more than ever, to stay right there in Chad's arms.

Chad looked over at the clock.

"Lisa, honey, you've got to go. He'll be home soon." She sat up.

"Already?"

Then she began to cry as she got ready to leave.

"I can't wait until tomorrow night, to be with you again, safe and protected. Oh, how I pray that David isn't in a violent mood, I'm sore enough."

Chad hugged her.

"Oh, darling, I ought to kill that bastard for what he's doing to you. He's destroying you and I can't stand watching you go home to him every night."

Lisa sighed, as she kissed him goodbye. "Nor can I. Listen I've really got to go now though. I love you, Chad, with all my heart and soul, I'll see you tomorrow night." Chad smiled and moved the hair out of her face.

"I love you too, princess. I'll see you soon."

She waved and blew him a kiss, and headed for home.

Lisa arrived home only minutes later, once again to find that David was with another woman. They were having sex, right there on the living room sofa, where she was supposed to sleep. She shook her head with disgust and went upstairs to change and found a note on the bed from David. The note read.

"Hey bitch, as you probably already know, I'm going to be a little busy tonight, so leave me the hell alone."

Then he added to the bottom.

"Oh and I found a dirty dish on the counter, this indicates to me, that you have been neglecting your housework. So you had better be prepared for tomorrow, when we discuss your punishment, because it won't be pretty. I guarantee you that you'll never leave another dirty dish lying around ever again. So, anyway, bitch, enjoy your night. Sleep well, ha-ha-ha."

Lisa was terrified; she knew that she was in a lot of trouble. She wanted to just pick up and run, but she knew that she would be caught before she made it to the door, as David had seen her come in. She was trapped like an animal in cage and there was no escaping David's intended abuse.

She tossed and turned all night, with the fear of what was coming to her. She knew that it was going to be bad, because David was never lenient with her, when it came to the housework. Then, finally, after hours of anticipating abuse, Lisa lulled herself to sleep.

The next morning, she was awakened by the feeling of cold metal on her throat, it was David. He was standing over her, holding a knife to her throat, snickering. Lisa slowly pulled away and jumped out of bed.

"David, what are you doing?" He laughed.

"What Lisa? Did you forget about your punishment?" With that he threw the knife and it lodged into the wall, only millimeters from Lisa's head. She screamed as the blade flew past her face, and David laughed. He grabbed her by the hair and threw her down on the floor, and then he kicked her over and over in the ribs. Lisa cried in pain and her cries seem to spawn more anger in David, as he kicked her harder and laughed with delight, at her intense pain.

Lisa reached up grabbing the knife, and then she held it up to David and ordered him to back off and leave her alone. David chuckled, as he kicked the knife out of her hand and slapped her across the face.

"Stupid foolish move bitch, you'll learn one of these days, I swear you will."

Then he slapped her again, splitting her lip.

"Do your housework and if I ever find another dirty dish lying around, your punishment will be ten times worse, that's a promise."

As always, Lisa did as she was told and started the housework. David followed her around, watching her every move and giving her instructions as to what she was to do. Then after hours of scrubbing, David finally decided that the house was clean and he let her off the hook.

He got changed and ready for the bar, but on his way out, he was sure to give Lisa another warning.

"There now, maybe next time, you'll think before you leave another dirty dish on the counter."

Lisa was in no mood to argue as she replied.

"Yes, David, I've learned my lesson. It won't happen again." David smirked and walked out slamming the door closed.

Lisa was furious, as she then threw a glass against the door and screamed.

"Yes master, no problem, I'll obey your every command, you stupid jerk."

Then she began to cry, while she cleaned up the broken glass and went to take her shower and get ready to go see Chad.

Tonight Chad had decided that he was going to take her to a motel and give her a night to remember. When she arrived at the motel, Chad was waiting right out front for her. He waved to her, as she walked toward him, then he grabbed her, threw his arms around her and kissed her passionately.

Lisa was stunned; he had kissed her right there in public, where people could see them. She loved Chad, but a part of her still felt guilty, because she was married and she feared being seen by somebody that David knew.

Chad took her by the hand and led her up to their room. He had booked the honeymoon suite and it was beautiful. There was a heart shaped bed, with bright red satin sheets and a huge Jacuzzi surrounded by mirrors.

Lisa was astounded with the room and her heart pounded with excitement. Chad looked at her with a seductive grin, as he took her into his arms and nuzzled her neck, while removing her blouse. Lisa's nipples became pebble hard, as he gently encircled them with his fingertips. Her breasts swelled with desire and she felt the crotch underneath her panties becoming moist, as the tingling sensation flowed from her hard nipples, right to the heart of her pussy.

Chad then slowly removed her skirt and panties and then began removing his own clothing, first his shirt and then his pants. He pressed his body up against hers, his heavy chest pressed against her breasts and his massive organ rested against her hot moist mound. Lisa's love button was erect, with the anticipation of his erection, thrusting deep inside of her, as Chad cupped her breasts, heightening the pleasure of her desire.

They kissed with their tongues touching sensuously; Lisa yearned for him, as he then bent down and began nibbling furiously at her clit. The waves robbed her of her control, as she began convulsing uncontrollably. The cries of pleasure sobbed from her throat, as the erotic sensations coursed through her body. Lisa now totally inflamed with desire, moved her hips and pelvis, intensifying the sensitivity and bringing her to orgasm.

She cried out involuntarily, as the flashes of pleasure raced through her body.

"Oh Chad, take me, take me now."

Chad guided her to the bed, where he slid his erection, deep into the whirlpool of her desire.

Chad drove her hard, in and out, his mound stroking vigorously against her already erect clit. Then as his thrusts became more intense, Lisa tightened her muscles, causing more friction and drawing him deeper into her channel of love. She raked her nails down his back in the heat of passion and pulled him harder to her.

Her hard nipples raced across his chest, with the movement of his thrusts. The tingling sensation, raced from her breasts to her love button, causing massive contractions as her orgasm began. Chad feeling the sexual contractions deep inside of her climaxed and was brought to orgasm.

As the pulsations tore through their bodies, they thrust together prolonging the pleasure. They embraced and kissed passionately, and then Chad led her to the Jacuzzi, where they enjoyed the soothing motion of the jets. Chad massaged her, the love in his eyes made it clear, that she meant the world to him, just as he did to her. They relaxed in each other's arms, while the hot moving water caressed their bodies.

Lisa felt like she was in heaven, it was as if the rest of the world had stopped. Chad's strong arms around her, gave her a sense of security that she had never felt before. His love was pure and he was all she lived for. The only thing that kept her strong, through all of the abuse at home, was Chad and the love that waited for her in his arms.

They got out of the Jacuzzi and dried off, and then they lay down on the bed and held each other close. Lisa was exhausted from all she had been through with David and soon fell asleep.

Chad lay next to her and watched her sleep, but soon he had to wake her to leave.

"Lisa, princess come on, honey it's getting late, I don't want David to freak out on you again. You have to get up, come on baby, up and Adam."

Lisa whined.

"Oh no, please tell me you're kidding, it can't be over yet, I don't want it to end so soon, I want it to be like this forever."

Chad sighed.

"I know, baby and soon it will be. I'm sorry, honey, I hate sending you home to him."

She sighed as she got up.

"Yeah, well I hate going, but it's the only way. If I stay, he'll find me and then we'll both be in danger, I've got to go."

Chad sighed.

"Yeah, I guess so; anyway I'll walk you to your car."

Lisa sighed and they left their beautiful room and headed to her car.

As they walked to her car, Chad put his arm around her. "Lisa, I love you and I promise you that someday, you'll be my wife and David will be nothing more than a bad memory. I can't stand seeing you living in such fear and in so much pain. I won't let him ruin your life, you're going to be happy and we're going to be together forever. We'll raise a family and spend the rest of our lives together. Oh Lisa I promise, I'm going to make you the happiest woman in the world."

Lisa hugged him.

"Oh Chad, I pray that you're right, because I truly do love you and I can't wait to be your wife. You are the most important person in my life; it's your love that keeps me going and gives me a reason to live. Without you I'd have nothing and nobody, your all I have and I need you in my life."

Chad kissed her.

"I need you, too and we will be together forever. I promise you, there's not a person on this earth who could keep us apart. We're in love and we need and deserve each other. Soon, baby, I promise you that we'll soon be free to have a life together and David won't be a problem."

Lisa felt the tears pooling in her eyes, as she kissed Chad sweetly.

"I guess I better go." Chad smiled.

"Yeah, I'll see you later baby, I love you."

Lisa sighed, her eyes filled with sadness as she pulled away and headed back home, to the drunken bum that she had married eight long years ago.

Chapter Three

Lisa and Chad's relationship was growing stronger by the day. They were sure. That their love could overcome anything, but the problem of David still remained. He was still refusing to let Lisa go and his abuse was becoming more unbearable. His beatings were harder and more severe; he was always putting her down and making her feel unworthy of love. He made her believe that she deserved what she was getting and it was her own fault. He convinced her that she was the one constantly messing up and she gave him reason punish her.

Lisa wanted to believe that it was all due to alcohol and that it was David's drinking that had sent him over the edge and destroyed their marriage. Yet with the thoughts David had implanted in her head, she did wonder if she was actually the cause, of all the pain and upset that had become her life.

Chad was forever telling her, that she shouldn't blame herself for all the abuse David had inflicted on her. That none of it was her fault. David was just a violently abusive man, who didn't care about anyone but himself.

Lisa wanted to believe that Chad was right but it wasn't easy, and still big part of her still wondered.

Lisa sat on the sofa, thinking about the mess her life had become and how desperately she wanted to change it. When suddenly out of the blue David came up behind her. He grabbed her by the hair and dragged her into the kitchen.

"Listen up, bitch, I'm heading over to my girlfriends place for the night and I said that I would bring dinner. So guess what, my dear? You get to cook it."

Lisa couldn't believe what she was hearing, this was ridiculous. David was having an affair and expected her to cater it for him.

David continued.

"I want lasagna and Caesar salad and it had better be good. This is a special evening and I want it to be a romantic one." Lisa was furious, he wouldn't set her free. Instead he expected her to help him make his relationship with another woman work out.

Lisa pulled away and yelled.

"No damn way, David, there's no way that I am going to help you make a romantic dinner for THAT woman! If you want to impress her, do it yourself. It's not me, who is screwing her, so why the hell should I have to make her happy?"

David went red in the face and the veins began to bulge in his neck as he turned and slapped her across the face.

"Her name is Paula, not THAT woman! And, yes, you will help me, Lisa, at least if you know what is good for you. You better get moving though, you only have four hours and I'm heading over there."

Lisa was still furious as she slammed at pan down on the counter top.

"Four hours or what David? What are you going to do if it's not ready?"

David chuckled and he turned back.

"Oh Lisa, silly, silly girl. Don't even think about getting brave with me. If you're not done, there's a closet with your name on it. I don't think you want to be locked up all night in the dark now do you?"

Lisa had closet phobia and was terrified of dark places. David knew it. Therefore, she couldn't allow for this to happen. Besides the fact of her fears there was also Chad to worry about. Lisa knew that if she didn't show up at his apartment that night, he would worry and come looking for her. Then she stood the chance of David finding out about him and destroying what they had.

Lisa still not happy with the chore at hand and tears rolling down her cheek began to cook for David and Paula.

Just then she heard footsteps coming toward the kitchen. She quickly wiped her tears away and acted calm about the whole situation.

David took a seat at the table.

"Thought I'd keep an eye on you for a bit. Don't want you doing something stupid to our meal now."

Lisa laughed.

"Yeah, wish it was that easy."

David shook his head and smirked. "Such a smart mouth for such a silly girl."

Lisa becoming brave again decided to try and reason with David.

"You know David; you really seem to want to be with this Paula. You know you're going about it all wrong. If you really want to be with her and be happy, why don't you just give me my divorce? Then you're free to be with her and have the happiness you're so sure you'll have with her."

Lisa had crossed the line; David slammed his fist down on the table and jumped up sending the chair flying across the kitchen. Then lunged at her slamming her head in to the cupboard.

"Listen, Lisa, I've told you a thousand times, I won't divorce you. Giving you a divorce with only make you happy. Now tell me why I would want to do something like that? Just forget it, Lisa, I'll never give you your divorce, you're stuck with me sweetheart, so get used to it."

Lisa, holding her hand to her forehead, sighed.

"Fine, David, but what about Paula?"

David still angry yelled.

"Oh, Paula is fantastic and more of a woman then you'll ever be. I just don't want to hurt her, exactly why I'm holding on to you; I need you here so I have someone to take all my frustrations out on. Paula gets the good stuff and you get the crap. That's all you deserve Lisa, the crap."

With that, David laughed ferociously and went back to sit down.

Lisa wanted David out of her life; he was a crazy alcoholic and wanted nothing more than to see her suffer. He expected her to sit by and watch him have a life with another woman, while she waited on him hand and foot.

All the while she herself was longing for a new life. A life with Chad, a life with a man who truly respected her and understood her deepest thoughts. David had his new life with Paula, but her life with Chad could not begin, at least not completely. Not until she had her divorce and was free from David.

After the food was prepared and David had left to be with Paula.

Lisa got ready and headed over to Chad's. She was feeling tired and worn from all the trouble at home, so decided to lie down and take a nap until Chad returned from work.

A few hours later, as Lisa lay peacefully sleeping in Chad's bed, he arrived home and Lisa awoke to the sensation of Chad's lips on hers and then his tongue caressing her ear lobes and neck.

Lisa sat up and returned the kiss. Their tongues touched sensuously as they kissed with great passion and lust. Her body became hot with desire and she slowly and gently stripped Chad of his clothing. Then laying him back on the bed, she began kissing his body and stroking his massive organ, getting him hard and ready.

Her crotch was becoming wet with the juices of her desire and her breast had become so hard with excitement they ached.

Lisa continued to stroke him as she whispered.

"I want to slide you deep inside of me. I want to ride you hard and fast, faster and faster until we both cum and scream with pleasure."

Chad groaned as he held her tightly.

"Yes, baby, yes, do it, baby, push me deep, give it to me, baby, give it to me hard."

Lisa climbed on top of him, driving him deep in her wet crevice. She rocked her pelvis up and down. The tightness of her opening seemed to swallow him up, as the friction sent sensations of pleasure coursing through her body.

Chat shuttered as the warm thrusts of her pussy rubbed up and down the stiffness of his manhood. He groaned as his eyes rolled back into his head and the pleasure dominated his body.

"Oh Lisa. Oh baby ride it, ride it hard baby, and come on baby make me cum."

Lisa hearing his pleas of arousal. Shrieked with excitement, as she thrust harder and faster. Pushing him deeper into the throbbing depth of her hot wet pussy. Her body began to quiver, as the flashes or pleasure raced through her body. She began convulsing uncontrollably, with the tingling of her arising orgasm and she screamed with erotic stimulation.

Chad's pulsating organ was hard with sexual enjoyment. As the waves of passion ripped through his exploding groin.

Then suddenly together they raced to the heights of sexual fulfillment and they burst in orgasm. They moaned and panted with the release of their sexual juices. Pooling together deep inside Lisa's channel of love.

Lisa sobbed involuntarily, as the hot juices shot from Chad and inflamed her desire.

"Oh Chad yes! That's it baby, cum, cum with me Chad, yes, oh yes."

They held each other tight, thrusting slowly with the contractions of their orgasms which shot through their sexes and they slowly floated down from the heights of sexual pleasure.

Then as they lay in each other's arms completely relaxed, Chad suddenly tapped her thigh and sat up.

"Boy, I don't know about you baby, but I sure worked up an appetite. What do you say we order out for dinner tonight? Something quick and easy."

Lisa smiled as she got up and slipped in to Chad's robe. "Yeah that sounds good; I'm kind of hungry myself. What do you feel like?"

Chad grinned a devilish grin.

"Well I feel like you again of course, but I guess pizza or Chinese will do for now. I'll let you decide."

Then as he got up from the bed and headed toward the bathroom he looked back.

"Listen while you're ordering something, I'm going to go grab a quick shower."

Lisa smiled as she walked toward him and kissed him sweetly.

"Okay, I'll call and order something, see you in a few minutes."

With that, she smacked his bottom and growled like a tiger as he walked away.

Then as Chad went in to take his shower, Lisa called and ordered dinner.

She ordered pizza and chicken wings, but not being used to making decisions without approval she yelled into Chad. "Baby, is pizza and wings okay with you? If not, I can call and change the order."

Chad turned the water off to answer.

"Of course it is anything you've ordered is fine with me. Don't forget Lisa, I'm not David; you don't have to get every little thing approved with me. You're free to make decisions and I'll always stand by you, too. Relax, baby, anything you want is just fine."

Lisa loved the idea that she could make decisions in their relationship. That was one thing that she couldn't do with David. With David, everything had to get by him first and he always had the final say.

As Lisa waited for the food to arrive, she set the table with candles and chilled some wine. Then she crept into the bathroom too see Chad.

She watched him, soaking wet in the shower as she walked closer.

"HI, Sexy, can I scrub your back for you?"

Chad turned, with a sensual smirk on his face and moaned.

"You sure can, baby, come here."

Then as Lisa reached into the shower and scrubbed his back, Chad found himself becoming aroused once more.

"Oh that feels so good, baby, how would you like to join me in here? I'll make it well worth your while."

Lisa smiled sweetly and raised her eyebrows.

"Oh, will you, now? I'd love to join you, my stallion."

Then as Lisa's robe hit the floor and she began to climb into the shower, there was a knock at the door.

Lisa stepped back out.

"Dam it! The food is here, I better get that." Then she leaned into Chad and whispered softly into his ear.

"Later, baby, after dinner and it will be even better."

With that, she threw the robe back on and ran out to answer the door and Chad headed out of the shower.

Then as they sat down to dinner, Chad insisted on feeding Lisa her pizza. He held it up to her mouth for her to take a bite and she did the same for him.

Chad took a bite as he groaned.

"Umm delicious, but nowhere near as delicious as you." Then he leaned over and kissed her. They passed the pizza back and forth, with seductive words each time, arousing each other once more.

Then before they knew it, Chad had cleared off the table and laid Lisa down, right in the middle of it.

Chad was straddled over her, pumping his hard love rod, deep into her hot wet loins. Their bodies bumped hard together, as the feeling of the cold table made Lisa's nipples so hard and erect; they felt as if they would burst. She felt Chad driving her long and hard, as her erect nipples brushed vigorously against his hairy and sweaty chest.

Lisa shrieked with excitement, as she felt the heat of Chad's hot love juices, pouring deep into her pussy. Then with the pleasures of Chad's moans she herself burst into erotic orgasm and began writing uncontrollably about the table.

Chad held her tight as he his kissed her gently.

"Oh Lisa, I love you more then you could ever know. You're one special lady and you mean the world to me. I hope you realize that."

The as Chad pulled away, Lisa leaned toward him and kissed him passionately.

"I love you too darling. You're my knight in shining armor."

Chad chuckled, as Lisa then got up and slipped back into his robe and began cleaning up the kitchen.

Chad went to put on some quiet music and then returned to help her. Lisa was shocked as she kissed his cheek.

"It's funny to see a man helping in the kitchen. I'm definitely not used to this."

Chad smiled and patted her bottom.

"Well, I don't mind helping out, the faster if gets done the sooner we get to sit and relax together."

Lisa smiled as Chad continued.

"You know, I really wish I could just take you away. Even for just a weekend. I want you all to myself so I can show you how much you really do mean to me. I want to show you just how happy we really could be, in a world with no David. No more abuse, no curfew, we'd do what we wanted, when we wanted. There would be nobody left to dominate our lives. Lisa baby, I love you and I want to make your world a safe one and free you from harm."

In her heart, Lisa loved the idea of going away with Chad, yet knew that David would never allow her to go away for the weekend. She could try, but he would only follow her and then find out about Chad.

Lisa stopped washing the dishes and turned to Chad, with a single tear running down her cheek, she hugged him. "Chad, I would love to get away with you. But you and I both know that I vacation right now is impossible. David would never allow it and I would get in one hell of a lot of trouble if I even tried to go against him."

Chad sighed as they went back to washing the dishes. "Yeah, I know, but you can't blame me for trying, can you?"

Lisa felt bad; it was obvious to her, how much Chad loved her and wanted to be with her. She hated to tell him no, but at this point had no choice.

"Oh, Chad, I'm so sorry things have to be this way right now. I'm hoping things will soon change, but until such time I have to be careful. Chad I truly love you and I just need you to understand, can you do that for me?"

Chad smiled and stroked her cheek.

"Yeah, I can understand, but that doesn't mean I have to like it."

Another tear streamed down Lisa's cheek as she drained the sink and hung up the dish towel.

Chad comforting her rubbed her shoulders and gently kissed her neck.

"It's okay, honey, everything will be fine. Eventually things will all work out and we'll be together and happy for the rest of our lives."

Lisa couldn't hold it back any longer and she began to cry as she listened to Chad's sweet words and felt the strong love he had for her. She wished they had gotten back together eight years ago rather then, her ending up with David. Life would have been completely different, there would have been no abuse and in Lisa's eyes that was a perfect life. Chad would have protected her rather then beat her and all of these problems never would have come to be.

Chad seeing Lisa's tears pulled her close and held her in his arms, as he stroked her hair.

Lisa wanted to hold on to him tight and never let go, yet once again time was running out and she was going to have to head back home.

"Well darling, it's that time again. I should really get going. David said he wasn't coming home tonight, and if I could trust that I would stay. But knowing him, it's just another stupid plan to catch me coming home late. I can't take that risk, so I have to be there."

Chad hugged her tighter and gently kissed her cheek. "Yeah guess it is that time again, I just wish you didn't have to go back there. I can't stand knowing what waits for you there."

Lisa kissed him long and passionately then gently touched his cheek.

"I have to go, see you tomorrow." Chad smiled as he led her to the door.

"Yeah, see you tomorrow. Keep your chin up and take care of yourself."

Lisa headed out, but turned back and blew him a kiss then waved.

As she drove home and thought about Chad and David and all the confusion of her life, she suddenly got a really sick feeling in the pit of her stomach. A sense that something wasn't right, she wasn't sure what it was but as she pulled into her driveway, she knew that her feelings were right and something was wrong. In her driveway sat a police officer waiting her to arrive home.

As she got out of her car, the officer approached her. "Are you Lisa Curtis? David Curtis's wife?"

Lisa's heart jumped to her throat as she answered. "Yes, is there's something wrong? What's happened?" The officer put his hand on her shoulder.

"It's your husband David. I'm sorry to say he was drinking and driving and he's been in an accident. He has been taken to hospital and you are needed there."

Lisa was worried and yet a big part of her hoped he died, so that she would be free. However playing the role of the loving wife, Lisa acted worried and horrified for David as she went with the officer to head for the hospital.

"How serious is it, officer? Is David going to make it?" The officer sighed as he replied.

"Well, to be honest with you, ma'am, your husband is a very lucky to be alive. His car is a total write off, I have no idea how he even came out of it alive."

Lisa was shocked that David had been so careless. "I suppose he'll be charged now, too?"

The officer nodded.

"Oh, yes, without a doubt. He'll be charged with driving under the influence, reckless endangerment and careless driving. He most likely got a hefty fine, lose his license and be sent to alcoholics anonymous."

Lisa couldn't believe what she was hearing; David had gone too far this time and really needed help. Now not only was his drinking affecting their lives, but the lives of innocent people as well. Each night when he drove home from the bar drunk, he was not only endangering his own life, but the lives of innocent and unsuspecting people. Lisa knew this couldn't go on, but there was no talking to David, he never listened to anything she had to say.

When they arrived at the hospital, a nurse took Lisa right in to see David.

He had a few broken ribs, a mild concussion and several cuts and bruises. Lisa had no sympathy for him what so ever, knowing that this had been brought on by himself and his stupidity.

Lisa walked over to his bed side where David looked up at her. Even the accident hadn't calmed him down any; he was still the same old David as he became angry with her.

"Well, gee, if it isn't my devoted wife. Where the hell have you been, Lisa? I've been here for six hours and you, my dear, were nowhere to be found."

Lisa wasn't sure how to answer knowing that no matter what she said; it would be good enough for David.

"I had to run some errands, David, I'm sorry I wasn't home when the police arrived, but I'm here now."

David snickered as he yelled.

"I swear, Lisa, if I wasn't in this bed, you would pay big time for this. You're supposed to be there at all times and you just decide to go out? Running errands, yeah right! You went out for a night on the town and I know it. You're nothing but a cheap whore Lisa, a slut out tramping around while her husband is away."

Lisa laughed and shook her head as she got brave.

"Oh, yeah, David, as if I expected anything better out you. After all you've done to me and all you've put me through, you expect me to just hover over you, like a loving wife. Ha, forget it you're not worth it! Besides you said you were spending the night at Paula's. Or was that just another of your foolish lies? I made up story to try and get to me? You're a fool David, this was all your own fault and you know it."

David was furious.

"How dare you take that tone with me, Lisa, who the hell do you think you are?"

Lisa laughed as she answered sarcastically.

"Someone smart enough to know, that it was your own stupidity that has landed you in this hospital bed. You expect me to sit here and feel sorry for you but that just isn't going to happen. You could have killed somebody, David."

David laughed.

"I only hit some bitch with kids in the car, no great loss there."

Lisa knew that David could be a horrible man, but this was too much.

"I don't believe you, David, you are so cold and definitely not the man I married. So where is your precious, Paula? I don't see her here hovering over you?"

David still angry reached out and grabbed Lisa by the wrist twisting it.

"For your information, Paula had an emergency at work and had to leave. So I went out to the bar before heading home. Paula doesn't know, or she would be here."

Lisa pulled away from David and stepped back.

"Well, it's too bad she isn't here, maybe then she'd see what an uncaring selfish ass-hole you really are."

David laughed.

"Yeah maybe, but you're stuck with me forever, baby, too bad for you now, isn't it?"

Lisa had listened to enough as she turned and headed out of the room.

David yelled.

"I'm out of here at noon tomorrow Lisa and I expect you to be here to pick me up."

Lisa wanted to just tell him to go to hell, but answered. "Yeah, I'll be here, now if you don't mind, I'm going home. I'm sick and tired of listening to your bullshit."

Then she left as David yelled to her in the hallway. "Yeah, we'll just see how brave you are tomorrow, won't we?"

Lisa ignored him as she kept walking and headed out to call a cab and go home.

While waiting for her cab, she decided she would call Chad and fill him in on everything that had happened.

Chad wasn't at all surprised to hear the news.

"I expected something like this sooner or later; David is nothing but a careless self-centered bum. He never takes anyone else into consideration, nor does he think about the consequences of his actions."

Lisa agreed.

"You're absolutely right; he doesn't care about anyone or anything. Any way I just wanted to let you know what's been going on. I'm not sure if I'll make it over there tomorrow night, David is coming home tomorrow and he'll expect me to hang around and take care of him."

Chad sighed,

"Yeah, he will. Listen, Lisa. Why don't you come here tonight? You can spend the night with me, rather than alone in that big house. I can always go in to work late tomorrow."

Lisa loved the idea.

"That sounds terrific, I'm just waiting for my cab, and then I'll swing by my place and pick up some things and be right over."

Chad growled like a tiger into the phone as he replied. "Great, I'll be waiting, see you soon."

Lisa hung up the phone from Chad and her cab had arrived. She headed for home, where she grabbed a change of clothes and left again to be with Chad.

When she arrived at his apartment, he greeted her at the door with a big hug and kiss and then asked Lisa exactly what had happened and if anyone had been hurt other than David. Lisa explained that the woman in the other car had two small children with her, one of which was a small infant and luckily they were all okay.

"I honestly can't believe how arrogant and uncaring David is. When he found out about the children, he didn't even care. He just said that it would have been two less brats in the world."

Chad was astonished.

"My God, Lisa, that bastard has no feeling what so ever. All he cares about is the bottle and keeping you trapped in his little torture chamber in hell. He could have killed that woman and her children and yet it doesn't even faze him. He's sick, honey, and he needs to be taken care of once and for all."

Lisa began to cry and explained to Chad, that she felt ashamed with herself for what she wished when she had heard about the accident.

"Chad, I wished he had died. How could I have been so cold as to have wished someone dead? The really scary part is that I still wish that."

Chad hugged her.

"Oh, Lisa, don't feel ashamed. It's completely understandable. David has put you through years of both mental and physical abuse. You have more than enough reasons to wish harm on him. I would never blame you for feeling that way, you have every right."

Chad held her close and told her everything would be okay. He was happy that she was there with him and for the first time, he could hold her in his arms all night long and watch her sleep.

"It's going to be wonderful waking up with you in my arms."

Lisa smiled as she agreed.

"Yes, it is, but please make sure I am awake by ten o'clock. I have to be at the hospital by noon to pick up David." Chad stroked her cheek.

"Don't worry, baby, I won't let you oversleep. I know how vicious David can be and I don't want you getting into any trouble with that idiot."

Lisa was exhausted as she yawned.

"Do you mind if we just go to sleep tonight? I'm really tired; this has just worn me out."

Chad smiled and kissed her sweetly on the cheek.

"I don't mind at all. You need your rest to be able to cope with that jerk tomorrow."

Lisa yawned again as they headed in to bed. "Yeah sure I do."

Chad and Lisa lay in each other's arms, warm and snug.

Lisa felt totally safe and protected, she hadn't felt this secure in a long time and she loved the feeling.

She kissed Chad goodnight and told him she loved him. Chad said he loved her too, as then held each other close and drifted off to sleep.

The next morning Lisa awoke feeling totally relaxed and refreshed. She had slept the best she had in years. Being with Chad, there was no fear and she didn't have to worry about what was coming in the morning.

As she lay there totally relaxed still in Chad's arms, she suddenly felt his tender touch as he caressed her body and kissed her gently.

She was a little shocked as she wasn't used to waking up this way, yet she loved it and found herself very turned on as she turned to him.

Chad kissed her passionately and hungrily as then went down and began licking her sensitive opening ferociously. He licked and fondled her sending erotic sensations of pleasure ripping through her body.

"Oh Lisa, baby I love waking you up this way. Being able to make love to you and please you before I go to work. I want to make you cum baby, cum real good and I won't stop until you do."

Chad was going nuts on her; each stroke of his tongue aroused her as he drove his finger deep into her wet crevice. Lisa groaned and writhed about the bed with stimulating bolts of energy coursing through her body. Then as she felt the tingling of her arising orgasm, she cried out.

"Oh Chad, oh yes baby, yes make me cum, make me cum good."

Chad hearing her lustful cries began going faster and faster on her. Deeper and harder each time, until she burst in to screams of erotic satisfaction.

Lisa rolled Chad over and jumped on top of him, driving his rock-hard rod deep into her hot wet pussy. She drove him long and hard and screamed with pleasure as the friction increased with the tightness of her sexual muscles. She rode him fast and slow and then fast again. She stimulated him and made him groan with pleasure and complete sexual arousal.

She felt the throbbing of Chad deep inside of her, as he began twitching erotically and exploded into massive orgasm. The hot juices of his desire flowed freely inside of her, she tingled as flashes of pleasure raced through her body and she was once again brought to orgasm. She screeched and grabbed Chad tight. He kissed her passionately and she then pulled away.

"Oh Chad, that was fantastic."

Chad smiled.

"Sure was. What a perfect way to start a day, I can't think of any better way to wake up."

Lisa agreed.

"Me, neither, I wish every morning could be like this. I love you Chad and waking up in your arms makes me happier than you could imagine. When I'm with you, I actually feel wanted and like I really do mean something."

Chad stroked her hair.

"You do mean something, baby, you mean a whole lot. You're one hell of a woman and I'm glad to have you in my life."

Lisa smiled and kissed his cheek.

"Thanks, baby, I'm glad to have you in my life too."

Then as they got up to grab a shower, Chad gave her a little love tap on her bottom.

Lisa jumped as she exclaimed. "Ooh baby!"

Then she wiggled her bottom at him and looking over her shoulder winked as she said.

"Guess you like what you see, eh?"

Chad chuckled.

"You bet I do, baby."

Then he chased her into the shower, where he began to wash her and she washed him. Then what had started out to be a normal everyday shower turned into an erotic event, as she got down on her knees and began sucking his dick while fondling his warm wet balls.

She sucked him long and fast, taking all of him in to her mouth. Chad moaned with the feeling her lips wrapped tightly around him.

"Oh, Lisa, oh yeah that's it. Take it all, suck me baby suck me good."

She continued to go at him faster and faster, all the while teasing him with her tongue until he burst with pleasure and his hot love juices shot into her mouth and she swallowed.

Chad pulled her up and turned her around leaning her against the shower wall. Then from behind he pushed his still hard manhood into her moist pussy. He pushed it hard and fast, deeper and deeper, faster and faster.

"Take it baby take it. Take it all, oh yeah baby take all of me."

Chad drove her harder and harder as he encircles her pebble hard nipples with his fingertips. The hot water drizzled down their steamy bodies, as they pumped hard bringing each other to the heights of desire, where they burst into erotic flames of ecstasy and were brought to orgasm.

Lisa screamed with excitement, as Chad's thrusts slowed and he pulled away.

"Well, baby, I have to say that is the best morning shower I've ever taken."

Lisa still catching her breath rubbed his shoulders.

"That's for sure; I've never taken a shower quite like it. Anyway Chad, sorry to say it, but I've got to get finished up here and get to the hospital to pick up David."

Chad sighed as he turned off the water.

"Yeah guess it is getting kind of late, I've got to get to work too so we better get ready."

They got out of the shower and began getting ready to go.

Lisa sighed as she got dressed and then explained.

"I guess I'll have to call you tonight, I'm sure David won't allow me to go out tonight. He'll want me there to take care of him; I'm going to try though. If I can get away for a bit, I'll be here. I can't guarantee it though, not with David and his attitude. I just can't stand the thought of not seeing you tonight."

Chad kissed her sweetly on the forehead.

"Well, if you can't get away, I'll see you tomorrow. Seriously baby, don't push it and piss him off. We can't have him finding out about me and I don't want him hurting you. Not even a few broken ribs will stop that jerk and you and I both know that."

Lisa sighed as she slipped into her jacket.

"I know Chad, but I really want to see you tonight. When I'm with you, nothing else matters, my life is perfect."

Chad hugged her.

"I know baby, but you know one night apart isn't going to hurt us any. You know that I will still be here waiting for you tomorrow. You can call me and we can talk, just don't push, David. Please, Lisa, for your own sake, don't push him."

Lisa kissed him then nodded.

"Yeah, I know you're right, but I'm still going to miss you. Anyway, I better get going. I love you, Chad, I'll call you tonight."

Chad returned the kiss as he stroked her hair.

"I love you, too and I'll be waiting to hear from you. Take care, baby, and keep your chin up."

Lisa smiled as she headed out. "I will. Bye, darling."

Lisa left Chad's apartment and headed for the hospital. She was sure that David would be in a fierce mood. After spending the night in the hospital without the bottle and her to yell at, he was sure to be horrible and she was not looking forward to it.

After the night, she had spent with Chad though, there was nothing David could really say to spoil her mood. She was relaxed and refreshed and happier than she had been in a long time.

Lisa arrived at the hospital at 11:30 A.M. To find that David was already set to leave.

As she looked at her watch, she questioned.

"What? Am I late? I thought you said noon?"

David was furious.

"I was discharged at 10:00 A.M. I called you and you weren't home. Where in the hell have you been?"

Lisa became extremely nervous.

"I, I, I had some bills to pay, so I left early this morning to get them paid and be here on time."

David snickered as he pounded his fist on to the bed. "Yeah, sure a likely excuse. I don't expect that you'll have to leave for the rest of the day then, eh, Lisa?"

Lisa holding back her anger answered.

"No David, I've done everything that needed to be done. I'll be home the rest of the day now."

David chuckled as he got up from the bed.

"Good, now let's get the hell out of here, this place is enough to make someone sick."

All the way home, all David did was yell and complain.

"Goddamn it, I can't believe my bloody car is a write off. This is total bullshit and the cops are taking away my license? Who the hell do they think they are? What right do they have, to tell me I can't drive? Stupid assholes, I wish I had hit one of them, it would have made it all worth it."

Lisa was angry with David's attitude as she replied. "Damn it, David, it's your own bloody fault. If you weren't such a drunk and you didn't drink and drive, this never would have happened. You could have killed that family and all you care about is the fact that you lost your license? My God, David, how can you be so selfish and uncaring. It really disgusts me to know that the man I married is so cold and heartless. You're positively unbelievable. Why don't you just think for a minute and realize that this whole mess was your own doing?"

David slapped her, causing her to lose control of the car for a second, swerving in the other lane and almost hitting an oncoming car.

Lisa yelled.

"You son of a bitch, what in the hell do you think you're doing? You could have caused another accident."

David laughed.

"Yeah, right, just because you women drivers don't know how to control a car, you blame me. Just like that bitch last night, you're all the same."

Lisa was furious.

"All right, whatever David, why don't you just give it a rest? I don't want to hear any more of your bullshit excuses, so just shut your bloody mouth."

To Lisa's surprise David never responded, he just sat quietly and for the rest of the ride home, he never said another word about the accident or anything else for that matter.

For the first time, David seemed speechless. Lisa was proud of herself, this was the first time she has stood up to David and actually won the argument.

They arrived home and went inside, David said he was going to lie down and told Lisa to put a case of beer in the fridge for him when he got up.

Lisa not wanting him drinking again shook her head as she replied.

"Forget it, David, I'm not doing it. If you want to get pissed out of your mind, put it in your own bar fridge, it's not going in mine. I won't condone your drinking any longer. It's become a serious problem and I am sick and tired of it."

David became furious as he turned and through his shoe at her, hitting her in the back of the head.

"Mouthy, are we? Damn it, Lisa! Just shut up and do it, if you know what is good for you. I swear, Lisa; if you don't, you'll be one sorry girl."

Lisa laughed, trying to remain brave. "Forget it, David. No way, I'm not doing it."

David grabbed the baseball bat from the corner and headed toward her, he raised the bat to hit her, but the pain in his ribs caused him to double over in pain and he dropped it.

Lisa laughed.

"Still going to try and get tough with me, David? Don't be so foolish, you dumb jerk."

David still furious walked into the kitchen and put his own beer in the fridge.

"You're a real bitch Lisa."

Lisa smirked.

"Yeah, I can be, can't I?"

Lisa couldn't believe it, David's being hurt was really working to her advantage and she was able to keep him under control and keep him from hurting her. She knew that it was only temporary and in a day or two, he would be right back to normal, but for the time being she had no real worries.

She waited until David had gone for his nap and then sat down on the sofa and called Chad.

"Hi sexy, you'll never believe this, I won the fight, well, at least this one."

Chad was confused.

"What do you mean? What happened?"

Lisa went on.

"Well, David was bitching and complaining all the way home about his car and the fact that he lost his license. Then when we got home, he was all demanding and wanted me to put a case of beer in the fridge for him. Anyway, I told him that I wouldn't do it and if he wanted to get drunk, he could put his own damn beer in the fridge. So, then he took a baseball bat and came at me."

Chad interrupted.

"Oh my God, Lisa, are you okay? Did he hurt you?"

Lisa continued.

"No, I'm fine, when he raised the bat to hit me, the pain in his ribs knocked him right back down and he dropped it. Then he just gave up and walked away from the fight. He put his own beer in the fridge and went to bed."

Chad was shocked.

"Wow, can't believe it, David walked away. You sound pretty excited, I mean you barely let me get in a word."

Lisa laughed.

"I'm sorry, I just can't believe it."

Chad agreed.

"Yeah, me neither and Lisa, honey, I think it's great but please be careful and watch your step. You know he won't be hurt forever and eventually, he will fight back. Don't get me wrong, baby, I am really proud of you for standing up for yourself, just be careful."

Lisa agreed.

"I will, Chad, don't you worry. Anyway, I better get going here; I'll call you later tonight. David is going to be drinking and will likely pass out early, so when he does, I'll call."

Chad sighed.

"You have to go so soon? All right then, I'll be waiting for you to call and I hope things are still okay then and you're all right. I love you, princess, talk to you later."

Lisa blew a kiss in to the phone.

"Bye, baby."

Lisa spent the rest of the day, watching movies and thinking about Chad. While David sat drowning his sorrows in beer and yelling about whatever he could. He found a spot on the kitchen counter and freaked out. Lisa walked in and washed it, but David swore the spot was moving.

Lisa laughed at him and took away his beer.

"David, I think you've had enough, why don't you just go to bed for the night and sleep it off?"

David became angry and reached out to hit her, but being so intoxicated, he passed out and did a face plant right on the kitchen floor.

Lisa dragged him in to the living room and pulled him up and got him settled on the sofa. He opened his eyes for a brief minute and grunted.

Lisa shook her head.

"Well, David, now you've done it. You're really going to pay for that one in the morning, falling on your ribs like that, not too bright."

David smirked as his yelled.

"Oh, just shut up and leave me the hell alone."

With that, he rolled over and went to sleep.

Lisa cleaned up the mess of beer bottles from around the house and then headed up to bed, where she then called Chad.

"Hi, baby, how are you?" Chad answered.

"I'm fine, honey, are you okay?" Lisa continued.

"I'm fine. I just miss you, I really wish I was there with you and not here alone in this dark room, with David right downstairs."

Chad sighed.

"Yeah, I know, Lisa. I miss you too. You know though, we could have some fun on the phone."

Lisa was confused.

"Chad, what do you mean? What are you getting at?" Chad began talking seductively.

"Oh baby, just imagine me there. I'm sucking your hard nipples and fingering your hot wet pussy. Now, I'm down licking your clit, while you're sucking my rock-hard dick."

Lisa felt the crotch of her panties becoming moist and her nipples getting hard as Chad spoke.

"Oh, Chad, you're getting me hot. I wish you were here to put your dick deep into my pussy."

Chad continued.

"Oh baby, I'm hard and ready. I want you so bad that I'm stroking myself. Up and down, faster and faster."

As Lisa listened to Chad's seductive voice and thought about his lips hard against her pussy. She reached down into her panties and began encircling her clit while she pushed her finger deep inside of herself.

"Ooh Chad, I'm playing with myself. I'm fingering my pussy and playing with my clit. I'm so hot and wet. I'm going to cum."

Chad was so aroused he groaned.

"Oh, Lisa, just thinking about you playing with your pussy has got me so horny that I'm going to shoot all over my bed."

Lisa fondled herself as she listened to Chad. The sensations of pleasure soared through her body as the juices of her desire flowed freely. She tingled as the waves dominated her body and she brought herself to orgasm.

"Oh, Chad, oh, I'm coming, baby, oh it's so good. Oh Chad, oh!"

Hearing Lisa's cries of pleasure Chad moaned.

"Oh Lisa, me too, baby, me too."

Chad groaned with satisfaction as Lisa panted with erotic stimulation.

"Oh Chad, that was great baby. I love you so much." Chad still overcome with erotic pleasure agreed.

"That was great, wasn't it? I love you, too, baby. Maybe now you can get a good night's rest."

Lisa still catching her breath answered.

"Yes, definitely, but I'll miss you though. I'll be there tomorrow night though, even if it kills me, I'm getting out of here to see you."

Chad chuckled.

"Okay, baby, I'll see you then. Now, I'm going to let you get some sleep. I'll see you tomorrow night, sleep well, angel. I love you."

Lisa blew a kiss into the phone. "I love you, too, bye."

Lisa hung up the phone and lay there thinking about Chad. She felt so loved as she quivered with happiness and she drifted off to sleep. That night she slept like a baby and dreamed that she was in Chad's arms, safe and secure and life was perfect.

The next morning Lisa awoke to sound of David yelling from downstairs.

"Lisa, why the hell am I on the sofa? It should be you down here, you should have put me in bed, you lazy tit."

Lisa sat up in bed as she said quietly to herself.

"Great! Things are back to normal, just when I thought things were going well, too."

She pulled herself out of bed and headed downstairs.

"What the hell are you bitching about now, David?"

David got up and slapped her across the face.

"Don't you speak to me like that, Lisa, or you'll be very sorry. Now, I want breakfast, eggs, bacon, toast and coffee. Get a move on it, I'm starving."

Lisa laughed.

"Ha! Go to hell, David, do it yourself."

David grabbed her and pinned her up against the wall, then bashed her head into it several times. Then he threw her down on the ground and began kicking her in the back.

"Go on, bitch; tell me to go to hell now. Come on, baby, what's your problem? Want me to stop? Beg me then, come on, baby. Beg me to stop."

Lisa refused. She was tired of giving him everything he wanted, so she tried to fight back. She reached up and hit him in the knee caps trying to knock him down, but didn't succeed. David began kicking her harder and harder, she was in pain and couldn't take it anymore, but she couldn't just lie there, she had to fight back.

Lisa pulled herself up and knowing that his ribs were already injured took it to her advantage and began hitting him over and over in the ribs. David soon doubled over and fell to the floor.

Lisa began kicking him in the back and threw his own words back at him.

"Come on, David, beg me, beg me to stop. What's your problem? Come on, beg me."

Then with one last kick to his back she walked away, while he yelled at her calling her a bitch and a whore.

Lisa paid him no attention as she kept walking. She believed that he had deserved what he got and she was proud of herself for fighting back. She had won and for once, David was hurt worse than she was and she was able to walk away.

David finally pulled himself up from the floor and went to take a shower and get dressed. Lisa was shocked that he hadn't even attempted to continue the argument, he just walked upstairs. Not wanting to give David a reason to start back up again, Lisa quickly cleaned things up.

David finished up and came back downstairs. To Lisa's surprise, he was calm and talked to her with some respect.

"Lisa, I'd like to go and see Paula. Do you think you could give me a ride over there? I know I shouldn't be asking you, but until I get my license back, I can't exactly drive myself."

Lisa was in a state of shock, who was this man and what had happened to David? She figured it was probably a set up and David was just playing mind games with her again, setting her up for a fall.

Yet she answered.

"Yeah, I guess I can do that, just give me some time to get ready to go."

David still acting respectful agreed.

"Yeah, sure no problem, I'm meeting her at the bar any way and it doesn't open for another forty-five minutes, so take your time."

As Lisa got ready to go, she wondered what David was up too. The last time he had acted like this, it was only to get what he wanted and then the next day, he beat her so bad that she was in bed for three days.

Lisa was scared, not knowing whether or not David was sincere or just playing another mind game, was terrifying and it was driving her crazy.

When she was ready to leave, she asked David which bar he was going to and if he needed her to pick him up.

"Oh, you can just drop me off downtown and I'll walk from there and you don't need to pick me up, I'm not sure what time I'll be home so I'll just find my own way."

Not knowing when he would be coming home and wanting to be safe to see Chad, she answered.

"That's fine, David, but I'm going out tonight with a couple of friends from school and I probably won't be home until around 3:00 A.M. You won't be able to reach me, so, are you sure you'll be able to get a ride with someone if needed?"

That was it, Lisa had pushed the wrong button and David exploded with anger once more.

"Typical, just bloody typical. Going out again, are you? Always out on the town and never there when I need something from you. You stupid little whore, you're my wife and you're supposed to be right there at home, waiting for me."

Lisa became angry as she yelled back.

"Get real, David, get bloody real. You just finished saying that I didn't have to pick you up. I offered and you refused so what the hell is your problem?"

David was quiet for a minute and then answered.

"Oh, what the hell does it matter anyway? I always knew that you were nothing but a useless tit and that you'd never do anything right. Besides, I've been meaning to tell you. Paula and I are going away on a four-day cruise, we leave Friday."

Lisa was stunned.

"Oh, you are, nice, really nice David!"

David laughed.

"Yeah, for me that is. You, however, have got your work cut out for you. There's a lot that needs to be done around the house and I expect you to get it all done. If I return to a mess, you're going to be sorry, you think I'm violent now? Ha! Just ignore the housework and you'll see just how violent I can be. You haven't seen anything yet, baby."

Lisa laughed.

"You're unbelievable, David, completely unbelievable. Just take off on vacation with your girlfriend and leave your wife at home to deal with everything else. You're an asshole and I'm really sick of your shit. Maybe I'll take off, too; maybe I'll just pack a bag and go away for a few days, too, what then?"

David chuckled as he shook his head.

"Go right ahead, at least if you're not there, I know the house will stay clean. Just make dam sure you're there by the time I return, if not, you'll pay the price, big time!"

Lisa was tired of arguing,

"Fine, David, whatever you say."

With that, she just tried to ignore him for the rest of the ride. The trip downtown seemed to take forever. Lisa couldn't wait to drop him off so she didn't have to listen to him anymore. Besides that, she couldn't wait to call Chad and tell him that David and Paula were going away, leaving them four full days to be alone together.

After dropping David off, Lisa tried to call Chad at work and tell him the good news, but found he was in a meeting. So, she decided that she would surprise him with the news that night over a nice dinner. So, she headed to Chad's apartment to cook a good meal and set things up for a very special evening.

She arrived at Chad's apartment, and went to the fridge to find that there wasn't much there to prepare a good meal with, so she headed back out to the grocery store, where she was stunned to run right into Paula and David.

David wasn't thrilled to see her there.

"What the hell are you doing here, Lisa? Following me around like a lost puppy?"

Lisa didn't want him to find out about Chad and she became nervous.

"No, David, I'm not following you around. I told you I had plans tonight with some old friends and I'm just picking some things up. We're cooking dinner before we go out."

David unsure whether or not to believe her, pulled her cart over.

"Then why do you only have two steaks in your cart?"

Lisa knew David was questioning her sincerity as she answered.

"Because each of us is going to pick up a few things. I was asked to bring two steaks and some stuff to make a salad. My God David, what is with the third degree?"

David continued.

"How many are going to be there?" Lisa answered quickly.

"Well, I think there is going to be six of us all together. I'm not quite sure as Kate may not make it."

David finally gave up questioning her.

"Well, fine then, see you tonight, but if you're not home by 3:00 A.M. there will be hell to pay."

Then as David walked away, Lisa sighed with relief; he had fallen for her lies and left her alone.

She then finished her shopping and headed out the car, but as she pulled away, she had a feeling that she was being watched.

Lisa looked into her rear-view mirror to discover that she was being followed. David and Paula were right behind her. She became terrified and wasn't sure where to go or how to lose them. She couldn't allow David to follow her to Chad's apartment. Then, in a panic, she began turning down streets she didn't even know and almost got lost. She had to find a way out of this mess, so she turned in to a variety store and David and Paula turned in as well.

Lisa jumped out of her car and walked over to see David. "What the hell are you doing? Why are you following me? Have you got nothing better to do?"

David got out of the car and started yelling.

"Don't you get it, Lisa? I don't trust you and I don't believe for a minute that you're going out with friends tonight. I think you're planning on leaving me and I won't have it."

With that, right there in public David began hitting her. Lisa yelled.

"Damn it, David, I'm not leaving you. I really am going out with friends tonight. I just stopped here to pick up a pack of smokes and noticed you behind me."

David was furious and continued hitting her and yelling. "You stupid damn whore, I don't believe a word you're saying. You're a liar, Lisa, a stupid foolish liar. In this marriage, you do only what I want. I don't care about you or your pathetic needs. I'm the only thing that matters and it's time you accepted that."

Right then Paula jumped in.

"David, leave her alone, she has a right to go out with her friends once in a while. I sure as hell hope you don't try to pull this crap with me. I won't put up with it, I'll walk away."

David stopped hitting Lisa and turned to Paula.

"Oh baby you're different, you don't have to worry about a thing. You mean something to me and I would never hurt you, or keep you from doing things. You're a totally different story, baby, trust me."

Paula wasn't sure whether or not to believe him; she just looked at him with a confused glazed look in her eyes.

Lisa laughed as she stepped back from David.

"Oh, yeah sure, David, you won't hurt her. At least, not until you have her wrapped around your little finger, right? You're an abusive alcoholic and all you care about is yourself. She'll find out, sooner or later that she'll be the one behind your iron fists."

Paula, seeing the fury in David's eyes, grabbed him by the arm.

"Come on David, let's go. I think we need to talk and Lisa has a dinner party to get to."

Then as they turned to get back into the car, Lisa yelled.

"If you're smart Paula, you'll run before it's too late for you, too."

Paula shrugged her shoulders as she pulled the car door closed and left with David.

Lisa was relieved they were finally gone, but got into her car to find that David had once again blackened her eye and split her lip. She knew that Chad was going to be furious and she worried that this was going to be the last straw and Chad would go after David.

She prayed that maybe the news of the vacation, would calm him down enough that he would just let things lie for now.

All the way to Chad's apartment, Lisa found herself constantly looking in her rear-view mirror, to see if she was being followed. The episode with David and Paula had left her frantic and terrified of being caught.

She arrived at Chad's building and parked her car in the back and out of sight then quickly ran inside. She couldn't believe how scared she was, David had never followed her before. Now knowing that he would, she was nervous to be out of the house and feared being caught with Chad.

Once in Chad's apartment, Lisa calmed down and got herself under control then began preparing a nice steak dinner for Chad. Just as she finished cooking and started setting the table, he arrived home. Lisa was still a little shaken and he noticed right away.

"Lisa, what's wrong? You look awful!"

Lisa sighed.

"I'm okay; well at least I am now. I had a little run in with David. He caught me at the grocery store and decided to follow me."

Chad jumped in.

"What! He followed you here?"

Lisa seeing Chad was worried answered quickly.

"No, no, baby, relax. I turned into a variety store to throw him off. Then he decided that he was going to start a fight with me right there in the parking lot and started beating on me."

Just as Lisa had suspected, Chad was furious.

"Who the hell does he think he is? How dare he do this to you and right there in public? What the hell was he doing driving anyway?"

Lisa jumped in.

"Oh he wasn't, Paula was with him. I can't believe how stupid she is, to stand there and watch David beat on me and then leave with him."

Chad shook his head still furious.

"Well, I guess they're meant for each other then. They're both idiots like two peas in a pod. Come here, baby; let me have a look at that eye."

Lisa walked over to Chad. As he looked at her eye, she could see the anger in his eyes.

"Lisa, that jerk is going to get it good. He has no right to beat on you, or anyone else for that matter. I swear to you, I'm going to get even with him."

Lisa wanted to just forget about David for now and just enjoy being with Chad.

"Come on, Chad, let's eat. I've made all your favorite foods, steak, mashed potatoes and tossed salad. Let's just enjoy out meal and forget about David for now okay? Besides, I've got a surprise for you."

Chad and Lisa sat down to dinner, but Chad was very anxious to find out what the surprise was.

"Well, honey, dinner looks fabulous, but what is this big surprise? Come on, don't keep me in suspense."

Lisa laughed as she went on to explain, that David and Paula were leaving on a cruise on Friday morning and would be gone for four whole days.

"If you could get the time off of work, we'd finally have or chance to get away together."

Chad was excited to hear the news.

"Lisa, that would be amazing. I can't see why I wouldn't be able to get the time off, I have two weeks of holidays owed to me so four days should be easy to get. I'll talk to my boss tomorrow and then we can work out the details."

Lisa smiled and kissed him.

"Oh Chad, four days alone together, without having to go home to David. It's going to be fantastic; I just hope it all works out."

Chad smiled and winked at her.

"Oh, I'm sure it will."

Then he raised his glass and made a toast.

"Here's to four days alone with the woman I fell hopelessly in love with. I love you Lisa and I always will."

A tear ran down Lisa's cheek as she replied.

"I love you, too, Chad, you're the best thing that has ever happened to me and I'll do whatever it takes to keep you happy."

Chad put his hand on hers as they finished up their meal, and then after they finished Lisa went into the kitchen to clean up.

As she stood at the counter, she suddenly felt the warmth of Chad's breath on her neck as he then whispered in to her ear.

"I've got a surprise for you, too, baby. I'm going to get it all set up while you're busy in here."

Lisa turned and raised her eyebrows as she smirked and replied

"Set it all up? Well Mr. Roberts, just what have you got planned?"

Chad laughed as he walked into the bedroom.

"You'll just have to wait and see now, won't you?"

Lisa laughed as she turned back and began washing the dishes. As she stood there at the sink, she couldn't help but wonder what it was Chad had planned. She was becoming overcome with suspense as her heart was beating a mile a minute and her hands were shaking. She couldn't wait to find out what it was Chad was doing in the other room.

Then as she finished up with the dishes, she yelled in to the other room.

"Chad, I'm finished in here, can I come in there now?"

Chad yelled back.

"No not just yet. Give me a few more minutes, just relax on the sofa and I'll come get you when I'm ready."

Lisa sat on the sofa and waited for Chad, the suspense was killing her. What was Chad doing and why was he being so secretive? Lisa was sweating as she tried to figure out what it was Chad was up too. Then she yelled to him again.

"Are you ready yet? I can't wait, I'm getting lonely, baby." Chad laughed as he yelled back.

"Oh, all right then. Since you put it that way, come on in."

Lisa jumped up off the sofa and headed inside the bedroom, where she walked in to find Chad laying on the bed.

He was laying naked with three different vibrators beside him and a porn movie playing on the big screen television. He had lit candles around the room and put red satin sheets on the bed and over on the bed side table, was several flavors of whipped cream, body gels and oils.

Lisa was shocked yet aroused as Chad then walked toward her and began pulling her pants off her using his teeth. As she looked down at him, now on his knees, she removed her top and bra. Her nipples were erect with anticipation and her crotch was becoming extremely wet, with thoughts of the events about to happen.

Chad stood up and took her by the arm and led her over to a chair in the corner of his room and sat her down. He then spread her legs wide apart and tied them to the chair so she couldn't close them and then tied her hands behind her back. Lisa had never been tied up for sex before, but something about it aroused her and made her feel totally erotic. Her nipples were so hard they ached and her pussy throbbed with anticipation.

Chad walked over to the bedside table and picked up a can of whipped cream then grabbed the vibrators off the bed. Lisa's body shook with excitement, as she thought about the things that Chad was going to do to her. She looked over at the television and noticed the woman in the movie was also tied in a chair. Seeing this aroused her more, Chad was living out a fantasy that she was a part of.

As Chad walked toward her, she groaned at the sight of his dick swaying with his movements. He got down on his knees and shot whipped cream on her nipples and began nibbling at them hungrily. Then moving downward, he shot more whipped cream on her mound and her sensitive opening and began licking her ferociously. His tongue was strong and the strokes made her shake with erotic stimulation.

Lisa felt completely at his mercy as she heard the hum of the vibrator moving slowly toward her hard clit. She shrieked with pleasure as she felt the tip of the vibrator, gently kiss her erect love button, sending chills quivering down her spine and leaving her completely at Chad's mercy.

Then as she felt the vibrator penetrate her hot yearning loins, Chad licked and gently kissed her clit, bringing her to massive orgasm.

Lisa shrieked with the erotic sensations coursing through her body and was so sensitive she was sure she couldn't take anymore, yet Chad continued. He stroked the vibrator faster and harder in and out of her pussy, while he sucked and caressed her breasts. Soon, her clit was hard again and ready for more and Chad once again began licking it and encircling it with the tip of the vibrator.

Chad then paused for moment, as he spread gel across Lisa's love-soaked pussy. It was cinnamon flavored and heated as the body became aroused. The heat of her pussy caused her to scream and squirm with pleasure, as Chad continued to lick her and push the vibrator deep inside of her. As Chad licked faster and faster and the gel got hotter, her body throbbed with intense pleasure. Chad, then switched to a ridged vibrator; he drove it in deeper and deeper harder and faster. The friction became so intense that Lisa once again raced to the sensual heights of desire and was brought to orgasm.

Then as Lisa sat there, still trying to catch her breath from the powerful explosion in her loins, Chad untied her. He then rubbed sensual oils all over her body and his own, then led her to the bed and laid her down.

He began teasing her with the head of his erect dick. He stroked it across her nipples and then slid it slowly across her mound as he spoke to her in a sensual voice.

"Do you want me, baby? Come on, tell me you want me, tell me you want my hard dick, deep in your wet pussy. Come on, baby, tell me."

Lisa writhed about as she shrieked and exclaimed.

"Yes, Chad, yes! I want you, I want you bad. Screw me, Chad, do it, screw my pussy. I want you, baby; I want you deep inside of me."

Chad then mounted her and pushed his hardness deep into her hot screaming loins.

"Take me, baby, take all of me."

Chad's throbbing rod was deep inside of her, sending pulsations of erotic joy, coursing through both of their bodies. As he drove himself in and out, Lisa's body convulsed uncontrollably. The pleasure that her body had already taken, made her so sensitive that with every stroke of his hardness, flashes of pleasure shot through her body and she raced once again to orgasm.

The heat from her exploding groin, forced sobs or pleasure shooting from her throat.

"Oh yes, Chad, yes, baby, oh yes I'm cumming. Oh I'm cumming so good."

Lisa panted and groaned seductively, as Chad then slid his hardness between the fullness of her breasts. He slid it back and forth faster and faster, bringing himself to orgasm and shooting his hot sensual juices across her chest.

Chad groaned as he then flopped down on the bed next to her.

"Oh Lisa, you're the best, baby. Your sexuality is so powerful; it seems to take over my entire body. You're the most sensual woman I've ever known, Oh God, how I love you."

Lisa rolled toward him, gently caressing his chest.

"Oh baby, without you, it would never be this good. It's you who brings out my sexuality; you've made me the woman I am today."

Chad kissed her sweetly.

"Well my lady, you sure do know how to send a man's ego through the ceiling now, don't you?"

Lisa laughed.

"Yeah okay Chad, funny ha-ha."

She then got up from the bed to head for the shower.

"I'm going to grab a shower baby; I have to get going soon."

Chad sighed.

"Yeah, it's that time again, isn't it?"

Lisa smiled sweetly as she went in to take her shower and then got ready to head back home.

As she got ready to leave, she reminded him about Friday.

"Don't forget about Friday now, I'm really looking forward to getting away with you, it will be fantastic."

Chad smiled a devilish grin.

"Oh, don't you worry, I won't forget and I promise you, we're going to have the time of our lives."

Lisa was so excited about it, she thought she'd burst. Finally a vacation with Chad, time alone with no David and no worries.

"I can't wait, baby, it's going to be wonderful."

She then grabbed on to him and gave him a long passionate kiss goodbye.

"I'll see you tomorrow baby, I love you."

Chad slapped her bottom as she turned to leave.

"See you later honey, I love you, too."

Lisa winked as she then headed down the corridor and headed for home.

When she arrived, she pulled in to see Paula's car parked in the driveway.

As she sat behind the wheel, she was almost afraid to get out of the car.

"What is she doing here? Just great, just wanted I needed tonight."

Lisa got out of her car and walked slowly toward the house, terrified to open the door. Who knows what would be waiting on the other side, David was there already and had Paula with him.

As she walked inside, she looked toward the living room where David and Paula sat together on the sofa in each other's arms.

David was still in a rage of fury as he began yelling. "Where the hell were you? Where have you been all night?" Lisa stopped short then answered calmly.

"I told you, David, I was out with the girls." David jumped up from the sofa.

"You were not, don't you lie to me. Andrea called here earlier and I know that weren't out with the girls at all, so where the hell have you been?"

Lisa in a panic quickly replied.

"I was so out with the girls. Andrea didn't know a thing about tonight, she was away and we couldn't get a hold of her to invite her."

David slapped her across the face.

"Yeah right! You're nothing but a lying bitch, Lisa. Do I have to call all of your friends to prove that?"

Lisa calling his bluff yelled back as she reached into her purse and took out her address book.

"Go right ahead, David, here do you want their numbers?"

David shoved her as he walked in to grab another beer.

"Oh just forget it, it's not worth it, but don't let me find out you were lying or you'll regret it. Damn I can't wait to leave on that cruise with Paula, she's a better woman then you'll ever be and the really great part is, I won't have to look at your disgusting face for four whole days."

Lisa was furious.

"Well, you know, if you really want to get away from me that bad, all you have to do is give me my divorce and let me go."

David was so angry he threw his beer up against the wall, then grabbed her by the throat and pinned her.

"Don't you ever mention a divorce to me again, Lisa, because you'll never get it. I've got you right where I want you, baby, and like it or not, you're stuck with me."

Lisa shoved him away from her and yelled right back. "Oh, well, we'll just see about that one, you stupid jerk."

David grabbed her by the hair and bashed her head into the wall, then threw her through the closet door. Then he and Paula laughed and went back to their television program. Then, as Lisa pulled herself up and was fixing the door, David continued.

"Why don't you just go to bed and get the hell out of our faces? I'm sick of looking at your pitiful mug."

Lisa growled as she glared at him and then headed upstairs yelling all the way.

"You're an asshole, David, why don't you go straight to hell? You treat people like shit and you're nothing but a no-good drunk."

David got up from the sofa and started coming after her, she laughed and shook her head.

"Oh yeah, David, that's it. Go ahead, hit me, prove you're a man and hit your wife. That is all you're really good at, so you may as well keep in practice."

David stopped, laughed an evil laugh and then returned to the sofa with Paula.

Lisa chuckled as she continued to be brave. "What's the matter, slugger? Can't do it?"

David snickered as he yelled back.

"Well, I would have, but you had to go and take all the fun out of it. You spoiled the moment."

Lisa shook her head and glared at him.

"That's all right, David, I'm sure you'll get even later anyway, you always do."

David chuckled.

"You know it, baby, the punishment is always worse the next day."

Right then Paula jumped in.

"Okay I've heard enough, come on, babe, just leave her alone and let's finish watching the show."

Lisa couldn't believe Paula could be so foolish as to sit and watch all of this and still want to be with him.

"God Paula, you are such an idiot! David is a woman beater, can't you see that? Sooner or later you're going to find out the hard way and then you'll know just how abusive and dominating he can be."

Paula laughed as she answered.

"Yeah sure, Lisa, I don't think so. You see I'm not a stupid little bitch like you, I please my men."

That was it, Lisa took enough from David and she wasn't about to take it from Paula too.

"You, Paula, you're nothing but a sleazy whore. You don't even have a clue how to be a real woman. Take a look in the mirror, sweet heart, you're the bitch."

Paula was furious and looked to David.

"That's it! David are you going to let her talk to me that way?"

David bashed his fist on the coffee table and jumped up.

"Take that back Lisa, you apologize to Paula, right now."

Lisa laughed as she yelled back.

"Not a chance, no way, she knows I'm right and I won't apologize for the truth."

David walked over to the corner and grabbed the baseball bat and then came at her. Then as he bashed her across the back with it, he demanded.

"Take it back, Lisa, I mean it, say you're sorry right this minute."

Lisa shook her head and refused.

"No damn it, I won't."

Then she turned and tripped David knocking him down the stairs.

As he lay at the bottom, he kicked the wall and pointed at Lisa.

"You'll pay for this, Lisa, you may have won tonight but you sure as hell won't win tomorrow. I'll get you for this, I'll get you good."

Lisa, not wanting to let her guard down, laughed.

"Yeah sure, David, whatever you say. Just so you know, I'm not letting you get away with this shit anymore. I'm not that stupid and I'll fight you every time."

David looked stunned as he dropped the argument and went back to join Paula on the sofa and Lisa went to bed.

As she lay there, all she thought about was Chad and the vacation they were going to take. For four whole days, she was going to be with him, she would fall asleep in his arms every night and wake up next to him every morning. There wasn't anything David could do at this point to ruin that for her or bring her down. She felt like she was floating on a cloud in a tropical paradise and Chad was her love slave. He meant the world to her and no matter what she went through at home; she knew he would always be there.

As she drifted off to sleep, her head was filled with nothing but pleasant thoughts and hopes for her life with Chad. She dreamed of someday being Chad's wife and raising a family. She has always wanted children, but with David children were a bad choice. With Chad on the other hand, she knew he would be a wonderful and loving father and she prayed someday that dream would be a reality.

The next morning Lisa awoke to a silent house, this was unusual as she always awoke to David yelling and demanding. She made her way downstairs unsure of what she was walking in to, only to find a letter on the kitchen table which read. Lisa I've gone with Paula with pick up the tickets for our cruise. I'll be home by 2:00 P.M. and I expect you to be there and have all of your housework done. The letter was signed your nightmare David.

Lisa became extremely nervous as she read the letter. She knew that there had to be a reason, why David was coming home at 2:00 P.M. when the bars were already open. This was not like him and she feared the worst.

As she looked at the clock and realized it was already 12:30 P.M. she panicked. She had over slept and now only an hour and a half to get the house completely in order.

As she frantically cleaned the house, she worried about what was going to happen when David came home and as always she feared for her life. Lisa was terrified of David and though she tried to act tough, she was actually a very fragile and emotional woman. She did whatever she had to, to stay alive and survive the abuse, but inside she was like a frightened little girl.

Just as the letter had read, at 2:00 P.M. right on the nose, David came in. He slammed the door behind him, to let Lisa know he was home. Then hearing his voice calling her in to the living room, Lisa shook with fear.

"Yes, David."

She called as she headed in to see him. David seemed calm as he answered.

"As you know, I'm leaving on a cruise with Paula on Friday morning. I wanted to let you know that since the cruise leaves at 6:00 A.M. I will be spending Thursday night over at Paula's place."

Lisa raised her eyebrows as she replied.

"Yeah so, why are you telling me?"

David grinned.

"Well my dear, I'm telling you because I want my laundry done. Tomorrow is Thursday and I want my things ready."

Lisa laughed with astonishment.

"Yeah sure, David, no problem. Little Miss Molly maid will get right on it."

David chuckled as he threw a pile of laundry at her.

"I certainly hope you have a better attitude when I get back, Lisa, because right now it really sucks and I'm sick of it."

Lisa was becoming angry and she dropped the laundry by the basement stairs.

"Oh well, David, sucks to be you doesn't it? Deal with it!" David raised his fist to hit her, but she stopped him.

"Hit me and you'll be sorry. Like I said last night, I'm not putting up with anymore of your shit."

With that, she picked up the laundry and headed down to the laundry room to do David's laundry.

David stomped around for a few minutes then yelled down to her.

"I'm out of here, I'll be home my usual time, make damn sure my laundry is washed, folded and ready to go."

Lisa yelled back.

"Yeah sure whatever, see ya!"

Lisa finished putting the laundry in and once she had heard David leave, went upstairs to call Chad.

"Hi baby, guess what? I've got some good news. David is spending tomorrow night at Paula's place, so he'll be gone and we'll be free to start our vacation."

Chad was happy to hear the news, but sighed as he replied. "That's great honey, but I have some bad news. I won't be able to see you tonight. I have to work late, I have a pile of client files I need to finish up with so I can take the four days off. I hope you're not too upset, I'm going to miss you but I need to do this so we can go away."

Lisa was a little disappointed but answered.

"That's okay darling, it's worth it if we can get away together. So where are you taking me, anyway?"

Chad had wanted to surprise her, but seeing as he couldn't see her that night, he told her.

"Well it was going to be a surprise, but I'm borrowing my boss's boat. I thought I would take you to this little abandoned island I know of, just off the coast. We'll be totally alone in paradise, with nothing and nobody to disturb us and seeing as David will be gone tomorrow, we can leave early."

Lisa was excited.

"Oh Chad, oh baby, sounds wonderful. I can't wait for David to leave, and then we can begin our romantic escapade. This is going to be the best four days of my life. I can't wait."

Chad laughed.

"I can't wait either, baby, glad you're excited. Anyway honey I have to get back to work here, I'll see you tomorrow."

Then he blew a kiss into the phone. "I love you, Lisa."

She returned the kiss.

"I love you too, Chad, see you tomorrow, my wild stallion."

Chapter Four

Thursday came quickly and Lisa was preparing for her vacation with Chad. She had to be careful not to be caught by David, who was busy giving her a list of demands and things that he wanted her to do while he was away.

Lisa knew that she wasn't going to be around, to fulfill his demands, but she didn't care. She was going to be alone with Chad on a romantic vacation and not even David could ruin that for her. These four days were going to be the happiest days, she had spent in over eight years and she couldn't wait for them to begin.

She was upstairs packing some her things, when she heard David calling to her.

"Lisa, where the hell is my swimsuit? I told you to pack everything that I would need and that included my swimsuit." David was headed up the stairs and toward their room.

Lisa, in a panic, quickly shoved her bag under the bed and then jumped up to reply.

"I thought I packed it, I'm sorry, I'll get it right away." With that, she walked over and took his swimsuit out of the drawer and handed it to him.

David however was angry and believed she was trying to ruin his cruise with Paula.

"You stupid bitch, you forgot it on purpose. You were trying to ruin my trip with Paula and I know you were. Lisa you're nothing but a selfish and inconsiderate whore and one day you'll pay for all your selfishness."

With that, his shoved her, pushing her up against the wall. Lisa turned back toward him and kicked him hard in the knees until he fell to the floor.

"You're the selfish one, David and you're not going to continue shoving me around. I'm not taking it anymore, so just leave me the hell alone."

David was furious as he reached and grabbed one of her spiked heeled shoes. Then he held her down and began pounding her with it in the back with it. He was hitting her so hard, that the heel was gouging her back. Lisa tried to fight back; she kicked him in the jaw and then grabbed his bat and began swinging it at him.

David was furious.

"Who in the hell do you think you are? You have no right to hit me, I'm the boss and you're nothing. I own you, Lisa and what I say goes, when are you going to learn that?"

Lisa still holding the bat yelled back.

"Sorry to burst your bubble, honey, but that is where you are wrong. Nobody owns me and I am something. I'm something special and there's nothing that you or anybody else can do about it. I'll always be whatever I want to be and sweet heart I want to be strong. So as long as I believe that and I believe in myself I will be. I fully intend to defend myself against you're abuse and bullshit and I refuse to let you win and get the best of me."

David laughed sarcastically and shook his head at her.
"Oh all right, Lisa! Ooh I'm shaking in my boots. Get real bitch, as if I'm afraid of your pitiful threats. You're nothing but a weak little suck and if you think you can win against me, you're wrong."

Lisa laughed right back.

"Fine, David, you go on believing whatever the hell you want to and I'll believe what I want to."

With that, she headed into the bathroom to take a shower, where not even ten minutes later David was at the door yelling.

"Get a move on in there, I want lunch. I'll give you ten more minutes and that's it, you had better be out of there and in the kitchen."

Lisa shook her head in disgust as she yelled back.

"Stick it David, do it yourself, it won't kill you."

Right then, David burst into the bathroom and yanked her out the shower and began bashing her head into the mirror, breaking it and cutting her face.

Lisa fought him and broke loose, throwing him into the shower, where he hit his head on the faucet.

"You foolish woman! You'll pay for this, you'll pay big time."

Then as David got up from the shower floor Lisa stepped back and even though she was terrified, responded.

"Ooh David, I'm shaking in my boots, I'm so scared."

David shoved past her and headed down the stairs.

"Fine, Lisa, have it your way. I'll let it go for now, but I promise you, before I leave, you're going to be punished and you'll be very sorry for fighting me."

Lisa was scared and in a lot of pain, but refused to let it show. She finished up in the bathroom and slowly headed downstairs, where she found that David had left and there was a note waiting the coffee table for her.

I've gone to pick up a few things and I'll be back shortly. I've haven't forgotten your punishment so just stew on that for a while. It won't be pretty my dear, see you soon.

Lisa was terrified and feared for her life, unsure of what to do, she called Chad.

"Hi baby, I'm sorry to bother you, but I'm really worried." Chad hearing the fear in her voice jumped in.

"It's okay Lisa, what is it, what is going on?" Lisa continued.

"David and I had a severe fight, my back is all gouged up and my face is cut pretty bad. He said that it's not over and he's going to punish me and it's going to be bad. I'm calling you because I'm not sure what's going to happen. Listen Chad, if I'm not at your place by 7:00 tonight, can you come over here and make sure that I'm okay? Chad I'm really afraid he's going to kill me this time."

Chad was terrified for Lisa as he jumped in.

"That's it, baby; I'm coming to get you right now. I won't let that bastard hurt you again."

Lisa pleaded with him.

"No Chad, you can't come over here, he'll be back soon. Please, Chad, if you come over here, David will find out about you and the consequences will be deadly. Oh maybe I shouldn't have called you, I'm sorry I just panicked, don't worry I'll be fine, just please don't come over here, I don't want David knowing about you."

Right then Lisa heard footsteps and then the door knob. "Oh God Chad, David is home I have to go, love you, bye." She quickly hung up the phone hoping not be caught, but David had heard her and began questioning her. "Who was that Lisa? Was it Paula?"

Lisa trying to keep things calm answered.

"No sorry, it was Andrea. She wanted me to go out shopping with her tonight and then maybe catch a movie."

David grinned sarcastically.

"Oh yeah and what did you tell her?" Lisa sighed as she answered.

"Don't worry David, I told her no. That way I can be your slave until you leave."

David chuckled.

"Oh good girl, maybe you're finally learning, but I'm leaving at 4:30 so you could go if you really wanted to. Unless of course, you're actually planning to be a good wife and do some work around the house. That would be a change."

Then he headed into the kitchen, where he suddenly stopped and turned back.

"Nice try, Lisa, bet you thought you were getting away with it didn't you?"

Lisa was confused.

"Getting away with what David?" He laughed.

"Trying to make me forget about your punishment. Sorry, my dear, it didn't work, I haven't forgotten and actually you couldn't have gone out tonight anyway. After I'm through with you, you won't be going anywhere."

Then he laughed and sneered at her with the devil in his eyes and Lisa shook with fear. She wasn't sure what it was David was going to do to her and she was terrified that this time that she wouldn't survive.

David was spending an awful lot of time, dreaming up her punishment, so she knew that it was going to be horrible. She thought about running, but knew that David would only find her and hurt her worse, so she headed back upstairs to make sure her things were all packed and ready to go. Then she went back and offered to help David get his ready.

"Do you need anything? Can I help you finish getting your things ready?"

David still angry laughed and slammed his fist down on the counter top.

"It's a little late to start sucking up now, Lisa, it won't work. You're going to be punished no matter what you do now. You need to be taught a lesson and I fully intend to follow through."

Lisa sighed.

"Fine, David, sorry for offering to help, do it yourself then." Then as she turned to walk away, he grabbed her arm. "Not so fast woman. Since you're here, you can cook my dinner. I don't have much time though, so sandwiches and coffee will be fine."

Lisa knew that she was already in enough trouble, so said nothing and went to make David his dinner, while he went to the basement to finish getting ready.

As she stood at the counter preparing his sandwiches, she heard the sound of something rustling in the basement. Unsure what it was she yelled down.

"David what is going on down there? Is everything okay?"

David yelled back with anger in his voice.

"Just don't you worry about what is going on down here and get my bloody dinner ready!"

Lisa wondered what is was David was doing, but not wanted to worsen the situation, just ignored it and went back to preparing his dinner. As she looked at the clock and noticed it was already 3:30 and David had planned to leave by 4:30, she prayed that she might be off the hook. David would be rushed now so may just let things go and leave for his cruise.

Lisa went back to the top of the stairs to let David know his dinner was ready.

"David, come on, your dinner is ready and it's already 3:30, if you want to be out of here in the next hour you better get moving."

David dashed up the stairs and shoved her on the way by.

"It's about time, it took you long enough. All I asked for was a couple of sandwiches and it seemed to take you forever."

Lisa sighed knowing that he was still in a mood. "Well sorry, David, but its ready now, so just eat."

David ate his dinner and then slid his plate across the table as he ordered.

"You have five minutes to get this kitchen spotless, so get moving."

Lisa didn't see the point as she responded.

"Why David? I'm not going anywhere, I can always do it later, it's not that big of a mess."

David jumped up and slapped her across the face. "You'll do it now, I want to see it done before I leave, so get you lazy ass moving."

Lisa walked over to the counter and started cleaning things up, while David went into the living room to get his bags ready. She hated doing whatever he wanted her too, but at this point she believed that she had no other choice.

As she finished up in the kitchen and then stood quietly at the counter, she heard David coming up behind her. He had crowbar and began bashing her across the back with it. Lisa tried to run, but he tripped her and then began hitting her even harder.

"You stupid slut, I told you, you were going get it. I bet you thought that you were getting out of it, didn't you? Well ha! Guess what, sweetie? You were wrong."

David continued to beat her, she was sure that he was going to kill her this time, but there was nothing more she could do. She was hurt bad and it was a struggle just to try and fight back.

David then bashed her in the head several times with the crowbar knocking her out cold.

"There, bitch, take that. I guess, I win this one now, don't I?"

Then with a vicious laugh, David dragged her limp body down to the basement and then tied her up to one of the support beams. She started to come around, as he then took his belt and whipped her with it over and over and she once again fell silent.

With that, David went back upstairs, locking the basement door behind him with paddle locks and chains that he had put in place so there was no way she could escape. Then not caring whether or not she lived or died, David walked out leaving for his vacation with Paula.

David, the man who had once loved Lisa, now hated her. He left her there, locked in the basement, tied to beam on a cold cement floor, with no food or water to die. David had no reservations about what he had done, she had talked back to him and disrespected his ways, so in his mind, she deserved to suffer.

Several hours later, Lisa awoke to find that she was tied up in the cold dark basement. She panicked and frantically tried to free herself, but the knots were tied too tight.

She looked down to see a note David had left on the floor. There written in big black letters so she could see it read. Ha-ha bitch, you lose this time, so suffer. See you in four days.

Lisa began to cry and started screaming, with hopes that someone would hear her, but she was in the basement and couldn't be heard from outside the house.

All she could do now was pray that Chad would find her before she died.

She was cold and terrified and in a lot of pain. She kept thinking that she was hearing things, but it was only her mind playing tricks on her. Lisa was suffering horrible fear but knew that she had to calm down, before she made herself crazy.

The only light to the basement came from a small opening where the dryer hose went outside, and with it becoming dark outside, that tiny bit of light was quickly vanishing.

Lisa was horrified and becoming claustrophobic, as her heart began pounding a mile a minute and she felt as though she were hyperventilating.

She couldn't breathe properly and she gasped for air as she felt like the room was closing in on her. She had to get out; somehow she had to free herself. She struggled and pulled, trying to break the ropes, but they wouldn't come free. All she did was cut her arms causing herself even more pain. She screamed once more, hoping that by some small chance someone would hear her, but there was nobody around and nobody knew she was there.

Lisa was trapped in David's little torture chamber in hell and there was no escape. She tried to think happy thoughts to calm herself down, but all that did was make her want to get free all the more, so she could be with Chad.

Hours past as she lay there cold in pain and bleeding from the ropes cutting her arms. Then suddenly in the darkness she heard a sound, it was knocking, someone was at the door.

She began screaming as loud as she could hoping to be heard.

"Help me, please someone help me. I'm trapped, Oh God please help me,"

It was Chad and he had heard Lisa's cries for help. Without even knowing what it was he was running in to, he burst through the door.

"Lisa, where are you? Lisa baby its Chad, where you baby?" Lisa heard Chad calling to her as she began to cry.

"Chad help me, I'm in the basement, help me baby I'm hurt bad and I'm so scared. Oh baby help me please help me."

Chad ran to the basement door, only to find that David had locked it with chains and he couldn't get in. Chad yelled down to her to let her know he was there.

"Hang in there Lisa, I'm coming. There's chains and locks on the door, I have to break them to get to you."

Lisa panicking screamed.

"Oh God, oh please hurry. I'm scared Chad, it's cold and dark down here and I hurt so badly."

Chad was frantic but wanted to try and calm her down yelled back.

"I know, honey, just stay calm. I promise you, I'll get you out of there, I'm not about to let you die."

Chad pried away at the chains, but they were too thick and he couldn't break them. So he ran out to his car to get a crowbar with hopes that he could pry them off. He pried and pulled as the chains began to loosen then finally broke, but that still left the problem of the paddle locks on the door.

Chad thought about trying to kick the door in, but being in a stair well it wasn't the best idea. He would most likely fly down there stairs along with the door and his being hurt was not an option. He needed to be there for Lisa and he was no good to her hurt.

Chad worked on breaking the locks as heard Lisa crying and begging him to hurry. He frantically picked away at the locks, trying to get to her. Chad knew that this was a well-planned stunt on David's part. Nobody could have dreamed this up in only one afternoon; David had planned this for some time. Chad was now even more determined, to help Lisa rid herself of David once and for all. Though he knew that it wouldn't be easy. David was insane and would fight them all the way, even to the death if it became necessary.

Lisa was quiet and Chad began to panic. "Baby, are you all right down there?"

Lisa didn't answer right away so he shouted to her once more.

"Lisa, baby, Lisa are you okay?"

Lisa finally answered with a weak yell.

"Yeah I'm okay; I can't catch my breath though."

Chad relieved to hear her voice and still picking away at the locks yelled back.

"Honey, just try to relax and take deep breaths, I should be in there in just a minute."

Right then Chad finally broke through the locks and the door flew open. He turned on the lights and ran down to get Lisa, but he couldn't see her.

"Lisa, where are you baby?" Lisa called to him.

"Chad I'm here, behind the water heater, help me."

Chad ran to her and quickly untied her, then held her in his arms.

"Oh Lisa, I'm here, baby, everything is going to be okay now."

Then he looked at her in astonishment.

"Look at what he's done to you, oh baby I should never had let you come home to that monster. Lisa this is the last straw, no more of this. We have got to find a way to get David out of your life for good."

Lisa agreed.

"Yes, baby, I know and after our vacation, we'll find a way." Chad was shocked.

"You mean, you still want to go away? Are you sure you're okay to go away?"

Lisa, even in extreme pain, smiled.

"I'll be fine, I'm not going to let him ruin our time together, we planned a vacation and we're going."

Chad smiled and stroked her cheek. "Okay baby, now let's get you out of here."

Lisa was still weak and cold, so Chad threw his coat around her and then picked her up and carried her out to his car, then went back in to grab her things and lock the door.

Then as they pulled away from her house, Chad concerned for Lisa's health asked.

"How long were you down there, baby? Do you know what time David left?"

Lisa kind of drowsy from her injuries, sighed as she answered.

"Well it was just after 4:00 when he first attacked me and started beating on me. He must have knocked me out, because the next thing I remember is waking up in the basement."

Chad looked at this watch.

"My God Lisa, it's almost 8:30. You were down there for over four hours, how long were you out?"

Lisa wasn't sure as she answered.

"I don't know exactly, I woke up not long before you arrived."

Chad was furious.

"My God, you're lucky you're even alive. I got there at 7:30, you must have been unconscious for at least three hours, you could have died."

Lisa sighed as she began to cry.

"Well dear, I think that was the whole idea. I'm just lucky I had you to save me. Thank you, Chad."

Lisa was hurting and still really shaken and jumpy. As they pulled up to a stop sign, she was sure that she saw David and Paula and she ducked under the seat.

David, seeing how horrified she was, put his hand on her shoulder.

"Lisa, honey relax, it's not them. Don't worry, baby, you're perfectly safe with me, no one can hurt you now."

Lisa began to cry harder as she turned to Chad with her tear-soaked face.

"Chad, I was scared, really scared. I thought that I was going to die and the worst part was that I was never going to see you again. I love you Chad and I need you. You're my whole world and I couldn't bear to lose you."

As they pulled into Chad parking lot, he patted her on the shoulder.

"I love you, too, sweetie and I promise that if it's the last thing I do, I'm going to make sure that you are safe and sound from here on out."

Chad then leaned over and kissed her sweetly on the cheek.

"Well this is it baby; we're alone for four whole days." Then trying to get a rise out of her he continued.

"Now let's just try and forget all about David and enjoy our vacation. If we think about him, we won't enjoy ourselves and we'd be letting him win. Now, I don't know about you, but I certainly don't want that to happen."

Lisa smiled as she put her hand on Chad's thigh.

"No, definitely not, you're right. Let's just forget about, David, I've been looking forward to this for too long and won't let him ruin it. This is our time now and there's no room from bad thoughts of David."

Chad smiled.

"That's my girl, now what do you say we head inside and get things ready to go and then get out of here? We're going to have the time of our lives and I fully intend to make you the happiest woman in the world."

Lisa smiled with tears in her eyes.

"You already have, Chad. When I'm with you, I'm always happy."

Chad got out and walked over to the passenger side to help Lisa out of the car, and then they went inside to get things ready for their trip.

Chad had bought several bottles of champagne and there was a huge box filled with passion fruits.

Lisa was shocked as she looked into the box. "Chad, what is all the fruit for?"

Chad grinned a devilish grin as he answered.

"Well baby, you can't have a romantic getaway on an abandoned island without passion fruit now, can you? That would just be wrong, it's a necessity."

Lisa smiled as she became dizzy and sat down.

"Okay, just thought I'd ask."

Chad walked over to her.

"Honey, are you okay? Are you sure you're up to this?" Lisa kissed him sweetly.

"Yeah, baby, I'll be okay. I just got a little dizzy for a second there and needed to sit for a second, I'm okay."

Chad still unsure went back to packing. He was packing body oils, whipped creams and vibrators.

Lisa, watching him, thought to herself.

Boy looks like it's going to be quite the trip, I can't wait, just wish I felt better.

Then she walked up behind Chad and gently kissed his neck. He turned to her with a smile.

"What was that for?"

She smiled and shrugged her shoulders.

"Oh I don't know, just for being such a romantic, I guess."

Chad laughed as they finished up the packing and headed out to the docks to pick up the boat.

When they arrived at the docks, Lisa was stunned. The boat was beautiful; it was just like a house on water. It had a huge kitchen and two big bedrooms with queen sized water beds, a living room and even an office. The boat was bigger than her entire house and she couldn't believe that for four days it was all theirs.

As she stood on the deck in total awe, Chad asked.

"Well, what do you think? Do you like it?"

Lisa exclaimed.

"Like it! I love it! It's absolutely beautiful." Chad smiled as he put his arms around her.

"Good, I'm glad you like it, because my boss said I can borrow it whenever I want and I figured that once you're rid of David, we could take it and head to the Bahamas for a real vacation."

Lisa sighed and shook her head.

"We're not supposed to be mentioning David remember? But the vacation sounds amazing, it would be fabulous."

Chad apologized.

"I know, I'm sorry and I won't mention him again. Now let's get set up and head out, shall we?"

Lisa agreed and went in to unpack their things and then rested a bit, while Chad began to cast off and they left for their own little tropical paradise.

As she lay there, she thought about Chad and how she couldn't wait to make love with him, with the warm sand at her back and the cool water at her feet. Her loins were on fire, with the deep desire to make passionate love with the man of her dreams. In her own little world, it was just her and Chad and the warm tropical breeze.

Lisa was getting hot, just thinking about her and Chad on the beach. Then as if he had read her mind, Chad dropped the anchor and walked into the bedroom. Then taking Lisa by the hand, he led her out on to the deck in the moonlight. Then right there, in the middle of the ocean under the stars, he began kissing her gently and removing her clothes. Chad then spread a blanket out on the deck and laid her down. He began nibbling at her breasts and caressing her hot loins as he whispered.

"I'm going to make love to you, now; I want to feel your hot wet pussy lips, wrapped tight around my thick hard dick."

Lisa tingled with Chad's words, she felt herself getting wet as he rubbed his hard dick across her hot pussy and then drove himself deep inside.

Chad's thrusts were strong and hard, he pushed himself deeper and deeper and then right when she thought she couldn't take anymore, he pushed himself even further.

As their bodies bumped together under the stars, in the cool ocean breeze, Lisa felt like she was in heaven. There was complete silence, other than the sounds of their passion and she was positive that this was truly the life she wanted.

Chad was going faster and faster, his thrusts were constant, as she felt the pulsations of his dick deep inside of her and she squirmed with pleasure.

Chad's balls slapped hard against her ass, as his thrusts became deeper and stronger. She felt her body becoming inflamed with erotic pleasure, as Chad's movements stimulated her.

Lisa became powerless, as the screams ripped from her throat and the erotic sensation or her orgasm took over.

"Oh Chad yes, that's it baby, oh yes."

Hearing Lisa's screams of passion, sent Chad quickly to the heights of desire. The contractions of their orgasms, going in rhythm with each other, made them feel as if their bodies had become one. As they pressed their bodies hard together and kissed each other passionately, with their tongues buried deep in each other's mouths, Chad held her tight.

"I love you, Lisa and you are truly the woman of my dreams."

Lisa smiled sweetly. "I love you too, baby."

Then as she went to get up from the deck, Chad saw her struggling.

"Here baby, let me help you. Are you okay? I didn't hurt you, did I?"

Lisa shook her head as she replied.

"No baby, not at all, I'm okay, just a little stiff and sore. Thanks for the hand."

With that, Lisa headed in to grab a bottle of champagne and glasses and then returned to the deck, where Chad was gazing out in to the ocean.

"I think we'll stay here for the night and I'll head to the island in the morning when there's more light. Is that okay with you, Lisa?"

Lisa handed him a glass of champagne.

"Yeah that's fine baby, I wouldn't want to get lost out here in the middle of ocean."

Then she thought for a second.

"Although, if we were lost in the ocean, I'd never have to go home to David."

Chad shook his head and raised his eye brows. "Uh-uh, Lisa! We're not talking about David, remember?"

Lisa looked out at the stars bouncing off the water as she replied.

"Yeah, I know. I'm sorry. It's just that I want to be free so bad. At this point Chad, I'd do anything."

Chad put his arm around her.

"I know baby, I know and I want him dead so bad I can taste it. But for now let's just enjoy our time together."

Lisa continued to look out at the water.

"It's so beautiful out here and peaceful, just you and me in the ocean breeze. I never imagined the ocean could be so calming, it's a wonderful feeling. I wish this vacation never had to end and we could be here forever."

Chad hugged her as he watched the reflection of the water in her eyes.

"Oh Lisa, you're such a sweet and gentle woman and so innocent. I honestly don't understand, how anyone could even think of hurting you. As I look at your face and see the way your eyes light up as you look out at the water, you remind me of a child on Christmas morning, filled with joy."

Lisa laughed.

"Oh Chad, I'm no child, I'm just a hurting soul, desperate to be free."

Chad pulled her closer.

"I know angel and I just wish you would let me help you."

Lisa knowing that the conversation was headed some where she didn't want to go right then, quickly changed the subject.

"So, are you hungry? Can I make you something to eat?" Chad patted his stomach.

"Yeah, I guess, I am a little hungry. Sorry for going on about you-know-who, I didn't mean to upset you."

Lisa smile and rubbed his cheek.

"Don't worry about it, you didn't upset me. Now can we drop it, please? I just don't want to talk about it right now."

Then she kissed him on the cheek and headed inside to get them something to each and Chad followed.

"So my darling, what would you like me to make for you? What are you hungry for?"

Chad picked up a strawberry and dipped it in chocolate sauce, then fed it to Lisa.

She smiled as she licked her lips. "Umm yum, sounds good to me."

Then she dipped a strawberry and fed it to Chad. They continued to feed each other strawberries, back and forth, tantalizing each other. Lisa found herself becoming aroused as she was soon down on her knees, kissing Chad's dick and caressing his balls.

Chad's dick was soon rock hard with sexual desire, as Lisa then began to suck him hungrily. She sucked him long and fast, while she stroked the base of it with her hand and fondled his balls.

Chad fully aroused with stimulation exclaimed.

"Oh Lisa. Oh yes baby, suck it, make me cum baby, do it baby do it."

Lisa sucked him quicker, taking all of him in her mouth.

Chad quivered and shook as his orgasm approached.

"Oh yes baby, oh yes, oh here it comes, oh yes I'm going to cum."

Lisa sucked faster with the contractions of Chad's throbbing orgasm, as the hot juices of his desire flowed down her throat. She moaned with satisfaction, knowing that she had pleased him and she kissed him gently moving upwards toward his lips.

Chad lifted her up and sat her down on the counter top. Where he then spread her thighs and began licking and kissing and hot already love soaked pussy.

He licked and sucked her clit, while he stroked his finger vigorously in and out of her. He nibbled at her ferociously and stimulated her bringing her racing to explosive orgasm. Lisa screeched with excitement and wriggled about the counter with the erotic sensations of Chad's touch coursing through her body.

"Ooh Chad, oh baby you're the best. You always know just what to do to please me. Oh God how I love you, you're wonderful baby."

Chad got up off his knees and kissed her cheek.

"No Lisa, it is you that is the best and I love you, too, honey."

With that, Chad headed in to take a shower and Lisa cleaned up the kitchen of strawberries and chocolate sauce, and then went into the bedroom to settle in to bed and wait for Chad.

When he finished up in the shower and came to bed, she curled up next to him and held him tight. Lisa felt like a baby in his arms, safe, protected and free from harm. She kissed his sweetly then put her head on his chest to listen to his heartbeat, as she became drowsy.

"Goodnight, darling. I love you."

Chad bent forward and kissed her forehead

"I love you, too, sleep well. See you in the morning."

Hearing those words 'see you in the morning' sent shivers of happiness up Lisa's spine. She was happier than she'd ever been, knowing that she was going to be waking up next to Chad in the morning, rather than David.

Lisa was so relaxed and comfortable, that in no time at all she had fallen fast asleep. Chad however was wide awake, thinking about all that had happened and how much he wanted to make Lisa's life a happy one once and for all. Then seeing as he was awake anyway, he decided he would get up and sail the boat to the island and surprise Lisa in the morning.

As he headed to the bridge to cast off, he thought of Lisa and how happy she made him. He wanted her to be free from harm, but know exactly how to go about it. He knew that he wasn't always going to be there to protect her from David, even though he wanted to be. Lisa had become his whole world and every time David hit her or hurt her in any way, he felt like his world was falling apart.

As Chad then set off for the island, he dreamed of having Lisa as his wife and raising a family with her. He wanted so much to make it happen, that he started thinking of ways to get rid of David and get her into his arms permanently.

He thought about bursting into their house and beating the crap out of David, then sweeping Lisa right off her feet and carrying her away to a whole new life of happiness. But then there was the fact of David's gun and what could happen, if he tried to get into their house and Chad refused to put Lisa's life on the line that way.

Chad couldn't imagine ever losing her and was living in constant fear of David going too far and killing her. He believed that Lisa was sweet and innocent and that David was using her innocence to hurt her and get what he wanted.

Then he thought that maybe if Lisa didn't act so innocent around David, he would lose interest and let her go, maybe he would just give up. But that was yet another plan that had great possibility of back firing, with Lisa ending up hurt or possibly killed.

Chad didn't know what to do, it was beginning to seem that the only way Lisa would ever be free from David, was if he were dead and at this point it seemed like the easiest way out. Chad thought about it over and over in his mind, but nothing seemed right or in any way easy. All he knew was that he had to help Lisa before it was too late. David had already locked her in a basement to die and Chad was sure that it wouldn't be is last attempt to kill her.

In no time at all, Chad arrived at the island. He looked around and thought about how great it was. He and Lisa were totally alone with no sign of life for miles; it was nothing but ocean, beach and trees. They had the whole island to themselves and could be together with no worries.

Chad was positive that Lisa would love it and would be completely surprised, to awake in the morning and find they were already there. Then as the sun began to rise over the ocean. Chad put on a pot of coffee and sat waiting for Lisa to awake.

He couldn't wait to see the look on her face, when she saw the island and how beautiful it was.

Shortly thereafter Lisa woke up, seeing that Chad wasn't in bed, she threw on a robe and headed out to the deck to see what was up.

As she looked around in astonishment she exclaimed. "We're here! Oh Chad it's so beautiful, oh you were so right, it's amazing out here."

Chad smiled as he put his arm around her and gave her a good morning kiss.

"Yes, it is and it's so peaceful and for the next few days, it's all ours. So are you surprised?"

Lisa still stunned with islands beauty, kissed him sweetly. "Yes, very surprised, you must have been up all night." Chad smiled.

"Yeah, I was, but it was worth it to see the look on your face this morning. I'm glad you're happy."

Lisa hugged him tighter.

"Oh yes baby, it's wonderful and so are you. Listen, I'm going to go and grab quick shower, but can I get you a coffee first?"

Chad looked down into his coffee cup.

"No that's fine; I've still got half a cup. You go take your shower and then we'll take a long walk on the beach."

Lisa kissed him then smacked his bottom. "Sounds great, I'll be back in a few minutes."

Lisa went to take her shower and Chad remained on the deck looking out at the water. Then as he looked down at his watch, he found himself once again thinking about David and how he and Paula should now have left on their cruise.

As he stood there thinking about it, he said to himself. "Good, maybe the ferry will sink and make the world a better place."

In Chad's mind, he really wished that David were dead, but he never had the guts to do anything about it. So he just prayed that by some freak accident, he and Paula would never return from their trip. Little did Chad know, Lisa was thinking the very same thing.

As she took her shower, she also thought about David and Paula on their cruise and prayed that the boat they were on, sunk to the bottom of the ocean and David died. Not wanting to spoil their vacation, Lisa wanted to keep her thoughts to herself. However as she finished her shower and walked back out on deck, she was surprised to hear Chad bring it up.

"Lisa, I know that we said we weren't going to talk about David, but you know? I've been standing here looking at the water and I can't help but think about how great it would be, if the boat he and Paula were on would sink."

Lisa laughed.

"Wow that is so weird." Chad was confused.

"Weird? What is weird?" Lisa continued.

"I was thinking the very same thing when I was in the shower. Could that be a good sign?"

Then she thought about it.

"Yeah right, like that would ever actually happen, it could never be that easy. David will be fine and return home ready to yell and scream and beat the hell out of me some more. I really wish I never had to go back, but I know that I do. David would only hunt me down and probably kill me if I didn't."

Chad sighed; he wanted to continue the conversation but could see Lisa becoming upset.

"Okay that's enough now, no more of this depressing talk. Let's just enjoy ourselves, we deserve it and after all that is what we're here for."

Lisa smiled as Chad then took her by the hand and led her down to the beach, where they walked with the cool water at their feet.

Lisa couldn't believe how beautiful and peaceful the island was, as she leaned into Chad's arm and they walked hand in hand.

"It's so peaceful out here and so calming." Then she looked up at him and questioned. "So how did you find this place anyway?" Chad grinned.

"Well, to be totally honest with you I found it by accident."

Lisa interrupted.

"By accident? How do you find a place so beautiful by accident?"

Chad laughed and began to blush as he continued. "Well..."

Chad paused then continued.

"A few years ago, I took a bunch of friends out on a sail boat. Not knowing a lot about sailing at that time, I got us all lost and this is where we ended up."

Lisa laughed as she teased.

"Oh yeah…leave it to Chad to get lost."

Chad walked further into the water, and then with his foot splashed water at her.

"What do you mean? Leave it to Chad?"

Lisa splashed water back at him as she laughed.

"Oh, I'm just kidding, I'm glad you found this place even if it was by accident. I love it here."

Chad grabbed her and started tickling her, she laughed so hard she fell to the ground. Then he sat on her and continued tickling her until she thought she would burst.

"Okay, okay, stop! Chad stop."

Chad stopped tickling her as he leaned in and kissed her passionately, as the waves can up and crashed against their bodies in the sand. They kissed each other so passionately, it was as if they were in their own little world and everything revolved around them.

Breaking away from the kiss, Lisa reached up and began tickling him, until he rolled off of her. Then with a devilish smile, she got up and ran into the water and began splashing him.

Chad jumped as the cold water hit him. "Oh it's cold!"

Lisa laughed and stuck her tongue out at him as she continued to splash him.

"Oh you big chicken, come on in, it's not that cold, it's actually refreshing."

Chad ran into the water. "Chicken, eh? I don't think so."

Then he grabbed her and kissed her as he scooped her up and carried her out the water and on to the beach, where he laid her in the warm sand, and began to pull off her wet clothes.

Lisa was becoming aroused, as Chad caressed her body and kissed her neck. Then as they lay there on the beach, Lisa reached down and began stroking his dick. Chad becoming so inflamed with desire as he felt his heart pounding in his chest, then slid his hard dick deep into her yearning pussy.

Their bodies were pressed hard together as the warm sand surrounded them and the cool water splashed at their feet. Chad pushed his hardness vigorously in and out as he sucked her breasts and then nibbled at her neck and earlobes.

Lisa was completely aroused, as she then rolled Chad off of her and on to his back. Then getting on top of him, she drove him deep in to her hot loins, as her pebble hard nipples gently rubbed back and forth across his chest.

Chad reached down and encircled her hard love button with his fingertips, while she rode him faster, driving him deeper and harder. Lisa moved her pelvis and hips in a circular motion, causing bolts of erotic energy coursing through her body and a tingling sensation coursing through Chad's hard dick, causing him to writhe about and groan with excitement.

She tightened her pussy muscles, increasing the intensity of the friction of her thrusts. Chad sucked her nipples and neck, sending signals of erotic pleasure from her breasts, right to the heart of her pussy and she burst in to orgasm. Then as the orgasm took over her body and her thrusts became harder, she screamed with pleasure, bringing Chad to cum right along with her.

They pressed their bodies hard together and held on to each other, as they sailed down from the heights of sexual satisfaction. Chad kissed her as he pulled himself up from the sand.

"That was amazing baby, you're the best. I'm kind of thirsty now though; think I'll go grab a coffee, would you like one?"

Lisa totally relaxed as she looked out the endless ocean, smiled as she answered.

"Yeah sure, that would be great, thank you darling."

Then as Chad went inside to get their coffee, Lisa decided she would wade in to the water. Once up to her chin in the water, so happy to finally be alone with Chad, she jumped up and screamed out across the ocean.

"YES, life is great, Oh Chad, I love you."

Chad heading back out to the beach with their coffee, heard her yelling.

"What are you yelling about?"

Lisa answered as she headed out of the water.

"Oh nothing really, I was just yelling because I'm so happy to be here with you, it's not like anyone can here me."

Chad laughed.

"Yeah okay, whatever. Lisa you're soaked, what, are you nuts? That water is freezing; it's only 10:00 A.M."

Lisa smiled and winked at him.

"Well baby, after making passionate love with you, my body was so hot that the water felt great."

Chad grinned as he raised his eye brows and shook his head.

"Oh yeah, I guess that's it then eh? Not nuts, just hot." Then he kissed her sweetly.

"You're one special lady, Lisa and I can't begin to tell you how happy I am to be here with you."

Lisa smiled.

"You don't have to tell me. I know."

As they sat on the beach, drinking their coffee and talking about all the things they could do, Chad made a suggestion. "Maybe, we should go and gather some wood, it will be cool tonight, it might be nice to sit by a warm fire. We could build one right down here on the beach and cuddle and do whatever else comes natural and…"

Lisa jumped in.

"Ooh you don't have to convince me, I think it's a great idea and very romantic."

Chad getting up then helping Lisa up replied.

"Well okay then, since we both agree, what do you say we go and get to gathering?"

Lisa agreed as the headed off into the woods, as they walked gathering wood, Lisa thought about how wonderful it would be to be rid of David and to be this happy all the time.

"Chad, what if we never went back? What do you think would happen?"

Chad trying to hold the mood answered.

"Well baby, I really wish I could say that we never had to go back, but we have too. We couldn't possibly make it out here forever, we'd have to go back to the city sooner or later and besides that, if I didn't return my boss's boat, they would come looking for us anyway."

Lisa sighed.

"Chad, I was being serious, I really am thinking about not going back."

Chad put his arm around her.

"Yeah I know honey; I was only trying to lighten things up because I knew where this conversation was going. I know you don't want to go back and I wish we didn't have too, but let's be practical. There's no way we could stay here and in the city, David would be sure to find you. All we can do right now is hope that he lets you go and if we play our cards right maybe we'll be rid of him soon."

Lisa sighed as she replied sarcastically.

"I know you are right, even though I really wish you were wrong. Since when did you get so practical anyway?"

Chad smiled as he kissed her sweetly on the cheek and answered.

"Sweetie I'm sorry, I don't mean to be such a big ogre, but we have to face reality. Now come on, let's just drop the subject and have a good time."

Lisa agreed and they went back to gathering wood.

As they continued to walk through the woods gathering, they came across a wild raspberry bush and Lisa decided to pick some, to feed them to Chad later. Chad saw her picking them and laughed as he snuck up behind her.

"Raspberries, ooh baby, now just what are those for?" Lisa turned and stuck her tongue out at him.

"What is so funny Mr.? Can't I pick berries to feed to my man?"

Chad growled into her ear then kissed her neck.

"Yeah of course you can. I was just imagining you lying naked on the beach covered in berries and me having to eat my way to you."

Lisa's jaw dropped as she raised her eye brows and shook her head.

"Oh God Chad! Get your mind out of the gutter; I'm picking raspberries not sucking your dick."

Chad laughed.

"Okay, okay, I'm sorry. I just can't help fantasizing about you, is that such a crime?"

Lisa threw some berries at him.

"Oh yeah, good come back, the perfect suck up."

Then she laughed as she threw him down on the ground and unzipped his pants. Then she placed some berries on his dick and slowly licked them off.

Chad became hard with the sensation of her tongue, sliding across his hard shaft. She then took him into her mouth and began sucking him hungrily; she sucked him faster and faster, while she caressed his inner thighs with her firm hard breasts.

Chad was completely aroused as he exclaimed. "Oh yes, Ooh baby, oh you're so good."

Lisa sucked him faster and longer as he writhed about beneath her and moments later shot his hot love juices deep in to her throat. Then after she finished and got up, Chad remarked.

"Oh yeah, I see and it's my mind that is in the gutter is it?" Lisa threw more berries at him as she smirked.

"Oh you just stop it, you love it and you know it." Chad smiled.

"You bet I did baby! You do it so well, I can never get enough."

Then he picked up the stack of wood.

"I'm getting kind of hungry, why don't we head back to the boat and get some lunch, then maybe take a swim?"

Lisa smiled a devilish grin.

"Yeah we could take a swim, or maybe we could have some desert first."

Then she winked at him and ran ahead back to the boat and he followed. He dropped the wood on the beach and ran on to the boat and grabbed her.

He started to kiss her and tickle her as she exclaimed. "Chad! I thought you were hungry?"

He growled as his nuzzled her neck.

"Yeah, I am, but how about some of that desert first?" Then he scooped her up and carried her in to the bedroom, where he began nibbling at her neck and removing her clothes. Lisa was stunned as she exclaimed.

"Wow Chad! A little hot, are we?"

Chad moaned as he responded. "Only for you baby."

He kissed her entire body and slid his finger in to the opening of her pussy. Then moving downward he began licking her clit and sliding his finger in and out of her. Lisa felt her pussy getting wet, as he nibbled at her like a ferocious tiger.

She shrieked and rolled about the bed, with Chad's touch inflaming her pussy with deep desire. He licked her faster and faster as her body tingled with excitement and she exclaimed.

"Oh Chad, oh yes, put it in me, baby, drive it in hard and deep, give it to me baby, screw my pussy hard."

Chad moved upwards and then slid his hard dick deep into her yearning pussy, then as he began driving her long and hard, she shrieked with pleasure as she cried out.

"Harder, baby, harder."

Chad's thrusts became harder and faster, as Lisa groaned and panted with flashes pleasure and stimulation, shooting through her body. She wrapped her legs tight around him, pushing him deeper and increasing the intensity of the friction and bringing on a massive explosion in her loins.

She screamed as the waves of pleasure dominated her spirit and her orgasm took over. Chad hearing the cries of pleasure shooting from her throat was instantly brought to orgasm himself. His thrusts slowed as he pumped with the rhythm of their orgasms, then he kissed Lisa sweetly as he pulled away and then got up.

"Well, now, I'm really hungry, time for lunch."

Lisa chuckled and she pulled herself up and then smacked his bottom.

"Okay love buns, I'll go and make us something, just let me get dressed."

Then as she reached for her clothes, Chad stopped her.

"What's the point of getting dressed? We're all alone here, who's going to care if we walk around naked? I don't know about you, but I find it a lot cooler, it's pretty hot out there and I haven't got anything you haven't seen anyway."

Lisa smiled as she dropped her clothes.

"You know you're right, it is cooler. What the hell! Forget the clothes."

Chad grinned.

"Yeah and without the clothes, I can spend the rest of the vacation admiring your firm beautiful body."

Lisa laughed sarcastically.

"Ha firm! Where do you see firm? I need to lose weight." Chad exclaimed.

"Yeah right! No you don't, baby your body is perfect, if you lost any weight, I wouldn't be able to find you."

Lisa laughed as headed in to the kitchen to make them some lunch.

"Yeah okay Chad, enough of the flattery, you can think whatever you want to, but I still think I need to lose some weight."

In the kitchen, Lisa prepared them some sandwiches and coffee for lunch and then called Chad in and they sat down to eat.

"Lisa, lunch looks great."

Lisa looking at the sandwiches on the table laughed. "Oh come on Chad, it's just sandwiches, not a three-course meal or something. Enough with the compliments, you've already got me, so you don't need to try and win me over."

Chad leaned across the table and kissed her.

"Lisa, I'm not David and I am thankful for everything you do, so just get used to the compliments. It is my way and everything about you, I find wonderful, that's love, baby and I love you."

Lisa was stunned and unsure what to say so sat quietly while they ate their lunch and got up to clean to kitchen.

Chad walked over and took her hand.

"Nope, come on, the mess can wait until later, let's go for a swim."

Lisa was shocked, she wasn't used to leaving a mess behind, David had never allowed that. With him, everything had to be sparkling all the time or she paid the price.

Once on the beach, they ran along the water, with the hot sun beating down on their naked bodies. Then they took each other's hand and walked out in to the water and when they were waist deep, they embraced each other and kissed passionately.

It was as if the rest of the world never existed, they were in paradise together and nothing else mattered. They swam together and kissed some more, their passion was so hot it seemed as if it were heating the ocean. Water that once seemed cold, now felt warm.

Lisa and Chad spent the rest of the day swimming, making out in the sand and frolicking naked in the sun. Then after a beautiful moon lit dinner, they started a fire on the beach and let the passion of their love take over.

Chad took her by the hand and led her into the cold ocean water, where he kissed her passionately and fondled her breasts. Then under the light of the stars, they held each other close and made love.

Lisa pulled herself up on Chad and wrapped her legs around him tight.

Chad slid his massive dick, deep inside of her and began pumping, as the waves crashed against their hot flesh. The light of the moon, sparkled across the water and with each passionate kiss, they became closer and even more in love.

Chad picked her up and kissing her sweetly he carried her to the shore, where he laid her down on the wet sand.

"Lisa I love you so much and making love with you had never felt more right. The passion between us is stronger than anything I've ever known, you are the most precious thing in my life and when I am with you, I feel like a whole person. I mean it darling, you're everything to me and I love you."

Lisa held him close as a tear rolled down her cheek.

"I love you, too, Chad and when I am with you, nothing else matters. You make my life full and worth living."

Chad caressed her naked body, as the tide came in and gently kissed their bodies in the sand. Lisa feeling extremely sensual pulled him closer.

"Chad, make love to me, I want to become one with you, let your passion free and make love to me, now."

Chad got on top of her and once again, pushed his hardness deep into her longing pussy. He stroked himself in and out, fast then slow. It was almost as if he were going in rhythm with the beating of their two hearts.

Lisa felt totally orgasmic, as she quivered with Chad's gentle loving touch. As his chest brushed against her hard, erect nipples and Chad kissed her sensuously, she felt as if their love had reached new heights and life were finally perfect.

For the first time, they were actually making real love and not just having sex. She felt closer than ever to Chad and wanted to hang on tight and never let go. She gently kissed his chest and rolled him over, then getting on top of him, she slowly moved up and down, pushing his manhood deep in to her channel of love.

Chad caressed her breasts and gently kissed her hard nipples, as he moaned and writhed about in the sand. Lisa held him tight, rocking her pelvis fast on his rock-hard shaft. As their bodies tingled with passionate desire, all at once the two burst into erotic flames of sexual desire and orgasmed into ecstasy together.

Lisa feeling closer than ever to Chad, whispered softly. "Chad, I feel like our love is stronger than ever, I love you more then you could possibly know." Chad held her in his arms.

"I know baby, I'm so in love with you, I feel like I'm floating on a cloud. I am so high on your love; nothing could possibly bring me down. Lisa I love you and I never want to lose you."

Lisa smiled and she stroked his hair.

"Well I hope you never have to, because I never want to be apart from you. I love you too much and I can't even imagine my life without you in it."

The two of them got up off the sand, held each other's hands and took a moonlit walk along the beach with the water at their feet. Then as the moon shone down on their wet bodies, they as if they were in heaven, together for an eternity.

Lisa prayed that she would never lose Chad, even though somewhere deep inside of her she sometimes wondered about their relationship.

She wondered if it was right for marriage or if their relationship was nothing more than a sexual friendship.

She believed in her heart that their relationship was a loving one, that would last forever, yet from time to time her mind drifted and she wondered.

As they walked, Chad looked up to the star filled sky. "You know Lisa, as I look up at all the stars in the sky, I feel like I am in a whole other world and you are by my side as my angel from heaven. Meeting you was the best thing that ever happened to me and I'm so glad I did."

Lisa was so taken in by Chad's words she felt as though she would cry, and then as she looked up at Chad and he yawned, she turned him around.

"Come on, my dear, let's get back and get some sleep. You must be exhausted after being up all last night and then all day long too."

Chad agreed as they headed back.

"Yeah, I am pretty wiped out, okay let's go get some sleep, guess the beach will still be here in the morning."

Lisa laughed as they walked hand in hand.

"Well, I sure hope so."

Chad grinned as they arrived back at the boat and headed inside to settle down in to bed. Then as Chad held her in his arms, he thought about how he needed to know that she was safe. He wanted to be able to protect her from all the abuse that she would be going back to, in only a few days.

As he lay there with a blank look on his face, Lisa knew that he was really thinking hard about something.

"Chad, what is wrong, baby? You look like you're off in another world, is something bothering you?"

Chad rolled toward her and stroked her cheek.

"No, baby, I'm fine. I am just thinking about how much you mean to me and day dreaming about our lives together."

Lisa knew there was more to it so asked. "Then why do you look so depressed?" Chad smiled.

"I'm not depressed baby, just deep in thought." Lisa smiled kissed him sweetly then turned away. "Okay then, good night, sleep well."

Chad knew that he had just lied to her, but he didn't want to upset her so thought it was best.

Chad kissed her shoulder gently, and then began to drift off to sleep. As Lisa lay there almost asleep herself, she thought about the ordeal she had been through at home. She thought about what she was going to tell David when she arrived home. He would be expecting to find her still locked in the basement and would want to know how she got free and she broke through those locks and chains.

Lisa was worried, she knew that is wasn't going to be easy to explain but that there was no way around it. She would just have to face the music and hope for the best. Then as she drifted off to sleep, she decided that she would talk to Chad about it in the morning and maybe together, they could think up and explanation that David would fall for.

The next morning, Lisa woke up in Chad's arms. It was a wonderful feeling to wake up safe and sound in his strong arms, knowing that she was protected and loved.

She kissed his sweetly on the lips, to wake him up and he opened his eyes to see her smiling face.

"Good morning beautiful how's my sweetheart this morning?"

Lisa rubbed his chest.

"Oh I'm fine, how are you? Did you sleep well?" Chad sat up at the side of the bed.

"Of course, I did, I was next to you. When I am with you, I'm so comfortable I sleep like a baby."

Lisa agreed as she sat up.

"Yeah so do I, it's really amazing how comfortable you can feel, when you're with someone you trust."

Lisa then got up out of bed.

"I'm going to go grab a shower and then I'll make the coffee."

Then as she got to the bathroom door she turned back. "Oh and Chad, I have something I need to talk to you about, it's kind of important."

Chad got up and put on his robe. "Oh okay, no problem."

Then he headed into the kitchen, he decided that while Lisa took her shower, he would make the coffee. Then as he waited, he sat pondering about what it was Lisa had to speak to him about and he feared that it wouldn't be good. He knew that Lisa was terrified of David finding out about them and a part of him always worried that she would leave him, to prevent him from ever knowing.

Chad was going out of his mind with worry and couldn't wait much longer, so he called to Lisa.

"Honey, coffee is ready, are you almost finished?" Lisa turning off the water yelled back.

"Yeah just finishing up, I'll be right out."

A few minutes later she walked in to the kitchen, and then as they sat down with their coffee, Chad asked.

"Well it's driving me crazy, what is it you have to talk to me about? Is it bad?"

Lisa jumped.

"Oh no, Chad, I'm sorry, I didn't mean to worry to you. I was just hoping that maybe we could talk and you could help me to figure a way out of a serious beating when I get home."

Chad interrupted.

"Why? What do you mean?" Lisa continued.

"Well think about it, David is going to be expecting to find me locked in that basement. How do I explain my getting out and how I broke those locks and chains on my own from the other side of the door?"

Chad sighed as he jumped up and began pacing around the kitchen.

"My God, I never even thought of that. I guess we really do need a good solid explanation now, don't we? What if you told him, a neighbor heard you screaming and broke you out?"

Lisa shook her head.

"No, that wouldn't work, David knows the neighbors on both sides and he would only check out my story. Besides that, as neighbor would have called the police and then they would have gone and picked up David from Paula's."

Chad shook his head.

"Well, I guess, telling him a passerby heard you and called the police wouldn't work then either. Especially since with police involvement there would be an investigation into it. After all, it was attempted murder. God Lisa, I just don't know what to say, this is really a tough one."

Right then Lisa exclaimed. "I know. I've got it!"

Chad extremely curious asked. "Well, what is it? What's your plan?" Lisa continued.

"Well right before David went crazy and then locked me up, I was talking to you on the phone and David walked in."

Chad was confused.

"Wait a minute, David heard you talking to me?" Lisa shook her head.

"No that's just it; he didn't hear me but asked who it was. I told him that is was Andrea calling to see if I wanted to go out shopping or something."

Chad completely interested in the plan jumped in. "Yes, go on."

"Well, I told David that I told her I couldn't go. So, I could tell David, that she decided to stop by for a visit and finding I was locked in the basement broke me out."

Chad rubbed his chin and nodded.

"Yeah that might work, but won't David check into that story as well?"

Lisa answered.

"Yes, he probably would, but as long as I get a hold of Andrea before I get home, I am sure she will back me up. She knows all about you and she also knows all about David's abuse and let's just say she doesn't like him much. If I call her as soon as we get back and explain everything to her, I am sure she will go along with it. All I have to do now, is pray that she's home when we return, or this plan could get blown out of the water."

Chad smiled and raised his coffee cup.

"Well, okay, sounds good. Now here's to hoping the plan doesn't fail."

Lisa raised her coffee cup and as she agreed. "Yes, let's just keep our fingers crossed." Then she took Chad by the hand.

"Well, now that this little matter is out of the way, what do you say we start enjoying the rest of our time together?"

Then she tugged his arm.

"Come on, handsome, let's got take a walk on the beach." Chad pulled back a bit.

"Sounds great, but first let me grab another coffee, would you like one?"

Lisa took her coffee cup off the table and handed it to him.

"Sure sounds great, thanks baby."

After getting their coffees, they headed down to the beach where they walked along the water in the gently morning sun. Chad pulled her close, wrapping his arm around her and holding her tight.

"I wish I could hold you like this forever and never let go." Lisa leaned into him resting her head on his arm.

"I know, Chad, I feel the same way."

Then becoming playful, she let go and ran into the water, then taking her coffee cup she began throwing water at him.

"Cold, baby?"

Chad chuckled and pointed to her. "Yes, it is, come here, you."

Lisa laughed as she shook her head no. "No way, if you want me, you come here."

Chad knew that the water was cold, but he had always loved the childlike qualities in Lisa. She was a mature woman and was going through a lot, yet she always seemed to find the best in everything and still find time to horse around and enjoy life. So he sat his coffee cup down in the sand and ran into the water to join her.

"Holy shit! Lisa, it's cold."

She laughed as she splashed more water at him and walked out further.

"Come on you, wimp, it's not that bad."

Chad laughed as he waded out to her, then grabbed her and swung her around.

"God, I love you, I love everything about you."

Lisa wrapped her legs around him, then pulling herself up, she kissed him passionately burring her tongue deep in his mouth. Chad held her tight and returned the kiss, and then he carried her out the water and on to the boat, where he laid her on the floor. Then continued to kiss her as he slowly and passionately began to make love to her.

He kissed her gently, while he caressed her yearning body, then moving downward he fondled her pussy and encircled her hard, sensitive clit. Lisa becoming aroused reached down and grabbed his already hard dick.

"Chad, I want to suck it, come on baby roll over and let me suck your hard dick."

Chad moaned as he rolled over on to his back and Lisa straddled him, with her pussy just above his mouth and he mouth at this rock-hard dick. She began sucking him hungrily, while Chad licked and fingered her pussy, sending waves of pleasure racing through her body. She moaned as she felt his lips pressed hard against her clit and she sucked him ferociously, while she stroked his warm balls.

The two moaned with sexual arousal as they climaxed to the peak of sexual delight. The erotic sensations ripped through their bodies, causing them to writhe about and convulse uncontrollably. Then as Chad reached the heights of sexual desire and his orgasm began, Lisa stroked him fast, allowing the juices of his sex to flow freely across her chest. Then feeling the heat of Chad's love shooting across her body, she herself was brought to orgasm.

Chad licked her fast burring his tongue deep inside her throbbing pussy as he moaned.

"Oh, Lisa, oh baby you taste so good, oh baby of yes let it go baby let it go."

Lisa writhed about on top of Chad and panted with sexual pleasure, as she sailed back down from her peak. Chad then rolled her over and putting her on her knees, entered her from behind. He pushed himself deeper and deeper and with another hard thrust, drove himself even further. Chad pumped and pumped, Lisa tightened her muscles increasing the friction as Chad exclaimed.

"Oh, baby, Oh God you're so tight, take it baby, take all of me."

Chad slapped her ass and grabbed on, pulling her to him harder and faster. She screamed and shrieked, with the tingling of her exploding groin and Chad drove himself even deeper. The contractions of her orgasm and the heat from her flowing juices immediately started his climax. Then as he reached his peak and began to orgasm, his thrusts slowed as he exclaimed.

"Yes! Oh yeah baby, yes baby, oh you make me cum so good, oh yes baby of yes."

Then he rubbed her shoulders, pulled out and flopped down on the floor next to her.

"Oh Lisa, I know that I've said it before, but you're the best and I love you."

Lisa rolled and put her head on his chest.

"I love you too baby, I just wish that we didn't have to head home tomorrow night. Oh and about that, I was wondering if maybe we should head back a little earlier in the day, so we can try and get a hold of Andrea before she heads out to the clubs."

Chad sat up and rubbed his chin.

"Yeah, that might be a good idea, although David and Paula aren't due back until after midnight, so we could still make it back in plenty of time."

Lisa sighed.

"Yeah, we could, but you know David, he never tells me the truth. He's forever telling me later times so that he'll be able to catch me coming home. He never trusts me to be there before he gets home. Although this time, he's expecting me to be locked in the basement or even dead, so it's possible that he will be late. I'm just not sure I want to take that chance though."

Chad sighed and he put his hand on her arm.

"Yeah, you're probably right. Okay, I'll just take you back to my place with me until midnight and we can finish up our vacation there and you'll be able to get a hold of Andrea."

Lisa agreed.

"Sounds like a plan."

Then as she looked at the clock she exclaimed.

"Wow, look at the time! Chad we've been here most of the day, it's almost time to start thinking about dinner. Boy, time really does fly when you're having a good time, doesn't it?"

Chad looked up at the clock.

"Sure does, anyway, baby, I'm going to go and grab a shower, I won't be long."

Lisa got up from the floor.

"Sure, baby, no problem, I'm going to go and start on dinner while you're in there. Listen, after your shower, why don't you rest a bit while I'm cooking dinner? We have a long trip tomorrow."

Chad yawned.

"Yeah, sounds good, maybe I'll take a short nap, you sure you don't mind?"

Lisa smiled.

"Not at all, baby, I'll wake you when dinner is ready."

Chad went to take his shower and Lisa headed into the kitchen to get started on dinner. She wanted it to be special because it was their last night on the island. She decided that she would prepare steaks and baked potatoes on the barbecue, with tossed salad and then fruit for dessert.

She chilled a bottle of champagne and set a table and chairs up on the beach, set with candles and quiet music.

Then once dinner was cooked and everything was set, she went in to wake Chad. She kissed him gently to wake him and he opened his eyes and kissed her sweetly.

"Hi baby, dinner ready?"

Lisa put her finger to her mouth. "Shh."

Then taking him by the hand, she led him out to the romantic setting on the beach and sat him down.

"Now, just relax darling and enjoy. You can get started on the salad and I'll be right back with the rest of the food."

Then while Chad poured the champagne and started on the salad, Lisa went inside and quickly slipped into a purple satin teddy, then grabbed the rest of the food and headed back out.

As Chad saw her walking across the beach, his jaw dropped and he exclaimed.

"Oh baby! Wow you look absolutely gorgeous." Lisa smiled as she replied.

"Thank you darling and I happen to think the same thing about you. You look wonderful sitting there with the glow of the candle light."

Chad handed Lisa a glass of champagne then lifted his glass.

"Here is to many more happy times and a life time of happiness and joy."

Lisa holding up her glass, then toasted.

"And may our love always be strong and survive whatever rough situations we are faced with and may we overcome all of the trouble and finally be free to let our love show."

Chad smiled and caressed her hand, and then they enjoyed their romantic dinner on the beach.

After the meal, Chad took her by the hand and led her out to the water's edge. Then hearing the quiet music playing in the background, they held each other tight and kissed passionately, as they danced slowly with the water at their feet.

Lisa grabbed on to him, held him tight and began to cry.

Chad wiped a tear away.

"Baby, what is it? What is wrong?"

Lisa began to cry harder as she put her head on his chest. "Nothing, that's just it, Chad, everything is perfect. I love You, Chad."

Chad kissed her sweetly as he led her back to the table. Then spreading the table cloth on the sand, he laid her down. He kissed her from head to toe and then held her in his arms. As they lay on the beach, gazing up at the stars, they spoke of their hopes and dreams to someday get married, have a huge house and fill it with their children.

Chad wanted two boy and two girls, Lisa laughed.

"Now, let's get realistic, that may not happen. We could get four of the same or three and one."

Chad grinned as he stroked her hair and responded. "Well that would be good, too, whatever God grants us will be wonderful and I hope they all look like you." Lisa sighed as she once again thought about her life.

"You know Chad? I always dreamed of having lots of children, but then with the way David turned out, I didn't want children to be involved so I held off. Now, I'm so glad that I did, children with David would be wrong, but with you, it feels so right."

The night air was now turning cold, as Chad stood up and then reached down to help Lisa up.

"Well, darling, it's getting chilly out here, what do you say we head back to the boat?"

Lisa agreed as she began cleaning up.

"Yeah it is, let's get this stuff cleaned up and get inside." Chad smiled as he smacked her bottom.

"We'll have a better time on the boat any way, remember I brought our toys."

Lisa laughed as she hurried gathering things up.

"Oh yeah. Right on! Well, come on then. Let's get this mess cleaned up."

Chad laughed as he quickly scooped up some stuff and ran toward the boat yelling.

"Just leave the table; I'll get it in the morning." Lisa ran to catch up with him.

"Hey, galloping stallion, wait up!"

Chad laughed as he stepped on to the boat. "Well then hurry up, my sexy love Goddess." Lisa laughed.

"Love Goddess? Is that the best you can do?" Chad smiled a devilish grin.

"Okay my princess of passion." Lisa smiled.

"Now, that one I can live with, but love Goddess? No, that one has got to go."

Chad laughed as he smacked her bottom and chased her into the boat and she ran right into the bedroom yelling.

"You better hurry up, stallion or I'm starting without you." As Chad walked in to the bedroom he responded.

"Oh yeah? Start without me, hey? I don't think so; I don't want to miss a second."

Lisa jumping on to the bed with a seductive look, meowed like the kitten as she called him over.

"I guess, you better get over here then."

Chad pulled a vibrator out of his bag and then jumped on to the bed next to her. Then turning it on, he began sliding it across her body and down toward her opening. He slid it up and down the slit of her pussy, making her hot and wet and inflamed with erotic desire, as he then pushed it deep in to her screaming pussy. He slid it in and out, fast then slow as he bent down and nibbled and licked her hard clit, making her squirm with excitement.

Lisa was soaked with erotic love juices, as she felt her climax beginning and she yelled out.

"Oh Chad, oh yes, oh don't stop, oh it feels so good, don't stop baby, don't stop."

Chad pushed it harder and faster, as she peaked and was brought to orgasm. Lisa was filled with erotic sensation, as she then rolled over and began sucking his hard dick, while she rolled the tip of the vibrator across his balls.

The sensation of the vibrator sent a tingling feeling shooting right up through hard dick. Lisa felt his massive organ becoming harder and stronger, as he groaned and writhed about with excitement. She sucked him longer and faster and licked his length, bringing him to cum in her mouth. She sucked and licked swallowing the juices of his desire as he exclaimed.

"Oh yes baby, swallow it baby, take it all baby, oh yes Lisa yes!"

Lisa groaned as she continued so suck him.

"Oh yes baby, that's it, cum in my mouth baby, oh you taste so good baby, oh yeah baby, that's it baby."

Lisa finished and sat up; Chad kissed her then looked deep in to her eyes.

"Baby, don't ever change, you are the best and truly my princess of passion."

Lisa blushed with his words as she looked down to the bed.

"Oh come on now, you don't have to go giving me a big head."

Chad laughed then trying to lighten things up responded. "Well, why not? You gave me one."

Lisa slapped him as she laughed.

"Oh Chad, ha-ha funny. You sure can be a sick puppy when you want to be. Now, come on, its late, let's get some sleep."

Chad laughed as they laid down and got comfortable in each other's arms.

Then as Chad drift off to sleep, Lisa lay thinking. She prayed that the night would be endless and she would be right there in Chad's arms forever, safe and secure with nothing to worry about.

The next morning came all too fast for Lisa, as they had to begin preparing to head home. As they stood on the deck enjoying their morning coffee, Lisa began to cry.

"Chad I don't think I can do it, I don't think I can face David and those iron fists, I'm scared. I know I have to go back to the city, but I don't think I can handle any more of his abuse. What should I do? Oh baby please, please tell me what to do."

Chad sighed as he pulled her close holding her in his arms.

"Oh Lisa, I wish I could just tell you that we never had to go back, but you and I both know that we have too. If you didn't go back, David would hunt you down and he wouldn't give up until he found you. We have to get you out of there for good, but right now running isn't the way to go about it."

Lisa began to cry harder.

"Then, what is Chad? What is the right way to about it?" Chad wiped her tears.

"I'm not sure, Lisa, but we definitely have to find a way and soon."

In no time at all, it was time to head back to the city. While Chad sailed the boat, Lisa cleaned and packed up their things. She wanted the ride home to last forever, but if didn't. An hour and a half later, they were back in the noisy city and on their way back to Chad's apartment.

Chad reminded her.

"Don't forget to call Andrea as soon as we get in, she has to know our plan, in case David tries to check out your story."

Lisa sighed.

"Yeah, I'll call her right away."

Chad reached out and put his hand on hers. "My God, Lisa, you're shaking."

Lisa sighed as a tear rolled down her cheek.

"Yeah, I know, I'm trying to stop, but I guess I'm a little more scared then I thought."

Chad held her hand.

"It's all right, baby, it will all be over soon. Just think of me and our love and it will get you through."

Lisa smiled then sighed.

"I just wish it were that easy."

They soon arrived at Chad's apartment and Lisa immediately called Andrea. She explained what had happened and how she got out, and then asked for her help.

"Andrea, I just need to know that you will back me up and tell David that you showed up and broke me out."

Andrea was disgusted with what David had done as she answered.

"Of course, I'll back you up, Lisa. My God, that guy is a real creep and anything I can do, to prevent you from being hurt, I'll do it. One of these days, Lisa, that jerk is going to kill you, he has to be stopped. Anyway, don't worry I'll back you up one hundred percent, you can count on me."

Lisa still shaking replied.

"Oh, thank you, Andrea, you're a really great friend and I really appreciate this, I'll talk to you later."

Lisa got off the phone and right away, Chad asked.

"Well what did she say? Will she back you up?" Lisa hugged Chad.

"Yeah, she said she would do anything she could to help." Chad let out a sigh of relief.

"Oh, thank goodness, that is one less thing to worry about." Right then the phone rang and Chad answered, it was Andrea.

"Lisa, its Andrea, for you." Lisa took the phone. "Hey Andrea, what is it?" Andrea seemed panicked.

"Lisa, you've got trouble. I was just talking to Cindy and she saw David this morning at the store, he's in town already."

Lisa became terrified as she panicked and began to shake. "Okay Andrea, thanks for calling."

Then she hung up the phone and turned to look at Chad. Chad taking one look at the fear in her eyes, knew instantly.

"Oh my God, he's back isn't he?"

Lisa holding back the tears and frantically grabbing her things answered.

"Yeah, he is, he got back early this morning. I've got to go." Chad grabbed her and kissed her.

"Try and calm yourself down, don't let him see you like this."

Lisa sighed and wiped her tears. "I'll try."

Chad kissed her goodbye and she headed for home.

When she arrived and walked inside, right away David jumped up from the sofa.

"Well, hello, Houdini."

Chapter Five

Chad was at home, unpacking and thinking about Lisa. He couldn't concentrate on much of anything and soon found himself staring out the window and worrying. He was no longer sure, that sending her home to David was the right thing to do and he feared losing her. Yet he knew sending her back to him, was the only way they could keep their relationship a secret. He couldn't stand the thought of her being hurt again, and he prayed that she was all right.

The more Chad stood thinking about the situation, the more frustrated and worried he became, as he said to himself.

"I'm an idiot, a total idiot, Lisa is my whole world and I've sent her back home to an abusive drunk, who's already made an attempt to kill her. What was I thinking? How could I be so foolish?"

Then taking a photo of Lisa out of his wallet, he kissed it. Then he began to shake as he felt the tears beginning to form in his eyes and he yelled out.

"What was I thinking? I am such a fool, Oh Lisa please be all right!"

Then sucking back the tears, Chad picked up the phone to call her, but knowing that it would only make things worse, he sat the phone back down and sat down on the sofa. Then looking at the phone and holding back the tears, he yelled out.

"Ring damn it, ring! Come on, Lisa, call."

Chad was terrified of what she was going through and now more than ever believed that David deserved to die. Then as he sat alone with his worries, Chad began thinking of ways to kill David and free Lisa once and for all. Ways that he wouldn't be caught and that wouldn't incriminate Lisa.

Meanwhile back at Lisa's, David was yelling and questioning her escape.

"Come on, Houdini, tell me your trick, how did you do it? How did you break through those chains and who helped you?"

Lisa was terrified and trying not to shake, as David then slammed his fists down cracking the coffee table.

"Well, Lisa? How did you do it? Answer me." Lisa hesitated and then nervously replied.

"Andrea…Andrea came over. She heard me scream out to her from the basement and she broke the chains with a crowbar to get me out."

David laughed and shook his head.

"Yeah right, you stupid bitch. What do you think I am stupid or something? You told Andrea that you couldn't go out, so why was she even here?"

Lisa trying to hide her fear quickly answered.

"She thought she would stop by and see if I was sure, that I didn't want to go."

David raised his eyebrows as snickered.

"Yeah, I'm not believing any of this, if this is how it happened, then how did she get into the house?"

Lisa knew that David wasn't falling for it, but answered. "She heard me screaming and she knew where the extra key was, so she unlocked the door and came in."

David laughed viciously as he punched the wall with his fist.

Lisa then responded.

"Well, first of all David, I want to tell you that you are a –"

"Bullshit, Lisa, that is total bullshit and you know why?" Lisa unsure how to answer backed away from David. "Why?"

David continued.

"Because, I never locked the door, Lisa, the door was unlocked the whole time, so you just lied to me."

Lisa knowing she was in trouble quickly exclaimed.

"No, David, I am not lying, I swear to you it's the truth. If you don't believe me, call Andrea, she'll tell you what happened."

David slapped her hard across the face and her head swung back.

"Fine, you stupid whore! I'll call your little friend, give me her number."

Lisa reached into her purse and pulled out Andrea's number and handed it to David, he then walked over to the phone to call her.

Lisa was scared as she prayed that Andrea would say the right things and confirm her story.

David asked Andrea, exactly what had happened. He wanted to know, why she came over, how she got in and how she got Lisa out. He wasn't leaving anything out, as he was determined to catch her in a lie.

He even put the call on speaker phone, so that Lisa would be able to hear when her friend messed up.

As Lisa stood listening, she worried that Andrea would forget about the spare key under the rock by the door and wouldn't say the right thing to David.

"Come on Andrea, think, remember the key, remember the key."

Lisa crossed her fingers and stood waiting to hear Andrea's response.

"Goddamned creep. How dare you tie Lisa up like that and leave her to die, you're an asshole, David and I hope you get exactly what you have coming for you."

David laughed as he glared at Lisa.

"Yeah, okay, Andrea, whatever. Just answer the questions, or don't you know the answers? Maybe you're just stalling because you don't know what to say."

Andrea was furious as she yelled into the phone.

"Fine, you stupid jerk! If you must know, I went over to see if she was sure she didn't want to go out, then when I heard her screaming from the basement, I went in with the spare key."

David still glaring at Lisa continued.

"Okay then, if you went in with the spare key, then where is it kept and how did you break those chains?"

Lisa panicked as she realized, that she hadn't told Andrea about the crowbar and was sure she was about to be caught. Andrea answered.

"God, David, you're a total idiot, but if it means helping Lisa, I'll answer your foolish questions. The key is under the rock by the front door and as for the chains; I broke them with a crowbar and then picked all those bloody locks on the door with a hair pin. Now, David, if that is all, I have got to go. Have Lisa call me later. Goodbye, David."

David hung up the phone from Andrea and turned to Lisa.

"Well I guess it's lucky for you, that your friends stick by you."

Lisa was stunned, she couldn't figure out how Andrea knew about the crowbar and the separate locks on the door as well. She hadn't told her about those, so how could she have known?

As Lisa stood confused, David came up to her; he grabbed her by the hair and bashed her head into the wall.

"Oh yeah bitch, we still have one more little matter to discuss."

Lisa holding her head asked.

"What is that, David? What did I do now?" David went on.

"Well my dear, I returned home at 8:30 this morning and no Lisa, where the hell were you?"

Lisa thought fast and answered.

"I went out for breakfast. I wasn't expecting you until tonight and I figured there wasn't much point in cooking when it was only me here. I woke up fairly early this morning and I left around 8:15 a.m. I must have just missed you."

David pushed her face harder in to the wall.

"Well then, where were you the rest of the morning? It doesn't take five hours to eat breakfast."

Lisa shuttered unsure what to say but answered.

"Well, like I said, David, I wasn't expecting you until tonight, so I went shopping, well just browsing actually, so don't worry, I didn't buy anything."

David punched her in the back and shoved her away.

"Fine! I'll let you off the hook, for now, anyway. Now get out of my sight, I'll call you when I want dinner."

Lisa went upstairs and called Andrea, to find out how she had known what to say to David.

"Hi, Andrea, its Lisa. I just called to find out how you knew about the crowbar and the chains. I was sure that I was caught and then you stunned me by knowing exactly what to say."

Andrea sighed as she answered.

"Chad called me; he wanted to make sure that I knew everything and what to say and if I had heard from you yet. Lisa, he is frantic with worry, you better call him before he goes out of his mind." Lisa agreed.

"Yeah, I'm sure he is worried, I was planning on calling him, right after I got off the phone with you. I just had to find out how you knew, that was all."

Andrea went on.

"Well, I guess, it was good that Chad called me, because if he hadn't, I wouldn't have had a clue what to say to David. Anyway Lisa, speaking of David, are you okay? What happened?"

Lisa sighed.

"Yeah, I'm okay; he bashed my face in to the wall, but other than that I'm all right. For now, anyway."

Andrea angry with David replied.

"Well, I sure hope you're okay and I hope that David gets exactly what he deserves and soon. Anyway Lisa, I have to get going, make sure you call Chad as soon as possible to save his sanity."

Lisa agreed.

"I sure will, right away. I'll talk to you later Andrea and thanks again."

Lisa hung up the phone from Andrea and right away called Chad, who picked up the phone before the first ring had even ended.

"Lisa, are you all right?"

Lisa knowing he was out of his mind with worry answered. "Yeah sweetie, relax, I'm okay. Andrea back me up all the way and David fell for it, hook line and sinker." Chad jumped in.

"Oh, thank God, I've been going crazy over here; I never realized how much I really do love you until now. Did he hurt you?"

Lisa sighed as she felt the tears beginning to form in her eyes.

"Chad, I love you, too. Thanks to Andrea, he didn't hurt me too bad this time."

Chad exclaimed.

"What do you mean by not too bad? What did he do?" Lisa went on to explain.

"Well, he got a little rough and bashed my face in to the wall. My cheek is a little swollen, but other than that I'm fine."

Chad freaked out.

"I'll kill him, I swear it Lisa, I am so sick of him hurting you, I am seriously considering killing him."

Lisa laughed as she exclaimed.

"I don't believe it! I was actually thinking the same thing, but the problem is finding a way to do it and not get caught. It's impossible it could never work."

Chad agreed.

"Yeah, that is a problem, but you know if we really thought it out, there are ways and we could even get away with it. Another problem though is actually having the guts to go through with it, that won't be easy either."

Lisa sighed.

"Oh, I know. I'm not even totally sure that killing him is the right thing to do, but at this point, it seems like the only way out."

Chad jumped in.

"Well we'll talk about it later when I see you. For now, you better get off the phone before you get caught. I love you Lisa, be careful and I'll see you later."

Lisa blew a kiss in to the phone.

"I love you, too, baby. See you later, bye for now."

After hanging up the phone from Chad, Lisa heard David yelling for her.

"Get down her bitch! I'm hungry and want my dinner." Lisa wanted to just tell him to go to hell, but answered.

"Yes, David, I'll be right down."

She got up and headed downstairs where he was waiting in the kitchen.

"What would you like for dinner David?" He laughed as he answered sarcastically.

"Food stupid! I don't give a shit what you cook, just do it and be quick about it."

Lisa sighed as she shook her head at him.

"Fine, David, relax. You know I only asked a question, you didn't have to yell about it. Why don't you just calm down, I mean hell, you would think that after a vacation, you would be a little more relaxed."

Lisa had just pushed the wrong button and David became furious. He jumped at her and began hitting her with a fierce look in his eyes. He punched her in the face, splitting her lip and giving her a black eye. She attempted to defend herself by kicking him in the groin, but that was a big mistake. David grabbed her by the throat and began choking her.

Lisa couldn't breathe and was becoming light headed, she was sure she was going to pass out, when suddenly he let go and began yelling.

"What are you stupid? Did you think that I would kill you? Ha I wouldn't give you the satisfaction, at least not until my dinner is cooked." With that, David laughed a vicious laugh and headed upstairs.

"Call me when my dinner is ready, bitch."

Lisa pulled herself up as she whispered to herself. "Yes master, anything you say master, I will obey."

She then slammed a pan on to the stove and then slammed a few cupboards. She was furious and tired of living her life as a slave. She had made up her mind, she was going to kill David, she didn't know how or when, but she was determined to do it.

David heard her banging things around in the kitchen and came back downstairs.

"What in the hell are you doing? Are you trying to piss me off?"

Lisa mumbled to herself.

"Well it wouldn't take much now would it?"

David slapped her in the back of the head and laughed. "You are such a fool, Lisa. One more sound out of you and you'll get another beating. Now hurry up, I may starve to death before you're finished."

Lisa was angry, she tried to hold it back but could resist and replied sarcastically.

"Oh goodie, you mean I get to watch you die?"

David lunged at her to hit her again, but she picked up a pan of hot grease and held it up to him.

"Lay a hand on me, or come even one step closer, and that pretty boy face of yours is going to look like a pizza. Come on, David, go for it!"

David backed off and walked in to the living room laughing and Lisa went back to cooking.

She cooked him pork chops and fries and then called him back in to the kitchen to eat.

David heading from the living room grunted.

"It's about time; you have got to be the slowest cook around."

Then as he sat down at the table and looked at his plate he complained.

"Pork chops and fries! It took you forty-five minutes to cook pork chops and fries? You are definitely lazy, bitch, stupid too."

Lisa slammed a pan into the sink and walked out of the kitchen yelling.

"You son of a bitch, I am sick of your bullshit. I don't have to sit here and take your abuse, I'm going out." David slammed the table and yelled.

"Good, go! I'll enjoy the peace and quiet, but you had better be home by 2:00 a.m. when I get in. If not, I'm going to find you and you and whoever you are with will die, because I will kill you."

Lisa grabbed her purse and walked out, slamming the door behind her. She walked out to her car and then burst into tears crying. The abuse had become too much for her to handle and she desperately needed a way out.

As she looked in the car mirror, at the mess that David had made of her face. She knew that she couldn't bear to walk around looking like this anymore. Her face was a mess and her neck had the imprints of his hands bruised on it. Lisa knew that Chad was going to be furious about this and she feared he would go after David.

As she drove over to his place, she thought of ways to kill David without being caught. She knew that she couldn't spend the rest of her life in jail; she had already done her time in David's prison at home. She knew the only way was to make it look like some kind of freak accident so that no one would suspect her.

Meanwhile back at Chad's, he was thinking the same thing. He had never wished harm on anyone before, but David was one person that he wanted to see burn in hell. Chad hated him for everything he was putting Lisa through, he was playing God with her life and he made all the decisions as to what she could and couldn't do and he beat her if she didn't obey him.

Chad couldn't understand how anyone could be so cruel and uncaring, especially to someone as sweet and innocent as Lisa. She didn't deserve to be treated that way and Chad was determined to put an end to it once and for all. No woman deserved to be abused and he could no longer just stand by and watch the woman he so deeply loved being hurt.

Lisa arrived at Chad's; she was still very distraught over the incidents that had taken place. She desperately needed to be held in Chad's loving arms, where she felt loved and secure.

She walked up to Chad's door with tears streaming down her cheek and knocked. Chad answered the door and right away exclaimed.

"Lisa! Baby what's wrong? What happened?"

Lisa began to cry harder as she looked up at him and he saw her face.

"Oh my God, Lisa! What has he done to you? When will it end?"

Lisa threw her arms around him.

"Oh baby hold me, I can't handle anymore. I have to kill him; it's the only way out and the only way to end all of this. Oh Chad hold me baby, just hold me."

Chad rubbed her back as he held her tight.

"Lisa, don't worry, I'm here for you and I'll help you no matter what you decide to do. David deserves what he gets and no matter what happens I will always love you. My love for you in unconditional and nothing could ever change that."

Lisa cried harder as she held Chad.

"My God Chad, I can't believe I am actually thinking about killing somebody. I've never hurt anyone in my life. Are you sure that killing him, is really the right thing to do?"

Chad sighed as he put his arm around her.

"Well right now, Lisa, I do believe that it is the right thing to do. Of course it has to be your decision, if you really don't want him dead and out of your life for good, then I'll just stop talking about it right now."

Lisa put her head on Chad's shoulder.

"Oh no, don't get me wrong. I am definitely sure that I want David out of my life for good and if dead is the only way, then there's no other choice."

Chad kissed her on the cheek.

"Come on, baby, let's go sit down. I really think you need to relax a bit."

As they sat down on the sofa, Chad rubbed her shoulders. "Here baby, lay back and relax and let me give you a massage, you're so tense." Lisa lay back on the sofa.

"Well gee, I wonder why? Of course, I'm tense, there is so much stress in my life right now. How could I not be?"

Chad began massaging her back and shoulders.

"Honey, just relax. You're with me now and you're safe and I hope that by now you believe that. I love you, Lisa and I would never do anything to hurt you."

Lisa turned head and gently kissed his hand.

"I know, Chad; I trust you and I've never once feared you hurting me. I just don't know how to deal with all of this anymore. Can you tell me Chad? Can you tell me how to deal with it?"

Chad began kissing her softly and caressing her body. "It's okay baby, we'll work it out and everything will soon straighten out. Our lives will be happy and there will be nothing to come between us."

Lisa rolled over and began kissing him passionately; she reached in to his pants and stroked his dick as she whispered.

"Make love to me, Chad, I need you, I need you now."

Chad began caressing her breasts, as she helped him out of his jeans and then bent down to suck his dick, making him hard and strong. He fondled her pussy, then slid his finger deep inside and stroked it in and out, getting her hot and wet.

Lisa squirmed with pleasure.

"Oh Chad, oh baby put it in me, put your hard dick deep in to my pussy. Make love to me baby, make love to me now."

Chad moved up, gently sliding himself deep into her hot yearning pussy. Then slid it slowly in and out. Trying to be gently with her, knowing that she was still bruised and hurting and he didn't want to cause her anymore pain.

Lisa however ignoring her pain grabbed his hips and pushed him deeper. She wrapped her legs around him tight as she shrieked.

"Harder baby harder. Screw my wet pussy, screw it hard."

Chad began driving her harder as he pushed himself deeper and deeper.

The tightness of her pussy wrapped hard around him, sent sensations of erotic stimulation shooting through his body. Chad pumped and pumped, with his warm balls slapping against the crack of her ass and the base of his hard dick pushing hard against her erect clit.

She squirmed and convulsed with pleasure.

"Oh Chad yes, that's it baby, make me cum. Screw my pussy and make me cum. Oh yeah! Oh yes baby, oh it feels so good."

Chad's thrusts became stronger and quicker, as the two of them raced to the heights of sexual desire and orgasmed into ecstasy.

Chad caressed her and kissed her gently, as their sexual juices flowed freely and pooled together deep inside of Lisa's hot soaked pussy. Then pulling away he kissed her lips sweetly. "I hope I didn't hurt you. I was trying to be gently with you because you're hurt, but you just make me so crazy I couldn't hold back."

Lisa smiled and stroked his cheek.

"Making love with you could never hurt me. You're just so sweet and passionate and you get me so hot that I just can't resist you. Don't you ever worry about hurting me, Chad, because you never could."

Chad smiled and stroked his fingers across her luscious lips.

"God I love you and I want everyone to know it too. I just wish we were free to go public with our relationship and let the world know just how in love we really are."

Lisa jumped up.

"Oh the hell with it, I'm tired of hiding, let's go." Chad was stunned.

"Go? Go where?"

She grabbed his arm and pulled him up.

"Get dressed, we're going out to the club and if David is there, oh well. I love you and I want everyone to know it."

Chad was shocked as he slipped into his jeans.

"Lisa, come on, now, honey. Are you really sure that you want to do this?"

Lisa buttoned her blouse.

"God Dammed right I do, we're going. Just let me call Andrea quickly and see if she wants to meet us there."

Chad still shocked replied.

"Well okay then. As long as you are positive this is what you want to do. I have to agree with you though, we have hidden this from everyone for long enough."

Lisa walked toward the phone as she agreed.

"Yes, we have and besides, David will be dead soon, so what he thinks really doesn't matter to me anymore."

With that, she picked up the phone to call Andrea and Chad finished getting ready, still shocked that they were actually going to go through with this.

Lisa hung up the phone and picked up her purse.

"Well, Andrea thinks it is great and she's going to meet us there in a bit. So we should get going."

As they headed to the door, Chad pulled her back and kissed her sweetly.

"Baby, I can't believe we are finally doing this. I have dreamed about this since the day we met and it's finally here, we're going public and everyone including David is going to know how much we love each other."

Lisa took his hand.

"You've got that right, now are you ready?" Chad smiled.

"I've been ready for a long time." Lisa smiled.

"Well then, ready or not, here we go."

As they drove to the club, Lisa sat with a blank look on her face.

Chad put his hand on her knee. "You're nervous, aren't you?"

She sighed.

"Yeah a little, but with you by my side, I know everything will be okay."

Chad smiled as he replied.

"Good baby, I want you to feel safe. I will protect you the best I can, but it's all up to you and whether or not you listen to David. I just hope that you will still be able to be with me, if he scares you into going home."

Lisa put her hand on his leg.

"Don't worry baby, even if I do end up at home, I'll still see you. David can't keep us apart, I won't let him."

They arrived at the club and as they drove around looking for a parking space Lisa exclaimed.

"Well here we go baby! It's show time."

Then as she looked around, she noticed Paula's car. "There is Paula's car, they're here."

They pulled into their parking space and Chad took her hand.

"Are you sure you still want to go through with this? I wouldn't blame you if you wanted to back out."

Lisa smiled and leaned into him and kissed his cheek. "No, let's do it, it's time."

As they got out of the car, Lisa noticed Andrea. "Chad, there's Andrea, call her over."

Chad yelled to her. "Andrea, over here."

She waved and headed right over.

"Hi guys, I am so glad that you two are finally doing this, but are you 100% positive this is what you want to do? David and Paula are here and David is already drunk as a skunk."

Lisa shook her head with disgust.

"Oh yeah that is typical! Yeah, I'm positive this is what I want to do. I'm going to prove to David that I really am something special and that he doesn't own me and I really can have a life without him."

Chad took her by the hand.

"Come on baby. Let's do it. It is time to face the music."

As they walked into the bar, they noticed David and Paula right away; sitting right at the end of the bar, but David and Paula never noticed them. They were looking right in Lisa's direction but never saw her.

Chad directed the girls to the only table left available in the entire club. A table which just happened to be directly in front of David. As they walked over and sat down, Andrea laughed.

"My God Lisa, he is so pathetic. He is just so wasted that he doesn't even notice his own wife, sitting right here in front of him."

Lisa shook her head and agreed. "Yes, he is pretty pathetic, isn't he?"

Chad leaned over and kissed her sweetly, then took her by the hand and led her out to the dance floor, where they began to dance seductively, right there in front of David.

Lisa couldn't believe it. She finally had the courage to face David and he didn't even know that she was there.

"God Chad, he's making a complete idiot out of himself. I can't believe what a fool he is. I don't even want to admit that I know him, much less that I'm married to him."

As they headed back to their table, Chad put his arm around her.

"Yeah, he is making a fool out himself, but as you told me before honey. When you married him, he was the perfect gentleman, he had a job and he didn't drink."

Lisa laughed.

"Yeah, isn't that funny? I marry him and he turns into a raving lunatic. Watch out, Chad, I might drive you to drink, too."

Andrea jumped in.

"Lisa you just stop that. The way David turned out wasn't your fault and you know it."

Chad agreed.

"Lisa Andrea is right, David did this by himself and you had nothing to do with it."

Lisa sighed as she looked down at the table.

"Yeah I know you're both right, but sometimes I still feel guilty."

Right then David spotted Andrea and waved to her, then started walking toward their table.

Lisa was stunned. He was walking right toward her and still hadn't realized that she was there. He was only feet away from her and still didn't know that it was her. How could he not have noticed her? Was he that drunk? Or did he actually believe that she would just go home and wait for another beating?

David walked right up to their table.

"Hey Andrea, how's it going? Who is your friend?"

Then as he turned his head and noticed it was Lisa, he freaked out and started yelling right there in the bar.

"Lisa! What the hell are you doing here? Get your ass home, this is my territory and you have no business here." Lisa yelled back.

"Go to hell David! I am not leaving; I have just as much right to be here as you do."

David grabbed her by the hair and yanked her up, then raised his hand to hit her.

Chad grabbed his arm.

"No, I don't think so, pal, not this time, just back off and let her go right now. This is my woman now, she may live with you, but she loves me and I love her. So, pal, from now on, every time you hurt her, I hurt you."

Lisa was in shock. She knew that Chad had been waiting a long time for this day, but she didn't think that he would become this defensive in public.

Andrea was applauding.

"Right on, Chad! You set him straight, he deserves it." David knocked Chad's arm down and back up.

"Excuse me pal, but this is my wife and my possession, you can't tell me what I can and can't do."

Chad leaned over the table and got right in David's face. "Oh yeah, you just watch me and if you have a problem with it, we can just take it outside right now."

Then to all of their surprise, David backed off and turned and walked away.

Lisa began to shake. Chad put his arm around her. "Baby, what's wrong? David knows about us now and he really doesn't seem to care."

A tear rolled down Lisa's cheek.

"No, Chad he cares, that was just too easy, he's planning something. I am in deep shit and I know it. David just doesn't give up that easily, he may have walked away for now, but he'll be back."

Andrea shook her head as she agreed.

"Yes, Chad, Lisa is right, that definitely wasn't the David we all know. He never walks away from a fight, even I'm scared. I really think that Lisa is going to need help and protection, because when David finally does blow, it's going to be fierce."

Chad sighed as he took Lisa's hand in his.

"Well, I'll do whatever is necessary to keep her safe, but if she goes home to him, there is not much I can do. It's all up to her; the decision is in her hands now."

Right then David came back to their table.

"Lisa, can I speak with you in private?"

Lisa held back the tears and tried not to shake as she responded.

"Yeah, okay, David, but it has to be right here in the bar, a table over there just opened, let's go there."

David looked angry as he nodded. "Fine then, let's go, move your ass."

Lisa went to get up from the table and Chad grabbed her.

He kissed her then whispered into her ear.

"Baby, if you need me just nod and I'll be right over, I'm here for you."

David and Lisa went and sat down at another table, it was across the bar, but could still be seen by Chad and Andrea.

Right away David started in on her.

"Lisa, if you have even half a brain in that head of yours, you'll show up at home tonight. I'm sure that you wouldn't want to see you're Mr. Pretty boy over there to turn up dead, now, would you?"

Lisa sucked back the tears.

"David, I want a divorce and your little threats aren't going to make me change my mind."

David laughed.

"Forget it, Lisa, there is no way in hell that I'm going to give you a divorce. I married you, now I own you; you made your bed, now you lay in it. If you continue to see this geek over there, that is your choice, but if I were him, I would watch my back, because I am going to do him in. Now as for you, it will be the same as always, you're to be home by 2:00 am. Every night or you're dead."

Lisa was afraid but didn't let it show.

"David, you wouldn't really kill him, would you?" He laughed a vicious laugh.

"Damn straight, I would. You cheated on me and betrayed our marital vows. If you want to save him, then you'll tell him that it's over right now in front of me."

Lisa yelled.

"No, David I won't. If anyone betrayed our marital vows, it was you. Why can't you just let me go? You don't love me and he does."

David was becoming furious his eyes were like daggers looking straight through her.

"Lisa, I've told you time and time again, I won't let you go. I need you to cook for me and do my housework like a good little wife and besides, without you, who would I yell at?"

As Chad and Andrea sat and watched, Chad worried. He wondered what they were talking about and prayed that he wouldn't lose Lisa. Then he looked to Andrea.

"What could they be talking about? Why hasn't he let her leave yet?"

Andrea sighed.

"I don't know, but Lisa doesn't look happy. Just give it a few more minutes and see what happens. If she hasn't come back by then, I'll go over."

David was slamming his fists on the table and demanding that Lisa dump Chad, she continued to refuse, and then David opened his jacket. He was carrying his gun.

"Do it, Lisa, or he dies tonight." Lisa began to shake.

"David, you're sick, I hate you."

David went to get up and had his hand in his jacket. Lisa jumped up.

"Okay, David, I'll do it. Under one condition though? You have to allow me to go out with my friends, whenever I want too."

David laughed.

"Okay fine. You don't have any friends that want to take you out anyway, so that is no big deal. Now get over there and dump that jerk, move it."

Lisa stepped in front of David.

"Okay fine, but I want to do it alone. Then we'll grab a cab and go home."

David shook his head with disgust. "Fine! Just do it."

Lisa walked over and acted like she was kissing Chad goodbye, but instead whispered into his ear.

"Baby, don't listen to a word I'm about to say, because it's not the truth. I'll call you later and explain everything. I'm okay, please don't worry."

Chad was confused but agreed, as Lisa pulled away and continued.

"I'm sorry, Chad, but it's over between us. I am married and committed to my husband. Therefore, this cannot go on between us. I can't see you anymore; I have to leave now with my husband, take care of yourself. Goodbye, Chad."

Then she turned and walked away.

Chad's jaw dropped, he was confused as he didn't know exactly what was going on. He looked as if he were about to cry but instead stood up slammed his fists down on the table and yelled.

"I'll kill him."

Then he yelled at David.

"Why can't you just let her go?"

David laughed.

"Oh well pal, looks like you lose and I win. Goodbye, pretty boy."

David then grabbed Lisa's arm hard enough to rip her sleeve and pulled her out of the bar.

Chad stayed out of the way. He knew that David had to have threatened her and he didn't want to make things worse. Still stunned he looked to Andrea.

"We have to help her; he's going to hurt her. What could he have said to make her go with him?"

Andrea still stunned herself responded.

"I don't know what he said, but Lisa was pretty shaky. Give it 20 minutes and I'll call her. I guarantee David will be back tonight. It's only 10:00 and he never stays home as long as the bar is open. Besides that, he left Paula sitting over there and I know that he'll come back for her, he wouldn't want to lose his little side dish."

Chad was worried sick as he replied.

"Okay 20 minutes and after you've talked to her, I'm heading over there, as long as David has left of course. I need to talk to her and you can call me if David leaves the bar so I have time to get out of there. I need to find out what exactly is going on, I can't help her if I don't know."

Andrea agreed.

"Yeah that sounds good, and then you can let me know if she's really okay, too."

Chad was worried sick, he only to wait 20 minutes, but it seemed like forever. He was terrified that David would kill Lisa and he would never again get to hold her and tell her how much he loved her. He couldn't bear the thought of living without her in his life, she was everything to him and nothing else mattered.

Andrea got up from the table and headed to the phone to call Lisa. She explained that Chad was planning on coming over there, after David left to come back to the bar and Lisa panicked.

"No, he can't! David is staying home; he doesn't trust me to stay put."

Andrea was worried.

"Lisa, are you okay? He must be furious if he's not coming back to the bar."

Lisa held back the tears as she replied.

"Yeah, I am okay, at least for now. David went to take a shower and sober up. Please, Andrea tell Chad that I will call him and not to worry because I will see him again. I refuse to let David keep us apart. I only left tonight because David had a gun in his jacket."

Andrea freaked out.

"What? Oh God, Lisa, please be careful. If you need any help, call Chad's. I am going to give him a ride home, he'll be there soon."

Lisa sighed as she answered.

"Oh, don't worry I'll be okay, I always survive. I only listened to David tonight because he said that he was going to kill Chad if I didn't and I couldn't take that chance. He had a gun and I really believed that he would do it."

Andrea was furious.

"Lisa, David is really sick and something has to be done about him. I wish you would just kill him and get it over with, nobody would blame you. Anyway Lisa I better let you go and get off the phone before you get caught. I'll explain everything to Chad and tell him that you're going to call him. Goodbye, Lisa, and please be careful."

After getting off the phone with Andrea, Lisa went and got David's gun. She then hid it so that she could use it to protect herself if needed. She never planned on using it, but she figured that David wouldn't take that chance and would back off.

Meanwhile at the bar, Andrea was explaining everything to Chad.

"Chad, David's not coming back to the bar tonight. I'm going to take you home and Lisa will call you there later."

Chad exclaimed.

"He's not coming back! Well, is she okay? What is going on?"

Andrea sighed as she answered.

"Well, she's okay for now. She is going to keep seeing you, she only left tonight, because David had a gun and he threatened to kill you."

Chad panicked.

"Oh, my God Andrea, he has a gun? He could kill her, I have to go over there and get her."

As Chad stood up, Andrea grabbed his arm.

"No, Chad, you can't. If you go over there, you are risking her being killed, now just calm down and let's get over to your place so she can call you. She said to tell you not to worry, that she will be okay."

Chad headed toward the door. "Let's get going, I can't miss her call."

Back at Lisa's, David had just finished up in the shower and came out yelling.

"Lisa, you're a stupid and foolish whore. I hope you realize that you have screwed up big this time. You're going to have to be taught yet another lesson. When will you learn?"

David walked to the corner of the room and picked up a baseball bat, then headed toward her.

Lisa in a panicked ran and grabbed the gun and pointed it at him.

"Back off, David. I mean it David, back off or I'll blow your bloody head off."

David rolled his eyes and began to laugh.

"Yeah right, nice try Lisa. It's not loaded. I only carry it for show and to scare fools like you."

Lisa wasn't sure what to believe as she frantically tried to fire the gun. Only to find that David wasn't lying and there were no bullets in the gun. She was horrified as she dropped the gun and tried to run. She knew that she was going to get it bad, but she couldn't get away fast enough.

David grinned fiercely and let out a horrifying laugh, as he raised the bat and swung, bashing Lisa across the back with it and knocking her to the ground.

Lisa was in pain and couldn't move. David raised the bat to hit her again, but just then there was a knock at the door and David answered it.

It was Paula and she was furious with David.

"Well, here you are you jerk! It was really sweet of you to ditch me at the bar like that."

Then as she walked into the room, she shook her head and smirked.

"Oh, this shit again. Good Lord woman, don't you ever learn?"

Then she turned to David.

"You know I'm really getting sick and tired of this shit. How about just letting it go for now, forget beating on the bitch and take me out for a coffee?"

To Lisa's surprise David agreed.

"Yeah, I suppose, I could do that, I think she's learned her lesson for now anyway. Just let me get ready and we're out of here."

As David got ready to leave with Paula, he continued to yell at Lisa, who still lay still and in pain on the living room floor.

"Listen up, bitch. You had better not even think about going back out tonight. I swear to you girl, if you disobey me this time, you'll pay worse than you ever have before and you'll never leave this house again either."

Lisa was furious as she yelled back sarcastically.

"Yes master, no problem master. You God damned jerk! Who the hell do you think you are? God?"

David laughed as he left with Paula.

"Yeah and I hold your fate in my hands."

With that, the door slammed shut and he and Paula left. Lisa crawled over to the sofa and pulled herself up. Her back was hurt badly and she was in extreme pain. Yet knowing that Chad would be going out of his mind with worry, she picked up the phone and called him.

A horrified Chad picked up the phone before the first ring had ended. Lisa spoke right away before he had time to even say hello.

"Baby it's me, I'm fine, please don't worry. I love you and I would never leave you."

Chad was relieved to hear from her.

"Oh Lisa, thank God you called. I have been going out of mind worrying about you. Are you okay? Did he hurt you?"

Lisa completely fed up with David answered.

"Yeah he did. He bashed me across the back with a baseball bad and its hurt really bad, it's just killing me. That isn't the worst part though; I pulled his gun on him, only to find out that it wasn't even loaded. Anyway darling I've had it, David has to die and I have to get out of here. I want to see you, I'm coming over. I'm going to leave a note for David, telling him that I've gone to stay with Andrea until he cools down. Can you call Andrea for me and ask her to pick me up at the variety store on the corner of my street?"

Chad was worried about her and couldn't wait to see her. "Yes baby of course I will, but why not take your car? It would be faster." Lisa sighed.

"Yeah it would, but if David were to look for me, the car wouldn't be hard to spot and he would know where I was. I don't want him finding me at your place and as far as I know he doesn't know where Andrea lives either, so he won't be able to find out that I am not really there. I will call him, later and try to reason with him, even though I know that reasoning is next to impossible."

Chad agreed.

"Yeah reasoning hasn't gotten you anywhere before so I doubt it will this time either. Anyway honey, I will call Andrea and send her to get you right away. I really want you here so I can take care of you, but Lisa sweetie, please be careful. You know David; he could be watching you, to see if you try to leave."

Lisa still in pain and shaken up replied.

"Yeah, I know, but I will be careful I promise. I'll see you in a little while, I love you, Chad."

Chad hung up the phone from Lisa and right away called Andrea. He explained what had happened and told her that Lisa was getting out of there, but needed to be picked up. Andrea, right away, jumped in.

"No problem I'm leaving right now, where is she?" Chad answered.

"Oh thank you so much Andrea, she's at the variety store on the corner of her street."

Andrea wanted nothing more than to see Lisa away from David as she answered.

"I'm on the way right now; see you in a bit, Chad."

With that, she hung up the phone and headed out to meet Lisa, who was frantically grabbing everything she thought she might need and tossing it into a bag, as to get out of there before David returned. Then out the door, she went to go and meet Andrea.

Lisa tried to be quick, but with a hurt back moving quickly was next to impossible. She found herself constantly looking over her shoulders to make sure she wasn't being followed, as she was terrified of being caught. If David knew that she was leaving him tonight to be with Chad, he would kill her for sure.

Lisa arrived at the store to find that Andrea was already there waiting.

"Hi Andrea. Sorry it took me so long, my back is killing me."

Andrea put her hand on Lisa's shoulder.

"It's okay, I'm just glad that you made it her safely. Now let's get you the hell out of here, Chad is waiting."

Lisa was scared of being caught, but couldn't wait to see Chad.

"So, how is Chad, anyway? I hope he's not too worried." Andrea nodded as she replied.

"Lisa, he is frantic. He can't even sit still; all he does is pace back and forth across the room waiting for the phone to ring. He loves you, Lisa and he it doesn't matter how many times you tell him not to worry about you, he's still going to."

Lisa was worried.

"Oh Andrea, I can't stand seeing him hurting like this. I have to fix this mess, so maybe we can all rest easy."

Andrea agreed.

"Yes and I sure hope that everything works out for you. Anyway Lisa. It's getting really late. If you don't mind, I'm just going to drop you off and then head home to bed. It's probably better that way too. That way if David does get a hold of my number and call me, I'll be there and I can just tell him you're sleeping or something, so he doesn't freak out."

Lisa laughed.

"David, not freak out? Yeah right, like that would ever happen. I'm going to call him later anyway and explain to him why I left and try and calm him down. Maybe then he'll get sick of me and give me my divorce."

They pulled into Chad's parking lot and Lisa opened the door. Andrea put her hand on Lisa's shoulder.

"Well, good luck, I hope everything works out okay. I'll call you tomorrow and see how you're doing."

Lisa smiled.

"Okay, Andrea, thanks for the lift, I'll talk to you tomorrow."

Andrea pulled away and Lisa headed toward Chad's door. She made it about half way up the walk and Chad came running out.

"Lisa, baby, are you okay? How is your back? Here let me help you inside, relax baby, you're safe now."

Chad then picked her up, carefully not to hurt her back and carried her inside.

"Oh Lisa, I love you so much. I'm sorry if I may seem like a little bit of a wimp, but when I heard that David had a gun, I was frantic with worry."

Lisa stopped him as she put her fingers to his lips.

"Shh, no more. Don't put yourself down, you're not a wimp, you were worried about me and I thank you for that. You really make me feel loved and

I'm glad to have you. There are so many other women out there, living their lives in the same situation that I am in and they have nobody. I am really lucky to someone who cares so much."

Chad hugged her.

"You mean the world to me Lisa. You are truly a sweet and kind woman and I want nothing more, then to make your world a safe and happy one. Now come on, let's sit down and figure out a way to do that."

Lisa sat down on the sofa.

"Yeah sounds good to me, but you know that is all I have done lately. All I keep thinking about is how to get rid of David and I have now come to the conclusion, that the only way to get rid of him is to kill him."

Chad agreed.

"Yeah I've come to that conclusion, too; the only problem is doing it without getting caught."

Lisa rested her head on the back of the sofa.

"Oh, I know. It's not the easiest thing to do. I have thought about it over and over. I thought about putting some sleeping pills into his beer, but that would be too easy to trace. Then I thought about getting a hold of some other drug and adding it to his food or drink so that he would over dose and look like he was just another addict. But I'm just not the type of person to go out and buy drugs; I'm more the type of person who would fight to get rid of them."

Chad rested his head in his hands.

"Well both of those ideas would work, but they're too risky. We have to think of something that would look like an accident, so that there would be no big investigation into his death. You and I both know Lisa that if questioned you would cave and confess. You're just too honest and I don't want to see you ending up behind bars, because of some idiot like David. You just don't deserve that, you've suffered enough already."

Lisa wasn't sure what to do, it all seemed so complicated.

"Well it's not going to be easy; I mean I've never even considered killing anyone before. I guess we had just better make sure we plan it all out well, so there is nothing to incriminate either of us. You know planning it isn't really the hard part though? The hardest part is going to be when it comes right down to actually doing it, can I actually go through with it? This all just seems like a dream. Anyway baby, why don't we just think it over for a while? Right now

I have to call David and see if I can't reason with him, or at least calm him down some." Chad laughed.

"Yeah right! Reason with David? What a joke, like that will ever happen." Lisa picked up the phone.

"Yeah, I know, but I have to at least try, otherwise he'll get a hold of Andrea's number and make her crazy, anyway here goes nothing, wish me luck."

Chad put his hand on her shoulder and watched as she called David.

After only two rings, David picked up and immediately started yelling.

"Lisa, if this is you, you're dead." Lisa laughed.

"Well, David it is me, but no, I'm not dead. In fact, I am very much alive." David continued to yell.

"You stupid bitch, I bet you think you're smart getting sarcastic with me." Lisa was nervous but laughed as she answered.

"Yes, I do, actually. What the hell are you going to do about it? I'm not there so you'll have an awful time trying to hit me now, won't you? Anyway, you drunken son of a bitch. I only called to see if you would be reasonable, but since you're not, I'm going to hang up now."

David calmed down some.

"No, Lisa, don't hang up. What did you want to talk about? I'll listen, just don't hang up yet."

Lisa was stunned.

"Well, this is a switch, getting to you, am I? Anyway, as you have already figured out, I walked out. Pretty gutsy, hey? I am at Andrea's and I have no intention to come home, until you calm down and can learn to control your temper. I have asked you over and over to give me a divorce and you just keep refusing. Therefore, David, until you can stop your shit, I'm gone. I refuse to come home to an abusive drunk, marriage isn't supposed to be that way."

David was becoming angry again, as he tried to play on Lisa's emotions and put the guilt on her.

"Oh, come on, now, Lisa, you deserved it and you know it. You're supposed to listen to your husband, not lip off and disobey him. However, if this is really what you want, I will do my best to control my temper. Now, just get your ass home."

Lisa chuckled.

"What a joke! No way, David, I'm not coming home tonight. I will call you tomorrow and we can discuss this matter further then. For now, however, I think you just need to calm down and think things through."

David raised his voice further.

"Oh, you'll be home tomorrow Lisa, because you'll be scared of what I might do to you if you're not and I have to go and find you. I think I have proven to you by now, just what I am capable of."

Lisa was scared but refused to let it show.

"What, David? What are you going to do? Are you going to kill me? You just think you rule the world, don't you? Listen asshole, you may think you rule the world, but you don't rule me."

David continued.

"Look, Lisa, I've already told you that I won't kill you. I wouldn't give you the satisfaction of death. I will just kill anyone else who gets in the way and I mean anybody. Now, I don't know what more you want from me. I have already promised you, that you can go out whenever you want to, as long as you are home every night by 2:00 am. You know, if you were smart you would just get your ass home here tonight, then I wouldn't have to prove myself."

Lisa felt the tear pooling in her eyes as the fear inside of her built up.

"No, David! I won't come home tonight. I will, however, talk to you tomorrow, but I'm not going to make any promises." David knew that his plan wasn't working, as he tried to act calm.

"Fine, Lisa. Look, I am really sorry and I promise I won't hurt you anymore if you come home, you have my word. I'll be the perfect gentleman, just please come home." Lisa leading him on continued.

"Well, like I said, I'll call you tomorrow. If you still feel that way then, I'll come home."

David, hiding his anger, sighed.

"Well, all right then, I'll talk to you tomorrow. Good night, Lisa, bye."

Lisa hung up the phone from David and turned to Chad with tears in her eyes.

"He's planning something, I don't know exactly what, but he is definitely planning something. That was just too weird; he gave up way too easy."

Chad sat forward.

"What exactly do you mean by weird?"

Lisa wiped a tear that was rolling down her cheek.

"Oh, I don't know. I'm just so tired of trying to figure him out. He was trying to be nice, which is totally unlike him unless he is up to something. He has a plan I know it, I just wish I knew what it was."

Meanwhile back at Lisa's place, David was drinking and his anger was becoming more intense. He was trying to figure out a way to prove to Lisa, that he really does mean business and make her understand that there really was no way out.

He found Lisa's phone book and started calling anyone who knew Andrea; trying to get a hold of her address. He told everyone he was an old boyfriend wanting to see her again. He knew he couldn't take the chance of letting them know who he really was, even though none of Andrea's friends had met him before. It took well over an hour, but finally someone gave it to him her home address.

"Yes, I've got her. Now I can prove just what a little liar she is, I know she's not there and I'm going to prove it. I'll show her just how serious I am, nobody double crosses David Curtis."

David was drunk and in a violent frenzy, as he called a cab and headed for Andrea's. He was determined to get even with Lisa for disobeying him and make damn sure it never happened again.

He arrived at Andrea's and he began pound on the door, demanding that she open it.

"Come on, your stupid, home-wrecking bitch, open the bloody door. Lisa is my wife and I have a right to see her. Now, open the damn door, move it you foolish whore, open up."

Andrea was extremely nervous as she yelled back.

"Go home, David. Lisa is asleep and you're not going to wake her. Whatever you have to say can wait until tomorrow, now leave."

David continued to pound and kick the door

"No, I won't leave, now open the door you stupid slut, before I kick it down."

Andrea became terrified as she knew what David was capable of.

"No David, I won't open the door. Leave now or I will call the police."

Right then David kicked the open and burst into Andrea's house in a fit of rage.

"Where is she, Andrea? Where in the hell is Lisa?"

David was running through the house searching everywhere.

"Tell me where she is, bitch; where in the hell is my wife?" Andrea was horrified as she tried to stay strong.

"David, it is none of your business, now get the hell out of my house or I'm calling the police."

David turned, picked the phone up and ripped it out of the wall.

"Oh, will you, Andrea? I think not."

Andrea was horrified as David hurdled toward her. Then grabbing her he began hitting her over and over. He was tossing her around like a rag doll, as she cried and screamed.

"David please. Leave me alone and just go home. You're drunk and you don't know what you're doing. Please David, please stop."

David continued to beat her, harder and harder.

"Oh yes, Andrea, I know exactly what I am doing. I am getting rid of a good for nothing trouble-maker."

Andrea lay on the floor in pain and too weak to fight back. David walked over to the fireplace and picked a brass poker. Then back to Andrea he began stabbing her over and over again with it.

"I am sorry, Andrea, but Lisa has to learn and your death will be a lesson to her. This will open her eyes to exactly what I am capable of, she'll never go against me again, and I am going to see to that."

After stabbing Andrea 18 times, David ran out, leaving her there on the floor in a pool of her own blood. He wasn't sure if she was dead or alive, as he looked over his shoulder, he noticed her body twitch, but never turned back. He had to get out of there, before someone called the police and he was caught.

As he ran away from the gruesome scene, he prayed that she hadn't survived and was indeed dead. He didn't want to end up behind bars and as long as she was dead, nobody would be able to point the finger at him. As far as anyone else knew, David didn't even know Andrea.

David walked all the way home as he thought to himself about what he done and how he felt his actions were justified.

"Lisa, I've got you now. I have proven myself and you'll never again ask me for a divorce. You're stuck with me, baby, for life and I will have my way. You'll never go against me again."

David was proud of himself for what he had done, to him it was a victory and one he wanted to celebrate as he sat down with a bottle of rye. He was still furious with Lisa and wondered where she was. But was positive that once she heard of Andrea's death, she would come crawling right back home.

Meanwhile, Lisa sat with Chad. Still talking about ways to kill David and get him out of the picture for good. They had no idea that David had just murdered Andrea or what was to come. All they knew was that they needed to free Lisa once and for all, before she ended up dead herself.

At this point, Lisa had finally figured out the perfect plan and it was only a matter of time, before she followed through. She prayed that her plan would work and she would finally be free to live a safe and happy life.

As she lay in Chad's arms in the sofa, he gently rubbed her sore and bruised back.

"I hope we get away with this. I love you, Lisa and I can't stand to lose you. This is a good plan though, fool proof and will definitely look like an accident. Now all we have to do is cross our fingers and hope it all plays out."

Lisa nodded.

"Yeah, I'm sure it will work out perfect. For now though, all I really want to do is get some sleep. I am exhausted and my back is really sore. Can I borrow one of your shirts to wear to bed?"

Chad smiled and kissed her sweetly.

"Of course you can, help yourself. You have had an exhausting day, I am sure you will rest better tonight though, knowing that you are here safe in my arms."

Lisa got up from the sofa.

"Yes it has been an exhausting day, total hell actually. Now let's go and get some sleep shall we."

Chad agreed as they headed into the bedroom. Then just as they started to settle down into bed, there was a knock at the door.

Lisa panicked.

"Oh no Chad! Who could it be at this hour? You don't think its David, do you?"

Chad jumped up.

"Relax, honey; I don't think he could possibly find you here. I'll go and see who it is."

Chad opened the door to find two police officers on the other side.

"Hello, sir, are you Chad Roberts?" Chad was stunned.

"Yes can I help you officers?" The officers continued.

"Well, I hope so. Do you by any chance know a woman by the name of Andrea Barker?"

Chad had a horrible feeling in the pit of his stomach. "Yeah, I do, she's a friend of my girlfriends. Is there something wrong?"

The officers had a blank look on their faces as they answered.

"Yes, I am afraid that there has been some foul play. Miss Barker is dead and it appears that she's been murdered. We found your name and address in her phone directory, along with several others. You're the first person we've actually been able to track down."

Chad freaked out.

"Andrea is dead? No, that is impossible, she couldn't be dead. She just drove Lisa and I home here a few hours ago and she was fine. How can this be? Andrea is such a sweet person and innocent, too. Who would kill her and why?"

The officers went on to further question Chad.

"Did she seem upset at all? Or angry? Did she have a date coming over that you know of? Someone she may have run into this evening?"

Chad shook his head.

"No, I don't think so. She was with Lisa and me all night, then said she was tired and went home to bed."

Right then Lisa came out of the bedroom.

"Chad, what is wrong? What is going on, you look upset? Chad has something happened?" Chad took her into his arms.

"Lisa, its Andrea. They found her tonight; it appears that she was murdered."

Lisa burst into tears and began screaming frantically. "No, not Andrea, it can't be. You're lying, how can you say something so horrible? She just left here a few hours ago, it can't be her, there's no way, not Andrea."

Chad hugged her and held her tight as she continued to cry.

"Andrea is my best friend. We've always been there for each other; we've been best friends for 15 years. If she had a problem with somebody, why didn't she tell me? Oh God this is crazy, it can't be her, it can't be Andrea."

The officers, knowing that this was a shock, continued.

"We are sorry to bring you this horrible news; we know that this must be a huge shock to you. But are you willing to help us, so that we can find her killer?"

Lisa jumped.

"How can you even ask that question? Of course I'll help; I'll do whatever I can."

Chad agreed. "Yes and so will I."

The officers went on.

"Great. Any information you can give us would help a great deal. We have not been able to locate any family and we need a positive identification for the record."

Lisa interrupted.

"Well her parents are both dead, she does have a sister who lives in New York. If would help, I suppose I could identify the body."

The officers agreed.

"That would be great, we know it won't be easy but we do need positive identification in order to proceed with the investigation. I do have to warn you though, it's not a pretty sight and she won't look as you remember her."

Lisa began to cry again.

"I understand. I just want to do whatever I can to help." Lisa went to grab her purse so she and Chad could go with the officers to identify Andrea's body. She was still in shock and very confused by all of this, as she asked.

"Where did it happen? How did she die? Or do I even want to know?"

The officers answered.

"It happened in her own home, she was stabbed to death."

Lisa still unbelieving of the whole situation wiped the tears that rolled down her cheeks.

"This is just so hard to believe. I keep thinking that I'm just having a bad nightmare and I'm going to wake up. Oh God, how I pray that it isn't her, I hope that you were mistaken and it isn't Andrea."

Lisa and Chad headed to morgue with the officers. Lisa was still hysterical and couldn't believe that Andrea was dead. She couldn't think of anyone that may have wanted her dead and the thought of David killing her, never even crossed her mind. As far as she knew David didn't have Andrea's address and he was already at home drunk and by this hour, he would most likely be passed out for the night.

They arrived at the morgue and one of the officers took Lisa and Chad into a tiny little room, where Andrea's body lay. The officer pulled back the sheet that covered her body and right away, Lisa screamed.

"Oh no. Andrea. It's her, its Andrea. Who did this to her? Why Andrea? I wanted to believe that it wasn't her; I prayed that it wasn't her, but it is. Why? How could this happen?"

Chad grabbed Lisa to hold her up, and then led her out of the room. She was a complete wreck and crying hysterically. When Andrea dropped her off at Chad's, she never expected that it would be the last time she saw her or that only hours later, she would be brutally murdered. This was a total shock and Lisa found it very hard to accept.

Chad told the officers everything that they knew, right up until the time that Andrea dropped Lisa off at his place.

"I wish I could have known. I could stop her from leaving. Andrea and Lisa have always been close and I think that if something were wrong. Andrea would have told her."

The officer shook Chad's hand.

"Well thanks for all of your help. We'll keep you informed of our findings and if we have any further questions, we will contact you. I'm really sorry about your friend. Now, why don't you take Lisa home, she's had a rough night."

Chad looked over at Lisa, sitting on a bench in the corner with a blank look on her face.

"Okay, thanks sir. Feel free to call with any questions; we'll do anything we can to help."

Chad walked over and helped Lisa up, then held her in his arms as he led her down to a cab to head home.

"Lisa. You don't think that David did this do you?" Lisa shook her head.

"No I don't think so, he was home drunk and he doesn't even know where Andrea lives. Besides that, what point would there be in David killing Andrea?"

Then Lisa thought about it for a minute and exclaimed.

"Oh my God Chad! The phone call tonight. David told me that he was going to prove to me just what he was capable of and how far he would go. He said he wouldn't kill me, but he would kill anybody who got in his way. Maybe he did do it, maybe he did kill Andrea. Oh God Chad, if this is true then it's all my fault."

Chad jumped in.

"No, it's not your fault Lisa so don't feel that way. But honey, if David did do this, then you are in more trouble than we ever thought. You can't go home now at all, it's too dangerous."

Lisa shook her head.

"No Chad that is where you're wrong. If he did do this, then I have to go home. If I don't turn up at home, he'll kill you too. I'm not about to take that chance. I was considering not killing David, but if I find out that he did kill Andrea, I'm following through with everything just as planned."

Chad was terrified for Lisa.

"Lisa no, you can't go home, he'll kill you too." Lisa was shaking.

"No, he won't kill me. He wants me around to take care of his needs."

Chad hated the idea of her going back home to David. "Maybe so, but I really wish you wouldn't go back. If you really believe this is what you have to do, I won't hold you back, but I really don't like the idea of you being there with him."

They arrived back at Chad's and right away Lisa called David.

He was furious and started yelling the second he picked up the phone.

"Lisa, I figured you'd be calling. Where in the hell are you? I know that you are not at Andrea's." Lisa cut in.

"How do you know that?" David laughed.

"Because I was there and I left you a little example of just what I will do, if you go against me."

Lisa was in shock. "You did it, didn't you?"

David snarled.

"Damn straight I did and Lisa, my dear, if you even dare to tell the police, I'll point the finger at you. Then, while you're in prison, I'll kill everyone else you know, including your Mr. Pretty boy. Now, you have 30 minutes to be home, or I'm going out to kill somebody else that you care about." Lisa began to cry and screamed into the phone.

"My God David, how could you do this? How could you kill Andrea?"

David laughed a vicious laugh, and then continued. "Look Lisa, just tell me that you're coming home and we'll talk then."

Lisa wanted to tell him to go to hell, but agreed. "Yes David, I'll be there soon. Goodbye."

Lisa hung up the phone from David. She was terrified to go home, but she was so brainwashed by David, that she believed anything he said and truly believed that there was nothing else she could do.

Chad saw the fear in her eyes and knew something was wrong.

"What is it, baby? What did he say?" Lisa began to cry.

"He did it, he killed her and if I'm not home in half an hour, he said he'll kill someone else, so I have to go. I can't let anyone else pay the price for my actions."

Chad panicked.

"You can't go home to him. Why don't we turn him in?" She continued.

"No Chad, I can't. If I turn him in, he's going to point the finger at me and then kill you. He'll do it Chad and we both know that."

Chad was frantic.

"Lisa please baby, don't go. He'll kill you and I can't bear to lose you. Please reconsider."

Lisa hugged him.

"Please, Chad calm down. I have to go, there's no other way. Besides remember the plan? If I don't go home, I can't go through with it. Just please relax honey. I'll be fine and I'll see you tomorrow night. I love you, Chad and I'll be all yours really soon."

Chad still didn't like the idea, but kissed her and walked her to the door. Lisa then left, to head back home to her abusive husband, who was now a murderer.

She was terrified and still in shock that David had killed Andrea. She was innocent in all of this and now she was dead needlessly. Lisa blamed herself, if she had only stayed home, this never would have happened. She was now more sure than ever that David deserved to die and that it was the right thing to do. Her only problem now, was finding the right moment and having the guts to go through with it.

As she pulled up her driveway, her heart began to pound as she feared what was coming. She knew that David was drunk and had already killed once, so she had to try and remain calm. Agitating him would only make things worse and she needed to play things as safe as possible.

Lisa sat in the car for a few minutes, to get herself under control. She had been through enough for one night and needed to just sit and relax and get a grip on things before heading inside.

Back at Chad's he was going out of his mind with worry. David had already killed Andrea and he believed that he wouldn't hesitate to kill Lisa too.

He sat alone in his room, staring up at the ceiling and waiting for the phone to ring. He became very shaky thinking about the hell that Lisa must be going through at home and all the pain that Andrea had suffered.

He couldn't believe how sick David was and how much pain he had caused to wonderful women. He was becoming extremely frustrated, as he picked up a glass off his bedside table and threw it across the room, smashing it on the wall.

"Goddammit. What the hell is this? Was does life have to be so bloody hard? Why do people have to suffer like this?"

Chad picked up Lisa's blouse off the bed and held it to his chest, as he began to cry.

"Oh Lisa, please baby, be okay. Don't let him win, make him suffer the way you have."

Then he looked up.

"Oh please, dear God, please take care of her, don't let him hurt her anymore, she doesn't deserve this."

Chad then laid down by the phone and soon drift off to sleep.

By this point, Lisa had finally made it out of the car and was headed into the house. Right as she walked through the door, she heard David calling to her.

"Lisa, is that you? I'm upstairs, I'll be right down."

Lisa was confused. David was acting cheery, as if nothing had happened, all the while, he had just committed murder. She was tired. She had been up all night, dealing with David's crap and Andrea's death. She couldn't handle much more, especially David's Mr. nice guy act.

David came downstairs, with a big smile on his face. "Hi dear, boy do you look tired. Don't worry I won't keep you up long, I just want to talk a bit and then you can go to sleep."

Lisa was in complete shock, it was like she was caught in the twilight zone. This couldn't be reality, it was just too strange. She pinched herself to make sure that she was awake.

"David, what has gotten into you? You just killed my best friend and yet, you're acting like you've just won the lottery or something. Are you completely insane? Have you lost what little mind you had left?" David smiled.

"Oh Lisa relax, get a grip. You asked me to control my temper with you, so I am. I took all my frustrations out on your little friend instead. Which by the way, my dear, was your fault."

This was just too much, David was right out of it.

"Sorry David, but you are wrong. It wasn't my fault at all, it was all you. If you would just let me go, then life would be a whole lot better. You're an abusive son of a bitch and I am not putting up with it anymore. You just murdered Andrea and why? Because you wanted to get even with me. I am sorry David but that is sick, so why don't you just get a grip?"

David continued to remain clam.

"Well Lisa, obviously you are too tired to talk reasonably right now."

David's attitude completely blew Lisa away. She was now more confused than ever and had no idea what was going on, or what was coming next. David had suddenly done a complete turn around and this terrified Lisa more than ever.

As she headed up to bed, she wondered what he was up to. She wondered if he would become violent again and kill her in her sleep. He had never acted this way before and she wasn't sure what to make of it. Now more than ever, she was convinced that he had completely lost his mind, this wasn't David he was acting like someone she never knew.

As Lisa got into bed, completely exhausted, she thought about the night's events. Tonight she had lost her best friend to David's violence and she now knew that it was time to get even. David has to be stopped before he killed again.

Chapter Six

After a long and restless night, with the past night events spiraling through her head, Lisa awoke. To her surprise, it was already two o'clock in the afternoon and shocking her further, David wasn't even angry. In fact, he seemed to be quite the opposite.

Lisa wondered how this could be, was it her that was losing her mind? Had she imagined everything and things were really okay? Nothing seemed right to her, this wasn't normal.

She slowly headed downstairs, unsure of what waited for her, to find David sitting on the sofa watching television.

"Good afternoon Lisa. Did you sleep well?"

Lisa was incredibly confused, thinking she was for sure losing her mind.

Then as she picked up the newspaper from the coffee table and read the headlines. "Woman brutally murdered in her own home" and saw Andrea's picture, it hit her. She knew that it hadn't been a dream and her nightmare was real, she was living with her best friend's killer and Andrea had died simply to prove a point.

Lisa began to shake and cry and she held the paper in hands, this infuriated David.

"Lisa, what the hell is your problem? Stop your damn blubbering, I haven't done anything to you today, so what's with the water works?"

Lisa was stunned with the cold blank look on David's face.

"What is with the water fall, David? How can you even say that? You know what you did, you killed my best friend! It wasn't enough, that you were already putting me through hell. Beating the tar out of me every day and making me live in this prison. You had to kill an innocent person."

"You're crazy, David, you've completely lost your mind!" David chuckled.

"It's you who makes me this way, Lisa!"

"If you would just listen to me and do what you're told, things like this wouldn't happen."

"I've warned you, time and time again, that if you ever went against me, you'd have to learn the hard way."

"Now perhaps with the influence, of your dear friend Andrea, you'll start doing as you're told, like a good wife should."

Lisa wasn't sure what to make of it all, as she shook with fear.

"David, you really are insane! If you wanted to punish me, then why didn't you just kill me? Why did you have to kill Andrea?"

David laughed and his got up from sofa.

"Lisa, Lisa, Lisa, you're such an idiot…don't you get it?"

Lisa shook her head.

"No, David, I don't get it. Why don't you explain it to me?" David continued.

"Killing Andrea, was the perfect way to make you suffer and feel guilty. There's no suffering in killing you. That just ends it painlessly. You needed to pay for crossing me."

Lisa became hysterical. She couldn't believe, that all of this had come down to murder. She was trapped in this marriage, stuck with David. Fighting day in and day out to survive. It was now apparent, there was only one way out and one way to free herself, David had to die.

Then as Lisa stood there a complete wreck, David pushed his way past.

"I'm going out!"

Lisa lifted her head and grinned sarcastically.

"What else is new?"

David let that one slide as he continued.

"I'll be home by three a.m. and you'd better be here. I don't care if you go out, I don't care what the hell you do. Just be in that door before I get here and not even a minute after. Do you understand that, Lisa? Or, do I have to spell it out for you darling?"

Lisa felt small as got up enough courage to yell back.

"Yes, you stupid jerk! I'm not totally stupid, you know? The only stupid thing, I've ever done was marry you! No worries David, I'll be here, so just go! Get out of here and leave me the hell alone!"

David shook his head.

Tsk, tsk, tsk.

"You'll never learn, will you? You're always so sarcastic. One of these days Lisa, one of these days." Lisa jumped in.

"What, David, what! One of these days you'll put me out my misery? Good! Then I'll be rid of you!"

David laughed as he walked out slamming the door behind him.

Lisa sat down on the sofa, hung her head and began to cry, as she mourned the loss of her dear friend. David had taken a life needlessly and it was all because of her and her stupidity.

"Oh God, I should never have left. What was I thinking? What am I doing?"

"Oh, how I pray, I pray that David never catches up with Chad."

As Lisa sat at home crying, Chad sat alone, beside himself with worry. He wondered if Lisa was okay. David had already killed once and there was nothing stopping him from killing Lisa too.

He reached over and picked up the phone to make sure it was working, then slammed it down.

"RING DAMN IT RING!"

"Lisa has to be okay, she just has to be. Please, baby, be okay!" Chad paced the house, waiting for the phone to ring, waiting for some word from Lisa. He was worried sick and knowing that there was nothing he could do, only made things harder to deal with.

The more he thought about the situation, the more frantic he became. He had to know she was alright.

He realized, that by calling her, he'd be taking a chance. A chance that David would pick, but he had to know.

Chad picked up the phone.

"If he answers I'll hang up, but I just have to speak to Lisa."

Chad's hands shook as he dialed the numbers and the phone began ring.

It rang once, twice…then on the third ring it was answered. Lisa picked up.

"Hello"

Chad jumped right in to it.

"Lisa, oh my God baby, are you alright?"

"I've been so worried."

"Is he there?"

"Can you talk?"

Lisa sighed as she replied. "Yea I can talk, he just left."

"I'm sorry I didn't call you sooner, I've just been so upset…"

Chad stopped her.

"Honey, it's okay, there's nothing to be sorry about. I'm just glad that you're okay."

"Did he hurt you?"

Lisa felt a lump her throat, as if she were going to cry again but held back.

"No he didn't hurt me, he was actually calm today, he even let me sleep in."

"Chad I really am getting tired of all this crap. I just can't take it anymore, I almost wish I was dead. None of this would be happening, if I were out of the picture. I just want to die."

Chad became furious.

"Lisa! What are you saying?"

"Stop that talk, right now! Killing yourself isn't going to solve anything. You'll just be letting him win."

Lisa began to cry uncontrollably.

"I just can't handle it anymore and killing myself would be so easy. I would finally be able to rest."

"I love you, Chad and I don't want to leave you. I just hate the fact, that I am endangering your life, by involving you in my problems. I'm sorry, Chad, but it really is the only way. Please forgive me, but this is goodbye."

Lisa then hung up the phone.

Chad was frantic. Lisa was about to take her own life and he wasn't there to stop her. He quickly grabbed his car keys and ran out without even shutting the door behind him and headed for Lisa's.

Chad was shaking with fear, that he would be too late. "Come on, Lisa, think baby, just calm down and think. Don't do it, don't let David win."

He tried calling her from his cell, but her phone just rang and rang with no answer.

Lisa was an emotional wreck and by this point, had already taken a bottle of sleeping pills, dissolved them in a glass of whisky and drank it.

Then as she lay on the sofa, becoming extremely drowsy. She thought about Andrea and how because of her and her screwed up marriage to David, she had been brutally murdered. Lisa blamed herself and believed, that by taking her own life. She would be saving other people from being hurt or possibly killed.

Then as she drifted off into a peaceful sleep, the door flew open and Chad ran in, to find her laying limp on the sofa. He ran to her side, praying she was still alive. He put his fingers to her neck and checked her pulse.

"Thank God, you're still alive! Lisa what have you done?" Then deciding there was no time to wait on an ambulance, Chad grabbed the empty bottle, scooped up Lisa and carried her to his car. As he rushed to the hospital he was in a panic. Lisa was dying, right there next to him and there was nothing he could do to save her. He wished he had been there to stop her and at that moment vowed, that he would always be there for her, no matter what it took. Nobody, not even David was going to keep him away from her, not anymore.

They arrived at the hospital and Chad ran through the doors with Lisa in his arms yelling for help.

"HELP! Somebody please hurry, you've got to help her, she's dying."

A doctor ran right over and took Lisa out of Chad's arms and rushed her in to an examination room and Chad followed.

As the doctor began to check her over, he turned to Chad. "What exactly happened here?"

Chad was shaking fearing for Lisa's life.

"She took a bottle of pills, I found the empty bottle on the counter next to an empty bottle of whiskey."

"She called me, she was really depressed and told me she was going to do this. I tried to get there, but I guess I wasn't quick enough."

The doctor took the empty bottle from Chad.

"Well, she's still alive, so I wouldn't say that. You got her here, where we can help her and that is the most important thing."

"Now just to get that stuff out of her and hope for the best."

"Do you have any idea, why she would want to take her own life?"

Chad wasn't sure Lisa would want him telling her story, but at this point he had no choice.

"Well she lost her best friend the other day, she was murdered. Then she's had other problems, so I'm sure it was a combination of it all."

The doctor continued to work on Lisa. "What kind of problems?"

Chad continued.

"Well, she's been having a lot of trouble at home. He husband abuses her, he's a drunk and beats on her every chance he gets. I've been trying to help her, but I guess, she needed more help than I could give her."

The doctor shook his head.

"Hmm I should have guessed. See, this all the time, abused women attempting to take their own life. They get so emotionally unstable, they believe the only way out is to end their lives and it's not."

"Unfortunately, all we can do here, is try to save them. We can't fix the problems at home, only they can do that."

"We can advise them though, to get out of the relationship and seek counseling. However, that is usually easier said than done."

Chad was listening to the doctor, but it all seemed distant as he worried about Lisa.

"Is she going to be okay? I really care about her and I need to know she'll be okay."

The doctor shook his head as he filled out Lisa's chart. "Well, we've done all we can do here, now it's just wait and see. She'll be closely monitored, until she awakes and then for a day or two afterwards. As it stands right now, she's stable and should pull through."

Chad was relieved yet still worried. "How long before she'll wake up?" Unsure the doctor answered.

"It's hard to say, everybody's body is different. Some wake up in a couple of hours and others longer. See, some stay out for more than a day. Do you know how to get in touch with her husband? He'll need to be contacted."

Chad sighed.

"Yeah, I figured as much. He'll be at the bar, he's always there between three in the afternoon until around two in the morning. The bar is called Sammy's, they all know him there so it shouldn't be hard to get in touch with him. His name is David."

The doctor wrote the information down on his note pad. "Same last name?"

Chad shook his head. "Yes, unfortunately."

The doctor headed out.

"Okay thanks, we'll get in touch with him. I'll check back a little later."

Chad sat at Lisa's bedside, holding her hand as she lay there looking lifeless and he began to cry.

"Lisa, how could this happen? I should have been there for you."

"Sweetie, come on, you have to pull through this, I love you, baby and I need you. I promise you this will never happen again, I won't let it. Just get well, baby, so we can be together."

Right then the doctor returned.

"Well we spoke with her husband, he's on his way. He said he would get Paula to drive him. Who's Paula?"

Chad smirked and shook his head.

"Oh, she's his girlfriend. Not only does he beat on Lisa, but he cheats on her as well and yet won't divorce her."

The doctor shook his head as he checked on Lisa. "He's one of those guys, is he? A real piece of work!"

"Well, as I said before, I can't help her with the problems at home. I can only help her while she's here and give her some much needed advice. Other than that, it's up to her to do the right thing and get out of the relationship."

"I'll be back to check on her a little later."

With that, the doctor left.

Chad knew that David was on the way and was confused. Torn between staying and leaving. He loved Lisa and needed to be with her and there when she woke up. Yet he worried, that if David found him there, he would take it out on Lisa and things would be worse.

Then before he could decide what to do, he heard the doctor talking to someone outside the door. It was David, he and Paula had already arrived.

Chad jumped up, unsure what to do. He knew that David would freak out when he found him there, but there was no way out now. He and Paula were outside the door.

Right then the door opened and David walked in. To Chad's surprise, he wasn't angry.

"Thank you for bringing Lisa to the hospital." David said. "I'm here now though, so you're free to leave. Lisa dumped you, so stay the hell away from her." Chad stood up and shook his head.

"No, I am here as Lisa's friend and I'm not leaving, until I know that she's okay."

David was shocked as Chad continued.

"Yeah, Lisa dumped me, but that doesn't mean I cannot remain her friend. Besides that, if I hadn't shown up, she would have died. You never would have gotten home in time."

David was impressed and gave Chad a shove. "FINE THEN STAY, for now anyway."

Then he turned to Lisa, still laying lifeless in her hospital bed.

"You stupid bloody, bitch!"

"If you think you're getting away from me that easily, you're wrong. Mr. Pretty Boy here may have saved you, but you're mine. Just wait until I get you home, you ruined a perfect bar night with this little stunt of you yours."

David then started slapping her cheek.

"Come on bitch, wake up! Wake up and face the music." Chad jumped up and grabbed David's arm.

"STOP! Why the hell don't you just leave her alone? It's your bloody fault that she's here in the first place. Isn't that enough for you? What more do you need? She almost died and all you can do is slap her and call her a bitch? Show a little respect, or is that too hard for you?"

David laughed as she shook Chad's hand off his arm. "Wow, you're a geek!"

"You know nothing about women man, this is what they deserve. If you treat them any different, they'll walk all over you."

"Come on, pal. I think it's time you faced reality." Chad was furious.

"Sorry buddy, but it's you who needs to face reality."

"You treat people like shit and it's you who walks all over people, not Lisa."

David became angry and he clenched his fists at Chad. "Listen pal! I said you could stay here, but I didn't say you could speak. If you want to remain here with MY wife, then just shut the hell up."

Chad wanted to just haul off and hit David, right in the mouth. Not wanting to risk being kicked out of the hospital though, he didn't.

"Fine David, I'll keep quiet, but not for you, for Lisa." Then as Lisa remained unconscious, David began yelling.

Demanding that she stop this game of hers and wake up, so he could get back to the bar.

Then Paula, who was getting tired of waiting, walked in. "Come on David, let's just leave."

"Obviously, she's not going to wake up tonight. So, why let her and her stupidity ruin the entire night?"

David laughed and snickered. "Yeah, you're probably right." Paula continued.

"Besides, there's not much point in yelling at her tonight anyway. It's not like she can hear you."

David agreed as he headed for the door.

"Yeah, no point crying over spilt milk I guess. If she wants to be an idiot and try something as stupid as this. Then she deserves to be alone, anyway."

Then he looked to Chad.

"Okay pretty boy, I'm out of here. I don't care if you stay, but you best realize, that once she's out of here, you're out of her life for good."

Then with that, he and Paula left, headed back to the bar. Chad was furious with the way David had treated Lisa. "What an asshole! I can't wait to see him six feet under, I hope he rots in hell!"

He walked back over to Lisa's beside and sat down. He took her hand into his.

"Baby, I don't know if you can hear me, but I love you. You don't deserve this and I promise you, baby, I will never treat you the way David does. You're my angel, just please get well."

With that, being totally exhausted. Chad laid his head down on the bed next to Lisa and closed his eyes.

As he rested there, thinking of Lisa, he suddenly felt the sweet caress of her hand, through his hair and heard the quiet whisper of her voice.

"Chad, where am I?"

Chad jumped up and a tear rolled down his cheek.

"Oh sweetie, thank God! I've never been happier to hear your voice."

"You're in the hospital baby. Luckily, I got to you in time and you're going to be alright."

"Let me get the doctor."

Lisa was still groggy as she took his hand and stopped him.

"Chad wait! I'm sorry baby, I didn't want to do this. I just couldn't see any other way out this mess. I love you and didn't want to leave you. I just can't take any more of this with David. I just can't."

Chad kissed her sweetly and then stroked his hand through her hair.

"Don't be sorry sweetheart, David is an ass and treats like shit. Killing yourself though, would have been letting him and win and he doesn't deserve to win. Not this battle, this battle is yours to win. Now let me get the doctor."

Chad headed out the nurse's desk to have the doctor paged and then back to Lisa, where he found her sitting silent and crying.

"Chad, I am so sorry for all of this. Can you ever forgive me?"

Chad wiped her tears away and winked.

"Sweetie, I've already forgiven you and I'm here for you." Then as Chad sat by her side, the doctor came in.

"Well, I see our sleeping beauty is awake."

Chad got up from the bed so the doctor could have a look at Lisa.

"You gave everybody a pretty big scare, Lisa. What were you thinking?"

Not knowing, how much the doctor already knew, Lisa was unsure how to respond.

"I don't know what I was thinking. It was stupid I know. I didn't really want to die."

The doctor continued.

"Well, Chad here has filled me in a little bit about your situation and I had the pleasure of meeting you husband. You really need to think about what you want to do. There are people who can help you, if you don't want to go back."

Lisa stopped him.

"I have to go back home, David won't let me go, he'll just find me and people will get hurt in the process."

The doctor wasn't impressed with Lisa's response.

"Well, it's too bad, you're making a mistake not getting out while you have the chance. Anyway dear, you seem to be doing a lot better, things look good. I'll be back to check on you in a bit. Please at least think about what I said, it's really for your own good."

With that, the doctor left and Chad sat back down with Lisa. She was shocked that David had been there.

"David, was here? He actually left the bar to come here? He'll be furious when I get home and…" Chad hushed her.

"Shh…Relax. Yes, he and Paula were both here, they've gone back to the bar now and he said he'd be back tomorrow. Honey, he acted like a royal asshole and proved how little he cares for you. I just don't understand why, he won't let you go."

Lisa was really confused.

"I don't understand it. He didn't flip out when he found you here? What did you say? That is totally unlike David." Chad went on.

"No, he didn't flip out at all. He actually stayed fairly calm and even thanked me for bringing you the hospital. He did, however, warn me, that once you were released from here, I was to stay away from you. I have no intentions on listening to that bullshit though. I'll see you, whether he likes it or not."

Lisa was stunned and more confused than ever before.

"David let you stay and didn't start a fight?"

"David is never calm. He's always piped up and arguing with somebody. All he ever does is yell and hit people. He's planning something. I don't know what it is, but he definitely has something up his sleeve. This just isn't normal and it scares the hell out of me."

Chad kissed her cheek. "Honey, relax!"

"I know David is acting strange lately, but you can't let it get to you."

"Who knows, maybe Paula is having a good effect on him. Although, she's pretty uncaring herself. She came here tonight with David and all she really cared about was getting back to the bar."

"I mean David was like that, too, but he's always been that way, so it didn't surprise me. Paula however, really stunned me. I never realized she could be so cold. Maybe those two are meant to be together, both cold ignorant people."

Lisa smirked.

"Well, I have seen that side of her before and she really can be selfish, when she wants to be."

Right then the doctor came back in. "How's our patient doing?"

Lisa sat up.

"I'm a little groggy, but other than that, I feel fine. You have to believe me, this was a stupid mistake and I don't plan on ever trying this again."

The doctor checked her pulse and then starting writing in her chart.

"Well, you're very lucky young lady, you could easily have died from what you took. I had better not see you back here in this condition, think long and hard about what I said earlier."

Lisa agreed as the doctor turned to Chad. "Can I speak with you in the hallway please?" Chad headed to the door.

"Certainly, Lisa I'll be right back."

Once in the hallway, the doctor explained the situation to Chad.

"Well, she's very lucky. She seems to have pulled right out of it and I can't see any serious side effects. Talking to her, I honestly don't believe she really wanted to die. I feel she was just very confused and still is, however I don't feel that she is a threat to herself any longer. Now provided she continues to recover and has no complications, she should be able to go home tomorrow."

Chad was thrilled.

"That's great, I am so happy to hear she's going to be okay. I agree that she never really wanted to die and was just confused. I don't believe she'll ever try this again either and from what she told me, she really does regret it."

The doctor shook Chad's hand.

"Well, let's just hope we're both right. This is no way for her to escape the abuse. If she does decide she wants to get out the right way, there's a battered women's group right here at the hospital. I would be more than happy to give her the name and number of the councilor, so she can get help to move on."

Chad thanked the doctor as he turned to head back. "Well, thank you, I will definitely let her know."

Chad rushed back in to be with Lisa, thrilled she was going to be okay.

"Well, sweetie, the doctor says you're doing well and you'll most likely be able to go home tomorrow. We both agree, that you're going to get through this and that you are no longer a threat to yourself."

Lisa was shocked.

"What do you mean, a threat to myself? The only threat to me is David, you and I both know that. God, I can't wait to get out of here, then I can finally take care of him once and for all. A threat to myself, yeah right!"

Chad kissed her cheek and took her hand.

"Calm down now, I'm sorry. I didn't mean to upset you, but you did try to commit suicide. So at one point, yes you were a threat to yourself. I didn't mean to imply that David wasn't a threat. I know better than anyone, that he is the real reason you're even here, it's his abuse that drove you to this. Please, forgive me if I came across wrong, I didn't mean too."

Lisa leaned in to him and put her head on his shoulder. "No Chad, you didn't. I've just been so damn frustrated with all of this, that sometimes I overreact and well, this was the result this time."

Chad held her close.

"I know sweetie, I know. It's just a matter of time though, before we set things right. Now listen honey, it's really getting late. I'm going to head home and get some rest and let you do the same. I'll stop by in the morning to see you, before you go home. It will be early though, so I don't run into David and cause a problem."

Lisa sighed.

"You do look pretty tired, baby. Okay, I guess I'll see you in the morning then. I love you."

Chad kissed her forehead.

"I love you, too, now get some rest. See you in the morning." Then as Chad turned to leave, Lisa stopped him.

"Oh and one more thing Chad. Tomorrow night is the night." Chad looked confused.

"The night? The night for what?" She went on.

"Tomorrow night I'm going to do it, I'm going to kill, David. Provided everything goes as planned, I'll be rid of him for good and nobody will ever know, that I had anything to do with it."

Chad kissed her one last time and then winked.

"Well, keep your fingers crossed, sweetie and we'll hope for the best. See you in the morning, bye, dear."

After Chad left, Lisa lay there in her hospital bed, dreaming about her life without David. She wanted to be happy and with him gone, she finally could be. By killing David, in her eyes, he was getting exactly what he deserved and she would never again have to suffer that raff of his abuse. As she lay there thinking, she tried to come up with reasons why she shouldn't go through with it and couldn't think of one.

David was cold and heartless and all he cared about, was himself and the bottle. She knew that Paula would be hurt, losing David. But believed she would soon realize, she was better off without him. After all, it was only a matter of time, before David turned on her and started beating her as well.

Lisa had now convinced herself, that this was the right thing to do. She would be freeing herself and Paula right along with her and avenging Andrea's death at the same time. She believed, the world would be a better place without David in it. He had pushed her to the limit and it was time to end it. After all, this was his doing, it was him who had driven her to this.

Meanwhile back at Chad's. He sat thinking about Lisa and their plan. He tried to justify to himself, what they were planning and it all seemed right. He also believed, that once David was dead, justice would finally be served and the world would be a much better place. Lisa had suffered the raff of David, for almost nine years now. She was constantly trying to find a way to escape the violence and he kept her in that prison he called a marriage. Now it seemed, the only way to escape, was to kill the one person holding her back, her husband.

Chad was proud of Lisa, for what she going to do. David was finally going to pay the ultimate price, for what he had done to her. He never before, thought he was capable of wishing someone dead. Or that he would ever be proud of someone for planning a murder, but this time he was. He couldn't wait until the moment that he saw David's body laid to rest, under six feet of earth.

Chad was a little stunned, that it had come to this, but was determined to help and set the woman he loved free from all of the abuse.

He was exhausted, yet nervous. So as he lay in bed, all he could do was toss and turn, unable to sleep and before long, the sun was coming up.

The next morning, bright and early the doctor returned to see Lisa.

"Good morning, Lisa."

"Well, I've gone over your chart and I don't see why you can't go home."

"So if you'd like to give someone a call to pick you up, you're free to go."

Lisa was thrilled.

"Really? Thank you for everything you did for me, I appreciate it."

The doctor tapped the bed.

"No problem, just don't try anything like this ever again, got it?"

Lisa agreed.

"No worries there, I plan on living a long and happy life. This was just a foolish mistake." He smiled and winked at her.

"Good to hear, bye Lisa, take care now."

Lisa wasn't sure what to do, if she waited for David to get up, call a cab and come to get her, she could wait all day. All she wanted to do now, was get out of there, so she decided to take the chance and call Chad.

"Good morning sexy, how are you? Did you sleep well?" Chad was thrilled to hear from her.

"Good morning sweetie, I'm good and you definitely sound better. What's up?"

She continued.

"Well darling, I've been discharged and need a ride home."

"I don't want to wait for David, that could take all day and I just want out of here. Could you come and…?" Chad stopped her.

"Of course, I'll come and get you. Just let me grab a quick shower, get dressed and I'll be there. See you soon, sweetie."

Lisa blew a kiss into the phone.

"Thank you baby, I love you, see you soon."

Then as Lisa got dressed and ready to go home, a nurse came in to get her.

"Lisa, you have a call at nurse's station." Lisa was shocked.

"A call, who is it? I don't think anybody knows I'm here." The nurse answered.

"It's a David Curtis, he says he's your husband." Lisa's heart began to pound.

"Oh great, just what I need right now. Okay."

She headed down to take the call, wondering why David would be calling her. Especially at this time of the morning, he was never up before noon.

"Hello David, what would you like?"

David chuckled.

"Well now, come on Lisa! Is that anyway to talk to me? Especially after your foolish little suicide attempt. I only called to see if you were alright and you snap at me?"

Lisa was becoming furious as she clenched her fists.

"Yeah right David! You only called to see if I was dead yet."

"Well sorry pal, I'm alive and well and I'll be home soon. A friend of mine is picking me up." David snarled.

"Oh, so you're getting a ride home from pretty boy, are you?"

"I hope he realizes, as soon as he drops you off, that's it? I warned him already, that he's to stay the hell away from you and he had better abide by my rules."

Lisa having taken enough, snapped back.

"David shut up! Just shut the hell up!"

"You just can't handle the fact that I've got somebody who cares about me. You're terrified, that I will get away from you and you'll have to learn to fend for yourself…"

David snapped right back. "Nervy today, are we? You can believe whatever you want to my dear, but you'll never get away from me. You can just get those thoughts of leaving me, right out of your head. You're my wife and you'll do what I say. Now just hurry up and get your little ass home, I'll be waiting."

With that, he slammed the phone down in her ear. Lisa was furious.

"Damn him! He deserves whatever he gets, it's my turn to win and I am going to."

Then as she headed back to her room, she noticed Chad getting off of the elevator and went to meet him, with a big kiss hello.

"Hi sexy, boy it's good to see you. David just called the nurses station for me."

Chad hugged her.

"It's great to see you back to your sweet self. So what did David have to say?"

Lisa continued as they headed to her room.

"He was just being himself, a perfect asshole. Making his usual threats, but you know what baby? For the first time, his threats don't scare me. He is the one who should be scared, after today he'll never hurt me or anyone else every again."

Chad pulled her closer to him and whispered.

"I know, sweetie, but keep your voice down. If anyone hears you talking like that, you're bound to get caught. You need to keep quiet about this, it cannot look even the slightest bit suspicious."

Lisa agreed.

"Yeah, I know, sorry. Just can't help it, my life is finally going to be my own. Anyway, let's get my things and get out of here."

Chad was a little concerned about David.

"Hun, won't David get mad, if he sees me bringing you home?"

Lisa kissed him sweetly.

"Don't worry about it baby. I already told him, you were bringing me home and he said he didn't care. Just as long as you disappear, after you drop me off. But don't worry, I'll be fine and I'll see you tonight."

Chad was still nervous about the whole thing.

"Well, as long as you're sure that he won't freak out. I don't want you to get into any trouble. If that bastard hurts you again, I swear baby, I'll go nuts."

With that, he helped her gather her things together and they headed out of the hospital. He still did not like the idea of bringing her back to David, especially after seeing his reaction to her suicide attempt, but what other choice did he have? Lisa wanted to go back there.

Chad was quiet on the road home and Lisa worried. "Are you okay? You're going to come over tonight and help me right? You seem kind of quiet. Would you rather, I just called you when it was done?"

Chad jumped.

"I just don't like the idea of bringing you back to David, that's all. I'm fine and yes, I am coming over to help you tonight. I would never let you do this on your own. Besides that, I honestly don't think, you could move David on your own. He'll be passed out and dead weight, don't worry dear, I'm here for you. Just give me a call, as soon as you're sure he's ready to pass out. I can be there in twenty to twenty-five minutes and by that time he should be out cold."

Lisa was happy to know Chad was there for her.

"Thank you, baby, for everything. Just make sure you're listening for the phone okay?"

He put his hand on hers.

"No worries there, baby, I'm always listening for the phone, when it comes to you."

Then as they pulled into Lisa's driveway, right away the front door opened and David rushed out.

"Come on Lisa, let's go, into the house." Then he looked at Chad.

"Thanks geek, now get the hell out of here and I don't expect to see your ugly mug around here again. I would think, that you would realize, another man's wife is owned property. Now if you're smart, you'll stay the hell away from her and my house."

Chad laughed.

"Listen pal, I'll do whatever the hell I please. You may control Lisa, but you sure as hell don't control me. So you my friend, can kiss my ass!"

With that, Chad tore out of the driveway and headed for home. He couldn't help but laugh, at the stunned look on David's face, when he told him off. He couldn't believe someone could be so arrogant and crazy enough to believe, that he could rule anybody and everybody.

"Sorry pal, this is one person you don't rule and if it's the last thing I do. I am going to see you burn in hell for everything you've done. You lose pal, it's finally the end of the road."

At this point, back at Lisa's. David was doing his usual yelling and putting her down.

"You are such a foolish woman!"

"If you thought, taking a few pills was going to free you from me, you were sadly mistaken. I've told you time and time again, you're never getting out of this marriage. Your Mr. Pretty boy there had better watch his step too. Nobody tells me off and gets away with it. That geeks got a real mouth on him and one of these days, it's going to get him into some real trouble."

"I swear Lisa, you have got to be the stupidest woman alive. If you honestly thought, you could see another man and get away with it, you were wrong."

Lisa decided this was it, she had taken more than enough and she was going to stand up for herself. "Oh shut your bloody mouth, David!"

"I am tired of listening to your sickening voice. All you ever say is worthless bullshit and your threats are really getting boring."

"Why don't you just shut up and fill your face with booze, at least when you're drunk, you make more sense."

David chuckled an evil and disturbing and laugh.

"You are such a little bitch! If you think my threats are bullshit, then maybe I will just have to prove once again, that they're not. Unless of course, you'd like to apologize?"

Lisa was afraid that David would go after Chad, like he did to Andrea so stooped to his level.

"Fine, David, if that is how you want it, then I'm sorry." He laughed as he smacked her ass.

"Oh darling, I've got you right where I want you. Wrapped tightly around my little finger. Now get your tight little ass upstairs and get the housework done, this place is a mess."

Lisa clenched her fists, all she wanted to do was hit him, but instead agreed.

"Yeah, this place is a mess and I wasn't even here. So I guess we know who the slob is now, don't we David?"

David slapped her across the face.

"You'll never learn, will you? You are not to speak to me in that tone! Now get moving, before you pay dearly for that one."

Lisa knew she had to listen, so went upstairs and started cleaning. As she cleaned, she worried about her plans to kill David. She was afraid, he would fight her and her plan would fail. She knew that if that happened, it would be her who ended up dead, as David would never put up with her fighting back.

Meanwhile, David was downstairs drinking as usual. However this time, Lisa was happy about it. David needed to be drunk for her plan to work.

She reached under the bed and pulled out a bottle of rum she had hidden and took it down to him.

"David, I found this bottle of rum while I was cleaning. It was under the bed, you must have put it there while you were drunk, do you want it?"

David reached out.

"Silly question, yeah pass it here, the more the better." Then as she turned to head back upstairs, he continued. "You know Lisa, you're the last person I expected to give me booze. You're usually trying to take it away from me." Lisa snickered.

"Well David, I guess I've just given up. I can't fight your drinking problem anymore."

He laughed and slapped the sofa.

"Ha, well good! Maybe now I can drink in peace." Lisa mumbled as she walked back up the stairs.

"Yeah or rest in peace. Come on, David, drink up now. Get hammered and pass out, you'll be right where I want you."

Meanwhile back at Chad's. He was going crazy worrying about Lisa. He was a nervous wreck, as he knew the time had finally come to finish David off for good.

The phone rang and he picked it up to find it was Lisa. "Hi baby! Well so far so good. I gave him the bottle of rum and he's already drank a bottle of whisky and about twelve beer, so it shouldn't be long before he's out of it and passes out."

"I know that things are moving quicker than expected, but I think that you should drive over now and maybe sit in the parking lot across the street from my house. Then when he's out, I can call your cell and you can leave your car there and come across the road."

Chad agreed

"Okay, that sounds good, I'm leaving now then. Be careful, sweetie, I love you and I will see you very soon. Good luck."

Chad became extremely nervous as all the pieces were falling into place.

He feared with their plan moving so fast, something would go wrong and they would fail. He quickly got ready and headed over and parked in the lot across from Lisa's house, waiting for show time.

Lisa was keeping a close eye on David, waiting for the right time to call Chad. She looked out the window and noticed that he had already arrived.

Her mind was now at ease, knowing that he was so close by and help was there if needed.

She walked into the living room with David. "Are you going out tonight?" David snarled at her.

"God, you're an idiot. Sammy's is closed tonight, they're waxing the dance floor. Why do you think I stayed home to drink? I swear, Lisa, sometimes ask you questions stupid, ah I mean, sometimes you ask stupid questions. Ah there I said it."

Lisa laughed.

"Oh, are we a little drunk there, David? You can't even speak."

David tried to get up, ready to hit her.

"Yeah, I am! Have you got a problem with that?" He reached out the hit her, but fell over.

"Holy shit, good rum! I wonder where I picked up this stuff, it's pretty good."

Lisa laughed as she mumbled to herself. "What a jackass."

David was becoming light headed and kept nodding in and out. Lisa knew it wouldn't be long now before he was down for the count.

"So David, have you spoken to Paula today?"

He mumbled.

"No…um…maybe I should call her." Lisa continue with her plan went on.

"Well if you'd like, you can just take my car and go over and surprise her."

David was really confused at this point.

"What? You would actually let me take your precious IROC?"

Lisa playing him continued. "Yeah sure, why not?"

David was so drunk, he couldn't even see, that Lisa was playing him like a deck of cards.

He got up from the sofa and started to walk. "Okay, sounds like a good idea, thanks, Lisa."

Then as he walked toward the garage, he fell flat on his face, passed out cold.

Lisa couldn't believe it. Everything was working perfectly.

She walked over and began to shake him. "David, David are you awake? David."

He was out and there was no waking him. Lisa immediately called Chad.

"Come on, baby, it's showtime, he's out cold."

Chad jumped out of the car and ran across the street, where Lisa met him at the door.

"Okay Lisa, you grab the keys and I will get him into the car."

Chad then picked up David and carried him to the car and strapped him into the driver's seat. Then when Lisa brought the keys out, they the car on, in the garage and walked away leaving him there to die.

They believed nothing could go wrong and then moments later, a sound came from the garage, it was David.

"Lisa, Lisa, Lisa, where am I?" Lisa panicked.

"Oh my God, Chad, he's waking up! Get out of here, quick you've got to go, hurry before he sees you."

Chad took her hand.

"No, Lisa, come with me. How are you going to explain this? He'll kill you, come with me baby."

Lisa quickly kissed him and then pulled her hand away. "No, I'll be fine, I'll work it out. Don't worry, just hurry up and get out of her."

"Oh and Chad, start thinking of plan B, would you?" Chad sighed.

"Yea okay. I'm going, be careful, I love you."

Then with one more, quick kiss, he headed back across the street to his car. Where he decided to stick around for a while and make sure all was okay. If there was even the slightest sign, that Lisa was in trouble, he was prepared to go right back over.

Lisa had to think fast. David was now fully awake and yelling.

"Lisa, what the hell is this? How did I get here? What the hell is going on?"

David had now turned off the car and opened the garage door. Lisa came out and acted surprised.

"David, what are you doing? I told you that you were too drunk to drive. Come on, get out of here. What are you trying to do, kill yourself?"

David was confused but still ignorant. "Kill myself? No Lisa, I'm not you. I must have started the car and then passed out. It's crazy though, I don't even remember coming out here."

Lisa shook her head.

"Well, you were in one of those moods, where anything you want, you get."

"I told you not to go, but you just yelled and said you would do what you wanted. Now, who was I to stop you? You're always telling me, to keep out of your business."

David still confused.

"Weird, all I remember is saying that I should call Paula. Since you're out here anyway, could you please give me a lift over to her place?" Lisa was stunned.

"PLEASE! David, you said please? My God, the exhaust fumes must have affected your brain. Wow please! Yeah, I'll drive you, just let me get my purse."

Chad watched from the parking lot and saw Lisa pulling out of the garage, with David in the car. Figuring things were okay, he headed for home, to wait for her to call.

"Good girl, Lisa, don't know how you got away with it, but good going, baby."

All the way to Paula's, David kept trying to figure out, how he had gotten in the car and why he couldn't remember.

Lisa tried to prevent him from knowing the truth. "Well David, it's pretty obvious. You just had far too much to drink and you blacked out. You should have stopped, when you started screwing up your sentences. But oh no, not you! You had to keep going, until you looked like a complete vegetable. You'll never learn David, you almost killed yourself and for what? A few moments of getting high on booze. Someday you'll quit and for your sake, hopefully before it quits you."

David was furious that she was lecturing him.

"Get real Lisa, I'm fine! I don't need to quit or even slow down for that matter. I can control my drinking any time I want to. I'm not that bad off and if you don't like it, too bad, bloody well deal with it!"

Lisa, not wanting to continue the argument, just kept her thoughts to herself.

"I don't have to deal with it, I'm going to kill you, instead. One of these days, your drinking will kill you and with my help it will be soon."

She wasn't about to let this first failed attempt stop her. Her freedom meant more to her then he did and she would continue, until once and for all he was dead and buried.

After dropping David off at Paula's, Lisa decided she'd better call Chad.

"Hi baby, everything is okay. David is at Paula's and won't be home until morning. I'm coming over, okay? We need to think of another way to get rid of him, this just wasn't good enough. First of all though baby, I want to take you into my arms and make passionate love to you. I've been aching for you all day and I can't wait any longer."

Chad wanted her just as bad.

"Ooh yea baby, I've been aching for you all day, too."

"I just can't believe our plan failed though. Everything seemed to be going so well, he was out cold. How in hell, did he wake up in that car? I was sure the fumes would kill him, before he had the chance to wake up. It's just so unbelievable. Anyway we'll talk later, I'll see you in a few minutes and make sure you're prepared for an erotic evening baby. I've been waiting, to feel your body next to mine all day, so hurry before I go crazy."

Lisa moaned into the phone.

"Well, be ready baby, because I'm on the way. See you in a few minutes."

Chad hung up the phone and began getting ready for Lisa. I wrote a note, telling her to come right in and taped it to the door. The turned out the lights and lit a trail of candles, from the living room to the bedroom. Where he then removed his clothes and lay naked on his bed. Waiting for his princess of passion to arrive.

Lisa arrived and seeing the note, headed right inside, to the candle lit path leading to Chad's room. She dropped her purse and headed to be with him, removing a piece of her clothing with each step toward him, until she arrived at his door completely naked.

There Chad was, laying naked on the bed, waiting for her. The room was lit by candle light and soft music was played in the background.

"Ooh Chad, Oh, baby you look good."

Chad sat up and put his arms out to her, leading her on to the bed next to him.

The as he kissed her passionately, she stopped him. "Wait a minute baby, I have a surprise."

She reached over and opened the night stand drawer and took out a pair of handcuffs. Then grabbed a couple of Chad's ties.

Chad was becoming aroused.

"Ooh baby, cool. You want me to tie you up?"

Lisa purred like a kitten.

"No baby, I'm going to tie you up."

Chad moaned, the thought of Lisa tying him up and having her way with him, really turned him on.

"Oh, Lisa! Baby, I hope you never change, every day you're more and more exciting. A true princess of passion, you're…"

She put her finger to his mouth.

"Shh, just keep quiet and enjoy baby, this night is all about you."

She then took the handcuffs and cuffed his hands behind his head, then took the ties and tied his legs to the bed posts. She gently kissed his chest, then slowly moving downward, she licked his inner thighs and then gently kissed his balls.

Chad was rock hard and more than ready for action, as she then began sucking him, long and fast. She took him deep into her throat and caressed his balls with her hand.

Chad tingled with sexual desire, as she then straddled his hot aroused body, pushing his hardness deep into her burning hot pussy.

She began rocking her pelvis, up and down, fast then slow, then fast again. Stroking his hard dick in and out of her wet pussy.

Chad moaned and quivered below her, as she bent forward allowing her hard nipples to brush against his firm hairy chest.

Lisa was becoming extremely wet, as the pleasure of his pulsating dick, deep inside of her, sent flashes of pleasure and erotic sensation coursing through her body.

She moved harder and faster, forcing him even deeper as they moaned and shrieked, with the sensation of their arising orgasms, dominating their bodies.

Lisa's pussy throbbed with excitement, as the contractions of her sexual peak began.

Chad hearing the sobs of pleasure shooting for her throat, screamed as his orgasm began. His body shook and his muscles tightened, as he writhed about. Completely taken over by sexual stimulation.

As the two of them came down, from the heights of sexual pleasure. Lisa untied him and they clung to each other and panted and groaned with satisfaction.

Chad kissed her forehead.

"God baby, it just keeps getting better with you."

"You really know how, to keep it interesting. The erotic feeling that I get with you, is like nothing I've ever known before. I love you Lisa and our love is right."

As Lisa held him close, she agreed.

"I love you too Chad. I've never felt this strongly about anyone before. I feel as if we're one and our two hearts beat together in rhythm with each other. I know that being with you, is the right thing for me and I never want our relationship to change. I feel safe when I'm in your arms and I know that you'll never hurt me or let me down. Everything with you is more perfect, then I ever could have imagined."

Then as the two lay holding each other close, Lisa began thinking of David again and how the plan had failed.

"Chad, I don't mean to ruin a perfect evening, but we really need to talk. We need a new plan, to get rid of David. I can't wait much longer, I'm afraid if I wait, I'll lose the nerve. I want it over with, once and for all."

Chad sat up.

"I know, baby. I realize we need a new plan, I'm just not sure what we should do. I mean we thought the first plan was fool proof and yet it failed. This just makes the whole situation a lot more difficult. I know how important your freedom is, it's important to me as well. Somehow it will work out, we'll find a way to make it happen."

Lisa got up and wrapped a sheet around herself and went to get her clothes.

"Chad, I just feel like I've lost the battle. I tried to kill him and he survived. Face it, baby. I've lost."

Chad wasn't happy with the negativity in Lisa's voice. "No baby, you haven't lost!"

"There are other ways of killing him that will look like an accident. We just have to think and come up with a way that he couldn't possibly escape. A way that even if he wakes up, he couldn't possibly save himself. Having him stay passed out however, does make things easier."

Lisa was listening to Chad, go on and on about killing David. She knew that it really was the only way out. Yet she still had her reservations about the whole situation.

"Listen Chad, why don't we just leave it for tonight? We'll talk about it tomorrow night, there's no big rush. After all, if we want the plan to work this time. We really have to work out every little detail and this time a backup plan would be good, too."

Chad agreed and he put his arm around her.

"Yea, you're right baby, an alternative plan would be best. Okay we'll talk tomorrow. Gives us both more time to think it over too."

Lisa finally admitted her fear.

"I love you Chad, but I'm really scared. What if what we're doing is the wrong thing? What will happen to us? I don't want to lose you."

Chad hugged her.

"Baby, you don't have to worry about that. I'm not going anywhere. I truly believe that our love is strong enough, to overcome anything and nothing will ever separate us. This is the right thing, we're fighting back for you and for Andrea as well, you…"

She stopped him.

"Okay, okay. You don't need to convince me anymore, I believe you and I know you're right. I just feel…Oh I don't know what I feel. All I know is I'm scared and I'm afraid of being caught. Our new plan has to go off without a hitch and the police need to believe it was an accident."

Lisa got up to get ready to go home.

"Well, it's late, baby and I think we both need some time alone to think and get a good night's rest. How about tomorrow I meet you at your work and we can come back to your place together and talk then?"

Chad took her by the hips and pulled her close. "Yeah we'll talk among other things."

Lisa pulled away and laughed a sweet laugh.

"WOW Chad! You're always so horny, don't you ever get enough?"

He pulled her back and kissed her neck. "I can never get enough of you, baby." Then he kissed her passionately.

"Well I better let you go, see you tomorrow. Sleep well angel."

Lisa turned to walk away.

"I better go, I love you, bye baby."

Lisa left and Chad sat down to think about things. There had to be a way, to pull off the perfect murder. He had to look accidental and Lisa could never be caught. He got up and paced back and forth, determined to come up with a way to free Lisa, once and for all.

By this point, Lisa had arrived at home, only to find that David was there, he had come home early.

"Well, be still my heart, it's Lisa and it's only midnight. What's the matter honey? Not having a good time tonight, without Andrea and pretty boy?"

Lisa wasn't in the mood for David and his games. "Sorry to burst your bubble David, but I had a great time tonight. I only came home early because I was tired. Why are you here? I thought you were spending the night with Paula?"

David laughed.

"Well, actually I thought I would come home and see if I could catch you sneaking in late. You ruined my fun by coming home early, guess I'll have to catch you next time."

Lisa was exhausted and didn't care.

"David, I'm really not in any mood for your shit. I am tired and I'm going to bed, so if you're finished, good night!"

He laughed and tossed a cushion off the sofa at her. "Oh yeah, go to bed you lazy bitch, that's all you ever do anymore."

She ignored him and continued to walk upstairs as she mumbled to herself.

"Yeah and if you only knew the things I was doing in bed with Chad. Ha! You burn, baby, you burn!"

Then she yelled down to David.

"Go to hell, David, go straight to hell!"

Lisa was becoming frustrated with the whole situation. She was beginning to think, that David was like a cat with nine lives and there was nothing going to kill him.

As she lay there in bed, she tried to make sense of her life, but she couldn't. Nothing made sense anymore, the only thing she knew for sure, was she wanted to be with Chad for the rest of her life and out of this nightmare she was living with David.

Chad was still awake, sitting on his sofa, trying to plan David's murder. He had written down of his ideas and finally figured out the perfect way to do it. Now it was just finding the right time to follow through with it. He was sure that Lisa would agree to it, even though it would mean her losing her car, which to her was her baby. Although there was the possibility, her insurance would cover it and her car would be replaced. This was the perfect plan and it was fool proof. All Chad had to do, was get a block of ice from the ice company and keep it in his freezer until the time came to follow through.

Chad couldn't wait to tell Lisa the plan, he was sure that she was going to like it and she would finally be able to relax. Knowing that it would all be over soon and there was no way this plan could possibly fail. Chad was finally able to relax and calm down enough to head to bed. However even still, found himself, doing nothing, but starring at the ceiling worrying about Lisa.

Lisa was at home doing pretty much the same. All she could do was toss and turn. She couldn't get comfortable with so much on her mind.

Her biggest fear, was that David would find out that she was still with Chad and try to kill him, like he had killed Andrea and she couldn't allow that to happen.

Lisa was exhausted from all the stress, so after hours of tossing and turning, she finally drifted off to sleep. It wasn't a peaceful sleep however, she had nightmares, of David killing Chad and woke back up in a cold sweat and began to cry with fear, over what her life had become.

Before long, she was awakened by the sound of David yelling. He was once again on a rampage.

"Come on you lazy bitch, get the hell out of that bed. I want this pig sty cleaned, but before that, you can make me some lunch. It's getting late, what the hell are you doing? Trying to starve me to death? Come on move it, get up you lazy whore."

Lisa pulled herself out of bed as she mumbled to herself. "I wish killing you was that easy."

David continued to yell as he headed back downstairs. "Come on! Hurry up! God damn, you're slow!"

Lisa was angry and couldn't hold back any longer.

"Yes master, anything you say, master. I'll be right there, just keep your pants on."

Lisa walked into the kitchen where David was waiting. "Okay, I'm here. Now what does master want for lunch?"

David stood up and punched her in the face, knocking her down.

"God, you're stupid! A stupid little whore! I am so sick of listening to all of your sarcastic remarks. You're really becoming mouthy lately, I guess a little bit of pretty boy had rubbed off on you. I'll be sure to fix that."

Then he kicked her repeatedly in the chest and back. "Now get the hell up and get my lunch ready, I'll have a few burgers and a beer."

With that, he walked into the living room and sat down in front of the television.

Lisa pulled herself up from the floor and went to work on David's lunch. She began to cry, as the pain from David's punch, became intense. She had hoped she would never have to suffer another beating from David, but being her plan hadn't worked, here she was, stuck in his grasp.

She was furious as she stood thinking about everything and feeling the pain, he had once again put her in. Then without even thinking, enraged with anger, she took the frying pan and went after David. She came up behind him and began beating him over the head with it.

Lisa wasn't strong enough to fight David and he took over. He grabbed the pan out of her hand and began beating her with it. He hit her over and over, each time harder than the time before. Lisa cried and begged him to stop, but that was only giving David what he wanted.

"Come on, bitch! Beg me again, beg for me to stop. Come on you little whore, beg me, beg me Lisa."

Lisa was in pain, but didn't want to give in to David. So he continued to hit her and kick her.

"Come on, Lisa, squirm, squirm with pain and beg me to stop."

Finally she couldn't take anymore and gave in.

"STOP! David please stop, please just let me be. I can't take anymore, please David, please stop."

He laughed a vicious laugh as he pulled away from her. "Good girl, just what I like. I love to see you beg, you're such a wimp!"

"Isn't it degrading to beg Lisa? Doesn't it make you feel small and worthless? I hope so, because you are!"

Lisa was hysterical, this was the end of the road. She had to make sure that her next attempt was the last and David was gone for good. She was in extreme pain and struggling to get up from the floor.

David kicked her again to get her moving.

"Get up! I still want my lunch and it had better be ready in the next thirty minutes or you're getting it again. For your sake, you had better get moving."

Lisa pulled herself up from the floor and slowly moved into the kitchen to make David his lunch. She was beaten bad and could barely move, yet still did as he had asked. She knew if she went against him, he would beat her again and she couldn't stand another beating. All she really wanted to do, was walk right out the door and go to be with Chad, but knew the consequences of that, could mean Chad's death.

She finished up cooking and called David into the kitchen.

"Your lunch is ready, better hurry up and eat it before it gets cold."

David walked in looking at his watch. "Hmm lucky you, 28 minutes, not bad."

"I don't have time to eat it now though. I'm supposed to meet Paula at the bar in an hour."

Lisa couldn't believe it as she thought to herself.

What a jerk! He beats me because he's hungry and then doesn't even eat it. All he wanted was a reason to beat me, he wasn't hungry. What a total asshole!

Lisa walked out of the kitchen and started on the housework. She was in pain, but wanted to get done so she could go and meet Chad at work.

David came out and said he was leaving, Lisa was relieved. "What time will you be home? I want to make sure I'm here."

He was surprised she asked.

"Good girl, getting smart and respecting my wishes, are you? I'll be home between two and three a.m. I don't want you leaving though, until this place is spotless."

Lisa sighed as she continued to clean.

"Yeah, I know, don't worry it will be. Goodbye."

As soon as he left, she continued to rush around, trying to get the housework done, so she could go and meet Chad at work. She was no longer thinking of the pain, all she thought of was getting to Chad.

Then as she finished and got ready to go, she walked into the garage only to find that David had siphoned the gas out of her car and left a note on the windshield.

The note read… "Ha-ha, got ya. I guess you'll have to stay home tonight, enjoy your day, bitch!"

Lisa was furious as she stormed back into the house. "Figures! Leave it to David to pull a stunt like this."

She then decided she would call a cab, but looking in her wallet to see if she had enough cash, she discovered he had also taken all of her money and credit cards, too. She was frantic, she had to get over to Chad's office, but because of David, she no longer had a way to get there.

Lisa picked up the phone and called Chad's office, his secretary answered.

"Hi Betty, its Lisa. Is Chad still there?" Betty answered.

"Oh hi Lisa, yes he is. I'll put you right through." Chad picked up.

"Hi honey, where are you? I thought you would have been here by now."

Lisa signed and almost began to cry.

"Well, I should have been, but I have a slight problem. David took all my cash and my credit cards and to make matters worse, siphoned the gas out of my car as well. I have no way to get there."

Chad snarled.

"What a jerk! Okay honey, call a cab and head over here. I'll watch for you and run down and pay for the cab. Other than that, are you okay?"

Lisa couldn't hold it back any longer and started to cry. "Well, to be honest with you, no I'm not. I'm a mess and pretty sore. David flipped out again and beat the hell out of me. I tried to stop him, but couldn't, he just kept going."

Chad growled and she could hear him slam his fist down on his desk.

"That son of a bitch! He'll get his and he'll get it really soon. We have to talk tonight, I've figured it out. The perfect plan and it can't fail. This time he dies and you'll never have to hurt again."

Lisa was thrilled hearing that from Chad.

"Thank God! I really can't take any more of these beatings, I hope this works. Anyway baby, I'll see you in a bit, watch for the cab, I'm on the way."

Shortly thereafter, Lisa arrived at Chad's office and he ran down to meet the cab. She stepped out and Chad was astonished with what David had done to her.

"Oh baby, oh sweetie, look at you, what has he done?"

Lisa tried to hold back the tears as a lump formed in her throat.

"I know, it's bad. He went crazy, I made the mistake of trying to fight him. I won't be doing that ever again."

Chad put his arm around her as they headed back up to his office.

Chad quickly tossed a few things in his brief case, grabbed his keys and they were off.

Chad smirked.

"No? I thought you were full of energy? I'm just kidding, baby. Seriously, I think they will replace your car, no questions asked and if not, you can always use my car. Besides, I thought you were going to move in with me after David was gone anyway?"

Lisa jumped.

Chapter Seven

They arrived a Chad's apartment and right away, he began filling Lisa in on his plan.

"Baby, I can't bear to see you going through this anymore. The time has come to free you from that monster. Now I have a plan that I am sure will work. There's one drawback though baby. You'll have to lose your car. I would use mine, but that would just look suspicious. Now…"

Lisa jumped in.

"Wait a minute, lose my car? Why would I lose my car?" Chad continued.

"Well we need to use your car, basically your car is the murder weapon. Well that and the block of ice I have in my freezer. I'm pretty sure, once it's proven it was an accident. Your insurance company will replace your car."

Lisa wasn't too sure.

"Well, I hope so. I love that car and it's kind of hard to get around without one. I mean I could walk, but its sixteen miles to your place and I'm not that energetic."

"Well, yes of course I am! But I can't exactly do it right away. I mean don't you think, it would look a little suspicious, if I moved in with you right after my husband was killed? Think about it Chad, I'll have to act like the perfect grieving widow, if not people will wonder."

Chad signed but agreed.

"Yeah I suppose you're right. You could come over and spend the night once in a while though right?"

She continued.

"Well, I don't know Chad. I mean, I am sure once David is dead, his family will show up for the funeral. He has always been close to his family and calls them at least five times a week. They see each other every holiday and special occasion, too. They have never really liked me and I am sure, that if I don't appear completely devastated. They will suspect that I had something to do with it and the whole thing, will blow up in my face. Don't you think that our love is strong enough, to survive a week or two apart? I mean…"

Chad stopped her.

"Don't even think that, of course I believe our love is strong enough to survive. It's just the thought of being away from you kills me, I'll miss you."

Lisa kissed him sweetly on the cheek.

"I will miss you, too, but I can call you. We'll talk every night. Now come enough about this for now. I thought we were going to have a romantic evening."

Chad moaned and growled. "Mmm yeah, don't you want to hear the rest of my plan first?"

She sighed as she ran her fingers through his hair.

"Oh okay baby, fill me in."

Then as Chad filled her, she kissed his neck and nibbled on his ear. As she whispered sweetly.

"Sounds good, now enough about this. I want you baby, I want you now."

Chad groaned as she began kissing his chest.

"I want to feel your hard dick, deep inside my wet pussy. Come on baby, make love to me, make love to me like only you can."

Chad moaned as he scooped her up and carried her into the bedroom and lay her on the bed. Then he slowly removed her clothes and began caressing her body passionately and kissing her gently. Then moving slowly downward and spreading her thighs apart, he began nibbling ferociously at her yearning clit and licking her hot moist pussy.

As Lisa felt his tongue, slowly sleeping into the depths of her now soaked pussy. She quivered and shook with complete erotic stimulation. Chad licked her fast and stroked his finger in and out. He fondled her ass and caressed her breast.

"Oh Lisa, your pussy tastes so good. Come on baby, let those juices flow and let me enjoy the sweet taste of your pleasure."

Chad kept going at her, stroking his finger faster and faster, as he encircled her hard clit, with the tip of his tongue. Lisa shrieked and writhed about the bed. Her body, completely overcome by sexual waves of pleasure. Then as she felt her arising orgasm, she sobbed with excitement. Stimulating bolts of energy coursed through her body and dominated her as she exploded in massive orgasm. She convulsed uncontrollably and screamed with pleasure.

"Oh yes, oh yes, Chad. Make me cum, make me cum good. Yes, Chad yeah!"

Chad then rolled her over and got on his knees behind her. He moaned as he slowly, slid his rock-hard dick, deep into her hot, love-soaked pussy. He pushed it long and hard and began pumping at her fast.

Lisa grabbed onto the headboard and pushed her pelvis back and forth, forcing him deeper and deeper inside of her. As she tightened her muscles to increase the intensity of the friction. She reached down between her legs and began fondling her clit.

Chad pumped at her, harder and harder, as the tightness of her pussy, sent erotic sensations coursing through his body, lightening.

Chad groaned with sheer pleasure.

"Oh yea baby, oh you're so tight. Take me baby, take all of me."

His thrusts became stronger and harder. They were now so constant, that it was hard to tell, when he pushed in and when he pulled back.

Lisa screamed and panted, as she felt, yet another orgasm, brewing deep inside of her throbbing pussy.

Chad grabbed her hips and pulled her harder to him. Forcing his pulsating organ deeper inside of her. Then as he climaxed and his orgasm began. He moaned and growled a passionate growl.

"Oh yeah, oh yea baby, yes! That's it, take me. Feel those hot juices flow deep inside of you, feel me cum baby, oh yea!"

Then as Lisa, felt the hot juices of Chad's sex, shooting deep into her channel of love. She was once again brought to orgasm.

She grabbed onto the pillows and bit on one, as the pleasure over whelmed her. She shrieked and convulsed with pure erotic stimulation, almost more then she could bare.

Chad still deep inside of her. Leaned forward, kissed her neck and whispered.

"Oh yes, baby, that's it baby. Cum, cum all of over my hard dick."

Lisa screamed with pure pleasure.

"Oh yes, oh yes, Oh Chad, you're the best baby. You truly are!"

Chad pulled out and laid down, on the bed next to her. "I'll tell you one thing, baby. We could never say, that we're not compatible sexually. Damn girl, it just keeps getting better and better. I swear, sex between us, is so explosive, it feels like the house is shaking."

Lisa kissed him sweetly on the cheek.

"It's more than just sex Chad, there's a passion between us. Something that is stronger than the both of us, something that only real love can create."

Chad smiled and ran his fingers through her hair. "You're right baby, everything with us is amazing and I truly do love you. I don't believe, I have ever loved anyone, the way I love you."

Lisa got up to head to the shower.

"I need to grab a shower, before I head home. Care to join me? I'll make it worth your while."

Chad jumped right up and tapped her on the bottom. "Oh yeah!"

"Let's go baby, I'm right behind you."

They jumped into the shower, Lisa looked at Chad and purred like a kitten.

"Damn baby, just look at the firm wet body of yours, glistening with the water pouring down it."

Then she tapped him on the bottom. Chad began to laugh jokingly.

"Talking about yourself, there baby?"

Lisa slapped him playfully.

"No silly, I'm talking about you and you know it!" Chad, leaned over and kissed her on the neck.

"I know baby. I was just trying to bug you and it worked now didn't it?"

Lisa reached down and taking his dick into her hand. She began stroking it up and down, then reached down to fondle his warm wet balls. Then getting down on her knees, she began to lick him. She licked him from balls, clear up to the tip of his rock-hard dick. Then pushing it into her mouth, she began to suck him, long and hard.

Chad quivered with the warm feeling of her tongue, gently caressing his dick and her soft sweet lips, wrapped tightly around him.

She sucked him longer and faster, taking more of him deep into her throat, as she caressed his balls with her hand. Chad moaned and shook, as he raced to the heights of sexual satisfaction. Then just as his began to cum, Lisa pulled back and allowed his cum, to shoot across her firm hard breasts.

Chad twitched with satisfaction.

"Oh God, oh baby. Lisa, I love you so much, I swear, you're the best and it's you and me forever, baby."

Lisa got up off her knees, her grabbed her, pulling her close and kissed her passionately and she kissed him right back. They buried their tongues, deep in each other's mouths and kissed with a passion so hot and for so long, the steam seemed to billow up in the room.

Suddenly, Lisa stopped and pushed Chad away.

"Baby, I have to stop. I would love to continue this, hell I could continue this forever. But I'm running out of time here, I need to be home in just over an hour and I need you to drive me. I can't be late, or you know, I'll pay for it."

Chad kissed her once more on the cheek.

"I really do hate him baby, I swear I do! He runs you like a battery-operated robot and beats on you and thinks that it's okay. Well it's not okay and I can't wait for the day that you never have to return home to that again."

Lisa grabbed a towel to dry off.

"I know, baby, I can't wait for that day to come either. Hopefully soon, it will all work out and we'll be free to be together forever. For now, however, I need to get home. If I don't go, this plan of ours will never work out so it has to be this way."

As they dried off and began getting dressed, Chad agreed, yet was still concerned.

"I know Lisa. I just worry about you, when you're not with me. I want to protect you and can't do that, when I'm here and you're there. It kills me, knowing what you're dealing with at home. I'm sorry if I seem over protective, but you're my life Lisa and I love you. I realize, that right now, you have to go home, but that doesn't mean I have to like it."

Lisa kissed him sweetly on the cheek.

"I know its hard baby, but it's how it is. I will call you later, I promise. I really don't mean to worry you so much, this isn't at all easy for me either. With any luck though, this will all be over soon and this will all be in the past."

Chad hugged her.

"I hope so sweetie. So are you ready to go?"

Lisa thought about it and worried that maybe David would already be home.

"Yeah I'm ready, but I think I should call a cab." Chad was shocked.

"A cab, why?"

Lisa picked up the phone.

"I'm just a little worried. What if David came home early? He'd see you and then we'd have trouble. I think it's too risky right now."

Chad wasn't pleased, but agreed.

"I suppose you're right, but I still hate this."

Lisa called a cab, then as she got ready to head downstairs to wait. She grabbed Chad and pulled him close. She kissed him and whispered in his ear.

"I love you, baby and I'll see you tomorrow. I'll be okay, don't worry, please."

Chad hugged her tightly.

"I love you, too, Lisa. Please, be safe."

Lisa headed downstairs to wait for her cab. As the door closed behind her, Chad became frustrated and punched a hole in the wall and yelled.

"Oh how wish, that had been David's face! Stupid son of a bitch, so help me God, I would love to beat him senseless. I can't wait until that ass is dead, he deserves what he has coming."

Chad sat down on the sofa and threw a cushion across the room in anger.

Meanwhile Lisa was arriving at home. Luckily David had not yet arrived. Knowing she wasn't supposed to be out. She quickly got ready and jumped into bed, making it appear, that she'd been there all night. She even turned the ringer off on the telephone, so she would have an excuse for not answering in case David had tried calling.

Shortly thereafter, she heard the slamming of the front door. David had arrived home. As always, he came right upstairs to make sure she was there. He chuckled to himself, seeing her laying there in bed.

"So Lisa, how was your night?"

Lisa not wanting to piss him off, tried to keep calm. "Yeah, I did actually! I stayed in and watched movies all night. I did try to go out and get cigarettes though. Thanks a helluva lot, you took my gas, but was it really necessary to take my money, too? It was actually a pretty foolish stunt, David. I had already changed my mind about going out and decided I would stay in. So the whole thing was pointless."

David snickered.

"Sure it was! Nice try, bitch! I tried calling three times and you never answered once."

Lisa knowing he was getting hyped up, tried to settle things.

"I'm sorry, David, but I was here all night and the phone never rang at all."

David started with his sarcasm.

"Oh yeah sure and I suppose, you're going to tell me the phone is broken or something now too. Come on Lisa, get real!"

Lisa was becoming frustrated.

"Well, I don't know David, maybe it is for all I know. It never rang all night, so who the hell knows!"

David walked over to check out the phone and noticed the ringer was turned off.

"The ringer is off. It was probably that stupid cat of yours again. The damn thing, is constantly walking across the phone. Stupid bloody animal."

Lisa couldn't believe how foolish David could be.

"Um, my stupid cat David? Don't you mean, your stupid cat? Remember, that cat is yours, so whatever it does, is your fault not mine. So don't put this one on me."

Lisa was right, so David wasn't quite sure how to respond. "Well, well whatever! Just shut the hell up Lisa, I'm going to bed. You take the sofa, I'm sleeping here tonight."

Lisa got up, laughing to herself and headed down to the sofa.

As she settled down to go to sleep. She started to think about Chad and hoped that he had calmed down and was able to get to sleep.

She worried about him and hated putting him through all of this. She was dragging him through, all of the problems of her abusive marriage and because of it, he was suffering right along with her.

At this point, back at Chad's apartment. He was still unable to sleep. He sat on his sofa, taking his frustrations out on a video game. He realized, Lisa didn't want him to worry, but how could he not? David was crazy. Kind of like a ticking time bomb, that could blow at any second. Lisa's life was in constant danger and he couldn't wait for the day that she would be safe in his arms for good. Protected and loved, with no worries of her lying somewhere hurt, or even worse, dead.

David's accident, could not come fast enough for Chad. He wanted all of this suffering over with and he knew, that he would not rest, until David was gone, dead, six feet under. The next morning, Lisa awoke to the sound the shower running. She wasn't sure who it was at first but as she approached the bathroom and heard a voice, she realized, that it was Paula. She must have come over in the night to be with David.

Lisa knocked on the door, assuming that David would be in there, too.

"David, is that you?"

Paula turned down the water.

"No Lisa, it's me Paula, I won't be long." Lisa wasn't at all impressed.

"Well I certainly hope not! You know Paula, you do have your own shower at home. Where the hell is David anyway?"

Paula was getting upset.

"He's gone out to run some errands for me. Now would you just leave me the hell alone and let me shower in peace."

Lisa laughed sarcastically.

"Ooh a little testy are we? Did somebody, wake up on the wrong side of MY bed?"

Then she laughed out loud and walked away from the bathroom door, shaking her head with disgust she said to herself.

"Wow that woman is unbelievable!"

Right as she turned to head downstairs, the bathroom door opened and the claws were out.

Paula began shaking her finger at Lisa, like she was the queen of the castle.

"You know Lisa, you really should try to be a little nicer to me. Perhaps if you did, things around here, would be a little easier. After all, we do share the same man. You may be his wife, but I'm the one who satisfies him completely. You better get used to it sweetheart, because I'm going to be around, a lot more often."

Lisa laughed.

"Ha! You want me to get along with you? I think NOT! Listen, Paula. Just because, you're screwing my husband, doesn't mean, you have to get to know me, too. Nor does it mean that you can just hang around here all the time, use my shower and do whatever you please. Why don't you just take David to your place? Like seriously, just because David and I no longer sleep together, doesn't make it okay, for you to sleep with him, in my room, or in my bed for that matter. I don't see a ring on your finger, or your name on the marriage certificate. So until I do sweetie, I don't have to put up with you, or your bullshit. So, why don't you just go to hell?"

Paula's just nearly hit the floor, she was stunned that Lisa would speak to her that way.

"Look, Lisa, you have no right speaking to me this way. You know, David will not be too happy, when he hears about this little argument."

Lisa was furious.

"I'll speak to you, however I see fit Paula. Remember, this is my home, not yours."

Paula was like a child, being sent the corner. She stomped her feet and began yelling.

"That's it, I've had it, Lisa! You're a bitch and I'm going to tell David, exactly how you treated me."

Lisa started to laugh.

"Aww, what's the matter, sweetie? Can't you stick up for yourself? You have to go running to someone else, to fight your battles for you? What the hell does David, see in you anyway? You're nothing but a little wimp. I'd like to see you, survive even one of David's beatings. I don't think you could handle it, you'd never make it."

Paula snickered and put her hand up.

"Yeah okay Lisa, you can stop right there. David is innocent. None of the bullshit you talk about has ever happened. David told me, it's all made up lies to make him look bad. You're just a lying, cheating little slut, so cut the crap!"

That was it, Lisa had taken enough of Paula's crap. She turned around, hauled off and punched her right in the mouth.

"Don't you ever, tell me that I'm a liar. You're not here 24/7 and have no idea, what goes on around here, behind closed doors. How in hell, do you think, I end up with all of these bruises, Paula? I'd have to be one helluva klutz to walk into that many walls! Get real, bitch, you have no idea! Why don't you just stop and think for once."

Paula just brushed Lisa off, as if what she was saying meant nothing at all.

"I don't have to listen to this shit. I'm going downstairs to wait for David."

Lisa laughed.

"Yeah that's it Paula, just walk away. It's not that you don't have to listen. It's that you don't want to listen, because you're too afraid to admit the obvious."

With that, Lisa headed in to take her shower, shaking her head at Paula's stupidity.

After showering and getting dressed, Lisa could hear David's voice. He was home and Paula was filling him in, on her version of the argument.

Lisa became terrified, to go downstairs. Yet knew, she would have to face the music sooner or later. So she headed down. David hearing her, met her at the bottom and right away began yelling.

"What the hell, did you think you were doing Lisa? Paula is a guest in this house and does not deserve, to be spoken to in the way you did. You should be showing her some respect, not being a total bitch to her."

With that, he grabbed Lisa by the hair and yanked her off the stairs, then began smacking her around and kicking her.

Lisa looked over at Paula.

"Do you see this, Paula? This is what goes on around here. What exactly, do you call this? Innocent arguing? You better pinch yourself sweetheart, because you're not dreaming, this is reality. Oh but wait a minute, I forgot, I'm a liar!"

David punched her, knocking her to her knees and Paula laughed and yelled at her.

"Shut the hell up, Lisa! This is your problem, not mine. I don't have to listen to your stupid complaints, because all of this, is your own bloody fault. Maybe if you learned some respect, things like this wouldn't happen."

Lisa was furious, this was happening to her and Paula just stood there, like it didn't even matter.

"Oh shut up, you stupid bitch! You don't even know what you're talking about, so just go to hell, Paula!"

David became even more enraged, punching Lisa in the mouth, splitting her lip. Then kicking her once more, he walked over and took Paula by the hand.

"Come on, baby, let's go over to your place for lunch, before the bar. I'm sick of looking at this pitiful bitch."

Then as they headed to the door, he looked back to Lisa. "I'll be home around two and expect you to be here."

Lisa pulled herself up from the floor as David and Paula left, slamming the door behind them. She went and got herself cleaned up, tidied the house and then sat down to call Chad.

She explained to him, what had happened, when she woke up to find Paula in the shower. Chad was shocked, when he heard, that Lisa had punched Paula in the mouth.

"Oh my God, Lisa, you did what? What did David do when he found out?"

Lisa explained.

"No, it wasn't good at all, David lost it on me, right there in front of her and she did nothing about it. I swear, he's got that woman so brainwashed, she truly believes, that all of this is my fault. Lucky for her though, she'll never have to live through David's abuse, because he'll be dead. If she only knew, how lucky she was, maybe she'd be a little less of a bitch."

Chad was concerned.

"Maybe. Anyway sweetie, are you sure you're okay? Are you hurt bad?"

Lisa was hurting, but not wanting to worry him too much, tried to change the subject.

"No more than usual, I'm okay. Anyway baby, I should let you get back to work. Are you free for lunch though? I could come by your office and meet you."

Chad growled into the phone.

"I'm always free, for you baby. Come by around 2:30, I should be able to take a break by then and we can have desert, if you know what I mean?"

Lisa purred like a kitten.

"Oh yeah, I know exactly what you mean. You really are insatiable now, aren't you?"

Chad laughed.

"Who me? I just can never get enough, of my princess, that's all. Anyway sweetie, I'll see you a little later. I love you."

Lisa hung up the phone from Chad, the quickly went through the house, making sure, what everything was in its place. Then went and prettied herself up, for her lunch with Chad.

Wanting to be a sexy as possible, to totally knock Chad to his knees. She put on her bright blue and black satin teddy, long trench coat and spiked heels. She was determined, to make sure Chad's lunch break, was one, he wouldn't soon forget.

As she drove over the Chad's office, she began to think, about her relationship with Chad and wondered. She wondered, if after David's death, their relationship, would still be as strong as it was right now. She worried, that the stress of committing a murder together, would take its toll on them and things would change. She prayed, they were strong enough, to get through it, but still worried.

What they were planning, was serious and nothing to joke about, yet Chad was handling it, like it really meant nothing. She wondered, if he was truly taking this seriously and if after David's death, they would be able to live with what they'd done. She wasn't sure, how she would handle it herself, yet knew in order to save herself and prevent anyone else from being hurt. This is what needed to be done. David was unstoppable, so this was the only option left, if she wanted to live a normal life again.

Lisa headed up to Chad's office. She walked in and locked the door behind her.

"Hello sexy, are you ready for dessert?"

Then she climbed up on Chad's desk and slowly removed her coat.

Chad's jaw dropped, as he watched her moving provocatively, in her blue and black satin teddy.

Lisa stood up and began to dance for him, right there on his desk, enticing him further. She waved her yearning pussy in his face, then bending down, she began kissing him passionately. Then slowly getting down off of his desk. She began removing his clothes, while she gently caressed his chest.

Chad moaned with excitement. As he reached forward and cupped the firmness of her breasts and encircled her erect nipples with his fingertips.

Lisa gently kissed his neck and earlobes, then reached between his legs and began stroking, his already hard dick.

Then moving down. She kissed his chest and slowly ran her tongue down his body. Then taking his massive organ deep into her mouth, she sucked and nibbled at him hungrily, running her tongue up and down, she licked him from the base of his dick, right to the tip, arousing him further.

Chad moaned and moved about his chair, with the erotic sensation, of Lisa's hot mouth, wrapped tightly around his dick. Explosive flashes of pleasure, rocketed through his body, as Lisa moaned and sucked him faster and faster, while fondling his balls with her hand.

Chad, now totally losing control of his sense, squirmed in the chair and yelled out.

"Oh yeah baby! Yes, yes Lisa. Suck it, suck it hard, baby."

Then as Lisa, sucked him faster, taking more of him, deep into her throat. Chad was brought to orgasm. His hot juices, flowed deep into her throat like bullets, as she continued to suck.

Chad groaned with satisfaction, as he picked her up and then laid her down, on the floor behind his desk. Then as he mounted, her hot yearning body and pushed his still hard dick, deep into her hot moist pussy. Lisa shrieked with pleasure.

"Oh yeah baby, yea, drive me, Chad, drive me hard!"

Chad pumped at her, pushing his hardness, deeper and deeper inside of her. Lisa writhed about with stimulating bolts of energy, coursing through her exploding groin. Chad pushed harder and deeper with each thrust, as he leaned forward, to nibble ferociously at her rock-hard nipples.

Then as the erotic sensations, took over her body. Lisa sailed to the heights of ecstasy was brought massive orgasm. Chad continued to push, in and out of her, as the contractions of her exploding groin, hugged him tightly, bringing him to cum once again, deep inside of her.

The two of them writhed about, holding each other close and kissing passionately, as their bodies, slowly drifted down, from the heights of pure sexual arousal.

Chad looked over the clock and couldn't believe, how much time had passed.

"Wow, I can't believe my break is almost over. Sure wish, all of my lunch breaks could be this good. Maybe, I should just bring you into work with me every day."

Lisa laughed.

"I wish you could! It would certainly make life interesting. Although, then we'd have the problem, of you, never wanting to leave the office."

Chad snickered jokingly.

"Well hey, it would save on rent!" Lisa hugged him.

"God, I love you! Don't ever change." Chad kissed her sweetly.

"I love you too baby and no I won't ever change. What you see, is what you get!"

Lisa got up, put her coat back on and did her best to fix her hair.

"I guess I better get out of here, before your boss comes in and catches us. I wouldn't want you, to get into trouble over this. I'm going to head over to your place and cook us a nice dinner for tonight."

Chad kissed her once more.

"Sounds great, baby, I'll see you after work. I love you Lisa." Lisa headed out of the office.

"I love you too babe, see you in a bit."

Lisa left Chad's office, but as she reached the door, she noticed that Betty, Chad's secretary, had already returned from her break.

"A little lunch break fun, there Lisa?" Lisa began to blush with embarrassment.

"Um yeah, what can I say? He's good, can you really blame me?"

Lisa heard Chad's laugh coming from behind her and turned back to see him standing there listening.

"Oh Chad, knock it off! What did you want me to say?" Chad chuckled.

"Oh I don't know. Exactly what you did say, I suppose. It's just, you look so sweet and innocent, standing there, blushing with embarrassment. I couldn't help but laugh."

Betty found the two of them amusing.

"Oh come on guys! There's really nothing to be embarrassed about. Hell, at least somebody's getting some!"

Chad and Lisa, both laughed, as they hugged once more.

Then saying good-bye, Lisa headed off to his place.

When she arrived, she went into the kitchen, to begin preparing dinner. She had decided on shepherd's pie, because that was Chad's favorite dish. Once she had things prepared, she looked around the apartment and decided that it needed some tidying and began cleaning things up.

"Wow, you can sure tell he's a bachelor. Nothing in the fridge and clothes all over the apartment."

As she cleaned and put things away, she then decided the furniture needed rearranging.

"This looks too much like a bachelor pad. If I'm going to be living here soon, it really should suit us both. Ah Chad won't mind, I'm sure he'll be pleased to have the place all cleaned up and organized."

Not long after she finished arranging things and the meal was fully prepared. Chad arrived home from work.

Hi honey, I'm home! Then he thought to himself.

"Wow did that ever sound funny, coming out of my mouth! I guess I'd better get used to it!"

Then looking around the apartment, he was shocked, with how organized it was.

"Wow Lisa, the place looks great! You've certainly been busy this afternoon."

Lisa wasn't sure, if actually meant that, or if he was only saying it, so he wouldn't offend her.

"Are you sure it's okay? I just thought, that since I will eventually be moving in. That maybe the place should be, how we both liked it."

Chad hugged her.

"Yes, I'm sure, its looks great! I don't think, I've ever seen the place this clean, it's terrific!"

Then he turned his head toward the kitchen.

"Yum, what is that smell? It smells delicious. Is that shepherd's pie?"

Lisa grinned.

"It sure is! I hope it is okay. I knew it was your favorite, so I decided to make it for dinner."

Chad was thrilled and his stomach began to rumble.

"Okay? Of course it's okay, hell it's more than okay. Shepherd's pie is my absolute favorite. This is awesome baby!"

Lisa laughed, Chad was like a little boy, getting cookies and milk after school.

"Well, okay then! Why don't you, go and grab your shower and I will get things set and dinner on the table."

Chad was anxious to dig in.

"Okay, but I'll make it quick. I can't wait, to dig into that shepherd's pie, it smells fabulous!"

While Chad, took his shower. Lisa quickly got things ready and put dinner out on the table. She couldn't help, but think to herself, about how different Chad was from David and how wonderful, her life would have been, if she had only stayed with Chad, all of those years before. Instead of letting him go and ending up married to David. The difference between the two of them, was like night and day.

Chad came out of the shower, too find Lisa starring off into space. She seemed miles away.

"Lisa…Lisa…Earth to Lisa" Lisa jumped.

"Sorry babe, how was your shower?" Chad rubbed her shoulder.

"My shower was fine, are you okay? You seemed very deep in thought. What were you thinking about?"

Lisa not really wanting to explain, quickly changed the subject.

"Yeah, I'm fine, sorry about that. Come on now, let's eat before dinner gets cold."

As they sat and ate dinner, Lisa seemed to drift off again.

She couldn't stop worrying about the 'what if's'.

"Chad…Baby, are you sure, that I'm the person, you want to spend the rest of your life with?"

Chad was shocked.

"Lisa, are you sure you're okay? Why would you ask that? Of course, you are. I love you and can't wait to make your mine forever. I want to grow old and gray with you. Raise a family and have plenty of grandchildren, to tell our love story to. How could you ever doubt my love for you?"

Chad took her hand and kissed it sweetly. She smiled, but was still unsure.

"I'm sorry, Chad. It's not that I doubt your love for me. It's that I sometimes worry, that once we're together for good and David is out of the way, things will change between us. I mean look at how my marriage turned out."

Chad leaned over and kissed her.

"Sweetie, you never have to worry about that. Our love, is the kind that lasts forever and I can promise you, you're mine and I won't let you go and I will never do anything to hurt you either. There's nothing you ever have to worry about, Princess, you have my word. Now let's eat this wonderful meal you've prepared for us, shall we?"

Lisa smiled.

"Okay, sorry babe. Let's eat, I wouldn't want all of this food to go to waste."

Chad winked at her as they continued their dinner. Lisa was surprised, at how much he was eating. She had never seen him, eat that much, at one meal before.

"Wow, Chad, you're sure putting it away tonight. It can't be that good?"

Chad laughed and patted his belly.

"Oh, yes it can be! This is fantastic sweetie. I wouldn't dare, tell my mother, but yours beats hers any day!"

Lisa grinned and winked.

"Keep it up baby, flattery will get you everywhere!"

After Dinner, to Lisa's surprise, Chad offered to clean up and do the dishes.

"Okay sweetie, you did all of the cooking and fixed this whole apartment up today. So I will clear the table and do the dinner dishes. Why don't you go and relax a bit? Maybe take a bubble bath. That will relax you and maybe calm your nerves too."

Lisa was stunned, a man offering to do the work, while she relaxed. Wow she could definitely get used to this!

"A bubble bath…really? That sounds wonderful, but are you sure? I could help you clean up, it won't take long."

Chad took her by the hand and led her toward the bathroom.

"No, I can handle it. You just go and relax in a nice hot bubble bath."

Lisa kissed him and looked into his eyes.

"You truly are amazing, how did I ever get so lucky? Okay babe, I'll see you in a bit then."

Lisa headed into the bathroom, lit some candles and settled into a nice hot bubble bath. While Chad turned on some music and went to work, cleaning up the kitchen.

While she soaked in the tub, she could hear the music playing and the sounds of Chad humming right along to the songs. She laid back, listening to him, as the lit from the candle, glistened off the bubbles that surrounded her. Chad in her eyes, was the perfect man and she couldn't wait, for their new life together to begin.

Lisa finished with her bath and walked out to the living room, wearing nothing but one of Chad's robes. She sat down on the sofa, in front of the blazing fire, that Chad had lit.

"Babe, that was amazing. Thank you, I really do feel more relaxed now."

Chad joined her on the sofa and began rubbing her shoulders.

"I know what my baby needs! I'm glad it helped, you really seemed stressed at dinner."

Lisa leaned into Chad's arms and put her head on his shoulder.

"It wasn't so much stressed, as worried. It's okay though, the moment has passed. I know in my heart, that things between us. Will always be, just as good as they are today, if not better!"

Chad kissed her shoulder.

"That's right baby! So please don't worry anymore."

The two of them sat on the sofa, holding each other, starring into the fire and listening to music, for hours. It seemed like only minutes, but the night quickly flew by.

Chad glanced at the clock.

"Lisa, its 12:45 already! What time is David due home tonight?"

Lisa got up from the sofa.

"Damn 12:45 already? He'll be home by 2:00, so I need to get moving here. I can't wait, until I know longer, have to race to home, worried about what David will do, if I'm late. Thank goodness, after tomorrow night, it will all be a thing of the past."

Chad was confused.

"Tomorrow? When did you decide, on tomorrow night?" Lisa explained.

"I was just about to discuss it with you, when you noticed the time. I found out, that tomorrow night, Sammy's bar, is closing at 11:00 and Paula is going to be out of town for the night. It would be the perfect night to do it. I can pick David up from the bar by 11:00 and without Paula around, there would be no interference."

Chad wasn't so sure this idea would work.

"It would be a perfect time, but if you pick him up from Sammy's, he'll be awake and we need him to be passed out. I don't see how this will work, if David is alert."

Lisa smirked.

"Well, you see, that is where the new part of the plan comes in. I'll have you, hidden the back seat of the car. Then when we reach our destination, or close to it. You can hit him from behind, knocking him out, then…"

Chad was shocked and quickly interrupted.

"Um, hit him from behind? Lisa, baby, if I do that, he'll have a bump on his head, making it just a slight bit suspicious. Don't you think, the police, are going to wonder, how he got the bump, on the back of his head?"

Lisa shook her head.

"Nah, not a chance! They'll just think, the bump was caused by his plunge to death. No one will ever be the wiser. As soon as it's done, I will head right home and get into bed. Then when the police arrive, I'll play them like a deck of cards. They will never suspect murder, much less that I, had anything to do with it."

Chad figured she was probably right, yet still had his concerns.

"You're probably right, but none the less. You still need to be careful and be sure, that David has had enough to drink, to make this believable. I mean, he needs to be really drunk!"

Lisa laughed.

"Ah come on Chad! When is David not drunk? Seriously, I don't think, we need to worry about that at all. That man drinks from the time he rolls out of bed in the morning, until passes back out at night. Having enough in his system, will not be an issue. Besides that, I will make sure, there is an open bottle of rye in the car too. It will appear to the police that he was drinking while driving. It will all get passed off, as another alcohol related fatality. No worries baby, this is all going to go smoothly."

Chad hugged her.

"Sheesh, I'm not sure why, but seeing the devil come out in your eyes, while you plan this, is kind of a turn on! Okay then, I guess this is it. Tomorrow night, your worst nightmare, comes to an end. I just pray, it all goes as planned. I'll have the block of ice with me, we'll need to transfer it to your trunk beforehand and I'll need to park my car, somewhere nearby, so we have a ride home afterwards."

Lisa looked at her watch and knew she needed to hurry home.

"Yea that's right we will and I'll have to follow you, so you can jump into the back of my car. I'm running late now though, so really have to run."

Chad agreed and kissed her.

"Yeah, the jerk will be home in 45 minutes, you better get going. I love you, Lisa."

Lisa crossed her fingers as she looked back.

"I love you, too, fingers crossed baby! See you tomorrow."

With that, she blew him one last kiss and headed home.

Chad headed back in to sit down, still unsure about it all and worried, that somehow, the plan would fail. He wondered, what would happen, if he didn't hit David hard enough, or if David noticed him in the back of the car. He knew, that if David caught him, it would be game over, for both him and Lisa. Everything to run like a well-oiled machine, there couldn't be any mistakes.

Lisa however, had become anxious to get this all over with. She was certain, it would all work as planned and she would finally be free of David and all of his abuse. In her mind, this no longer felt like murder. It felt more like a self-defense action and in her eyes, she was doing the world a favor. One less abuser in the world, meant less pain and suffering for more innocent people.

Lisa arrived home and quickly rushed into the house, hoping to beat David. Too her surprise however, David was right behind her.

"Cutting it a little close to the line, aren't we Lisa? You're damn lucky, you were in that door before me." Lisa jumped and her heart pounded.

"Holy hell, David! What are you doing, sneaking up on me like that? You scared the hell out of me!"

David laughed as he tossed his jacket down on the sofa. "Good, that was the plan!"

Then he shoved her aside, to push his way by.

"Now, let me check out this house. I'm willing to bet, that nothing was done, before you left to go out. You never seem to care about our home anymore, everything gets ignored and left in a shambles." Lisa laughed.

"Oh yeah, sure it does David! If anything is in a shambles, it's because you left it that way. Maybe if you, made this place seem more like a home, rather than a torture chamber in hell, I'd care a little more."

David slapped her across the face.

"Don't you ever use that tone with me. Just keep that mouth of yours shut and learn to deal with it!"

Lisa laughed and thought to herself.

Oh I'll deal with it alright! Permanently!

Lisa headed upstairs and David followed behind her. "Paula is going away tomorrow night and Sammy's is closing early. I'll need a ride home, so be there by 10:30. I would suggest you don't make any plans, because so help me God, if you're late Lisa, you'll pay for it. I'm expecting a call by 11:30 from Paula and if I miss the call, you're dead!"

Lisa thought to herself.

No, you'll be dead!

However, replied.

"Fine, David, I'll be there and with time to spare, too."

David headed back downstairs, Lisa sat on the side of her bed and couldn't help but smile. Her plan was falling right into place and little did David know, he was paving the way, for his own demise.

Lisa decided, she'd better call Chad and let him know what time to meet her.

"Hey babe, were you sleeping? I hope I didn't wake you." Chad sounded tired.

"No, I was still up, headed to bed though. What's up sweetie?"

Lisa filled in him.

"Oh okay, I'll be quick. I thought I would let you know, David wants me to pick him up by 10:30 tomorrow night. So you'll need to meet me, by 10:15 everything is falling, right into place baby."

Chad perked up a bit.

"It sounds that way! Okay sweetie, I'll be there by 10:15 and I'll have the ice in my trunk to transfer to yours. Thank you for keeping me up to date, it won't be long now and we'll both be able to rest easy."

Lisa could hear David coming up the stairs.

"David is coming! I have to get off the phone. I love you, see you tomorrow."

She quickly hung up the phone, just in time for David, to walk through the bedroom door,

"What are you doing, Lisa? You should have been, back downstairs by now."

Lisa was confused.

"Excuse me? Why would I be back downstairs?"

David grabbed her pillow and threw it toward the door. "Because, you're sleeping the sofa. I get the bed, remember?" Lisa laughed as she got brave.

"Yeah, no I don't think so David. You take the sofa, I'm staying right here and if you don't bloody like it, oh well, I'm not moving."

David raised his hand to hit her, however Lisa grabbed his arm.

"Yeah that's it David! Win the argument, by hitting me. That will make it all better! All you know how to do is hit, but sorry to tell you, sweetheart. It doesn't matter whether you hit me or not, because I'm still not moving. I am sleeping right here in my bed. So it's your choice David. You can hit me, or you can walk away, but either way, you're still sleeping on the sofa."

David yanked his arm away and stepped back.

"Fine, if you're going to be a bitch about it! Come to think about it, there's a movie on, I wouldn't mind seeing anyway."

David turned to walk away, Lisa laughed.

"Yeah, sure there is, just can't admit, that you lost the fight and I won."

David turned back with daggers in his eyes, yet did nothing.

"Watch your step girl, you're treading on very thin ice." With that, he walked away and headed back downstairs.

Lisa was in shock, yet proud of herself. She had stood up to David and actually won. As she settled down to sleep, all she could think about, was how all of this, would be a thing of the past very soon. Her nightmare, was going to come to a crashing end and she and Chad, would finally be free, to spend the rest of their lives together, in complete happiness.

Lisa woke up the next morning, fully expecting David to be in a foul mood, over the events of the night before, but her surprise, he had already left. She went into the kitchen, to make some coffee and found a note, taped to the coffee maker.

"Gone out, be at Sammy's by 10:30, don't be late, or else!" Signed David.

Lisa was relieved, everything was going to go off without a hitch and to make things even better. She was going to get to spend a relaxing day at home, without David and his bullshit. He had left early and now, would never have a chance, to hit her again. He was going to meet with sudden death tonight and Lisa would finally be freed. Never again, would she have to feel, the sting of his fists, or have to walk around bruised and covering up black eyes behind sun glasses. Lisa had won the abuse and would no longer, have her life dominated by her abuser.

From this day forward, she would be free to once again, enjoy her life and follow her dreams for happiness. She and Chad, would be together and finally be able to have the life they'd dreamed of and even start a family together. She was over the moon with excitement over the thought of David being gone and couldn't wait for the day to be over.

Meanwhile, Chad was at work and finding it very hard to concentrate on his work. He wondered if Lisa, was really strong enough, to be able to handle something as serious, as killing someone. He feared, that maybe after it was all said and done, Lisa wouldn't handle it well and be sent right over the edge, she'd already been teetering on for months.

The rest of the day, passed by quickly and before long, it was time for Lisa to go and meet Chad. She was nervous, but at this point, there was no turning back. She wanted this over with and the time had come. She was becoming shaky, as she drove around the side streets, by Sammy's bar, watching for Chad.

After a few minutes of driving around, she spotted him, parked in an alley, not far from the bar.

She pulled up beside him, got out and opened the trunk. Chad got out of his car and opened his trunk to grab the ice.

"Are you ready Chad?"

He looked nervous, but answered.

"Yep, I'm ready, as ready as I'll ever be, let's do this!"

He grabbed the block of ice and moved it into Lisa's trunk, then jumped in the back seat.

"Lisa, open all the window's now, we have to move quickly later and there won't be time."

Lisa agreed, as she rolled down all the windows and Chad, hid under and old blanket in the back seat.

They then, headed over to pick up David, who was already, waiting outside Sammy's, for her to arrive. He was so drunk, that he could barely stand up and was using a pole, to steady himself. Seeing that he was alone, Lisa turned to the back seat.

"Chad, he's alone and there's nobody at all around. So there won't be any witnesses that I picked him up."

Chad let out a sigh of relief. "Oh, thank God! That's perfect!"

Lisa pulled up and honked for David. He staggered over to the car and got in.

"It's about bloody time, bitch! It's cold out there, what the hell took you so long?"

Lisa shook her head at him, thinking to herself. *What an idiot* but replied.

"What's the problem David? I'm here on time, actually 5 minutes early. So relax would ya?"

David reached over and punched her in the side of the head. Nearly causing her to swerve off the road.

"David, what the hell are you doing? Are you nuts? I nearly went off the road."

David being sarcastic answered.

"No I'm not nuts, but you must be. What the hell are you doing, with all of the windows open? It's near freezing outside."

Lisa grabbed a cigarette and lit it.

"I'm smoking dumbass and you know, I always open the windows to smoke in the car. If you have a problem with it, too bloody bad."

David then hit her again and snickered.

"Damn, I love smacking you around. I love the sound, my fist makes when it connects with your empty head!"

Right then, Chad jumped up from the back seat and yelled.

"THAT IS IT! I'VE HAD IT!" and with that, he hit David in the back of the head with a crowbar, knocking him out cold.

"I'm sorry Lisa, I couldn't wait. He's a damned asshole and I was really getting sick of listening to his bullshit. Besides that, I wasn't about to sit here and watch him, hit you again."

Lisa slowed the car.

"It's okay baby, it was actually right on time, we're here." Then she pulled the car up to the hill, at the top of the bridge and they both quickly got out. Chad pulled David over, into the driver's seat. Lisa threw an open bottle on the floor and Chad got the block of ice out of the trunk and wedged it, on to the accelerator. Then they put the car into drive, turned it on and quickly slammed the door and got out of the way.

Then as they stood by watching, the car sped down the hill, crashed through the barricades, where the bridge turned and David plunged into the lake and to his death.

Lisa and Chad, then quickly ran to Chad's car and took off. Lisa was pumped with adrenaline.

"Oh my God, it's over! He's dead! We did it Chad, we actually did it!"

Chad's heart was still pounding.

"Yes, we did, didn't we? Now to get you, back to your place. Before the police find him and arrive to inform you, of your husband's tragic accident."

They pulled into Lisa's driveway and Chad leaned over and kissed her.

"Okay sweetie, stay strong and call me, after the police have been and let me know how it all went."

Lisa hugged him.

"I will baby, wish me luck."

Then she headed inside, she put on her nightgown and robe and messed up her hair a bit, to make it appear that she had been home all night. Then sat and waited for the police to arrive.

As Lisa sat waiting, the reality of what she'd done, finally kicked in and she became upset. She had just murdered her husband and she wasn't quite sure how to handle it. A big part of her was happy to finally be free and knowing that Andrea's killer, had now paid for what he'd done to her and she could rest in peace, gave Lisa her a sense of peace. Yet, she still felt the guilt, starting to build up inside of her.

Right then, the phone rang. Lisa looked up at the clock, to realize it was 11:30, so knew, it had to be Paula.

"Hello"

Paula was shocked, that Lisa had answered and not David. "Oh Lisa. Hi, it's Paula, David around?"

"No, Paula, he's not home yet."

Paula seemed angry that he wasn't there.

"What do you mean, he's not there? Are you sure? He said he would be home by 11:30 for my call. Are you sure you're not lying to me? And why are you home, anyway? You're never home this early."

Lisa was becoming infuriated with Paula.

"No, I'm not lying to you Paula, he hasn't come in yet and for your information, I didn't go out tonight. I've been in bed all day with the flu. Have you got a problem with that? Hey, you should come over for a visit and maybe you'll catch it!"

Paula hated Lisa's constant sarcasm with her.

"Um, no Lisa, I don't think so. Just tell David I called." Then she slammed the phone down, in Lisa's ear.

Lisa couldn't believe, what a witch Paula could be. What business was it of hers, whether he was home or not?

"Wow, that woman is too much! Thank God, I'll finally be rid of her, too. No David, No Paula. That woman, has interfered in my life too much already and with David gone, there's no longer a reason, for her to be around."

Lisa began thinking, about everything she would do now, that David was gone. She decided, that she would likely sell the house now. She figured, she'd be moving in with Chad and really, the house held too many bad memories. For her to ever live there happily.

Then she decided, she would offer most of David's things to his brother. However, when she thought of David's brother, she thought about his family.

"Oh know, David's family! What am I going to tell them?"

She knew his family would be devastated by this and would expect her, to be devastated herself. David's family knew, that their marriage was on the rocks, but she would still, need to act like the grieving widow, to keep them from suspecting anything.

Lisa was making herself crazy, thinking about everything, that she would have to do now and how she would need to act, to keep things believable. When suddenly, there was a knock at the door. She knew right away, it had to be the police. So she pulled herself together and went to answer.

When she opened the door, two police officers stood before her.

"Good evening ma'am, can was speak with you, please? It won't take long."

Lisa opened the door further.

"Yes sure, come in. Please excuse the way I look. It's this darn flu bug, I can't seem to shake it."

The officers stepped inside.

"It's quite alright ma'am. We just a few questions for you. We'd hate to bring you such bad news, with you being so under the weather and all."

Lisa cut them off.

"Bad news? What's wrong?"

The officers led her to a chair and she sat down. "Ma'am, do you own a purple IROC? And if so, can you tell us of its whereabouts?"

Lisa, trying to play stupid, answered.

"Well yes, it's in the garage. I haven't been out all day and my husband lost his license."

The officers continued.

"Ma'am, do you know where your husband is?" Lisa acted worried.

"Well yeah. He said he was going out to Sammy's bar, the one on Station street, why?"

One of the officers took her hand and helped her up from the chair.

"Ma'am, is there any way, that your husband could have taken your car? Could you please, take a look for us?"

Lisa still playing stupid agreed.

"Well okay, I'll take a look, but I'm sure, he would have called a cab. He lost his license 6 months ago, after driving drunk and nearly killing a family. Let me tell you, his losing his license, was a huge load off my mind. I was forever worrying, something would happen with him drinking as much as he did. Anyway, he's never touched my car since, he's always called a cab. So I can't see him taking my car tonight, either. I'll just grab my keys and open the garage."

Lisa walked over to her purse to grab her keys, then playing the unsuspecting wife. She reached into her purse and became upset.

"They're gone! My keys aren't here! The garage must be unlocked then, let's look. I can't believe, that he would drive without a license, what was he thinking?"

Lisa took the officers out to the garage, where they found that her car was gone.

Lisa acting like she had no idea, yelled.

"Oh my God, he took my car! I don't believe this! Where is he? Was he arrested? There wasn't another accident, was there?"

The officers led her back into the house and sat her back down.

"Ma'am, we're sorry to have to tell you this. But we pulled your car, out of the lake tonight and the person driving it was killed. We cannot however, be positive, that is was your husband, until the body has been identified. He didn't have any identification on him and it seems that, he was drunk and drove right through the barricades on Lake View Bridge and drowned. Ma'am, we're terribly sorry, if it was your husband, it was truly a tragic accident."

Lisa began to shake and forced out some tears to make it look good.

"No! Please tell me, this is some kind of sick joke. Where's David? It can't be him, it can't be David."

Lisa became hysterical and cried even harder.

"No, it can't be him, you're wrong, you've got to be wrong." The officers tried to calm her.

"Ma'am, we need you to come with us, to identify the body. We cannot be sure, until you do. We are terribly sorry."

Lisa continued to cry and sob, playing right up to the officers. As they tried to console her.

Lisa began blaming herself.

"This is all my fault. If I hadn't been sick in bed, I would have been out and he wouldn't have been able to take my car. I should have been paying attention. How did I not see him, take off in my car?"

One of the officers put his arm around her.

"You cannot blame yourself for this, it was not in any way your fault. You were sick in bed."

The officers were convinced, it was just an accident and Lisa had been home sick, in bed all night. Lisa knew right then, that she had gotten away with it. They had played right into her web of lies, David was dead and nobody would ever know, the truth of how he met his demise.

The officers took Lisa, over to the morgue, so she could identify the body. She was nervous and not sure, she wanted to see him, but knew she had to.

She walked into the room, they pulled back the sheet and right away, she began to scream and sob.

"Oh my God, it's him! It's David! Oh No, David No! How did this happen. No..."

One of the officers, then led Lisa out of the room.

"I'm sorry for your loss, Ma'am, but in order to close the case, we needed a positive identification. We're deeply sorry to have put you through, such an ordeal. One of the officers will drive you home."

Lisa pulled away.

"Thanks, but that's okay, I think I'll walk. I don't live far from here and could use the air."

The officers were pretty insistent.

"Ma'am, it's pretty late. Are you sure? It's not a problem, for someone to drive you home."

Lisa still playing the grieving widow, started to walk away. "My husband is dead! I need some fresh air. I'll walk, but thank you."

Lisa left and then called Chad and explained what had happened and that it had worked as planned and the case was now closed.

"I'm heading home now, pick me up there."

Chapter Eight

Lisa walked home, in a state of shock. Seeing David, laying there dead, made what she'd done, all the more real. In her mind, she kept seeing him lying there, completely lifeless and put there, by her doing. She wasn't sure how to handle it all, she just felt numb and lost.

She arrived home and sat on her front porch, to wait for Chad. She wasn't even dressed. With all of the confusion and upset, she had gone to the morgue in her robe. Shortly after she arrived, Chad pulled into the driveway. She was so distant, she hadn't even noticed his headlights. Chad got out and walked over to meet her.

"Lisa…Lisa…Honey are you okay?"

Lisa looked up with a tear rolling down her cheek.

"Yeah I suppose so. I'm just a little upset I guess. Seeing David lying there on that table like that, really got to me."

Chad took her by the hand. "Come on baby, let's go."

Once they were in the car and headed to his place. Lisa still sat, quiet and distant. Chad knew, she wasn't handling things well.

"For someone who's just been freed Lisa, you certainly don't seem too happy."

Lisa began to cry.

"Of course, I'm not happy! I just killed someone. Sure, I am glad that I'm free from all of the crap he put me through and that Andrea's killer has paid the price for her death. But Chad, I'm no better than him! I killed him, just like he killed Andrea. I know they say, an eye for an eye, but it was murder. What am I supposed to do, celebrate the fact that I did this?"

Chad was shocked.

"No baby, not at all. I don't expect you to celebrate it at all. I mean you have every right, to be upset about it. I'd be worried if you weren't! You do need to look at it another way though. You were being put through hell, all you really did, was free yourself from the pain you were suffering. I'm sure in time, you'll see the brighter side of things and be happy you did what you did."

Lisa sighed.

"I don't know, maybe. But what about his family? I'm going to have to call them and let them know, that David is dead. They will be devastated and it's all my fault. How do I explain his death to them, without letting on that I had something to do with it? It won't be easy to explain and I'm terrified, that I'll mess up and they will suspect me."

Chad put his hand on her shoulder.

"Lisa, honey relax. I'm sure you'll do just fine. If you can convince the police, then I'm sure, you can convince his family. All you have to do, is act like you are completely overcome with grief. As far as they knew, you loved David. They'll never suspect a thing, I'm sure of it."

Lisa hoped he was right, but still had her doubts. "You're probably right, but I'm still worried. It won't be easy to call and tell them."

Chad trying to reassure her, reached over and held her hand.

"If it makes it any easier, you can call them tonight, from my place. I will sit right there with you, while you make the call."

Once again, tears were rolling down her cheek.

"Chad, you're too sweet. I'm sure it would make it a little easier for me, thank you."

They arrived at Chad's apartment and went inside, Lisa was still very distant, as she went to sit down.

"You know Chad, after tonight. I won't be able to see you, for at least a week, maybe even two."

Chad interrupted her.

"What? A week or two? Why?"

She continued.

"Well, as soon as David's family hears the news. I'm sure, they will leave Washington right away, to come and help me with the funeral preparations. Then with the funeral and getting all of David's affairs in order, I'm sure they will be here for a while."

Chad sighed as he sat down beside her.

"Yea I suppose you're right. It won't be easy, being away from you that long though. We've never been apart more than a day. I guess I'll have to settle for phone calls. But a week or two, wow that's a long time without you."

Then he picked up the phone and handed it to Lisa. "Speaking of phone calls, I think it's time to call David's family and get it over with."

Lisa took the phone and began to dial. "Yeah I suppose I better, I can't wait forever."

After 3 rings, David's mother Janet, picked up the phone and Lisa got all choked up.

"Hi Janet, it's me, Lisa."

Janet knew right away, that something wasn't right. "Lisa, you sound upset. Is there something wrong?"

Lisa began to sob and cry.

"Yes, Janet. It's David, there's been an accident." Janet became frantic.

"An accident. Oh my God, Lisa, how serious? Is David okay?"

Lisa sobbed harder.

"Oh Janet, he was drunk and he drove off of lake view bridge. He's dead Janet, David was killed in the crash."

Janet began to cry and screamed into the phone.

"No! Not my boy, not my son! How can this be, Lisa? He doesn't even have a car. How can he be gone, how can my boy be dead?"

Lisa at this point was frantically trying to make it through the call, without completely losing control. The guilt she felt was unbearable, hearing the devastation in his mother's voice. "He took my car. I was sick in bed and I didn't hear him leave, but it was my car, that he had the accident in. I don't know why he took my car, but he did and now he's dead."

Janet could tell, that Lisa felt guilty because David had taken her car.

"Oh Lisa, he was always so stubborn. He never listened to anyone. Even if, you had tried to stop him, he still would have taken the car. That was how he was, he always had to be right."

Then she sobbed harder.

"Oh God, my boy is dead. I just can't believe this, it's like a bad dream. Oh why was he so foolish? Why couldn't he just think with his head for once? He was always drinking, like that was all that ever mattered."

Lisa tried to calm Janet down.

"Janet. I really don't think, that I can handle all of this on my own. Will come and help me, with all of the arrangements?" Janet was quick to answer.

"Of course, I will dear. I wouldn't hear of letting you go through all of this on your own. I will just call his father and the rest of the family and then I'll be there, on the first flight tomorrow morning. I'll call you when I get in."

Lisa was a little relieved, knowing she would have help with everything.

"Thank you, Janet. I really do need help with all of this. Right now, I think I am still in shock. It hasn't really sunk in yet. It just seems so impossible. I mean why David? He was so young."

Janet agreed, but tried to calm down for Lisa.

"Yes, he was my dear and what makes this all the more difficult, is the fact. That you two, never even had the chance to have children. I never even got to see my son's child. Anyway dear, don't you worry. I will be there for you and we will get through this together. I'll take a week off from work and I can stay with you and help you get things in order. It will be okay, somehow, together, we'll get through this tragedy."

Lisa tried to hold back the tears.

"Thank you, Janet, I really appreciate it. I will see you tomorrow, bye for now."

Lisa hung up the phone and was shaking. That was the hardest telephone conversation, she had ever had. She might have made her own life easier, by killing David, but in the process. She had devastated other lives.

Lisa began to cry hysterically. Chad rubbed her shoulders and did his best to console her, but her crying had become out of control.

"Lisa, baby, it's okay. I am here for you, try and relax. It's important that you try and calm down. We will get through this together. We both know, that this had to be done, there was no way around it."

Lisa was becoming angry.

"Oh stop it Chad, just stop it! All you are doing, is trying to justify what we did, to save your own conscience. I realize, that it was the only way out, but I still cannot help being upset. We took a life tonight Chad, we killed my husband."

Chad was shocked, Lisa had never gotten upset with him before.

"I'm sorry sweetie, I was only trying to help. I realize, that killing David, was a serious thing to do, but I was only trying to calm you down. I wasn't trying to justify what we've done at all. I know that we cannot change this, but we cannot dwell on it either, or it will just make us both crazy."

Lisa sighed.

"Oh I know and I'm sorry I yelled at you. I'm just really stressed out right now. I'm sure, once the funeral is over with and everything is in order and Janet's gone back home. I'll be fine and our lives will be right back on track. No more sneaking around now though, we're free to do as we please."

Chad kissed her on the cheek.

"I love you, Lisa and I promise you, that everything will be okay."

Lisa leaned into him and put her head on his shoulder. "I love you, too, Chad."

Chad started to kiss her neck and stroke her hair. Lisa stopped him.

"Chad, no. Not tonight, I'm really not in the mood and besides that, it wouldn't be right, not right now."

Chad put his arm around her and pulled her close. "Okay baby. Do you mind, if I just hold you then?" A tear rolled down Lisa's cheek.

"No not all, in fact I'd really like that. Thank you for understanding, Chad."

After a while of sitting on the sofa in Chad's arms, Lisa started to nod off. She was completely worn out from everything. Chad, gently shook her to wake her.

"Come on baby, let's go to bed. You can sleep here tonight." Chad put his arm around her and led her to the bedroom. "Thank you Chad. I really am exhausted and tomorrow morning, I have to be prepared to face a grieving mother. I'm not sure how I'll handle that, at all."

They got to the bedroom and as they started to get into bed. Chad pulled her close and once again, started to kiss her neck and nibble on her ear. Lisa shoved him away.

"Seriously, Chad, No! I don't even understand, how after tonight, you could be in the mood. I mean really, it's not like it's going to shrivel up and die, if you don't get any for bit."

Chad couldn't believe Lisa's sarcasm and was a little upset, by the fact, Lisa was cutting him off for a while.

"Lisa, baby, what's with all of the attitude. This isn't at all like you and what do you mean, won't get any for a bit. How long is a bit?"

She couldn't believe what she was hearing.

"What attitude, Chad? We just killed someone, I'm sorry if sex isn't the first thing on my mind right now. As for it being a bit, yeah it will be. At least a few weeks, until this is all over with. What kind of wife would I look like, if

I started running around, with you on my arm, when my husband has just died? Think about it baby, if you really love me, you'll understand this."

Chad wasn't at all thrilled, but not wanting to lose Lisa, he agreed.

"Yeah, I suppose you're right, it won't be easy being without you though. Okay sweetie, let's just try and get some sleep."

With that, Lisa rolled over and faced the other way, Chad moved closer and put his arms around her and held her.

"Is this okay?"

Lisa sighed.

"Yes, it's fine, let's just sleep now."

Within minutes, Chad was fast asleep. It was as if killing David, had no effect on him what so ever. Lisa however, laid there quietly, starring at the wall. She still could not believe, what they had done. David had treated her horribly and in her mind, she believed, he got what he deserved, but in her heart, she felt she had made a horrible mistake. She thought about dozens of ways, she could have dealt with it, without killing him, but now it was too late and she needed to live with what she had done.

While she lay there next to Chad, she also began to think about their relationship and wondered, how Chad could be so uncaring about all of this. He really seemed, to be happy that David was dead and had no regrets about it what so ever. All that seemed to matter to him that evening, was having sex with her. Even after she had told him, it was not the time. Lisa wondered, if maybe her relationship with Chad, was nothing more than a sexual thing and if being together on another level, would ever work out.

So many thoughts raced through her head and she now more than ever, was unsure of her future. Chad had shown her a side of him, which she never knew existed. A cold side that she was not sure she liked. Before this, he had always seemed loving and caring. Now she wondered, if all of that, was simply to get her where he wanted her and into his bed. Before long, the sun was coming up. Lisa still laid there, wide awake and deep in thought.

Chad rolled over and kissed her sweetly on the lips. "Good morning princess. I hope you got some sleep." Lisa kissed him back.

"Morning babe. No actually, I didn't. There were so many thoughts racing through my head. All I could do was lie here, starring at the wall."

Chad sat up at the side of the bed.

"Sorry to hear that sweetie, things will get better though, you'll see. I'm going to make some coffee, would you like some? Then I think I'd better get you home, before Janet's flight arrives."

Lisa got up and grabbed her robe.

"Yeah sure, I'd love some, but yes, I do have to get going very soon."

They sat down in the kitchen drinking their coffee. Lisa was quiet, with so many things running through her head. Chad reached across the table and took her hand in his.

"I'm going to miss you Lisa, it won't be easy, being away from you. I can't wait, until this is all over with and you're finally mine forever."

Lisa looked up at him and tried to force a smile.

"I'll miss you too Chad and no none of this will be easy. I just hope, that this long road I have been on, will finally end with you. All of this, is so very difficult to deal with and I pray, that you will stick by me, the best you can and be understanding, during it all."

Chad kissed her hand.

"I'm trying Lisa and I will continue to try. I won't give you up, that I can promise you. So no matter what happens baby, you're mine and I won't let go."

Lisa wasn't sure what to make of that. It was starting to seem, almost as if Chad were more obsessed with her, than in love. All he kept mentioning, was never letting her go and her being his forever and when they were together, he could never get enough of her sexually. Lisa began to have some serious doubts about things. It had been Chad's idea to get rid of David and now that he was dead, Chad didn't seem to care at all. Lisa prayed, she was wrong, but things were starting to turn in a direction, that she didn't like.

"Okay Chad, I've really got to get going. Can you drive me home?"

Chad got up from the table.

"Of course, I can baby, but are you sure, you don't want another coffee first? It's still pretty early."

Lisa went and grabbed her purse.

"No, I really should get going, Janet could arrive at any time."

Chad grabbed his keys and slipped on his shoes. "Okay princess, let's go then."

As they drove back to Lisa's, Chad continued to talk, about what their lives were going to be like, now that she was his forever. He talked of wonderful things that Lisa had only dreamed of, while married to David.

Yet a part of her, still worried, if he was for real.

As they turned down her street, Lisa quickly stopped him. "Oh my God, stop the car, Chad stop the car, let me out here."

Chad was confused.

"Why? I can drive you to your house. What's the matter?" Lisa pointed to her driveway.

"That's Paula's car in the driveway. She's there and she has no idea that David is dead. If she sees me with you, she's going to suspect something. I need to show up at home alone."

Chad reached over and hugged her, then gave her a long passionate kiss.

"I'm sure going to miss you sweetie. Hang in there and keep strong."

Lisa kissed him once more before getting out the car. "I will baby and I'll miss you, too. Talk to you soon."

Lisa headed home, where Paula met her at the door, with her usual attitude.

"It's about time, Lisa! Where the hell is David? And why are you, walking the streets in your bath robe? You're one weird woman, I'm telling ya!"

Lisa shoved her aside.

"Shut the hell up, Paula. After the night I've had, who the hell cares if I'm in my bath robe. It's been a long and very difficult night and I really don't have the time, or the patience, to deal with your shit. Now, why don't you just get the hell off of my property and out of my life. I've had enough grief and upset, to last me a lifetime."

Paula was furious.

"Look, here Lisa! I will come over here, whenever I want to. I'm not here to see you, I'm here to see David. I am his girlfriend, remember?"

Lisa, was tired of listening to her and gave up the whole of idea, of breaking it to her gently.

"Not anymore, Paula! David is dead. He was in a car wreck last night and didn't make it. I've been up all night, with police and notifying family etc. Now, would you care, to upset me any further? Or do you think, you could just back the hell off now?"

Paula stepped back and grabbed the porch banister to support herself.

"Dead? David's dead? How can that be? He doesn't even have a car, so how could he have been in a wreck?"

Lisa sat down on the porch.

"Look, Paula, I am sorry that I had to break it to you like this, but yes, David is dead. He had my car, he took it while I was asleep in bed, sick with this flu bug. I guess he took it with him to Sammy's and after having a few too many, he drove it off of the lake view bridge. He's dead Paula, he drowned in the car."

Paula refused to believe her.

"Yeah right, Lisa, this story is so far-fetched, it's pathetic. You never let David drive your car and even if you did, he wouldn't have taken it. He hated your IROC, because you had it painted that awful purple. He said he'd never be caught dead in a purple car."

Lisa couldn't handle much more of Paula.

"Ha-ha-ha, funny Paula, because he was found dead in a purple car! Look, I have no idea why he took my car. The fact is, he did and now he's dead. I'm sorry, Paula, but there is nothing I can do, to change this. David died last night, because of he's stubborn, careless attitude. Even if I'd tried to stop him from taking my car, I wouldn't have been able to. You know that, as well as I do."

Paula began yelling and pointing at Lisa.

"This is all your fault, Lisa. If it wasn't for you, he never would have become an alcoholic. You treated him like dirt, you never gave him what he needed and never cared either. Why do you think he had me? You deserved every beating you got. You're nothing, but a bitch and a stupid little whore."

Lisa began to cry.

"Look, Paula. David's drinking problem, was not my fault, now please just leave, get off of my property."

Just then, Janet walked up the driveway. She had heard most the argument and jumped in, to help Lisa.

"Lisa is right, it wasn't her fault. My son was an alcoholic for years, even before he and Lisa met. It was his love for her that actually made him slow down for a bit. Alcoholism, however, is a sickness and David wasn't strong enough, to fight it. Now, I don't know who you are Ma'am and I'm not sure I care to know. But I think, that you should do as my daughter-in-law has asked and leave. We don't need your upsetting comments. My son, Lisa's husband, has just died and we don't need the likes of you hanging around."

Paula tried to suck up to David's mother.

"You're David's mother? Oh, I am so sorry for your loss. David spoke of you often, he really loved you." Janet knew right away, just who Paula was.

"Oh lovely! I take it you're the little tramp that he was with last? You know, I had always hoped, that he would change and for once, learn to love and respect his beautiful wife. But when I look at the likes of you, it becomes very obvious that you don't always get what you hope for. I guess that old saying, like father like son, is very true. David and his father, were like two peas in a pod. Now, get the hell out of here, before I kick your ass down the driveway myself."

Paula began to cry.

"Fine Ma'am, I'll leave, but I want you to know that I really did love your son."

Janet totally ignored her and she and Lisa went inside.

Lisa hugged her.

"Oh Janet, it is so good to see you. I thought you were going to call when you got in?"

Janet set down her bags.

"Well I did call, but I didn't get an answer. I just figured you were sleeping and not wanting to disturb you, I just headed right over. I know where the spare key is, so I figured, just let you sleep. Lord knows, you probably needed it."

Lisa sighed.

"Well, actually, I didn't get any sleep at all last night. All of this, has just been far too upsetting. Sometimes, it's even hard to breath, I just feel numb and lost. Anyway, so this morning I decided to go out for some air and when I returned, there was Paula, on my front door step and as usual, she only made things worse."

Janet put her arms around Lisa.

"Oh my dear, I am so sorry, for the way, that my son treated you. He treated you badly and was downright cruel. You never deserved that, hell nobody does. I'm just glad, that you were able to stick it out and try and save the marriage. Believe me, I know how hard it is, I tried for over 20 years, before I finally gave up. Unfortunately, David turned out, just like his father. I had prayed he would straighten around, but I suppose now, it's too late for all of that, he's dead."

Janet sucked back the tears.

"I'm not going to cry. I promised myself, I would be strong for you, my dear."

Lisa hugged her again. "It's okay Janet, really it is."

The two of them sat down at the kitchen table and began making all of the arrangements. Janet explained that David's father, brothers and sister, would all be arriving before the funeral, then began planning the service.

"Lisa, honey. Is there anything special, you would like to be done at the funeral? Or anything you'd like said about David?"

Lisa began to cry.

"I don't know, I really don't know Janet. I'm only 29 years old and already a widow. I never thought I'd have to deal with this, not for a long time. Life is just so crazy and far too short. I'm sorry Janet, but I just don't think I can handle this, it's just too hard."

Janet wiped away her tears and hugged her.

"I know, sweetie. Don't you worry, I'll take care of everything. Why don't you go and lay down for a bit. You didn't get any rest last night and I'm sure you're exhausted. Grief can really take its toll on people, you need your rest."

Lisa yawned as she wiped more of her tears away.

"I am pretty worn out. I didn't sleep a wink, all night. I'm sorry Janet. I really thought, that I could handle this, but I guess I'm not as strong, as I thought."

Janet hugged her once more, as she headed upstairs to lay down.

She wasn't at all sure, how she would get through the next week. There was so much grief and pain and she was the reason for it all. Then as she lay down in bed, she began to miss Chad and wondered, how he was feeling about it all. She figured, that by now, the reality of what they'd done, would have hit him. So she picked up the phone, to give him a call.

"Hi baby, it's me. How are you?" Chad was thrilled to hear from her.

"Hi sweetie, I'm fantastic! How is everything going over there?"

Lisa was bit shocked.

"You're fantastic? Chad, has none of what's happened, had any effect on you at all? I'm going crazy. This is a lot harder, than I ever thought possible. Janet, is taking it better than I am and handling pretty much everything. I just can't do it and you're fantastic?"

Chad wasn't quite sure how to respond.

"Well, maybe not fantastic, but I'm okay with everything. This is how it was meant to be, so I've dealt with it and I'm moving on. We knew, this wouldn't be easy for you Lisa, so I'm not surprised, to hear you're having problems handling it. It will get easier though as time passes."

Lisa couldn't believe her ears.

"You're moving on? It hasn't even been 24 hours and already, you're moving on? Wow!"

Chad knew that Lisa wasn't impressed with him.

"You know what I mean sweetie. I'm dealing with it, that's all I meant. Anyway, so what happened with Paula this morning? How did she take it?"

Lisa sighed.

"Oh…she was a bitch as usual. She blamed me, for all of David's problems and called me a whore. It was pretty horrible and Janet showed up, right in the middle of it all. That's when things, really got interesting. Janet called Paula a tramp and said, that she didn't want anything to do, with the likes of her and then told her to leave, before she kicked her ass. The look on Paula's face, was priceless."

Chad started to laugh.

"Oh boy, that would have been awesome to see. Anyway, sweetie, I was thinking, that I would come to the funeral, to be there for you, what do you think?" Lisa wasn't at all sure about that.

"Oh babe, I don't know. I mean how would we explain you to people? There would be a lot of questions."

Chad didn't see a problem with it.

"Nah, nobody would question a thing. We just make it appear, that we're friends and that I was friends with David as well. Nobody would think anything of it. I'm just a friend, there to say goodbye to one friend and support another. Nothing to it, sweetie, it will all be fine."

Lisa wasn't at all sure, that she liked this side of Chad. Deceiving people, seemed to really come easy to him and she wondered, if he'd ever deceived her. Unsure what to make of it all, she ended their call.

"Well, I'll think about it. Anyway, Chad, I've got to get off the phone. Janet will be needing it soon and I'm supposed to be resting. I will talk to you later."

Chad understood.

"Oh okay sweetie, I love you, keep your chin up, this will all be over soon. Talk to you later."

Lisa hung up the phone from Chad and lay down on her bed, trying to get some rest. She tossed and turned, but just couldn't fall asleep. The pain of what she'd done, was eating away at her. Visions of David, crashing to his death, kept running through her mind and she kept hearing his voice. Telling her, that she'd never be able to live with herself, because of what she'd done. David's face and the sound of his voice, was stuck in head like glue.

Lisa was sure, that she would never make it through this, without the guilt eating her alive. She tossed and turned some more, hoping to drift off, but no luck. She pulled herself back up out of bed and went down to see how Janet was doing with the arrangements.

Janet heard her coming down the stairs.

"Lisa, is that you? I thought you were resting? I've cooked some dinner, if you're hungry." Lisa walked into the kitchen.

"It smells great Janet, but really, I don't think I could eat a thing. My stomach is in knots. How did things go with the arrangements?"

Janet pulled out a chair for Lisa.

"I think everything is all set. The funeral will be, the day after tomorrow. There will be visitation tomorrow and then the service the next morning. The family will all be arriving, first thing in the morning."

Lisa hadn't thought about the funeral home visitation. She would have to be there, with all of David's grieving family and David's body, right there in front of her. She had no idea, how she would hold it together, seeing his body lying there, knowing that she was the reason for it.

"Visitation, I hadn't thought about that. Oh Janet, I don't know, how I will get through it. Seeing him, there in a casket, will make all of this real. I don't know how to deal with this, I just don't."

Janet hugged her, Lisa sobbed on her shoulder.

"Honey, we will get through it together. Just remember, you're not alone. I will be right there with you through it all." Lisa couldn't take much more. Being there in the house, knowing that David was gone, was becoming more than she could bare.

"Thanks, Mom, I really appreciate, all you are doing for me. I need to get out of here for a bit though, do you mind? I just need to get out for coffee or something, do anything, but sit around here. It's too hard, sitting here, knowing that David, is never going to come through that door again. I just need to get out for a while."

Janet wiped Lisa's tears.

"Of course dear, I don't blame you at all. You go out and relax for a bit. I'm sure it would do you some good. Do you need any money or anything?" Lisa got up from the table. "No, I'm fine, but thanks."

Lisa quickly got herself fixed up, then headed out. She stopped at the variety store to call Chad, but he wasn't home. Instead, he'd left a message on his machine for her. Telling her, that he was at Sammy's bar.

Lisa was shocked. Why would Chad go to David's hang out, it wasn't like him to even be caught, in a place like that. She called a cab and headed over there, to find out what was going on. As the cab pulled up in front. Lisa noticed Chad, standing out front. Paula was with him and they appeared to be arguing. Unsure of what was happening, she rushed over. "Chad! What is going on here? What are you doing, here with her?"

Chad knew, Lisa wasn't impressed.

"Hi sweetie, it's okay, everything is under control. Paula just decided, to pick a fight with me, over David's funeral arrangements. She seems to feel, that she has to the right to be involved in it all and I am simply telling her, to just leave you and Janet alone, to deal with it."

Paula interrupted.

"Why don't you tell her everything, Chad? Why don't you tell her, that you're making threats? Telling me, that if I don't stay away from her, how sorry I'll be. Tell her the truth Chad, or aren't you man enough?"

Lisa wasn't sure what to think.

"Oh shut up, Paula! Chad, what does she mean? Did you threaten her?"

Chad laughed.

"Oh please! I wouldn't waste my breath! You know me, Lisa. How could you believe that? She is exaggerating again, just like she always does."

Lisa was becoming furious.

"You know, Paula, I've about had enough of your shit! David was my husband, not yours, so just stay the hell out of my life."

Paula grabbed Lisa's arm.

"Look bitch! If you think, I'm falling for your little grieving widow charade, you have another thing coming. What would David's mother think, if she were to find out, about Chad here? How would she feel, to know what a slut, you really are?"

That was it, the claws were out! Lisa lunged at Paula, but Chad pulled her back.

"You stupid slut, you bitch! You don't know anything about me and even so, Janet wouldn't care. She knows all about you and would never, believe you over me."

Paula waved her hand, as if she didn't care and turned to walk away. Lisa and Chad, headed in the bar, but Chad turned back to Paula.

"You disgust me, Paula. You're nothing but a cheap whore, who should be standing out on a street corner somewhere. Don't go forgetting our conversation now, I meant it."

Lisa seemed confused.

"What conversation, Chad? Is there something, you're not telling me?"

Chad hugged her.

"No baby, it's all good. So how are things? Are you holding up okay?"

Lisa held back the tears, she could feel whelming up in her eyes.

"As well as to be expected I suppose. It's been really difficult. I needed to get out for a bit, away from it all. So, I told Janet I was going for coffee. She's expecting me back shortly though, so I don't have much time."

Chad leaned over and kissed her neck.

"Well, what do you say, we make the most of the time we have then. There's a motel, right next door. Want to check in for a bit?"

Lisa shoved Chad away.

"You have got to be kidding me! Is that all you think about? Come on Chad, you know this isn't the time to be messing around."

Chad was stunned.

"What has gotten into you, sweetie? You've never turned me down before and now, you seem to want nothing to do with me. Why? Lisa, I miss you so much that it hurts and I really do need you, right now, tonight."

Lisa knew in that moment, that Chad only had one thing in mind, when they were together and it wasn't her company, it was sex.

"I'm sorry that you cannot understand, Chad. I miss you too, but I need time right now, to get things in order. If you can't handle that, then I'm sorry. Anyway, I really should be heading home. I told Janet I wouldn't be long."

With that, she got up to leave and Chad grabbed her hand.

"Sweetie, I'm sorry, don't leave. Stay with me a bit." Lisa pulled away and headed toward the door.

"I'm sorry Chad, but I need to get home. I will talk to you later."

Chad was furious with Lisa. She had never before, let him down like this and he was starting to believe, that this was the beginning of the end for them. The road seemed to be coming to an end, a dead end.

"No way am I letting her go, not like this and not because of David."

As Chad sat there alone, Paula walked back into the bar. "What's the matter stud? Did she ditch you for something better?"

Chad growled and slammed his fist down on the table. "Look, you stupid bitch, I've about had it, with you and all of your bullshit. Your time is coming and you will, get exactly what you deserve."

Paula laughed.

"Ooh I'm shaking, Mr. Tough guy is going to get me, ooh I'm so scared!"

Chad got up from the table and headed out of the bar. "Watch your back, bitch!"

Paula laughed, as he walked out, then went to the phone and called Lisa, warning her, that Chad was making threats and she believed that he was dangerous.

Lisa never wanted to believe her, yet a part of her feared she could be right. Chad was acting like a completely different person, since David's death. Almost like he enjoyed it and had won her, like she was prize in a carnival.

Janet walked in the room, just as Lisa was hanging up the phone.

"Who was that, dear? You sounded upset?" Lisa signed as she laid down on the sofa.

"Oh, it was that woman again, the one David was seeing." Janet was disgusted, that her son, could have taken up, with such a woman.

"I'm sorry, Lisa. I don't mean to speak ill of the dead, but my son, really wasn't the sharpest tool in the shed. He had no clue, what a great thing, he had at home and continued, to take up, with women like her. I'm sorry you're now left, to deal with her."

Lisa was finally starting to nod off. "It's okay, Janet, I can handle her."

With that, Lisa had finally drifted off to sleep. Janet covered her with a blanket, then headed to bed herself.

Meanwhile, back at Sammy's, Paula was leaving the bar.

She walked out the front door and around the side.

As she came up to the alley, all she could see, was a car with its high beams on, shining right in her face. Then suddenly, there was the sound of screeching tires, as the car sped forward toward her. She let out a scream and tried to get out of the way, but there was nowhere to turn, the car was coming too fast. The car, then struck her and pushed her, crushing her up against the brick wall.

As she stood there pinned and dying, she looked into the windshield, to see Chad laughing. He had kept his promise and she was paying the ultimate price, for upsetting Lisa. One more death, planned and executed by Chad, that man, Lisa, believed, was her dream come true.

Chad sat there, watching Paula die, then spun his car around and took off. He drove his car, out into the woods and set it on fire. Then walked home and shortly after, called the police, to report his car had been stolen.

Another perfect murder and one more less person, to interfere in his and Lisa's lives.

Chapter Nine

The next morning, Lisa awoke to the sound of voices. Lots of voices. As she rolled over on the sofa, she realized, that David's family had arrived. She pulled herself up and headed into the kitchen, where she was greeted by all of David's siblings. All hugging her and telling her, how sorry they were. Lisa knew, that this, was just the beginning, of what would prove to be, one of the hardest days of her life.

She grabbed a coffee and sat down at the table. Janet passed her the paper, to show her, that the write up about David's service was listed. Lisa quickly glanced at it, seeing it in print like that, wasn't easy, so she turned over the paper. Then as she sat there, sipping her coffee, she suddenly screamed.

"Oh my God! No way! Paula?" Janet moved over beside Lisa. "What is it, dear?"

Lisa pointed to the paper.

"It's Paula, David's girlfriend, Paula, she's dead!" Janet couldn't believe it.

"Are you sure that it's her? How did it happen?"

Janet took the paper to read the article and sure enough, it was Paula's picture.

"It says here, that she was run down last night, in an alley by that bar. The same bar, that David was always at. I'm telling you, that place is trouble."

Lisa was terrified. Paula had called her and warned her. She told her, that Chad was making threats and she believed he was dangerous. Then just hours later, she's run down and killed. Lisa never wanted to believe, that Chad was capable of such a thing, but it was all pointing to him.

Lisa was in shock and really not sure, what she believed. It could just be coincidence, or was it that Chad, the man she trusted was really a cold-blooded killer. It had been his idea, to kill David and then once they did, it never seemed to faze him. Then, he made threats to Paula and hours later, she turns up dead, too. Lisa began to fear the worst, yet prayed she was wrong.

Lisa finished her coffee, then decided she'd better get herself ready for the funeral home. She knew Chad would be there and wasn't quite sure, how to handle the thoughts that were running through her head.

"Janet, I'm going to go and grab a shower and get ready for the funeral home. What time do we need to be there?"

Janet looked at her watch.

"Oh, yes, it's getting late. We need to be there in about an hour dear. You go and get ready and I will quickly tidy up the kitchen."

Lisa quickly grabbed a shower and then went and got herself dressed. She put on her off the shoulder black dress. The one that David had bought her, on their first wedding anniversary. Back then, things were still good between them and David loved seeing her wear it. Then she headed downstairs, where the rest of the family, was all preparing to leave. Janet took her by the hand.

"Are you ready, my dear? You and I are going to ride with Bobby."

Lisa sighed and once again sucked back the tears. "I'm as ready as I'll ever be. Let's go."

They arrived at the funeral home and headed inside.

Before visitors arrived, the family was given a few minutes alone, with David's body. Lisa walked into the room, took one look at David in his casket and fell to the floor weeping. Bobby, David's brother, walked over and helped her up and walked her to a chair. Seeing David there like that, made it all so real. He was gone, never coming back and his blood, was on her hands.

As she sat in the funeral home. She watched, as family members and friends, all paid their respects to David. Each of them, shocked over his sudden death and devastated by the loss.

It was tearing her up inside, knowing the pain she'd caused. She could barely breath, she couldn't speak and at this point couldn't even cry. She just sat still and silent, watching everything happen around her. When suddenly, she felt a hand on her shoulder and she jumped, looking up to see, that it was Chad.

"Hi sweetie, how are you holding up?"

Lisa shrugged her shoulder, knocking his hand off.

"I'm holding up, okay. What took you so long to get here? I thought you were going to be here for noon?" Chad sat down beside her.

"I know, I'm sorry sweetie. It's really a long story, my car was stolen last night. The police found it, but it was out in the woods and was torched. Probably some kids out joy riding or something."

Lisa could feel a lump in her throat and her heart was pounding. Paula had been run down and the same night, Chad's car was stolen and torched. All of this was too much of a coincidence and she knew right then, that Chad, had killed Paula.

"Chad, what happened with you and Paula, after I left last night?"

Chad sensed that Lisa suspected him.

"Nothing at all, I left right after you did, why?"

Lisa knew that Chad was lying, because Paula had called her.

"Chad, Paula is dead. She was run down last night, after leaving Sammy's bar. Right after she called me and warned me, that you were making threats. Chad, I want to believe that you had nothing to do with it, but now you walk in here, telling me that your car was stolen. Chad, please tell me I'm wrong, tell me you didn't kill Paula."

Chad wasn't sure what to say. Lisa was on to him and he didn't want to lose her.

"Lisa, baby. Come on, Paula was trouble. She was going to make things difficult for us and you know it. I'm not saying that I killed her, but I will say, that I'm happy she's dead."

Lisa knew that Chad had killed her and really couldn't handle being with him anymore. He was obsessed with her. So much so, that he was willing to kill for her and that she couldn't accept.

"Chad, I think you should leave. I can't handle this right now, it's all too much."

Chad was stunned.

"Are you kidding me, Lisa? You seriously want me to leave? Baby, please, don't do this! Come on baby, I love you, don't do this to us. Let me stay. You need me and you know you do."

Lisa shoved him away.

"Yeah, I thought I did, Chad, but now I know, that I don't. You don't really love me, you're obsessed with me and that isn't love. I cannot be with you, knowing that you have killed someone. I know you say you didn't, but I know in my heart you did. Chad, I loved you with all of my heart and I prayed that the road had finally ended with you and me together. Then you changed. You showed me a side of you that I don't like. A cold and vicious side. I can't handle it Chad, please leave, it's over for us. This is the end of the road."

Chad stood up, shoving the chair into the wall.

"No, it's not, Lisa, I won't let you go, I refuse to let you go. I will leave, but we are far from over."

With that, Chad stormed out of the funeral home. Lisa was devastated. All of her hopes and dreams, had come crashing down on her and they had all began, with the death of her husband. How things had gone so badly, so quickly, was beyond her, but everything in her world, had suddenly changed.

Before long, the visitation was over. Janet came over to get Lisa.

"Sweetie, it's time to go. We'll give you a few minutes alone with David, to say your good-byes and then we have to leave."

Lisa walked over to David's casket and began to sob.

"I am so sorry, David that things ended this way. Please forgive me, David. I did love you, I really did. I hope that you are now at peace, goodbye."

Then she leaned forward and kissed his forehead. Saying her final farewell, to the man she'd married and vowed to love.

Lisa was in total and complete shock, as they arrived back at her place. She walked right up to her room and sat down, silent in the dark. She could hear the family downstairs, sitting down to eat dinner. Yet she couldn't move. She just sat there, numb and motionless, starring out the window.

Janet walked into the room.

"Sweetie, are you hungry? You really should try to eat something."

Lisa shrugged her shoulders.

"No not really, but thanks Janet. I think, I'm just going to try and get some sleep."

Janet hugged her.

"Okay sweetie, if you need anything, I'm right downstairs."

Lisa laid back on her bed and all she could think about was Chad. She wondered, if there had been others that had died at his hand. They had been apart for years, before finding each other again. She had no idea, what he had been doing during those years and couldn't help but think, he may have killed other people. Killing David and Paula, came far too easy for him and this terrified her.

As she lay there thinking and looking out her window, the phone rang. She looked at her call display and realized it was Chad. She picked up the phone, then quickly hung it back up. A few moments later, it rang again.

"He's not going to let up." She picked up the phone.

"Chad, I don't want to talk. I told you, we're finished, over with, a thing of the past. Please, just leave me alone now."

Chad trying to win her back began to beg.

"Lisa, please, don't do this. I love you and I will prove that to you. Just don't do this, please!"

Lisa was becoming upset.

"Chad, it's over. After all of this, I can no longer trust you. Without trust, there's no relationship. I know that you killed Paula, it's obvious and I cannot be with someone, who would do that. Please Chad, leave me alone, or I will have to turn you over to the police."

Chad became angry.

"Turn me over to the police! You have got be kidding me? Are you that foolish? If you turn me over sweetie, you're going down, too. Remember, you helped kill your asshole husband."

Lisa couldn't believe her ears. Chad was not at all, the man she'd believed he was. He was cold and vicious and couldn't be trusted.

"At this point Chad, I don't care. I would spend the rest of my life in prison, if it meant saving other lives. Now please, leave me alone. Move on with your life and forget about me, we're done."

With that, she hung up the phone and unplugged it, so that he couldn't call her back.

Then she crawled into bed, pulled the covers up over her head and lay there thinking, tossing and turning, until she finally drifted off to sleep.

Her life had completely changed and would never again be the same.

The night quickly passed and before long, the sun was coming up. Lisa rolled over in bed and looked out at the sunrise. Today was the day, she bid her final farewell to David and the first day, of the rest of her life. Unsure of how her life would now be, she lay there, afraid to face today.

She could hear David's family, downstairs, getting ready for the funeral. She knew, that she didn't have much time to get ready herself, yet found it hard getting out of bed. She pulled herself up, just as Janet walked in, with a coffee in hand.

"Good morning Lisa, I thought you could use this." Lisa took the cup from Janet's hand.

"Thank you, I really could. So I guess this is it, the official end of the road."

Janet put her arm around her.

"But it's the start of a new one my dear. I'll head downstairs and let you get ready. We need to head out, in about half an hour."

Lisa laid out her dress on the end of her bed and then headed to the shower. She worried, that Chad would show up at the funeral and cause a scene, but prayed that he wouldn't.

Seeing him, today, of all days, would only make things more difficult.

She hurried to get ready and then met the family downstairs. His sister was having a hard morning and sobbing uncontrollably, Janet was doing her best to stay strong, but broke down and cried herself. This was her final good-bye to her son and all of the dreams she once held for him.

At the funeral, everyone seemed distant and quiet. Almost as if they were in disbelief that this was really happening. Friend of David's spoke of the good times they'd had with him and all of the crazy things, he'd done growing up. David's sister gave a speech, about him and Lisa. She spoke of them, like they were a match made in heaven and how Lisa stood by him, through all of his faults.

Lisa found it hard, to get through it. Hearing all of the stories, knowing she was the reason he was dead. She hadn't stood by him at all, instead, she killed him taking the easy way out.

At the cemetery, as she watched David's casket, lowered into the ground. Lisa broke down and knelt down at the graveside and prayed for forgiveness. As she pulled herself up, she looked across the way and noticed Chad standing beside a tree. She tried to ignore him, but he saw her look at him and came over to her.

"Lisa, can we talk?"

Lisa stood up and looked at him with her tear-soaked face.

"There is nothing to talk about, Chad, it's over and I never want to see you again. Please, understand this, Chad. I can longer be with you, knowing what I know."

Chad was furious.

"Fine, have it your way, but you'll regret this and that is a promise."

With that, Chad stormed off, got into his rental car and sped off.

Lisa headed home, to deal with David's family, who was now preparing to head home themselves.

Janet hugged Lisa.

"Sweetie, if you need anything, anything at all, I'm only a phone call away."

Lisa began to cry.

"Thank you, I really appreciate it. I'm going to miss you guys."

At this point, Janet was crying right along with her. "We'll miss you too Lisa, but you're still family and we will always be there for you."

Lisa hugged her again, as she walked them to the door to see them out.

"Have a safe trip and call me when you get home, to let me know you got there safely."

Janet waved as they all walked away.

"I will, my dear, stay strong, I'll be in touch soon."

Lisa closed the door and was heading into the kitchen. When suddenly there was a knock on the door. Assuming that Janet had forgotten something, she rushed to answer.

"Did you forget something Janet?"

Then as she unlocked the door, it suddenly burst open. It was Chad.

"Chad, you cannot be here. Please leave."

Chad seemed distant, almost as if he were somebody else. He walked toward her, with a vicious and evil look on his face.

"I warned you, baby. I warned you not to end us. I love you and you're mine. I won't let you go, not like this. If you won't be with me, then you won't be with anybody."

Lisa was horrified as she began to back up.

"What do you mean, Chad?"

Chad never answered, he just reached into his pocket and pulled out a gun, he pointed it at Lisa.

"This is the end of the road, Lisa, a road that ends with you."

Then he fired the gun 5 times and Lisa fell lifeless to the floor.

Chad stood over her, weeping.

"Look what you made me do! My sweet princess, my beautiful Lisa. Just look what you made me do!"

Chad walked away, only turning back once to look at her lying there, cold and lifeless on the floor.

"Goodbye Lisa. True lust always, baby, true lust always."

The incomparable E.J. Van Amelsvoort will steal your heart. She captivates the reader with her artistic ability to paint her story and characters with imagination, vitality, and pure magic.

Lisa Curtis, a married woman of eight years, finds love in the arms of another man. While suffering abuse brought on by the man, she vowed to love. Does betraying her marital vows mean death? Or will she free herself to live a life of happiness, with her newfound love? Will her new lover give her the respect and love that she deserves, or is their relationship purely sexual? What happens when they take their love to new heights? Will they go too far? What will happen to her husband? How far will her lover go to keep her?

This sexy erotic thriller will keep you guessing.

Few writers can convey the style and bridge to cross over that E.J. uses to paint the picture for her adult novels as well as her riveting poetry. E.J. was born and raised in London, Ontario, Canada. Even as a child growing up, E.J. had a true passion for writing.

Whether it was letter to one of her many pen pals, a poem or short story, E.J. would spend many hours writing. Her dream was to grow up and become an author, like some of her favorite writers. Then in 1993, E.J. began working on making her dream a reality, when she began writing her young adult, children's, and adult fiction books.

Aside from writing books, E.J. has a great love for animals and nature. She has completed courses in animal sciences and forestry wildlife conservation and is a supporter of the Canadian Wildlife Federation, other forestry and wildlife foundations, Habitat for Humanity and other charitable organizations.

Presently, E.J. resides in London, Ontario, Canada, with her children and husband, Leonard, and has made herself well-known across Canada, the United States, and the rest of the world.